From the Pages of the *Purgatorio*

To run o'er better waters hoists its sail
The little vessel of my genius now,
That leaves behind itself a sea so cruel;
And of that second kingdom will I sing
Wherein the human spirit doth purge itself,
And to ascend to heaven becometh worthy.
(Canto I, lines 1–6, page 3)

O noble conscience, and without a stain,
How sharp a sting is trivial fault to thee!
(Canto III, lines 8–9, page 13)

"For to lose time irks him most who most knows."
(Canto III, line 78, page 16)

Horrible my iniquities had been;
But Infinite Goodness hath such ample arms,
That it receives whatever turns to it.
(Canto III, lines 121–123, page 17)

"Verily, in so deep a questioning
Do not decide, unless she tell it thee,
Who light 'twixt truth and intellect shall be.
I know not if thou understand; I speak
Of Beatrice; her shalt thou see above,
Smiling and happy, on this mountain's top."
(Canto VI, lines 43–48, page 32)

'Twas now the hour that turneth back desire
In those who sail the sea, and melts the heart,
The day they've said to their sweet friends farewell,
And the new pilgrim penetrates with love,

If he doth hear from far away a bell
That seemeth to deplore the dying day.
(Canto VIII, lines 1–6, page 43)

O human creatures, born to soar aloft,
Why fall ye thus before a little wind?
(Canto XII, lines 95–96, page 68)

"The world is blind, and sooth thou comest from it!
Ye who are living every cause refer
Still upward to the heavens, as if all things
They of necessity moved with themselves.
If this were so, in you would be destroyed
Free will, nor any justice would there be
In having joy for good, or grief for evil."
(Canto XVI, lines 66–72, page 91)

"To greater force and to a better nature,
Though free, ye subject are, and that creates
The mind in you the heavens have not in charge.
Hence, if the present world doth go astray,
In you the cause is; be it sought in you."
(Canto XVI, lines 79–83, page 91)

With such care is it needful, and such food,
That the last wound of all should be closed up.
(Canto XXV, lines 138–139, page 142)

"But so much more malignant and more savage
Becomes the land untilled and with bad seed,
The more good earthly vigor it possesses."
(Canto XXX, lines 118–120, page 169)

From the most holy water I returned
Regenerate, in the manner of new trees
That are renewed with a new foliage,
Pure and disposed to mount unto the stars.
(Canto XXXIII, lines 142–145, page 188)

THE PURGATORIO DANTE ALIGHIERI

TRANSLATED BY

HENRY WADSWORTH LONGFELLOW

With an Introduction and Notes
by Peter Bondanella
and Julia Conaway Bondanella

Illustrations by
Gustave Doré

George Stade
Consulting Editorial Director

BARNES & NOBLE CLASSICS
NEW YORK

_JB_

BARNES & NOBLE CLASSICS
NEW YORK

Published by Barnes & Noble Books
122 Fifth Avenue
New York, NY 10011

www.barnesandnoble.com/classics

Dante is believed to have composed _The Divine Comedy_ between 1308 and 1321, just before his death. Longfellow's translation of the _Purgatorio_ first appeared in 1867; the present text derives from the Bigelow, Smith & Co. edition published in 1909.

Published in 2005 by Barnes & Noble Classics with new Introduction, Notes, Biography, Chronology, Map of Purgatory, Inspired By, Comments & Questions, and For Further Reading.

The Purgatorio
ISBN 1-59308-219-3
LC Control Number 2004116954

Produced and published in conjunction with:
Fine Creative Media, Inc.
322 Eighth Avenue
New York, NY 10001
Michael J. Fine, President and Publisher

Printed in the United States of America
QM
1 3 5 7 9 10 8 6 4 2
FIRST PRINTING

Dante Alighieri

Dante Alighieri was born in Florence in 1265 to Alighiero Alighieri, who appears to have been a moneylender and property holder, and his wife, Bella. Alighieri's was a family of good standing. Much of what we know of Dante's earliest years comes to us from *La Vita Nuova* (*The New Life*, completed around 1293), in which he tells the story of his idealized love for Beatrice Portinari, whom he encountered just before his ninth birthday. Beatrice died in 1290 but remained Dante's idealized love and muse throughout his life. Sometime around 1285 Dante married Gemma Donati, with whom he had three sons and a daughter.

Dante's public life is better documented than his private life. It is known that he counted among his closest friends the poet Guido Cavalcanti and the philosopher and writer Brunetto Latini, who is generally credited with bringing classical literature to thirteenth-century Florence. Dante began an intense study of theology at the churches of Santa Maria Novella and Santa Croce in 1292, and was well-versed in classical literature and philosophy as well as religious thought. Membership in a guild was a requirement to participate in the government of Florence, and Dante partook of this privilege after enrolling in the Arte dei Medici e Speziali (Guild of Physicians and Apothecaries), in 1295. He was elected to serve as a prior, the city's highest office, in 1300.

By early 1302, however, Dante had fallen out of favor in Florence. The Guelphs, the ruling body with whom Dante's family had long been associated, had split into two factions, the White and the Black Guelphs. Dante aligned himself with the Whites, who were opposed to the intervention of Pope Boniface VIII and his representative, Charles of Valois, in Florentine politics. While Dante was in Rome with a delegation protesting papal policy, Charles of Valois entered the city and a proclamation was issued banishing Dante and others, ordering them to be burned alive should they fall into the hands of the Florentine government.

Dante never returned to Florence, even after the exiles were granted a pardon. He probably began *La Divina Commedia* (*The Divine Comedy*) around 1308, during his extensive travels throughout Italy. The work brought him fame as soon as it began to circulate (in hand-copied form, at a time when the printing press had not yet been invented). Dante's travels took him to Verona, where he resided on and off for some six years, and finally to Ravenna, where he died on September 14, 1321, after falling ill in Venice.

Dante Alighieri is considered to be one of the world's greatest poets. In the words of the twentieth-century poet T. S. Eliot, "Dante and Shakespeare, divide the world between them. There is no third."

Table of Contents

The World of Dante and
the *Purgatorio*

1265 In May or June (exact date unknown), Dante Alighieri is born to Alighiero Alighieri, a Florentine moneylender and renter of properties, and his wife, Bella, daughter of a family of good standing. (Dante discusses his ancestry in *Paradiso* [*Paradise*], cantos XV and XVI.)

1272 Bella dies.

1274 According to his later collection of poetry and prose *La Vita Nuova* (*The New Life*), Dante lays eyes on Beatrice Portinari for the first time during festivities on May 1. Throughout his life and career Dante cites Beatrice as his muse and as the benevolent force in his life, maintaining that she inspired the best part of his work.

1281 Dante, some scholars contend, studies at the universities of Bologna and Padua.

1282 Dante's father dies, leaving a modest inheritance of property.

1283 Dante passes Beatrice in the street and she greets him. The encounter inspires a visionlike dream, which Dante recounts in a sonnet that he circulates around Florence. One of the readers, the poet Guido Cavalcanti, becomes Dante's friend and mentor. About the same time Dante finds a role model and teacher in Brunetto Latini, a writer and influential Florentine politician and man of letters.

c.1285 Dante is married to Gemma Donati, to whom he was betrothed when he was twelve and Gemma was ten.

1287 Beatrice marries Simone de' Bardi, member of a wealthy clan.

1288 Dante's son, Giovanni, is born. Dante and Gemma will have three more children, Pietro, Iacopo, and Antonia.

1289   It is believed that Dante, having been trained in knightly warfare, fights in the battle of Campaldino on June 11, when the Guelphs, with whom Dante sympathizes, defeat the Ghibellines. On August 16 Dante goes into battle again, this time against the Pisans to restore the fortress at the village of Caprona to the Guelphs, from whom the Ghibellines have captured it.

1290   Beatrice dies in June.

1292   Dante begins to study theology, first at the Dominican church of Santa Maria Novella, then at the Franciscan church of Santa Croce. His theological readings will have a profound influence on his works.

c.1293   Dante completes *La Vita Nuova*, which he had begun around 1283 to celebrate his beloved Beatrice.

1295   Dante enrolls in the Arte dei Medici e Speziali (Guild of Doctors and Apothecaries), which includes philosophers as well. Membership in a guild gives him a say in the Florentine government. Dante's friend and mentor Brunetto Latini dies.

1300   Dante, a persuasive and eloquent speaker, is appointed to Florence's highest office as one of the city priors. He holds this office from June 15 to August 15. Florence is once again divided into warring factions, the White and the Black Guelphs. Dante's sympathies lie with the Whites, who favor independence from papal authority; in what he considers to be the best interests of Florence, he must concur with the priors when they send Guido Cavalcanti, a Black and his longtime friend, into exile on the Tuscan coast, where he dies of malaria. Dante travels as part of a mission to the city of San Gimignano to rally Tuscan cities against the territorial ambitions of Pope Boniface VIII.

1301   Dante goes to Rome to ask Pope Boniface VIII to help prevent the French Charles of Valois, a papist sympathizer, from entering Florence. Charles takes the city in November, and the Blacks harshly regain power.

1302   On January 27 Dante is accused of corruption and bribery, fined, and sentenced to two years in exile. When he does not reply to the charges, his home and possessions are confiscated, and on March 10 his sentence is increased; he is now banished for life and condemned to be burned alive if he ever returns to the city.

1303–1304   Dante travels throughout central and northern Italy and affiliates himself with other Florentine exiles. He appears to have been much dissatisfied with his colleagues. Dante arrives for a stay in Verona, as a guest of Bartolomeo della Scala, son of a local ruling family.

1306–1308   Dante works on *Il Convivio* (*The Banquet*), a philosophical treatise on poetry influenced, in part, by the writings of Aristotle. Throughout these years he travels to Lucca (where some think he encounters his eldest son, Giovanni), Arezzo, Padua, Venice, and other cities. It is believed that Dante probably begins work on *La Divina Commedia* (*The Divine Comedy*), turning first to the *Inferno* (*Hell*), in 1308; he will complete the larger work shortly before his death in 1321.

1309–1311   In January Dante attends the coronation, in Milan, of Henry VII of Luxemburg as king of Lombardy. Dante views Henry as the rightful ruler of Italy and writes two impassioned letters to the Florentines, imploring them to open their gates to Henry.

1312   Dante begins a six-year stay in Verona, interrupted by frequent travels, as a guest of Cangrande della Scala, a powerful political leader. While in Verona, Dante revises the *Inferno*, writes and revises *Purgatorio* (*Purgatory*), and begins *Paradiso*. His second son, Pietro, joins him in Verona.

1313   Henry VII dies, putting an end to Dante's hopes of returning to Florence.

1315   Dante refuses an offer from Florence allowing him to return if he pays a reduced portion of a fine imposed upon him at the time of his exile; he calls the pardon "ridiculous and ill-advised." Another decree is issued against Dante, as well as his sons, condemning them to beheading if they are captured. The *Inferno* gains recognition throughout Italy.

1319–1321   Dante stays in Ravenna as a guest of Guido Novello da Polenta. Two of Dante's sons, Pietro and Iacopo, his daughter, Antonia, and his wife, Gemma, join him. Antonia enters the convent of Santo Stefano degli Olivi in Ravenna, taking the name Sister Beatrice.

1321   Dante travels to Venice to help negotiate a peaceful resolution
        to a disagreement that has arisen between Ravenna and Venice.
        During his return to Ravenna across marshy lands, he con-
        tracts malarial fever; he dies on the night of September 13–14.
        He is buried "with all the honors deemed worthy of such an
        illustrious deceased man," writes Giovanni Boccaccio, the
        author of another great fourteenth-century Italian master-
        piece, the *Decameron*. Dante's remains are in Ravenna's church
        of San Francesco, though Florence has tried repeatedly to have
        them moved to the poet's place of birth.

1337   Florence establishes the Chair of Dante, an academic position
        for the preservation and study of Dante's works. This position
        was first held by Giovanni Boccaccio, who was not only a
        friend of Dante's, but whose own literary perspective was
        influenced by the poet's writings and who was one of Dante's
        first biographers.

The Story of the *Purgatorio* in Brief

BY HENRY FRANCES CAREY

CANTO I. The Poet describes the delight he experienced at issuing a little before dawn from the infernal regions, into the pure air that surrounds the isle of Purgatory; and then relates how, turning to the right, he beheld four stars never seen before but by our first parents, and met on his left the shade of Cato of Utica, who, having warned him and Virgil what is needful to be done before they proceed on their way through Purgatory, disappears; and the two poets go toward the shore, where Virgil cleanses Dante's face with the dew, and girds him with a reed, as Cato had commanded.

CANTO II. They behold a vessel under conduct of an angel, coming over the waves with spirits to Purgatory, among whom, when the passengers have landed, Dante recognizes his friend Casella; but, while they are entertained by him with a song, they hear Cato exclaiming against their negligent loitering, and at that rebuke hasten forward to the mountain.

CANTO III. Our Poet, perceiving no shadow except that cast by his own body, is fearful that Virgil has deserted him; but he is freed from that error, and both arrive together at the foot of the mountain; on finding it too steep to climb, they inquire the way from a troop of spirits that are coming toward them, and are by them shown which is the easiest ascent. Manfredi, king of Naples, who is one of these spirits, bids Dante inform his daughter Costanza, queen of Arragon, of the manner in which he had died.

CANTO IV. Dante and Virgil ascend the mountain of Purgatory, by a steep and narrow path pent in on each side by rock, till they reach a part of it that opens into a ledge or cornice. There seating themselves, and turning to the east, Dante wonders at seeing the sun on their left, the cause of which is explained to him by Virgil; and while they continue their discourse, a voice addresses them, at which they turn, and find several spirits behind the rock, and among the rest one named Belacque, who had been known to our Poet on earth, and who tells that he is doomed to linger there on account of his having delayed his repentance to the last.

CANTO V. They meet with others, who had deferred their repentance till they were overtaken by a violent death, when sufficient space being allowed them, they were then saved; and among these, Giacopo del Cassero, Buonconte da Montefeltro, and Pia, a lady of Sienna.

CANTO VI. Many besides, who are in like case with those spoken of in the last Canto, beseech our poet to obtain for them the prayers of their friends, when he shall be returned to this world. This moves him to express a doubt to his guide, how the dead can be profited by the prayers of the living; for the solution of which doubt he is referred to Beatrice. Afterwards he meets with Sordello the Mantuan, whose affection, shown to Virgil his countryman, leads Dante to break forth into an invective against the unnatural divisions with which Italy, and more especially Florence, was distracted.

CANTO VII. The approach of night hindering further ascent, Sordello conducts our Poet apart to an eminence, from whence they behold a pleasant recess, in form of a flowery valley, scooped out of the mountain, where are many famous spirits, and among them the Emperor Rudolph, Ottocar king of Bohemia, Philip III of France, Henry of Navarre, Peter III of Aragon, Charles I of Naples, Henry III of England, and William, Marquis of Montferrat.

CANTO VIII. Two angels, with flaming swords broken at the points, descend to keep watch over the valley, into which Virgil and Dante entering by desire of Sordello, our Poet meets with joy the spirit of Nino, the judge of Gallura, one who was well known to him. Meantime three exceedingly bright stars appear near the pole, and a serpent creeps subtly into the valley, but flees at hearing the approach of those angelic guards. Lastly, Conrad Malaspina predicts to our Poet his future banishment.

CANTO IX. Dante is carried up the mountain, asleep and dreaming, by Lucia; and, on wakening, finds himself, two hours after sunrise, with Virgil, near the gate of Purgatory, through which they are admitted by the angel deputed by Saint Peter to keep it.

CANTO X. Being admitted at the gate of Purgatory, our Poets ascend a winding path up the rock, till they reach an open and level space that extends each way round the mountain. On the side that rises, and which is of white marble, are seen artfully engraven many stories of humility, which while they are contemplating, there approach the souls of those who expiate the sin of pride, and who are bent down beneath the weight of heavy stones.

CANTO XI. After a prayer uttered by the spirits, who were spoken of in the last Canto, Virgil inquires the way upward, and is answered by one, who declares himself to have been Omberto, son of the Count of Santafiore. Next our Poet distinguishes Oderigi, the illuminator, who discourses on the vanity of worldly fame, and points out to him the soul of Provenzano Salvani.

CANTO XII. Dante being desired by Virgil to look down on the ground which they are treading, observes that it is wrought over with imagery exhibiting various instances of pride recorded in history and fable. They leave the first cornice, and are ushered to the next by an angel who points out the way.

CANTO XIII. They gain the second cornice, where the sin of envy is purged; and having proceeded a little to the right, they hear voices uttered by invisible spirits recounting famous examples of charity, and next behold the shades, or souls, of the envious clad in sackcloth, and having their eyes sewed up with an iron thread. Among these Dante finds Sapia, a Siennese lady, from whom he learns the cause of her being there.

CANTO XIV. Our Poet on this second cornice finds also the souls of Guido del Duca of Brettinoro, and Rinieri da Calboli of Romagna; the latter of whom, hearing that he comes from the banks of the Arno, inveighs against the degeneracy of all those who dwell in the cities visited by that stream; and the former, in like manner, against the inhabitants of Romagna. On leaving these, our Poets hear voices recording noted instances of envy.

CANTO XV. An angel invites them to ascend the next step. On their way Dante suggests certain doubts, which are resolved by Virgil; and, when they reach the third cornice, where the sin of anger is purged, our Poet, in a kind of waking dream, beholds remarkable instances of patience; and soon after they are enveloped in a dense fog.

CANTO XVI. As they proceed through the mist, they hear the voices of spirits praying. Marco Lombardo, one of these, points out to Dante the error of such as impute our actions to necessity; explains to him that man is endued with free will; and shows that much of human depravity results from the undue mixture of spiritual and temporal authority in rulers.

CANTO XVII. The Poet issues from that thick vapor; and soon after his fancy represents to him in lively portraiture some noted examples of anger. This imagination is dissipated by the appearance of an angel, who marshals them onward to the fourth cornice, on which the sin of sloth is purged; and here Virgil shows him that this vice proceeds from a defect of love, and that all love can be only of two sorts, either natural, or of the soul: of which sorts the former is always right, but the latter may err either in respect of object or of degree.

CANTO XVIII. Virgil discourses further concerning the nature of love. Then a multitude of spirits rush by; two of whom in van of the rest, record instances of zeal and fervent affection, and another, who was abbot of San Zeno in Verona, declares himself to Virgil and Dante; and lastly follow other spirits, shouting forth memorable examples of the sin for which they suffer. The Poet, pursuing his meditations, falls into a dreamy slumber.

CANTO XIX. The Poet, after describing his dream, relates how, at the summoning of an angel, he ascends with Virgil to the fifth cornice, where the sin of avarice is cleansed, and where he finds Pope Adrian the fifth.

CANTO XX. Among those on the fifth cornice, Hugh Capet records illustrious examples of voluntary poverty and of bounty; then tells who himself is, and speaks of his descendants on the French throne; and, lastly, adds some noted instances of avarice. When he has ended, the mountain shakes, and all the spirits sing "Glory to God."

CANTO XXI. The two poets are overtaken by the spirit of Statius, who, being cleansed, is on his way to Paradise, and who explains the cause of the mountain shaking, and of the hymn; his joy at beholding Virgil.

CANTO XXII. Dante, Virgil and Statius mount to the sixth cornice, where the sin of gluttony is cleansed, the two Latin Poets discoursing by the way. Turning to the right, they find a tree hung with sweet-smelling fruit, and watered by a shower that issues from the rock. Voices are heard to proceed from among the leaves, recording examples of temperance.

CANTO XXIII. They are overtaken by the spirit of Forese, who had been a friend of our Poet's on earth, and who now inveighs bitterly against the immodest dress of their countrywomen at Florence.

CANTO XXIV. Forese points out several others by name who are here, like himself, purifying themselves from the vice of gluttony; and among the rest, Buonaggiunta of Lucca, with whom our Poet converses. Forese then predicts the violent end of Dante's political enemy, Corso Donati; and, when he has quitted them, the Poet, in company with Statius and Virgil, arrives at another tree, from whence issue voices that record ancient examples of gluttony; and proceeding forward, they are directed by an angel which way to ascend to the next cornice of the mountain.

CANTO XXV. Virgil and Statius resolve some doubts that have arisen in the mind of Dante from what he had just seen. They all arrive on the seventh and last cornice, where the sin of lust is purged in fire; and the spirits of those suffering therein are heard to record illustrious instances of chastity.

CANTO XXVI. The spirits wonder at seeing the shadow cast by the body of Dante on the flames as he passes it. This moves one of them to address him. It proves to be Guido Guinicelli, the Italian Poet, who points out to him the spirit of Arnault Daniel, the Provençal, with whom he also speaks.

CANTO XXVII. An angel sends them forward through the fire to the last ascent, which leads to the terrestrial Paradise, situated on the summit of the mountain. They have not proceeded many steps on their way upward, when the fall of night hinders them from going further; and our Poet, who has lain down with Virgil and Statius to rest, beholds in a dream two females, figuring the active and contemplative life. With the return of morning, they reach the height; and here Virgil gives Dante full liberty to use his own pleasure and judgment in the choice of his way, till he shall meet with Beatrice.

CANTO XXVIII. Dante wanders through the forest of the terrestrial Paradise, till he is stopped by a stream, on the other side of which he beholds a fair lady, culling flowers. He speaks to her; and she, in reply, explains to him certain things touching the nature of that place, and tells that the water, which flows between them, is here called Lethe, and in another place has the name of Eunoe.

CANTO XXIX. The lady, who in a following Canto is called Matilda, moves along the side of the stream in a contrary direction to the current, and Dante keeps equal pace with her on the opposite bank. A marvelous sight, preceded by music, appears in view.

CANTO XXX. Beatrice descends from heaven, and rebukes the poet.

CANTO XXXI. Beatrice continues her reprehension of Dante, who confesses his error, and falls to the ground: coming to himself again, he is by Matilda drawn through the waters of Lethe, and presented first to the four virgins who figure the cardinal virtues; these in their turn lead him to the Gryphon, a symbol of our Saviour; and the three virgins, representing the evangelical virtues, intercede for him with Beatrice, that she would display to him her second beauty.

CANTO XXXII. Dante is warned not to gaze too fixedly on Beatrice. The procession moves on, accompanied by Matilda, Statius and Dante, till they reach an exceedingly lofty tree, where divers strange chances befall.

CANTO XXXIII. After a hymn sung, Beatrice leaves the tree, and takes with her the seven virgins, Matilda, Statius, and Dante. She then darkly predicts to our Poets some future events. Lastly, the whole band arrive at the fountain, from whence the two streams, Lethe and Eunoe, separating, flow different ways; and Matilda, at the desire of Beatrice, causes our Poet to drink of the latter stream.

Introduction

Dante's Life and Times

We know little about the private lives of Homer and Shakespeare, the only two poets who may be said to rival Dante's influence in the Western tradition or, indeed, his genius. Some critics have raised doubts about the authorship of the *Iliad* and the *Odyssey*, and about the rich poetry and drama of Shakespeare. But Dante Alighieri, the man whom the nineteenth-century British writer and critic John Ruskin called "the central man of all the world," is unquestionably the author of the great epic poem we call *The Divine Comedy*, of which *Purgatorio* is just one of three parts. Dante the man remains inextricably tied to the content and action of *The Divine Comedy*, both as its narrator and as its central protagonist. Many of the important events in his life figure prominently in the work, and the reader, to whom a good many of these biographical details are not immediately transparent, must seek out information in annotations that centuries of scholars and commentators have compiled.

The problematic quality of autobiographical details in Dante's works is that they may allude to real, historical events that actually occurred or to fictional events from Dante's fertile imagination. It is not always easy to separate fact from fiction. Dante the Poet is also the epic's protagonist, Dante the Pilgrim. It required a breathtaking act of poetic license for Dante to make himself the hero of an epic, a genre usually populated by warriors and heroes. The results, however, have silenced any critical objections to such presumption. Scholarly debate over Dante's poem has continued since its first appearance in manuscript in the early fourteenth century. The unbroken tradition of writing about Dante from that time to the present remains unparalleled in its complexity and breadth by that on any other major Western author, including Shakespeare. Yet despite all we know about Dante (much of this gained from the poem itself), problems arise because there is not a single extant autograph manuscript of his many works, including his poetic masterpiece. Every one of his many works has come down to us in such a complicated manuscript tradition that his contemporary editors can still carry on heated debates about which text should be accepted as the best one or whether, indeed, some of his minor works are actually to be attributed to his own hand.

A child born on a day between May 14 and June 13, 1265, in the Tuscan city of Florence, Italy, was christened in the Baptistery of San Giovanni on March 26, 1266, with the name Durante Alighieri, later contracted to Dante Alighieri. Dante's family—the father Alighiero and the mother Bella—was not particularly wealthy or distinguished but was sufficiently well off that Dante could later participate in the republican government of Florence, eligibility for which rested primarily upon economic status. According to Dante's testimony in *La Vita Nuova* (*The New Life*), he first encountered a girl named Beatrice Portinari when they were both eight years of age; he saw her again nine years later, in 1283. A decisive encounter in his poetic and intellectual development, this meeting inspired Dante's unrequited love for Beatrice (who died in 1290) and led him to begin writing poetry. Dante married a woman named Gemma Donati (the marriage contract is dated 1277), and he apparently had four children.

Dante must have enjoyed a very good education, probably from the schools that had grown up around the ecclesiastical centers in Florence—the Dominican church of Santa Maria Novella; the Augustinian church of Santo Spirito; and the Franciscan church of Santa Croce. He certainly received stellar training in Latin grammar (he would later compose a number of works in Latin) and must have read extensively in the Latin classics and rhetoric books typically employed in medieval education. The poet also came under the influence of Brunetto Latini (1220–1295), under whose tutelage he probably encountered not only the works of Aristotle and Cicero but also important works written in Old French, such as *The Romance of the Rose*, and the troubadour lyrics written in Old Provençal. One work attributed to Dante but still contested by some scholars, and probably written between 1285 and 1295, is *Il Fiore* (*The Flower*), a series of 232 sonnets summarizing *The Romance of the Rose*.

The lyric poetry Dante produced between the early 1280s and the mid-1290s holds much greater importance in his poetic development. These ninety or so poems of undoubted attribution represent a kind of artistic workshop for the young aspiring lyric poet. The poems display a variety of metrical forms: sonnets, sestinas, *ballate* (dance songs with repeating refrains), and *canzoni*, ode-like "songs," as the name implies, consisting of a number of stanzas of varying lengths and a shorter envoy. Dante considered the *canzone* to be the noblest form of poetry. This kind of poetry was popular among the major groups of lyric poets Dante admired, imitated, and sometimes criticized: the Provençal troubadours, such as Arnaut Daniel and Bertran de Born; the Sicilian School of poetry that flourished from around 1230 to 1250, the members of which included Pier della Vigna and Giacomo da Lentini, the probable inventor of the sonnet; the Tuscan school led by Guittone d'Arezzo; the Bolognese group of poets led by Guido Guinizzelli; and what came to be known as poets of the *dolce stil novo* ("sweet new style"), a group of Tuscans including not only Bonagiunta da Lucca, Cino da Pistoia, and Guido Cavalcanti, but also Dante himself. Dante places a number of these individuals in *The Divine Comedy* as testimony to his own literary development and to his argument that poetry represents one of humanity's most noble callings.

Had Dante stopped writing poetry with his lyric production and never composed *The Divine Comedy*, he would be remembered only by medievalists as the author of two works. These are a moderately interesting Latin treatise on political theory, *De Monarchia* (*Monarchy*), completed during the last decade of his life, and an unfinished Latin treatise on vernacular language and its use in poetry, *De Vulgari Eloquentia* (*On Eloquence in the Vernacular Tongue*), probably written between 1302 and 1305. Without *The Divine Comedy*, there would have been little reason for Dante to have composed the unfinished Italian work *Il Convivio* (*The Banquet*), a philosophical consideration of poetry that is also inspired by religion. In fact, rather than being admired for the often abstract and ethereal love lyrics typical of the "sweet new style" (the term itself comes from a line in *The Divine Comedy*), Dante would be recognized primarily for *La Vita Nuova* and four explicitly sensual lyrics called the *rime petrose* (literally, "rocky rhymes"). These reveal his interest in metrical experimentation and a highly sophisticated understanding that the courtly love celebrated by the Provençal poets—often Dante's models—was firmly based on requited lust rather than unrequited love. Such a poetic reputation would not have attracted much critical attention during the past six centuries from anyone but highly specialized scholars.

Dante's love poetry, however, led to the stroke of genius that ultimately saved him from so unremarkable a future. Dante had the immensely clever idea of taking thirty-one of the lyric poems he had composed concerning an unrequited love for the girl named Beatrice and setting them within a prose frame. Although not widely read and immediately eclipsed by the appearance of his great epic, *La Vita Nuova* (probably completed around 1293) represents a fundamental step forward in Dante's poetic and intellectual development. The Italian prose framework of the work allowed Dante to comment on his own work. This idea of a poet who presents a series of poems on love and then includes his own readings of the works was a unique invention that flirts with a postmodern conception of literature as an ironic revisitation of what has been written in the past. *La Vita Nuova* represents a precocious first step toward Dante's decision to become the protagonist hero of an epic poem filled with self-critical images of its author. This little work already contains the key distinction in *The Divine Comedy* between protagonist and narrator, who are the same person but are viewed from different perspectives. But even more important was the revolutionary role of Beatrice in *La Vita Nuova*. By the addition of the prose commentary, Dante projects Beatrice as one whose name, life, and effects upon the narrator are associated with blessing and salvation and especially with the number nine (the square of three, the number of the Trinity). Her death nearly destroys the narrator of *La Vita Nuova*, but in the process of mourning, Dante envisions a Beatrice who has become a figuration of Christ and a guide to his salvation, even before her dramatic appearance in *The Divine Comedy*.

Did Beatrice really exist? We know that there was a real person named Beatrice Portinari who died around the time Dante says his Beatrice did. Did she really have such an influence upon the young Dante, or does Dante simply invent this conceit in order to embark on a revolutionary treatment of a woman's role in a poet's life? It is impossible to prove or disprove this influence, for we only have Dante's word. Whether or not the young Dante was so struck by Beatrice at the age of eight that she led him to poetic glory, Dante does state that this early *innamoramento* transformed his life and mind. In the process, Dante raised the poetry of praise, the most traditional role of medieval love poetry, to the highest possible level, surpassing the traditional claims of courtly poetry that a woman's love (sexual or chaste) refined a man. Dante affirmed that a woman's love could lead a man or a poet to God with its Platonic overtones, and this bordered on blasphemy. At the same time, Dante stepped back from the avowed sensuality of troubadour lyrics and created a literary relationship between the lover and his beloved that would later come to be labeled "platonic."

For approximately a decade between the time *La Vita Nuova* was completed and his exile from Florence in 1302, Dante divided his activities between writing and active participation in the communal government. In 1289 Dante took part as a cavalryman in the battle of Campaldino, in which the Florentine Guelphs were victorious against the Ghibellines of the nearby Tuscan city of Arezzo. Guelph and Ghibelline traditionally refer to Italian political factions allied, respectively, to the papacy and to the Holy Roman Empire. But the intense and bitter rivalries within the city-state governments of Italy made things more complicated than that. If your enemy was a Guelph, you became a Ghibelline, and vice versa. Conflicts between families and clans were often more important than the more weighty issues of empire versus papacy. Florence was traditionally Guelph, as were most of the city-state republics intent upon removing themselves from the restrictions of either church or state, but even the Guelphs divided into warring factions. The Black Guelphs were most extreme and had the closest ties to the papacy. The White Guelphs (Dante's party) were generally more moderate in their politics.

In 1300 Florence boasted a population of around 100,000; it may have risen to 120,000 before the Black Plague of 1348 devastated the city, as it did most of Western Europe. This Italian city-state was a crucial player in the politics of the period because of its central location, its vibrant republican government, and particularly its enormous wealth. Its flourishing textile industry (specializing in luxury goods of wool and silk but also more humble fabrics made from cotton and linen) and its international banking business dominated world trade and commerce—even rivaling that of Venice, a commercial city and seafaring republic. Florentine politics reflected not only the struggle between Ghibellines and the two factions of Guelphs but also the class conflict between the impoverished mass of humble workers, on the one hand, and the two groups of economically well-off people who governed and who were themselves often in conflict. These were the elite, upper-class patricians who represented a small number of powerful families and were not really noble in the medieval or feudal sense, and the more numerous but less prestigious middle-class merchants, artisans, notaries, lawyers, manufacturers, and shopkeepers who were members of the various guilds and corporations in the city-state. The politics of the city remained turbulent because of friction between various groups. Although members of the groups were often connected to each other by ties of family, religion, and friendship, conflicts often turned into violence, riot, and warfare, with financial ruin and exile being the favorite punishment for those who lost the struggle. Constant internal conflict led quite naturally to a search for outside allies, further complicating the situation within Florence.

In the fourteenth century, the Florentine florin served as the standard currency for the entire European economy. Its value was carefully maintained: 24 karats of purely refined gold, accepted almost everywhere in the known world as legal tender. Rapid commercial communications operated by the Florentine banks, the invention of double-entry bookkeeping, and shrewd dealings abroad made Florence the capital of the major service industry of the Middle Ages. When Tuscan banks began to collect papal revenues all over Europe, the profits were enormous. Based upon high banking charges and incredible profits from the luxury goods produced by the textile industry, the Florentine economy supported a huge building program between 1250 and 1320. The popular monuments now visited by busloads of foreign tourists each year—the Bargello, the churches of Santa Croce and Santa Maria Novella, the Duomo of Santa Maria del Fiore, the Palazzo Vecchio, numerous family palaces—were all begun during Dante's lifetime. Florentines were so omnipresent in the economic life of Western Europe that they were called the "fifth element" by a pope—the other four elements, of course, were earth, fire, air, and water. Florentine bankers collected taxes for various foreign monarchs and loaned money to both sides in European wars, gaining a reputation as usurers for their trouble. Florentines ran at least one European navy, and like their counterparts in Venice, they journeyed as far as China and India in search of profit. In the process, they began to patronize architects, painters, and sculptors in such an enthusiastic and sophisticated manner that the city soon became the artistic capital of the known world. By the time Dante, Petrarch, and Boccaccio died, they had virtually created Italian literature and fixed the Italian language in the form that we know it today. Unlike Old French or Old English, Old Italian is just Italian, thanks to the example of Dante and his two brilliant successors, together known as the "three crowns of Florence."

Religious life in Florence was vibrant, and the cloister and pulpit concerned Florentine citizens as much as the bank and the factory did. In fact, a significant part of the city's remarkable artistic production was directly linked to religious patronage. Religious organizations also contributed a great deal to the daily life of the city. The life of a medieval Florentine was marked from the cradle to the grave by religious ritual; time was told by canonical hours, and the passing of the seasons was marked by religious holidays, saint's days, and church processions. Moreover, the city's clerics provided much of the education and religious confraternities supplied much of the social assistance before the advent of a welfare state. One of Tuscany's wealthiest citizens in the next century, Francesco Datini, began his ledger book with the telling phrase "In the name of God and profit." The relationship between economic wealth and moral corruption, the latter caused by a society that avidly pursued profit and tried to retain its religious devotion, would provide Dante with one of the key themes in *Inferno* and *Purgatorio*—the moral and ethical corruption of both Church and society brought about by the wealth produced by the "new people" that Dante's essentially conservative social views could not abide. Florence also boasted some of the greatest reformist, fire-and-brimstone preachers of the time, figures who reflected the great popular piety of both the masses and members of the ruling classes and the intelligentsia. Echoing the concerns of these preachers, Dante sometimes seems like an outraged Jeremiah, but his moral indignation over corruption and evildoing was shared by many of his fellow citizens. In spite of Dante's reservations about the "new people" who were busily making Florence into the most exciting place in the Western world, Florence, between the thirteenth and the sixteenth centuries, became a cultural and commercial center that would rival Athens and Rome in its brilliance.

Once the merchant class determined that internal conflict was bad for business, the city government found a novel way to limit the strife. In 1293 a fundamental constitutional change, the *Ordinamenti di Giustizia* (Ordinances of Justice), took effect in Florence, supported by the Guelph faction. Essentially, it limited political participation in the republican government of the city to members of the major guilds or corporations—basically merchants, bankers, magistrates, notaries, and the moneyed classes. It is important to remember that medieval guilds were not modern labor unions: Membership usually excluded common workers and included only people with property or money. In 1295 Dante joined the Arte dei Medici e Speziali (Guild of Physicians and Apothecaries)—the same guild to which most artists in Renaissance Florence subsequently belonged, because apothecaries provided the materials for paintings. He was elected to serve a two-month term as one of the seven city priors, but fulfilling his civic duty proved to be disastrous for Dante. The elevation to this office identified him as an important White Guelph and made him a target when the more radical Black Guelphs seized power from the White Guelphs. While serving as one of three Florentine ambassadors to Pope Boniface VIII in Rome in 1302, Dante was sentenced first to exile and then to death if he should ever again set foot in his beloved native city of Florence.

Dante's exile lasted until his death, in 1321, from malaria at Ravenna, where he enjoyed the protection and patronage of Guido Novello of Polenta, after receiving the same type of hospitality from Cangrande della Scala in Verona. He wrote *The Divine Comedy* during his long years in exile, and his body was laid to rest not in Florence but in Ravenna, where it remains to this day. In spite of Dante's life in exile and the composition of the poem outside his native city, *The Divine Comedy* has a distinctive Florentine and Tuscan character. The poem often reflects the partisan struggles that swept over Italy during Dante's day, and in so doing it allowed the poet ample opportunity to pay back his political foes. Many of the most memorable figures in the poem are essentially minor historical characters who played a role in the internecine factional struggles of fourteenth-century Florence and who had a personal effect on Dante's life. The depictions inspired by Dante's rancor and righteous indignation—or, occasionally, by his admiration—have transformed many of these minor figures, condemned to a Hell or saved in a Purgatory or Paradise of Dante's invention, into major literary characters.

An Overview of The Divine Comedy

Several times in the poem, Dante refers simply to his creation as the *Comedy*. A subsequent sixteenth-century edition of a manuscript published in Venice during the Renaissance added the adjective "divine" to the title, where it has remained ever since. The poem is an epic, owing a good deal of its structure and content to the epic tradition that began in Western literature with Homer's *Iliad* and *Odyssey*—works Dante could not have read, since he knew no Greek. Few readers of Virgil's *Aeneid*, however, would ever know the Latin epic better than Dante, who absorbed many of the lessons he might have learned from a direct reading of Homer through an indirect encounter with Homer in Virgil's poem. In celebrating the birth of the city of Rome, destined to rule the classical world by Virgil's lifetime, the Latin poet could not have predicted that his imperial capital would eventually become the capital of Christianity, or that the Latin race would be fully Christianized. The link of medieval Rome to both the Roman Republic and Empire, on the one hand, and to the rise of Christianity, on the other, was never far from Dante's mind when he considered what Rome meant to his own times. Virgil's Latin epic became the single most important work in the formation of the ideas that would eventually produce *The Divine Comedy*. Dante also read carefully other Latin epics that are less popular today. One such book was Lucan's *Pharsalia*, a work that described the Roman civil wars and was also full of horrible monsters and marvelous sights. He admired two Latin epics by Statius: the unfinished *Achilleid*, a treatment of Achilles in the Trojan War, and the more important *Thebeid*, a poem treating the fratricidal struggles of the sons of Oedipus in the city of Thebes. Ovid's *Metamorphoses* provided Dante with the most influential repository of poetry about classical mythology.

Nonetheless, no classical precedent really exists for the overall structure of *The Divine Comedy*, in which the author is also the epic protagonist, an Everyman who is not a warrior or a city founder. Homer or Virgil would never have dreamed of making themselves the heroes of their epic works. Dante the Pilgrim in Dante the Poet's epic takes a journey that the poet believes must be taken by every human being. No matter how many trappings of the classical epic *The Divine Comedy* may contain—invocations to the muses, masterful epic similes, divine messengers sent from the deities, lofty verse, and monsters and other figures cited from the literature or mythology of ancient Greece and Rome—the underpinning of the entire poem is fundamentally religious. It is a Christian epic and, more specifically, a Catholic epic. For the first time in Western literature, the values and ideals of an epic poem derive from the fundamental tenets of Christianity as they were understood during the Middle Ages. This means Catholicism as mediated by the dominant theology of the time—the scholasticism of Saint Thomas Aquinas—as well as the writings, teachings, and examples of such figures as Saint Augustine, Saint Francis, Saint Benedict, Saint Dominic, Saint Bernard, and Saint Bonaventure. Ancient philosophy, in particular the works of Cicero, Boethius, and Aristotle, came to Dante filtered through these Christian lenses, as did the traditional Ptolemaic picture of the universe as earth-centered and the classical rhetoric and erudition often based on either Scholastic commentaries in Latin or Latin translations of Arabic commentaries on Greek texts. It is important to remember, however, that all of Dante's sources are filtered through his own unique poetic intelligence to serve his own personal, historical, religious, and literary purposes.

The most important philosopher of the Middle Ages in Italy as in Europe was Aristotle, the sage Dante calls the master of "those who know" (*Inferno* IV: 131). By the time Dante was born, more than fifty of Aristotle's works had been translated into Latin, although these works were often read alongside Scholastic or Arabic commentaries. Plato was virtually unknown during Dante's time, except for an incomplete Latin translation of the *Timaeus*. Certainly Dante would also have gained some insight into Platonic thought through some of the neo-Platonists to whom Augustine refers in his *Confessions*. The emergence of Plato as a rival for Aristotle would not occur until the Medici family of fifteenth-century Florence sponsored the publication of Latin translations of the entire body of Plato's works.

In addition to his profound knowledge of Christian philosophy and theology, Dante had a familiarity with the Bible that was extensive for his time, an era when most Catholics may have heard scripture cited only in sermons, or read to them out loud during the celebration of the mass, or even depicted in narrative fresco painting and tempera altar pieces in the churches. In the centuries before the Reformation declared that every man could be his own priest, few laymen actually read the Bible. Dante was certainly an exception to this general practice, and the Bible he would have read would have been some version of Saint Jerome's Latin Vulgate. In *The Divine Comedy*, Dante draws almost 600 references or citations from the Bible, compared to almost 400 from Aristotle and almost 200 from Virgil. Interestingly enough, the number of classical and biblical citations is almost identical, an eloquent testimony to Dante's conscious desire to synthesize the classical and Christian traditions in his poem. Dante's familiarity with Catholic ritual and music also shines forth in the poetry, mainly in *Purgatorio* and *Paradiso*, where it is associated with harmony and order.

The theme of Dante's epic work is the state of souls after death. Consequently, the entire work is subdivided into three parts, each corresponding to one of the three possibilities in the Christian afterlife. In *Inferno* XX: 1–3, Dante refers to the part of the poem devoted to Hell as "the first song" ("la prima canzon"). *Canzone* means "song" in a generic sense but may also refer to a specific poetic genre, a relatively long composition, the rough equivalent of the ode, with a number of stanzas and an envoy. Dante valued the Italian *canzone* form for its rich poetic possibilities. At the end of *Purgatorio*, in canto XXXIII: 140, he employs another, even more suggestive term for the three major parts of the work—referring to *Purgatorio* as "this second canticle" (*questa cantica seconda*). If labeling his complete epic poem a *canzone* recalls Dante's origins in his secular lyrics, both the amorous and the moralizing variety, calling each of the poem's three parts (*Inferno, Purgatorio, Paradiso*) a *cantica*, or canticle, reminds us of the religious nature of their content, since the term retains the biblical suggestion of Song of

Songs (*Cantica canticorum* in the Vulgate Bible). The two terms Dante employs when referring to his poem also reflect Dante's intention to synthesize very different literary and philosophical traditions in his epic, blending the secular love lyrics of *La Vita Nuova* and the tradition of courtly love with the greatest lyric poetry of the Bible.

Besides the terms Dante uses to refer to the three parts of his epic poem (the number of parts suggesting the holy trinity), Dante employs the term *canto* (first mentioned in *Inferno* XX: 2) for the name he gives to the 100 subdivisions of the three canticles of his poem. The word suggests both poetry and song and singing in Italian, appropriate to the epic tradition, which emphasized the act of singing. The cantos in the poem are divided as follows: thirty-four in *Inferno* and thirty-three in both *Purgatorio* and *Paradiso*. Dante obviously considers canto I of *Inferno* to be a kind of general prologue to the work. Thus the poem may be said to reflect the following numerical structure: 1 + 33 (*Inferno*) + 33 (*Purgatorio*) + 33 (*Paradiso*) = 100. Given Dante's fascination with symbolic numbers, the suggestive quality of this arrangement is certainly intentional.

Dante's poem contains 14,233 lines of hendecasyllabic verse in *terza rima*. The length of each canto may vary from between 115 and 160 lines. Hendecasyllabic verse, following Dante's noble example, became the elevated poetic line of choice in Italian literature, just as the peerless example of Shakespeare's blank verse of iambic pentameter has privileged that poetic form in English. In general, the most successful English translations of Dante, such as Longfellow's, have always been in blank verse, not in rhymed verse. Italian poetry is not scanned by feet but by counting the number of syllables in a line. Since most Italian words are accented on the penultimate syllable, hendecasyllabic verse generally contains eleven syllables with the tenth accented. Lines of ten syllables or even twelve syllables occur in the poem infrequently but still follow the general rule governing accents: In the first case, the tenth or last syllable is accented, while in the second case, the tenth syllable of a twelve syllable line retains the accent.

Dante's great metric invention was *terza rima*. This incomparable narrative form has stanzas of three lines (tercets) in which the first and third lines rhyme with each other, and the second lines rhyme with the first and third lines of the next tercet. The formula for *terza rima* may be written as follows: *aba bcb cdc d . . . wxw xyx yzy z*. Note that each canto begins with a pair of alternating rhymes but ends on a single line. The rhyme scheme also makes run-on lines (*enjambement*) infrequent in the poem, since the focus is upon rhymes at the end of lines. English, compared to Italian, is relatively impoverished with rhymes, and this explains in large measure why most attempts to repeat Dante's *terza rima* have met with dismal failure in English translations. The Trinitarian association with a rhyme scheme that relentlessly repeats itself in series of threes seems obvious. What is less obvious but probably also intended by Dante is that *terza rima* helped to protect his manuscripts from changes by scribes (either accidental or intentional) and eventually by proofreaders after the advent of printing. We may not have an autograph manuscript of *The Divine Comedy*, but even after the passage of nearly seven centuries, the text of Dante's poem that has been established for us today represents an amazingly accurate version of what Dante must have written, thanks in part to the meter the poet invented that has helped to insure the integrity of the text.

Dante's Purgatorio: *Conception, Geography, and Its System of Punishments*

No writer has expressed more creatively and concretely the relationship between this life and the next than Dante, nor has any other writer more clearly defined the responsibility of the individual for his or her actions. Dante's *Divine Comedy* not only depicts through the character of his Pilgrim protagonist the way in which human beings can learn—and earn—their way to heaven, but also demonstrates that all human actions have consequences. Dante views sin as the result of poor choices, and daily choices create the individual human personality, the Aristotelian *habitus*. The Christian Church, affirmed by the theology of such major writers as Origen, Saint Augustine, Gregory the Great, Albertus Magnus, and Thomas Aquinas, proposed an afterlife in which true justice was assured. The good would find their blessings in heaven, the evil their punishments in Hell, and those neither too good nor too wicked would be punished harshly in Purgatory but rewarded generously for their penitence in Paradise. Many late Roman and early medieval literary accounts of the afterlife, including a variety of early medieval Christian visions, give form and shape to the ideas discussed by the Church fathers. Drawing on this rich tradition as well as traditions of the classical world, Dante provides a carefully wrought and fully interrelated vision of the afterlife in the context of God's universal order through a tangible depiction of punishments and rewards. His goal is to show his readers the path to salvation through the education of his Pilgrim, who is their representative in the journey.

Dante's originality lies not only in the beauty and intellectual power of his poetry but also in his creation of an unusual epic hero—himself. His fiction is that Dante the Poet, now older and wiser, looks back on his own pilgrimage to the other world, a journey made by his protagonist, Dante the Pilgrim, who suffers a midlife crisis of faith. Dante the Pilgrim is so burdened by sin that he cannot climb the mountain toward the light and requires the assistance of three heavenly ladies and the revered Latin poet Virgil. In order to complete his journey of salvation, he must travel through the three realms of the afterlife to learn about the true nature of sin and death. The freshness of this invention grabs the reader's attention and makes the poem the kind of tension-filled drama that has created readers for it over many centuries.

Dante's *Inferno* colorfully exposes the nature of sin and damnation in his depiction of wicked souls whose failure to repent and whose choices in life have determined their punishments. The damned are eager for punishment and never ask to be released from it. *Purgatorio* shows saved and hopeful souls enduring the harsh punishments that purify them and prepare them for Paradise. They, too, are eager to serve their time as quickly as possible and to enter Paradise. *Paradiso* reveals the nature and beauty of virtue and goodness and how the human soul can ascend, slowly gaining an understanding of the divine. All three canticles provide lessons for the spiritually needy Pilgrim, who is both Dante himself and Everyman. Through his allegory, Dante ties together the many meanings of the poem. He states in his letter to Cangrande della Scala that his subject "taken in its literal sense, is the state of souls after death." He also adds that "if the work is taken allegorically, its subject is how man by the exercise of his free will justly merits reward or punishment."[1]

Dante never mindlessly parrots theology or literary tradition. His

Divine Comedy is filled with his own creative synthesis of theology, philosophy, history, literary, and artistic tradition, as well as his own idiosyncratic views and opinions, including his political aspirations. A number of his ideas, themes, poetic images, and characters appear in more than one of the three canticles. Among the numerous links between the three realms to which souls travel after death is the image of the stars that ends each of the three canticles. The stars raise the Pilgrim's eyes—and those of the reader—toward the heavens and carry with them a reminder of the perfect order of creation and of the perfection of God's every decision. Christianity's system of divine justice, based on the conception of a universe perfectly ordered by its Creator, takes inspiration from the Old Testament as well as from pagan philosophers and such writers as Plato, Cicero, and Virgil. They all conceived of other worlds in which punishments would be proportionate to the crimes and rewards proportionate to good deeds. Dante's poem draws on a vast range of sources and themes, but he transforms them into a gripping adventure in the other world and a poem of transcendent beauty.

In Dante's *Divine Comedy*, the regions of Hell, Purgatory, and Paradise are linked spatially, geographically, cosmologically, poetically, and thematically. The science of Dante's day followed the Ptolemaic system of the universe in astronomy and Aristotle's teachings on physics and biology. In designing his other world, Dante draws on the Ptolemaic-Aristotelian cosmology of the spheres as well as upon the symbolic number three. The universe was organized into nine concentric spheres, which reflected circular orbits of seven "planets" (the moon, Mercury, Venus, the sun, Mars, Jupiter, and Saturn), the heaven of the fixed stars, and the Primum Mobile, beyond which was the Empyrean, or heaven, and God. Earth was at the center of the universe, with the sun revolving around it along with the moon and planets. Hell was thought to be in the center of earth, which was farthest from the Empyrean. A great chain of being extended from gross matter, animals, and humanity on earth, through the heavens, to the nine orders of the angels, and then to God in the Empyrean.

This cosmology serves as a template for organizing the three canticles, each of which is divided into nine circular, or spherical, spaces. Underlying the nine circular regions in each of the three realms is a tripartite division. In Hell, the tripartite division is based on Dante's classification of sins, for which he is indebted to Aristotle and Cicero. In Purgatory, this structure rests upon three separate regions: Antepurgatory, Purgatory, and the Garden of Eden. In Paradise, the combination of the universal order of the spheres, the heavenly rose, and the orders of angels creates a similar spatial effect.

Dante's three realms of the afterlife generally reflect traditional medieval thinking on astronomy and science, but the poet is also capable of enriching this tradition with his own ideas to enliven his picture of the other world. Hell and Purgatory are both places of punishment and expiation. In Hell, those entering are warned to abandon all hope, because punishments are eternal. Even worse than the incredibly original and grotesque physical punishments Dante invents for his sinners in Hell is the eternal loss of communion with God that is enjoyed by the blessed. The miscreants of Hell do not qualify for the purifying penalties of Purgatory, where souls who do not die in mortal sin suffer temporary but painful expiation before receiving their blissful reward in Paradise. The penitent sinners in Purgatory qualify for heaven, but they must be improved before going there through the purifying penalties for their sins.

Punishments are not eternal in Dante's Purgatory. Hope motivates the penitents to "do their time," because they know that eventually they will attain the greatest possible reward, the vision of God and the communion of the saints. In this sense, Purgatory is even more tightly linked to Paradise: Sinners in both these realms are saved. From this knowledge, the souls undergoing the process of purgation in Dante's "second realm" gain both hope and strength. Since these souls are eager to endure the punishments they know they deserve, they are often reluctant to spend too much time talking to the Pilgrim, because every minute they remain with him delays their ascent to blessedness. Nonetheless, some sinners ask the Pilgrim to remember them when he returns to earth, so that family members, clerics, or friends might pray for them and reduce the length of time they must suffer.

In Dante's time, the doctrine of Purgatory had yet to be formulated by the Church, but it had evolved over the first millennium of Christianity into a place of temporary punishments with a rather vague geography.[2] During the thirteenth century, it began to assume more specific characteristics. Yet it required the poetic power and vision of Dante to create a place that appealed to the imagination. Dante's extraordinary achievement is to have invented Purgatory as a palpable, although presumably temporary, part of the other world. He draws on a number of elements central to the history of Purgatory, especially the idea that salvation is determined by the state of the soul at the moment of death. Other elements are the emphasis on harsh punishments for serious sins committed repeatedly, even though an individual has sincerely repented for having sinned; the creation of ongoing bonds among members of the Christian community, especially family members; the importance of prayer in relieving the punishment of the saved who require purgation; and the concept of Purgatory as a place that, unlike Hell, is not eternal. Church doctrine, which rests on biblical authority, always defined Hell as an eternal place of punishment for human souls who died in mortal sin without a sincere confession of their faults and an expression of true repentance for their misdeeds. Church teaching on Purgatory has always been less specific but consistently defines Purgatory as a place or condition of temporary punishments for those who died in God's grace without repenting fully for venial, less serious faults or who have not yet sufficiently paid for their sins. The logic of Purgatory is clearly linked to the Christian idea of divine justice and to the tradition of praying to or for the dead. Those who have not renounced sinning in life must pay appropriately in death, even if they have repented.

The fifth cantos in both *Inferno* and *Purgatorio* illustrate this logic of salvation. Whereas Hell is a place where souls "abandon all hope" and seek their punishment with perverse eagerness, Purgatory is the exact opposite. Here the souls' hope and love of God allow them eagerly to seek their punishment. Buonconte da Montefeltro, the saved sinner of *Purgatorio* V in the region of Antepurgatory populated by the souls of the unabsolved, has only to murmur the name of the Virgin Mary at the time of his death to reach Purgatory. On the contrary, Francesca and Paolo, the adulterers killed by her jealous husband and Paolo's deformed brother in *Inferno* V, are consumed by their sinful love, and they fail at the moment of their death to take advantage of the opportunity of salvation. Their unholy love is so powerful and their love of God so dim that they doom themselves to an eternity of suffering, reflecting the mindlessness and lack of self-discipline typical of their sin.

The unspoken comparison between another of the murdered souls, the gentle Pia of *Purgatorio* V and the damned Francesca of *Inferno* V, helps to define other differences between the damned and the saved. Pia gently and briefly asks the Pilgrim to remember her after he has recovered from his journey to Paradise. She is humble and focused upon her need to be remembered among the living. Francesca, on the contrary, uses language to manipulate the Pilgrim by presenting a lengthy, distorted version of her story in the poetic language of love, demonstrating her blindness and selfishness, but also seducing the Pilgrim, who is still weak with sin. The linkage between the two canticles is complicated further by the familial connection between characters in *Inferno* and *Purgatorio*. Buonconte da Montefeltro in *Purgatorio* V is the son of the damned Guido da Montefeltro in *Inferno* XXVII, whose repentance turns out to be just another example of his ability to twist the truth as well as his delusion that a pope has the power to forgive a sin before it is committed. Like Francesca, Guido seems oblivious to the fact that his words to the Pilgrim provide clear evidence of his wicked and damnable nature.

Such interconnections forcefully demonstrate to the Pilgrim and to the reader that Purgatory offers hope to those who have not led perfectly righteous lives and that one's situation in the afterlife can be improved, with sincere repentance and contrition. Like souls in Hell, many of those in Purgatory ask to be remembered, but in Purgatory, the goal is more specifically to be remembered in the prayers of the living. In canto VI of *Purgatorio*, the Pilgrim is puzzled by the insistence of "all those shades / Who only prayed that some one else may pray, / So as to hasten their becoming holy" (VI: 25–27). In canto VI: 34–48, Virgil explains that prayers offered by the righteous can help to satisfy the debts of penance owed by souls in Purgatory, but he tells Dante that he must await the explanations of Beatrice for a fuller understanding. Since prayers for the dead had long been part of Christian tradition, it was not an enormous leap to link them to the second realm of the afterlife, where they could hasten a soul's journey toward God. Without Purgatory, there would be no strong reason to pray for the souls of the departed. Thus, Dante makes prayers for the dead, central to the Christian tradition from its beginnings, a central rule of his Purgatory.

Although Dante's *Purgatorio* draws on earlier pagan and Christian discussions and representations of a place of purification in the afterlife, the actual Catholic doctrine of Purgatory was formulated long after Dante wrote his poem, at the Councils of Florence (1439) and Trent (1547, 1562, 1563). As a work of art, *Purgatorio* shares in Dante's great and original synthesis of the Christian and the classical worlds he presents in *The Divine Comedy* as a whole. His intellectual and poetic achievement in the second realm of the afterlife is no less extraordinary than that in *Inferno*. Dante draws a refined, elegant, and enduring image of Purgatory out of diverse, sometimes equivocal and conflicting theological, philosophical, visionary, and poetic literature from pagan and Christian traditions.

Dante's Purgatory is as fresh and fascinating as his Hell. It is a place full of the colors and expressions of faith, hope, and love. Dante designs his Purgatory like Hell and Paradise: All three realms are based on what Dante took to be the divine plan—the nine spheres of the Ptolemaic universe. An almost physical connection exists between Hell and Purgatory, both of which are located on earth. Dante's Hell is a hollow cone shaped by the land displaced from the southern hemisphere after Lucifer, expelled from Heaven, fell to earth. It is situated under Jerusalem and consists of nine concentric circles that grow ever smaller and house more and more evil sinners, a kind of perversion of the celestial spheres of Paradise. Dante knew virtually nothing of the southern hemisphere and, like other thinkers of his time, thought that the northern hemisphere contained all of earth's land, while the southern hemisphere contained the oceans. Dante conjectured that Satan's collision with the southern hemisphere caused all the land to rush northward to avoid contact with his tainted corpse.

Ultimately, Hell ends at earth's core, where Lucifer is imprisoned in ice. Dante the Pilgrim and Virgil climb up Lucifer's legs to enter the southern hemisphere. As Dante conceives it, Purgatory is a kind of inverted image of Hell: It is a solitary island atop which sits a mountain full of the kind of terraces he might have seen in his native Tuscany. The mountain reaches toward the heavens, the only land remaining in the southern hemisphere since Satan's fall. Atop the mountain lies the Garden of Eden, closed to the living, all marked with Adam's sin, and now a place of refreshment, through which the purified souls must pass to leave behind the last taints of their earthly existence. In preparation for their admission to Paradise, the souls are bathed in the waters of the rivers Lethe and Eunoë, which cleanse their memories of bad deeds, leaving only those of the good.

Like the other two canticles, *Purgatorio* provides the reader with a rich, textured world of real individuals as well as imaginary ones within a poetic universe that has its own specifically Dantesque regulations and customs. As in Hell, Purgatory is governed by a series of the usual entertaining and ingenious "house rules" that Dante invented. The Pilgrim undergoes certain cleansing rituals. When he arrives from Hell, Virgil must wipe the infernal dust from his brow to prepare him for a holier realm. In moving to Purgatory proper, the Pilgrim must ascend three steps to the gates, and these steps seem to represent the three parts of Christian penitence: confession, contrition, and satisfaction of the sinner's debt. In Purgatory proper, an angel inscribes seven *P*s on the Pilgrim's forehead to represent the seven deadly sins, of which he must be cleansed during his purificatory journey through Purgatory. At the end of each ledge on the mountain, an angel removes a *P*, and the Pilgrim becomes progressively lighter as he is progressively relieved of the burden of a particular deadly transgression. As a consequence, it becomes paradoxically easier to climb up the Mountain of Purgatory than it does to climb down into the depths of Hell.

Besides rituals of this sort, all of which suggest various ecclesiastical rituals of the Church, Dante the Pilgrim discovers a wide range of rules that govern this second realm. The souls in Purgatory are not restricted to one spot, but since darkness affects the will, they cannot climb at night. To achieve true penitence, the individual soul requires the illumination of divine grace. Dante the Poet informs the reader that purgatorial punishments cannot go beyond "the mighty sentence" (X: 106–111), or Judgment Day. In *Inferno*, souls can see only the future, since part of their punishment is to be cut off from the present. In *Purgatorio*, souls both know the present and see into the future, although they are never omniscient. Dante the Pilgrim learns that souls are not required to spend time on a terrace if they are not guilty of the sin punished there (XIX: 79–81). The Pilgrim also learns about the meteorological and geophysical characteristics of Purgatory from the classical poet Statius. In an event reminiscent of Hell, the mountain shakes (XX: 124–129) and the Pilgrim is "scared to death." Statius informs him that each time a soul arises of its own free will to heaven, an earthquake occurs and causes rejoicing among the community of the saved (XXI: 55–72).

Surprisingly, Statius turns out to be the soul who is moving on to Paradise, a demonstration of Dante's belief that not all good pagans have been condemned to Limbo, whereas Virgil (a much greater poet) remains blocked there. On his way to Paradise, Statius joins Dante the Pilgrim and Virgil as they move toward the Earthly Paradise. He eventually explains to Dante the nature of the aerial bodies that make it possible for the bodies of the gluttonous to be so lean and for Dante to see the souls in the afterlife (XXV: 16–108). In this invention of the aerial body, Dante goes far beyond the theology of his times, which held that the soul remains without its body until the Final Judgment. At the moment of death, according to Dante's fantasy, the soul freed of the body still contains both human faculties and the divine intellective soul, and a formative power then creates from air a shade, which has all the sensory organs and feelings of the body.

The Pilgrim encounters classical figures, either historical or mythological, along the way through Purgatory, as he did in his visit to Hell. The figures who serve as guardians in the second canticle of the poem are much less demonic than those watching over the damned. Figures from classical mythology (many taken from Ovid's poetry), along with biblical characters, often provide the exemplary lessons of vice and virtue on each of the terraces the souls pass through to purge their sins. Among the saved, we find numerous historical characters from Christian times in the Roman Empire and Europe. Virgil[3] remains the central classical figure in *Purgatorio*, even though Statius joins him and the Pilgrim near the top of the Mountain of Purgatory (XXV). Virgil remains Dante's choice as the only possible guide for the Pilgrim's journey toward salvation. He was Dante's model, a revered epic poet who had written about the other world in some detail in the sixth book of the *Aeneid*, where he describes a place of eternal punishment called Tartarus. According to legend, Virgil had also descended into the depths of the Christian Hell that Dante the Pilgrim has just visited.

Virgil remains an appropriate guide for most of the journey through Purgatory, despite the fact that he cannot be saved, for he continues to represent the best that reason without revelation can achieve in the moral sphere. The medieval belief that Virgil had written about the coming of Christ in his *Fourth Eclogue* also gave him a special status. More importantly, his *Aeneid* provides one of the literary sources for the idea of a place of purgation and for the development of the Christian Purgatory. Virgil depicts Aeneas glancing upward toward the light above, a typical image in the development of the idea of Purgatory that is also found in the biblical passages used to argue the existence of Purgatory by Christian thinkers. In the biblical story of Lazarus and the wicked rich man (Luke 16: 23), the latter lifts up his eyes and sees Lazarus in the bosom of Abraham. Dante also imitates Virgil's idea that the duration of the journey to the other world has specific limits. Furthermore, Virgil describes a process of purgatorial punishment undergone by those whose souls are tainted but are not so thoroughly wicked that they cannot be cleansed, unlike the wicked that he consigns to Tartarus. Moreover, in Virgil's view, the soul was shut in the prison of flesh and tainted by the evil of the physical. In the *Aeneid*, souls pay for their wicked acts through penalties based on wind, water, and fire, and most important, Virgil sets out the idea of proportional punishments, which lies at the center of both Hell and Purgatory.

Only one angel appears in *Inferno*, in canto IX, when he descends into Hell to open the gates of Dis, and like Beatrice in *Inferno* II, he cannot leave Hell fast enough. But angels regularly appear in Purgatory to assist the Pilgrim in his quest for salvation, and their attitude is loving. Directing the craft that bears souls to Purgatory in canto II is a winged angel of dazzling white who blesses his passengers with the sign of the cross as they sing "In exitu Israel de Aegypto," a figure diametrically opposed to Hell's Charon (*Inferno* III) or Phlegyas (*Inferno* VIII). Two guardian angels clothed in green protect the souls in the Valley of the Princes (*Purgatorio* VIII: 22–39, 97–108). An angel as majestic as the one in *Inferno* IX, dressed in robes the color of earth or ashes, courteously guides the remorseful Pilgrim up the steps of white, black, and red into Purgatory proper and inscribes seven *P*s on his forehead (*Purgatorio* IX: 73–117). On each terrace an angel representing the virtue opposed to the sin punished there appears to remove the *P* representing the sin of which he has been purged and to aid him in his journey.

Dante also includes historical characters among the guardians of Purgatory. In contrast to the dreaded Charon, boatman of the Styx, there is the unnamed noble Roman hero, Cato of Utica, the passionate republican and statesman of the crumbling Roman republic who opposed the efforts of both Caesar and Pompey to subvert and destroy republican government. Although Cato was a legendary example of natural moral virtue, he did not know Christ. He also chose suicide rather than a life under tyranny. Dante never explains if Cato must retreat to Limbo or advance to Paradise through God's grace, but he certainly employs this virtuous pagan as a figure of Christian liberty. Whereas the damned in Hell require guardians or bureaucrats (not to mention torturers enjoying their work), just as a prison requires jailors and executioners, the souls in Purgatory are generally focused upon their expiatory work. Although Cato serves as a guardian to ensure that only the saved pass into his realm, he indicates that Purgatory is quite different from Hell. He tells the Pilgrim and Virgil that they need not flatter him to gain safe passage as they had in the infernal places, and he urges them to move forward on their journey, helping them gain their bearings. Cato suddenly reappears in the second canto to rebuke all the recent arrivals listening to the music of Casella, whom Dante may have known. He urges them not to lose precious time on mere music and to hurry to the mountain to begin their ascent toward true bliss.

Dante's Purgatory exhibits the possibility of the hope of salvation. Its souls are not wholly deformed by the dehumanizing power of sin, a power reflected throughout Hell in the conditions, both physical and mental, of the damned. Reflecting the story of the Garden of Eden in Genesis 3, the damned in Dante's Hell are separated not only from God but from their fellow humans as they were on earth, by mistrust, despair, and hatred. In Dante's *Purgatorio*, the poet's central themes are freedom, love, repentance, hope, and charity—qualities that define the virtuous on earth. Relationships in Purgatory are defined by love rather than by Hellish hate, deception, and separation. The saved sinners are learning the virtues required to become members of the "communion of saints," required for admission to Paradise. In the first canto, the "beauteous planet" (I: 19) is Venus, the morning star, whose power now originates in the Holy Spirit and causes all things to love. In the pagan pantheon, Venus was the goddess of sensual love, but the poet's fantasy transposes her into a symbol of Christian love—love of God, one's neighbor, and oneself.

The most engaging inhabitants in Purgatory are not classical monsters, mythological figures, or heroes as they are in Hell. Instead, they are contemporary Italians, and among them are famous figures and virtually unknown characters from all over the peninsula. In Dante's afterlife, Purgatory is a world that, like Hell, depicts human weakness, but with an essential difference. The purgatorial realm sounds the note of freedom with the first appearance of Cato, who renounced his life in the name of political and individual liberty. In Virgil's *Aeneid*, Cato is depicted as the one who gives "laws" to the virtuous in the Underworld. Just as Virgil serves as an ideal guide to the Pilgrim, Cato is the perfect guardian for the saved. In introducing Dante to Cato, Virgil explains that Dante the Pilgrim also "seeketh Liberty" (I: 71). But the freedom for which the Pilgrim searches is the liberty of exercising one's free will to follow God's laws and ultimately to return to God in Paradise. The freedom of Purgatory is to pay for one's transgressions, to experience God's mercy for those who truly repent of their sins, and, ultimately, to enjoy the blessings of Paradise. It is precisely this freedom to obey and to love God that the damned in Dante's Hell have forever lost.

The most counterintuitive aspect of Dante's *Divine Comedy* is that the seven deadly sins of lust, gluttony, avarice/prodigality, sloth, wrath, envy, and pride (the obvious scheme for organizing the punishment of the sins of damnation) serve to organize the physical layout of Purgatory. Hell is ordered by a definition of three categories (incontinence, fraud, and violence) indebted more to Aristotle and Cicero than to Christian theology. Purgatory's structure directly embodies these traditional seven deadly sins. Yet, the repeated transgressions purged in Purgatory are also part of Hell. The shape of the Mountain of

Purgatory resembles a reverse image of the shape of Hell. Instead of a hollow cone becoming narrower and narrower, the image of Purgatory is that of a mountain with two levels that precede seven terraces. Each terrace is smaller than the one below, and each is devoted to one of the traditional sins. The structuring theme of the number nine displays itself in the overall structure of Purgatory that includes, in addition to the seven terraces of Purgatory proper, an Antepurgatory with two groups of sinners, the excommunicated and the late repentant. In Paradise, Dante employs the nine angelic orders to organize the geography of heaven into different regions leading up to the Empyrean. He also associates these different realms with planetary bodies, as well as with the classical virtues (prudence, fortitude, justice, and temperance) and the three Christian virtues (faith, hope, and charity, or love).

A thin line divides the saved from the damned: The state of the soul at the time of its death determines its damnation or salvation. It is sufficient to shed one sincere tear or to say one sincere prayer of repentance to be saved. The unabsolved souls in canto V describe themselves as sinners right to the end who were saved when a divine light illuminated their souls and brought them penitence and pardon. In the same canto, Buonconte, son of Guido da Montefeltro damned in *Inferno* XXVII for failing to repent sincerely, describes how he earned salvation by "one poor little tear" (V: 107). Just as the damned in Hell are organized into groups according to the type and severity of their sins, the souls in Purgatory are grouped according to their sinful inclinations. In Hell, a soul is punished for one wicked habit; in Purgatory, a soul might be purged of more than one sin while climbing the Mountain toward heaven. Furthermore, whereas the souls in Hell led lives controlled by their sins, the souls in Purgatory earn their freedom through painful penance. In the end, they will themselves to move on to Paradise, but they must first suffer the purgatorial punishments devised for their sins in order to learn the way to Paradise through discipline and love.

Penalties in Hell are never remedial, because the damned are defined for eternity by their sins. In Purgatory, each sin has its opposite virtue, and on each terrace, the souls are offered exempla not only of the vice for which they are punished but of the virtue toward which they must strive before proceeding to Paradise. In *Inferno* I the Pilgrim found the brightly lit mountaintop as unattainable as the mountain seen by Ulysses (*Inferno* XXVI: 133), but in *Purgatorio* I he is able, once cleansed of the filth of Hell, to move upward in the light, with the climb becoming ever easier as he leaves each terrace. His time in Hell has taught him the true nature of sin; it has hardened him against it, but he, too, must pay the penalty for sinning while he passes through Purgatory. His lessons continue, but with a difference. Rather than the painful despair of Hell, the Pilgrim now feels the hope of the souls who focus upon their punishment in order to pay their penalties as quickly as possible, given the rules. He discovers a community of souls, since the souls in Purgatory never try to deceive or injure the Pilgrim and his guide. Rather they assist him in finding his way. Indeed, at the very beginning, the disciplined Cato urges them all to focus on the task at hand: gaining their freedom and access to heaven.

The geography of Purgatory resembles that of Hell with its conical shape and basic tripartite structure. Beginning from the bottom, there is first Antepurgatory, then Purgatory proper, and finally the Garden of Eden at the top. The three parts are tied together poetically by the Pilgrim's three dreams. The mountain of the second canticle has been prefigured in Hell by both the mountain that the Pilgrim attempts to climb in *Inferno* I and the mountain in *Inferno* XXVI, near which Ulysses and his men drown as they sail past the Pillars of Hercules and through the waters of the southern hemisphere. Interestingly, Dante begins *Purgatorio* in a manner that recalls *Inferno*. He utilizes a seafaring image (*Purgatorio* I: 1–3), recalling his image of himself as a swimmer in *Inferno* I: 22–24. The Poet also invokes the muses in both canticles: In *Inferno* he calls upon the muses and his memory to assist his poetry; in *Purgatorio* he again invokes the muses, specifically calling upon Calliope, the muse of heroic epic poetry. During his journey down through Hell, Dante has begun to learn about the right kind of love and the humility before God that makes him ready to attempt the ascent of the mountain once again.

Virgil and the Pilgrim arrive in the southern hemisphere and find themselves looking at the stars from the shores of Purgatory. They have returned to the world of real time, where the changes from day to night govern the behavior of the souls. Night, the time of darkness, is a time to sleep and, perhaps, to dream, as in the case of the Pilgrim; day is for climbing, allowed only during daylight. The entrance to Purgatory is treated in the first two cantos, where, just as in Hell, Virgil and the Pilgrim find their way blocked by a severe old man, a guardian quite different from those in Hell:

- Canto I: Arrival at dawn on the shores of Purgatory (the appearance of Cato, the cleansing of the Pilgrim, and the goal of freedom)
- Canto II: Wandering of saved souls (Casella's explanation of the journey of saved souls, Purgatory as a passageway for the saved, and Cato's admonition that salvation requires hard work).

Challenged by Cato, who apparently believes the travelers have escaped from Hell, Virgil once again explains that their journey is sponsored by three heavenly women to earn Dante's salvation, with the goal of freedom. At Cato's behest, Virgil cleanses the Pilgrim of the dirt of Hell and they see dawn rising (canto II), symbolic of the Pilgrim's spiritual progress and of the rebirth of all the souls who have crossed over to the shores of Purgatory. Virgil discovers that an angel to whom he bows—not a mythological creature like Charon or Phlegyas—ferries souls from the delta of the Tiber to the shores of the Mountain of Purgatory. The Pilgrim witnesses the landing of the craft bearing "more than a hundred" saved souls (II: 45), so many less than the damned, who are as numerous as the leaves falling from trees in autumn (*Inferno* III: 112). These souls to be purged and saved, however, are singing about the joyful exodus in unison and in happiness, even though they will suffer to expiate their sins. The damned blaspheme, gnash their teeth, and weep as they throw themselves into Charon's boat.

In Dante's *Purgatorio* music plays a crucial role and is often linked to poetry, another increasingly important theme in the canticle. In Hell, we find no music, only groans, screams, and curses. The only music we remember from that infernal realm is an ironic perversion of the opening line of the sixth-century liturgical hymn "Vexilla Regis prodeunt Inferni" ("The banners of the King of hell are advancing") in the first line of *Inferno* XXXIV. It announces to the Pilgrim and the reader that they have arrived at the center of this icy, evil kingdom with all its horror and where all hearts are frozen against the feelings crucial to the essential bonds, both human and divine. Dante introduces us to the use of song in the second canto of *Purgatorio*, where it symbolizes the harmony typical of the communities of the saved. The hundred or more souls who arrive on the shores of Purgatory in canto II: 46–47 are singing in unison the hymn about the biblical exodus, "In exitu Israel de Aegypto," from Psalms 114: 1. This song prefigures the struggle of the Pilgrim and all the souls in Purgatory to free themselves from the slavery of their sinful habits and finally to arrive in Paradise.

Nonetheless, Dante makes it clear that not all music is beneficial. Upon their arrival in Purgatory, the souls wander around asking directions, as if they have forgotten their goal and purpose. When they realize that Dante is alive, they gather around him and Virgil, staring and curious. Among them, Dante recognizes his old friend Casella, who explains that Purgatory is a passageway for all the saved souls—both those who must suffer the purgatorial punishments and those who will go directly to Paradise (*Purgatorio* II: 103–105). All the souls seem easily distracted from their purpose—not yet ready for heaven—and Dante asks Casella to sing for him as he had in the past on earth. The Pilgrim, Virgil, and the other souls then stand around enjoying Casella's musical rendition of one of Dante's love songs, the second *canzone* discussed in book III of *Il Convivio: Amor che ne la mente mi ragiona*—in Longfellow's translation, "Love, that within my mind discourses with me" (II: 112).⁴ Cato suddenly reappears to rebuke them sharply for their spiritual defect—for losing themselves in poetry and song, too reminiscent of their earthly pursuits. Dante's reactions are still flawed and inappropriate, but in this respect, he is like other penitent souls who require purgation. Even refined earthly pursuits such as poetry and music find no place or purpose in the Christian realms of the saved, where loving God is the single focus. Purgatory is a place where the souls must labor to earn Paradise, but this is not the last time Dante brings up the subject of poetry and its purpose. Virgil himself is profoundly embarrassed by his *lapsus*, and all the souls move quickly in search of the path upward.

After having met the new arrivals and Casella, the Pilgrim proceeds to the area for souls not yet prepared to enter Purgatory proper, Antepurgatory, depicted in the next six cantos (III–VIII) of *Purgatorio*. This first region in the second realm temporarily confines souls who repented late in life but must make satisfaction for their spiritual laziness. The four groups of late repentant include the excommunicated; the indolent; the unabsolved; and negligent or preoccupied rulers:

- Canto III: The excommunicated (the initial explanation of the aery bodies or shades of souls by Virgil; Manfredi; discussion of length of punishments of the excommunicates in Antepurgatory)
- Canto IV: The indolent (Virgil's discussion of human psychology and astronomy; Belacqua)
- Cantos V–VII: The unabsolved (Jacopo del Cassero; Buonconte da Montefeltro and the Pia; Virgil's discussion of the power of prayer; Sordello; the Poet's invective against Italy)
- Cantos VII and VIII: Preoccupied or negligent rulers (Nino Visconti and Currado Malaspina in the Valley of the Princes).

Interestingly, the sequence of sinners follows an order based on the severity of the sin, ascending from the most serious to the least serious. This is a switch from the organization of Hell, where Dante met the least culpable of the damned in the first six circles. Also, the regions of Antepurgatory seem rather undistinguishable, except for the Valley of the Princes, unlike those in Hell, where sinners seem to be strictly confined to one distinct place for eternity. After the first group of arrivals, the Pilgrim encounters four groups of souls, including one solitary sinner, Sordello (VI: 74), the Italian who wrote troubadour lyrics in Provençal and who left Italy amid scandal to work as a court functionary in France. As in Hell, groups of sinners are normally represented by particular individuals to whom the Pilgrim speaks. The punishment of the souls who were late falls into the category of *contrapasso* (on which more below), because the delay of their entry into Purgatory parallels their delay in repenting and formally reconciling themselves with God.

Manfredi (III: 112) represents the excommunicate, having been expelled from the Church at least twice without ever being reconciled to the papacy when he died and therefore having been refused burial. The excommunicate were not simply late to repent; they also had in life presumably committed sins so serious that they were excommunicated and died in a state of contemptuous disobedience—excluded from the sacraments, guidance, and community of the Church. Excommunication itself is not a sin, nor could it guarantee damnation, but failing to take the matter seriously or treating it without respect was considered a sin. Although the Church often tried to use excommunication as a weapon to make people fear damnation, Dante displays a belief that God, rather than the Church, makes the final judgment of souls, each of whom is responsible for his or her ultimate fate in the afterlife. Despite having lived in sin, far from God, Manfredi is saved at the end by a small but sincere act of contrition and repentance as he lay dying, showing how great and how mysterious a thing is God's mercy. The excommunicates are depicted as lost sheep, trying to find their way but doing so together, as if to reconcile themselves once again with a Christian community. The excommunicate show the Pilgrim the path upward by crying out in unison (IV: 18).

The length of punishment of the excommunicates differs from that of the other three groups in Antepurgatory. Awaiting their entrance into Purgatory proper and into heaven, the excommunicates must spend thirty years for every year that they spent at odds with the Church. The indolent, the unabsolved, and the negligent rulers pay a penalty of only one year for each year they failed to repent. All the late repentant can, however, be helped by the intervention of prayers offered by their living loved ones (III: 140–141). The early Christian belief that the living could lessen the purgatorial suffering of the souls of the dead in the masses, prayers, alms, and pious works remains allied with the doctrine of Purgatory. The prayers of the good are the most efficacious, and it is a duty of relatives to pray for dead family members to help them pay their debt to God. Virgil's discourse on intercessory prayer in canto III explains that the delay in Antepurgatory is entirely penal and that a soul in a state of grace can, through the right kind of love, reduce the debt owed by the souls of the late repentant (III: 24–48).

The indolent are the second of the four groups of sinners whom Dante meets in Antepurgatory. Like the other sinners, the indolent delayed repenting up to the time of their deaths. Belacqua (IV: 123) and his compatriots display a fatigue and droopiness in the afterlife that reflects their willful laziness in attending to their spiritual welfare when alive. They never actively challenged the Church, but neither did they heed its call. Their behavior, which originates in sloth, prevents the mind from asking for forgiveness in a timely way. Virgil's discourse on human psychology (IV: 1–14) is partly an attempt to explain how the soul can be distracted by earthly concerns, which turn them away from God. Belacqua explains to the Pilgrim that God's angel prevents him passing through the gate of Purgatory until he has completed his punishment. He mentions that sincere holy prayers may speed him on his way through the gate (IV: 130–134). Dante reminds the reader of these rules in his depiction of Provenzan Salvani (XI: 127–132) and Forese Donati, whose presence on the sixth terrace puzzles Dante (XXIII: 83–90), who expected to find them in Antepurgatory with the late repentant.

The singing of the final two groups in Antepurgatory, whose lives ended violently (the unabsolved) or who remained focused upon matters of state (the negligent rulers), reflects the less serious nature of their sins. Their delay in repenting seems in some way excused by the helplessness of those who died by combat or murder and by the high purpose of the rulers and leaders who bore the burden of sustaining the earthly social order. Yet they, too, require moral improvement. Although the indolent are singing the *Miserere*, they cut it short when they are distracted by the Pilgrim's shadow, as if acting out their inability to move toward God.

As they move on, Virgil and Dante meet the Italian troubadour poet and knight, Sordello, whose work at courts in Italy and, especially, in Provence, no doubt gave him the insights into political shenanigans. Sordello, whose presence is not clearly explained by Dante, becomes a central figure in cantos VI–VIII. Sordello greets Virgil as a fellow Mantuan, and Dante the Poet devotes the next seventy-six lines (VI: 76–151) to the internecine horror of conflicts in Italy and within the Florentine republic. This invective clearly demonstrates that Dante was a political partisan who deplored the chaos of continual wars. The Edenic Valley of the Princes, where Dante sees many of the rulers of the day who were so preoccupied with their worldly burdens that they neglected the state of their own souls, constitutes a clear change in the environment. The beauty and deliberation of the princes' song transports the Pilgrim, making him forget himself. He is especially moved by the second of their two evening hymns sung at compline, the latest service of the day—the *Te lucis ante* ("Before daylight fades"; VIII: 13). The hymn is sung to request protection from the evil represented by the serpent and from dreams, and it precedes the Pilgrim's first dream, in canto IX. This music prefigures the songs of Purgatory proper and the music of Paradise, which symbolizes the divine order through its harmony and beauty.

In Purgatory proper, the middle region of the mountain, punishments are stark and severe in comparison to those in Antepurgatory. There, the stars, brilliant lights, sapphire or vermillion skies, and the verdant valley with its sparkling grass and sweet-smelling flowers are all earthly signs of nature, more typical of the lower regions. The Pilgrim later learns, in canto XXI, that, unlike in Hell, weather and its attendant meteorological changes do not exist in Purgatory. The angel at the gate of Purgatory inscribes seven *P*s upon the Pilgrim's forehead (IX: 112), each of which another angel will remove after he has experienced the lessons of sin, punishment, hope, and salvation on each of the seven terraces into which the mountain is divided. Although its punishments are severe, Purgatory is a place of calm and concentration, where the sounds of music bring serenity and solace to hopeful souls. Beyond the gate, the tranquil, unhurried atmosphere gives way to the steep and hard path up the stony peak of punishment.

Like Hell and Paradise, Purgatory is carefully organized into seven concentric circular ledges, where sinners purge their sins in ritualistic fashion, eagerly accepting punishments for all the sins they have committed and hopeful of their eventual ascension to heaven. Dante the Pilgrim discovers that on each terrace of Purgatory, souls cleanse themselves of one of the seven deadly sins not simply through punishment, as in Hell, but through a process of education. They are educated through vivid illustrations not only of the virtue they must pursue but also of the vice they must avoid.

- Canto IX: The Pilgrim's first dream
- Cantos X–XII: Terrace I, misdirected love—the proud

(Omberto Altobranceschi, Oderisi da Agobbio, Provenzan Salvani)

- Cantos XIII–XVI: Terrace II, misdirected love—the envious (Sapìa of Siena, Guido del Duca, Renier da Calboli)
- Cantos XV–XVII: Terrace III, misdirected love—the wrathful (Marco the Lombard)
- Cantos XVII and XVIII: Terrace IV, deficient love—the slothful (the Abbot of San Zeno in Verona)
- Cantos XIX–XXII: Terrace V, excessive love—the avaricious and the prodigal (Pope Adrian V and Hugh Capet; the appearance of Statius)
- Cantos XXII–XXV: Terrace VI, excessive love—the Gluttonous (Dante's friend Forese Donati and Buonagiunta of Lucca)
- Cantos XXV and XXVI: Terrace VII, excessive love—the lustful (Guido Guinicelli and Arnaut Daniel, both famous poets).

Not surprisingly, the sin of pride is punished in the first terrace to which all souls proceed. Theologians of Dante's time considered pride to be the source of all sin, the worst and most common human fault. It was, after all, the archetypal sin, which led to Lucifer's challenge and the first humans' disobedience. In Dante's Hell, pride is ubiquitous, affecting a spectrum of characters from the self-involved Francesca to Farinata and to Lucifer himself. Dante admits that pride is a significant fault in his Pilgrim, for which he will do far longer penance than for envy (*Purgatorio* XIII: 133–138).

At the beginning of canto X, establishing the theme of love as central to *The Divine Comedy*, Dante the Poet describes the gates of Purgatory as a barrier eternally closed to souls whose loves are perverted (X: 2). In this canto, Dante also depicts the pattern of punishment and purgation that will govern all the terraces. As Virgil and the Pilgrim enter each of the seven terraces, they find *exempla* of the virtue opposite each sin, after which they meet the sinners and learn of their punishments. Each group of sinners says a special prayer, usually one that reflects what they need to learn. As they are leaving each terrace, they see or hear representations of the sin being purged. Dante creates

Purgatory as a place of harsh punishments that involve heavy stones (pride); eyes sewn shut (envy); smoke (wrath); running (sloth); prostration on the ground (avarice); starvation (gluttony); and fire (lust). It is also a place of learning and purification. The representations of virtue and vice, designed to teach the souls and to inspire them to virtue, take various forms, visual or auditory, including carvings, voices, and visions.

The general rule regulating the actual physical punishments in Purgatory, as opposed to their geographical location or their moral hierarchy from more serious to least serious, derives from the system of punishments in Hell, the *contrapasso*. Finally defined relatively late in *Inferno* (XXVIII: 142), *contrapasso* is a variation on the Old Testament's *lex talionis*, the law of retaliation or retribution, the proverbial "eye for an eye, a tooth for a tooth." Longfellow translates *contrapasso* quite neatly as "counterpoise." Dante's Italian term comes from the Latin translation of a Greek word found in Aristotle's *Nicomachean Ethics* and discussed extensively by Saint Thomas Aquinas in his commentary on the Aristotelian passage. The original Greek word meant "retaliation," clearly relating it to the *lex talionis*. The purgatorial punishments in the form of the *contrapasso* are harsh, but that is in keeping with the preventive concept of Purgatory shared by many of the early Christian writers from Augustine onward, who wished to lead Christians down the straight and narrow path of virtue. *Purgatorio*, carrying on the teachings of *Inferno*, strongly emphasizes that sin has consequences. In the second realm, however, sinners eagerly submit to their punishments, because, unlike the damned, they have the hope of heaven. Many readers of Dante's *Divine Comedy* are puzzled by a lack of compassion for sinners, since nothing seems more foreign to the moral teachings of Christ than righteous indignation or eternal damnation. But even in Purgatory, sinners, who have taken too long to repent their evil ways, must endure their sufferings to expiate their evil deeds.

Inversely from the levels of Hell, the first and lowest terraces on the Mountain of Purgatory punish the most serious sins (pride, envy, and wrath) that involve the misapplication of intellect, a special gift from God. As in *Inferno*, Dante here looks upon sins of appetite or incontinence (love of money, food, or sex) that reflect a loss of self-control as being less serious than sins committed by willful misuse of reason.

Once again, Dante, in contrast to prudish religious thinkers, does not consider lust to be a very serious sin. Lust may prevent the individual from focusing upon love of God or his Christian neighbor, but it is not a sin about which the poet is obsessed. Anything but a puritan or a religious fundamentalist, Dante considers the perversions of love in pride, envy, and wrath more likely to lead to the shattering of human bonds than indulging one's sexual desires.

The moral and political core of *Purgatorio* lies in Virgil's lectures on the nature of love and Marco Lombardo's discourse on evil in the central cantos of the second canticle. In canto XV: 40–81, responding to a question from the Pilgrim, Virgil discusses the essential difference between love for earthly and heavenly things, the former being diminished when divided and the latter increased when shared. Marco the Lombard discusses the psychology and politics of evil and its origin in ignorance, bad leadership, and lack of restraints or curbs in canto XVI: 63–145, then Virgil continues his discussion of love as the motivating force of all human action in canto XVII: 85–139. He explains that God embeds two kinds of love in the human heart prior to birth. The first is the natural, instinctive desire to return to God, which can never in itself be wrong. The second kind of love—misdirected, deficient, and excessive love—is governed by our free will; given human fallibility, it can lead to evil actions. Dante's *Divine Comedy*, in its focus upon love of God as the ultimate goal of every human soul, and in its exploration of the sociological and political ramifications of misdirected love, has an Augustinian cast.

Dante utilizes the popular classical and medieval literary device of the dream as a way of marking the Pilgrim's progress and linking the three regions of Purgatory thematically. Having utilized various visionary experiences in *La Vita Nuova*, Dante creates his *Divine Comedy* as a vision on a large scale, in which spells of fainting, sleeping, and dreaming are central to the narrative.

- Canto IX: 13–42: The Pilgrim's first dream
- Canto XIX: 7–33: The Pilgrim's second dream
- Canto XXVII: 91–114: The Pilgrim's third dream.

Virgil and the Pilgrim arrive on the shores of the Mountain of Purgatory on Easter Sunday at dawn, after which they spend several days ascending the mountain. It is impossible for the souls to climb up the mountain at night, due to human weakness in the absence of divine light (VII: 43–45). Instead, they sleep, and to sleep for the Pilgrim is to dream—specifically, to dream at dawn, the traditional time for the kind of truthful dreams that would be sent by a divinity. These dreams punctuate the Pilgrim's movement from region to region of Purgatory and occur in a ritualistic numerical pattern based on the number three (three regions, three dreams, three stages in the Pilgrim's moral development) and permutations of the number nine (in cantos IX, XIX, and XXVII). The erotic aspect of these dreams no doubt reflects the Pilgrim's own worst sin—lust.

During the first night, before crossing the threshold of Purgatory proper, the Pilgrim dreams of an eagle that hovers in the sky then swoops down and transports him upward into a region of fire, the burning heat of which interrupts the dream and his sleep (IX: 19–42). The Pilgrim compares himself to Ganymede, the beautiful boy who becomes a lover of Zeus, giving the episode an erotic quality. The fiery region looks forward not only to the Pilgrim's ascent, but also to the wall of fire through which he must pass on the last terrace—the terrace of the lustful.

After the long discussion of love and political and moral leadership in which Virgil and Marco the Lombard engage, the sleepy Pilgrim sinks into his second dream on his second night in Purgatory and sees a repulsively ugly and deformed woman (XIX: 7–33). Gradually his eyes betray him and transform her into the figure of a siren, like the one who tested Ulysses and Aeneas, signifying the seductive—even erotic—power of familiar vices over human senses. A saintly lady interrupts the siren's song, countering her evil spell and revealing her once again in her ugliness, both physical and moral, emphasized by the disgusting stench that pours from her body and awakens the Pilgrim from his dream.

After his purifying experience on the terrace of the lustful, the Pilgrim experiences his third dream on his third night in Purgatory (XXVII: 91–114). He sees a lovely young woman, Leah, who picks flowers to weave in a garland to adorn herself as she looks in her mirror. She explains that her sister Rachel always sits before her mirror, contemplating her eyes. These two figures, symbolic of the active and contemplative lives, resemble Matilda and Beatrice, whom the Pilgrim meets in the Earthly Paradise. The erotic aspect of this final dream reflects a marked change in the Pilgrim, an orientation toward heavenly love. At the end of this canto, the Pilgrim hears Virgil's final words in which he pronounces the Pilgrim master of his fate (XXVII: 127–142), now that his soul has been restored to true freedom. Virgil indicates he is ready to follow his desires, and that being good, they will be satisfied (XXVII: 115–116), preparing him for Paradise, his next stop.

At the end of the Pilgrim's purgatorial journey, such longing comes upon him that he rises easily to the Earthly Paradise (XXVII: 120–XXXIII: 145), and he enters upon a new phase in his spiritual development. Although Dante never specifically employs the term "Earthly Paradise" in *Purgatorio*, the term was a common medieval expression for the Garden of Eden. In early *mappamondi* (maps of the world) the Garden of Eden was located on the easternmost edge of inhabitable space, and was possibly an island or a mountain that reached into the heavens, entirely inaccessible to humans. Dante invents a Purgatory that is a mountain topped by a garden, on which the journey of purification ends in a return to the original Paradise in which humankind was born, where the Pilgrim, whose soul is reoriented to love of God, regains the freedom, innocence, and harmony destroyed by original sin. The Earthly Paradise represents the happiness that can be acquired in this life through the proper use of reason and the practice of the moral virtues—the right use of reason that Virgil could teach the Pilgrim. In *Purgatorio*, Dante emphasizes that the responsibility for moral leadership lies with those at the top of the social ladder— particularly the emperor and pope, who, in his view, have failed their subjects.

The journey out of the "dark wood" at the beginning of *The Divine Comedy* leads to the primordial forest of the Garden of Eden, an environment that bears no resemblance to those the Pilgrim has experienced earlier in his journey. Once Virgil tells Dante that he may choose either to wait for Beatrice or to explore the garden (XXVII: 127–142), the Pilgrim's choice is to seek his pleasure in the midst of the "heavenly forest," the "ancient wood" (XXVIII: 2, 23), where he finds a gentle breeze, flowers, a sweet smell, and the song of birds. He then comes to two streams of crystal clarity flowing from a single source, the Lethe and the Eunoë, each of which has a separate moral purpose. The Lethe, in keeping with its function in Virgil, cleanses the soul from sin through forgetfulness; the Eunoë fosters the opposite, the remembrance of good.

Across the rivers the Pilgrim sees a lovely woman reminiscent of Leah in his third dream and who remains unnamed until Beatrice refers to her as Matilda (XXXIII: 119). Recalling the Pilgrim's dream just prior to entering the Earthly Paradise, she is gathering flowers and singing praise of God's creations. Her significance has been debated, but she clearly represents the active and happy life lived according to natural justice, or possibly, humanity restored to its original purity and earthly wisdom. She welcomes the three poets, glowing with love (XXVIII: 43–45), and becomes their guide and teacher in the Earthly Paradise. She addresses Dante the Pilgrim and answers his question about the weather, which he had been told never changed in Purgatory. She explains the significance of Adam's sin and the miraculous character of a place in which plants grow without seeds and water comes from an eternal source (XXVIII: 115–117 and 121–126). Dante's Earthly Paradise represents the highest goodness in nature at its intersection with the supernatural. The air, revolving with the sphere of the moon and broken by the peak of the mountain, blows through the Earthly Paradise and is the source of the power of the spring that feeds the two rivers and controls the natural growth in the garden. Bringing a smile to the lips of Virgil and Statius, she even notes that pagan poets who wrote of the Golden Age may have had an inkling of humankind's original perfection and goodness (XXVIII: 139–144).

Dante's experiences at the end of *Purgatorio* include lessons from Christian history as well as episodes from his own personal life, especially those involving his love for Beatrice. The pageantry that is part of his experiences in the Earthly Paradise seems to be inspired by the Book of Revelation (the Apocalypse). The happiness found in the Earthly Paradise fulfills the first of the Pilgrim's two goals. It is quite different from the heavenly bliss of Paradise, presented by Beatrice, which can be attained only with the help of God's grace and revealed truth and through the enlightenment of the theological virtues (faith, hope, and charity, or love). The ascent up the mountain has been a preparation of the Pilgrim's heart and mind to receive Christian revelation and to enter Paradise. Matilda leads him and his two classical companions (Virgil and Statius) along the riverbanks toward the east to witness the first of visionary pageants that present the early history of Christianity. The pageant displays figures representing the books of the Bible; the theological and cardinal virtues (faith, hope, charity or love, prudence, justice, fortitude, and temperance); and the coming of Christ, depicted as the griffin drawing a chariot (XXIX: 106–120). This vision, with its focus on Christ in glory, is based primarily upon the Book of Revelation. The pageant continues with the procession in canto XXX that brings Beatrice from heaven, whose coming is announced by angels with words from the Bible that applied to Christ: "Benedictus qui venis!" or "Blessed art Thou that comest" (Matthew 21: 9).

At the moment of Beatrice's appearance, Dante turns to Virgil, but finds himself alone with Statius. Virgil's disappearance is as sudden and unanticipated as his appearance in *Inferno*. Here it is linked to Dante's idea of salvation as a personal responsibility that cannot depend on reason or any other individual, even the pope himself. In the confrontation with Beatrice, the Pilgrim, cowed, trembling, and ashamed before her eyes, must face the guilty realization that his early sinful love for Beatrice distracted him from true virtue, divine love, and the goal of earning salvation. Provoking the Pilgrim to tears, she speaks of her efforts to guide him until she died and he strayed from her. She accuses him of squandering his gifts and ignoring the good, despite her prayers, until she had to send him to Hell to learn it by observing the damned (XXX: 72–141).

Before crossing the Lethe, the Pilgrim must repent, and recalling examples such as Buonconte (V), he expresses his repentance in tears (XXX: 142–145). At the beginning of canto XXXI, Beatrice continues to scold him for his failures. Dante offers his confession: He has been too distracted by worldly joys, or "Sirens" (XXXI: 34–36, 45). Recognizing the depth of his guilt, he falls into a swoon, reminiscent of that he experienced after hearing the story of Francesca (*Inferno* V), but here, his emotion has been redirected toward the right kind of love (XXXI: 85–90). Once he has confessed and expressed true remorse, Matilda leads him, gliding Christ-like across the water of the Lethe, from which he drinks to erase sin from his memory (XXXI: 97–102). Thereafter he can find true pleasure by gazing into Beatrice's eyes, where he finds his reward in a double vision. The four pagan virtues lead him to the first vision, of Christ as the griffin. The three Christian virtues lead him to the second vision, of the mouth of Beatrice unveiled, a brilliant symbol of the wisdom that leads to salvation (XXXI: 103–138; XXXII: 1–12). The description of Beatrice's ineffable beauty at the end of canto XXXI foreshadows the technique used in describing the Pilgrim's vision of God in *Paradiso* (XXXI: 139–145).

The triumphal processions depict the ideal state of the world restored by Christ's birth, its current corruption, and the hope for the present and future; Christ's Second Coming will see the Church triumphant and the saved in Paradise. Blinded by the sight of Beatrice's face, the Pilgrim looks away, and as his eyes become accustomed to the dimness outside Beatrice's face, he sees the procession in retreat (XXXII: 10–27). With Statius and Matilda, the Pilgrim follows the procession, which circles a tall tree stripped bare because of Adam's sin, the prefiguration of the cross and God's gift of Redemption (XXXI: 28–42). The griffin, representing Christ and strong in his obedience to God, refrains from touching the tree, symbolic of God's justice, which then renews itself (XXXII: 43–60). Like the apostles at the transfiguration in the Bible (Matthew 17: 5), the Pilgrim, overcome, falls asleep and is reawakened by Matilda. He once again gazes upon the pageant, now in transformation with the return of the griffin and his host to heaven (XXXII: 61–90). Beatrice instructs him to give an account of what he sees as a moral message to those still living on earth (XXXII: 100–105).

The Pilgrim now sees Beatrice and the seven virtues guarding the chariot, which represents the Church (XXXII: 91–99). The new vision comes in the form of seven tableaux that symbolize a succession of attacks on the Church. In the first tableau, an eagle, that of Jove, swoops down and destroys the leaves, bark, and blooms on the tree and strikes the chariot, which behaves like a ship in a tempest (XXXII: 109–117); this is an allusion to the persecution of Christianity by some Roman emperors. Subsequent tableaux depict such historical issues as internal heresies and the defense of tradition (XXXII: 118–123); the Donation of Constantine and the Church's acquisition of secular power and wealth (XXXII: 124–129); the later corruption and schisms, symbolized by a dragon (XXXII: 130–135); and the Church's subsequent acquisitions of even greater temporal influence (XXXII: 136–141). The chariot then sprouts seven heads, perhaps representing the seven deadly sins (XXXII: 142–147). In the last tableau, the whore replaces Beatrice on the chariot and is accompanied by a giant, symbolizing the control of the Church by the kings of France. When the whore looks at the Pilgrim, the giant beats her and moves the chariot to a position in the woods and out of the Pilgrim's view (XXXII: 148–160), just as the French kings moved the papacy to the French city of Avignon during the so-called Babylonian Captivity of the Church (1309–1378). Dante the Poet here marks a future time in the fiction of his epic narrative, since his journey to the afterlife occurs in the year 1300, nine years before this widely criticized move.

In the last canto of this canticle, Beatrice reassures those lamenting that the Church will eventually triumph and organizes a new procession of the seven virtues that includes herself, Matilda, and the two poets, Dante and Statius (XXXIII: 1–15). Explaining the pageant's meaning (XXXIII: 34–72), Beatrice announces Dante's task of telling humankind upon his return to the world that "life . . . is a running unto death" (XXXIII: 54) and that the Church requires reform, perhaps through the agency of the empire (XXXIII: 55–78). Earlier, she has prophesied the coming of an avenger, perhaps a good emperor, programmed as the Arabic number 515, or the Roman number DXV (XXXIII: 43). This avenger will bring the world and the Church back to order and truth, preparing them for the Second Coming. When Dante the Pilgrim expresses his intellectual confusion, Beatrice declares that "from this time forward shall [her] words / Be naked, so far as is befitting / To lay them open unto thy rude gaze" (XXXIII: 100–102).

Beatrice's role as wisdom is clearly evident, and she tells the Pilgrim to ask Matilda for an explanation (XXXIII: 118–119), instructing her to lead him to the Eunoë, where the waters will revive his memory of good and strengthen his "half-dead virtue" (XXXIII: 129). Both Dante and Statius are led forward, but the Poet says that the experience is indescribable, just as he claimed was the case when he saw Beatrice's face (XXXIII: 136–141; XXXI: 139–145). Reborn by his journey and the cleansing waters of the rivers of the Earthly Paradise, the Pilgrim returns to Beatrice "pure and disposed to mount unto the stars"

(XXXIII: 145), the stellar symbol of his ultimate goal of paradise regained. At the beginning of *Paradiso*, Beatrice looks into the sun, and Dante, receiving the power to do so too, sees the whole sky joined in sunlight, because he has already left the Earthly Paradise for the heavenly (*Paradiso* I: 37–93).

Purgatorio *and Allegory*

Dante constantly insists that what he saw in a journey through the afterlife was true. As Charles S. Singleton, one of Dante's greatest American interpreters, never tired of emphasizing, the key fiction of *The Divine Comedy* is that the poem is true. Dante wants his readers to believe that what they see, feel, and hear in his poem did actually occur. The work is not just an intellectual pastime for an exiled intellectual. Medieval literature is often described as a literature of allegory. In an allegorical reading of *Purgatorio*, the reader would constantly be forced to identify characters with abstract ideas: Dante becomes Everyman, Virgil becomes human reason, Cato becomes liberty, Beatrice revelation and wisdom, and so forth. Everything in the poem would thus become a vast and impersonal puzzle. The reader's function would involve identifying what each of the characters stood for and observing the relationships and interplay among them. The result would be a lifting of the veil of allegory and a revealing or uncovering of the secret meaning underneath. That concealed meaning would of necessity involve even more abstract ideas: love, death, evil, sin, heresy, treachery, and so forth.

Such allegorical abstractions, however, are simply not what Dante's great poem is all about. To understand Dante's position on allegory and historical truth, it is first necessary to understand that serious medieval thinkers (theologians, philosophers—not poets) considered poetry to be a fiction that did not tell the truth. Quite rightly, allegorical poems that used characters to represent abstract qualities could not be literally true and were considered "fables" in the pejorative sense. Dante wanted his readers—including serious thinkers—to consider his poem to be a true account of an actual journey. Even if the reader willfully suspends his or her disbelief in the reality of the poem's action and believes that this fantastical journey actually took place, a traditional allegorical poem would simply not serve his purposes, for it would place more emphasis on the abstract ideas contained in the poem than on the characters themselves, and the historical reality some represent.

The method that Dante employed in his work, and one that he suggests in a late letter to Cangrande della Scala, is quite different from the traditional allegory typical of works such as *The Romance of the Rose* or *The Pilgrim's Progress*. Contrary to the allegory of the poets, Dante accepted at least in part what was known as the allegory of the theologians, which involved bearing in mind four possible senses of a text: the historical or literal; the allegorical; the moral or tropological; and the anagogical. Such a method derived from reading Holy Scriptures, particularly in determining the relationship between the historical and the allegorical senses. For example, in most Christian services, regardless of the denomination, the ritual requires a reading of a passage from the Old Testament followed by, or juxtaposed to, a reading of a passage from the New Testament. In most cases, the Old Testament text prefigures or anticipates that of the New Testament, which fulfills or explains elements of the Old Testament. The classic example of how these four senses operate may be taken from the event to which Dante himself refers in *Purgatorio* II: 46–47. There, an angelic boatman (the counterpart to the infernal Charon) delivers souls to the shore of Purgatory. As the souls arrive, they sing in Latin the words "In exitu Israel de Aegypto" ("When Israel out of Egypt came)," a biblical citation from Psalms 114: 1.

What are we to make of this moment in the poem? According to the four senses of the allegory of the theologians, we can read the passage in various ways. The event celebrated by the souls about to undergo purgation points us to the exodus of the Hebrews led by Moses. This event was and is historically and literally true. Still, leading the Hebrews out of captivity may be explained allegorically as a prefiguration of Christ's redemption of lost souls, bringing mankind out of bondage to sin. In a real sense, then, Christ fulfills Moses and Moses prefigures or foreshadows Christ. This kind of figural interpretation is common to Christian thought. It explains why Job's suffering might be compared to Christ's passion; why Jonah's three days in the whale's belly was frequently compared to Christ's resurrection three days after the Crucifixion, during which he descended into hell; and why Abraham's sacrifice of Isaac could be viewed as a prefiguration of God's sacrifice of His son, Jesus. In the case of Jonah, Christ even refers to the story in the Bible (Matthew 12: 40) as a prefiguration of what will happen to him, and in the Gospels Christ consciously seeks to fulfill the prophecies of the Old Testament.

Such a "figural" realism, as the literary historian Erich Auerbach has labeled it, makes sense from a Christian point of view, and it is one kind of meaning that Dante certainly understood and employed on occasion in his poem, when another medieval poet might have employed traditional allegory. Another interesting example of this kind of figural realism may be demonstrated by an analysis of why Dante places Cato of Utica, a suicide and a pagan who died before the birth of Christ, in canto I of *Purgatorio* rather than in *Inferno* XIII, the spot reserved for suicides. Dante might also have placed him in the Limbo of the Virtuous Pagans along with other positive classical figures, such as Virgil, who are mentioned in *Inferno* IV. Applying the principles of figural realism, Auerbach has argued persuasively that Cato fulfills in the afterlife his historical identity on earth: Once the embodiment of love for political freedom, he now constitutes a figural symbol for the freedom of the immortal soul. Dante's counterintuitive treatments of such pagans as Virgil or Cato point us to the final "house rule" of his poem. Our poet does not concern himself overly much with consistency. He makes the rules to fit his poetic design, not to satisfy logicians, philosophers, theologians, historians, or politicians. In Hell, he condemns popes to eternal damnation just as easily as he rewards Statius, a pagan poet we now consider to be far less a writer than Virgil, with eternal salvation.

Returning to the four senses of a text, the third and fourth senses—the moral (tropological) and the anagogical senses—always seem more ambiguous. If we take our example from Exodus, the moral sense would refer to the soul of the individual Christian seeking an "exodus" from a life of sin in the present. The anagogical sense would refer to the end of time after the Last Judgment when the saved believe they will arrive in the Promised Land—for Christians, this is heaven and not the land of Israel. Frankly, Dante infrequently concerns himself with the third and fourth senses of a text, for he is most fascinated by suggesting ways in which historical events, ideas, or characters may suggest (foreshadow, prefigure) other interesting events, ideas, or characters.

The best advice to the reader of *The Divine Comedy* in general and to *Purgatorio* in particular is to pay attention to the literal sense of the poem. The greatest poetry in Dante resides in the literal sense of the work, its graphic descriptions of the sinners, their characters, and their punishments. In like manner, the greatest and most satisfying intellectual achievement of the poem comes from the reader's understanding of (and not necessarily agreement with) Dante's complex view of morality, or the sinful world that God's punishment is designed to correct. In most cases, a concrete appreciation of the small details of his poem will almost always lead to surprising but satisfying discoveries about the universe Dante's poetry has created.

We read the classics because they offer us different perspectives on timeless questions. Very few people today who encounter *The Divine Comedy*, even Catholics, accept most of Dante's assumptions about the universe. We have gone from the Ptolemaic universe Dante understood through the Newtonian universe that overturned the classical and medieval world views and into the Einsteinian universe of black holes and relativity, learning that both Newton and Einstein have valuable applications. In religion, we have experienced the complete schism of a single Christian church after the Reformation into many different Christian churches, and while Western society is clearly more secular in spirit than was the Florence of Dante's day, other non-Christian cultures seem to be returning to a religious fundamentalism not seen in the West for centuries. The confusing politics involving the petty squabbles of Guelf and Ghibelline have long since vanished and have been submerged since Dante's day by various kinds of political systems, most of which are far worse than those he experienced.

Perhaps Dante might recognize a similarity between the nascent capitalism of medieval Florence and our own contemporary multinational economic system. Both produced inordinate and unexpected quantities of wealth, although neither ever arrived at a fully equitable means of distributing it, and both economic systems have suffered periodical and frequent cyclical waves of boom and bust that sometimes threaten the lives and fortunes of those who depend on them. Dante would not have been surprised by the many religious, social, political, scientific, intellectual, or economic changes that have taken place since his time. He would have been surprised only if the characters that inhabit *Inferno* seem dated, almost denizens of another planet. But, of course, Dante's characters are all too contemporary. It would not be difficult to compile a list of our acquaintances or colleagues and to place them in the appropriate places in Hell. A humor magazine in 1998 announced a new circle opening in Hell for the "corpadverticus"—publicists, lobbyists, marketers, demographers, media whores, franchisers and licensers, and awards-show hosts!⁵ More difficult, perhaps, would be a similar assignment of those we know to appropriate places in Purgatory or Paradise.

What explains our contemporary fascination with Dante is his attitude toward his characters. As members of a liberal, diverse, and tolerant culture typical of twenty-first-century democracies, at least in our ideals we tend to see everything and everyone from a variety of positive perspectives. We are asked to respect those with whom we disagree. The French maxim says it all—*tout comprendre, c'est tout pardoner* ("to understand all is to forgive all"). Dante stands entirely outside such a "civilized," politically correct perspective. For him, understanding does not imply justification, and Dante is the most judgmental of all poets. He believes that civilization involves understanding, an act of the intellect, but for Dante understanding leads inevitably to evaluation, judgment, and the assumption of a moral position based on very simple but immutable ethical and religious precepts. No situational ethics, no "I'm OK, you're OK," no automatic and naive acceptances of every point of view, no matter how ill founded. His energy derives from moral indignation—indignation about the corruption of the Church, about the corruption of Florence and most Italian or European cities, about the weakness of the Holy Roman Empire, and about the general wretched state of humanity. But his genius is based on something even more precious and more unusual—his love for truth and his ability to express it in timeless poetic form.

―――

JULIA CONAWAY BONDANELLA is Professor of Italian at Indiana University. She has served as President of the National Collegiate Honors Council and as Assistant Chairman of the National Endowment for the Humanities. Her publications include a book on

Petrarch, *The Cassell Dictionary of Italian Literature*, and translations of Italian classics by Benvenuto Cellini, Niccolò Machiavelli, and Giorgio Vasari.

———

PETER BONDANELLA is Distinguished Professor of Comparative Literature and Italian at Indiana University and has been President of the American Association for Italian Studies. His publications include a number of translations of Italian classics, books on Italian Renaissance literature, and studies of Italian cinema. His latest book is *Hollywood Italians: Dagos, Palookas, Romeos, Wise Guys, and Sopranos*, a history of how Italian Americans have been depicted in Hollywood.

Notes to the Introduction

1. Dante Alighieri, *Literary Criticism of Dante*, translated and edited by Robert S. Haller (Lincoln: University of Nebraska Press, 1973), p. 99.

2. The classic study of Purgatory is Jacques Le Goff's *The Birth of Purgatory*, translated by Arthur Goldhammer (Chicago: University of Chicago Press, 1984).

3. Although Longfellow calls the poet Virgilius, we have consistently used the more common contemporary form Virgil throughout the introduction and the notes.

4. For an English translation of this work, see Dante, *The Banquet*, translated and edited by Christopher Ryan, Stanford French and Italian Studies, volume 61 (Saratoga, CA: ANMA Libri, 1989), pp. 77–78. Ryan translates this poem's first line as "Love, which discourses to me *yearningly* in my mind."

5. *The Onion*, volume 34, number 8 (September 24, 1998).

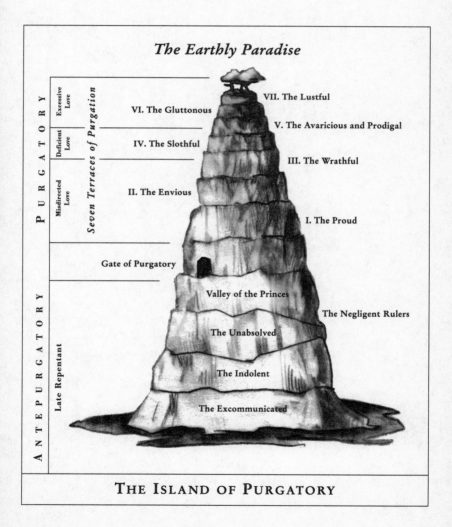

The Earthly Paradise

PURGATORY

- Excessive Love
- Deficient Love
- Misdirected Love

Seven Terraces of Purgation

VI. The Gluttonous

VII. The Lustful

V. The Avaricious and Prodigal

IV. The Slothful

III. The Wrathful

II. The Envious

I. The Proud

Gate of Purgatory

Valley of the Princes

The Negligent Rulers

The Unabsolved

The Indolent

The Excommunicated

ANTEPURGATORY

Late Repentant

THE ISLAND OF PURGATORY

THE
PURGATORIO

CANTO I

To run o'er better waters hoists its sail
    The little vessel of my genius now,
    That leaves behind itself a sea so cruel;[1]
And of that second kingdom will I sing
    Wherein the human spirit doth purge itself,   5
    And to ascend to heaven becometh worthy.[2]
But let dead Poesy here rise again,[3]
    O holy Muses,[4] since that I am yours,
    And here Calliope[5] somewhat ascend,
My song accompanying with that sound,   10
    Of which the miserable magpies[6] felt
    The blow so great, that they despaired of pardon.[7]
Sweet color of the oriental sapphire,[8]
    That was upgathered in the cloudless aspect
    Of the pure air, as far as the first circle,[9]   15
Unto mine eyes did recommence delight
    Soon as I issued forth from the dead air,[10]
    Which had with sadness filled mine eyes and breast.
The beauteous planet, that to love incites,
    Was making all the orient to laugh,   20
    Veiling the Fishes that were in her escort.[11]
To the right hand I turned,[12] and fixed my mind
    Upon the other pole, and saw four stars
    Ne'er seen before save by the primal people.[13]
Rejoicing in their flamelets seemed the heaven.   25
    O thou septentrional and widowed site,[14]
    Because thou art deprived of seeing these!

When from regarding them I had withdrawn,
>> Turning a little to the other pole,
>> There where the Wain had disappeared already,[15]   30
I saw beside me an old man alone,[16]
>> Worthy of so much reverence in his look,
>> That more owes not to father any son.
A long beard and with white hair intermingled
>> He wore, in semblance like unto the tresses,   35
>> Of which a double list[17] fell on his breast.
The rays of the four consecrated stars
>> Did so adorn his countenance with light,[18]
>> That him I saw as were the sun before him.
"Who are you? ye who, counter the blind river,   40
>> Have fled away from the eternal prison?"[19]
>> Moving those venerable plumes, he said:
"Who guided you? or who has been your lamp
>> In issuing forth out of the night profound,
>> That ever black makes the infernal valley?   45
The laws of the abyss, are they thus broken?[20]
>> Or is there changed in heaven some counsel new,
>> That being damned ye come unto my grottos?"
Then did my Leader lay his grasp upon me,
>> And with his words, and with his hands and signs   50
>> Reverent he made in me my knees and brow;
Then answered him: "I came not of myself;[21]
>> A Lady from Heaven descended, at whose prayers
>> I aided this one with my company.
But since it is thy will more be unfolded   55
>> Of our condition, how it truly is,
>> Mine cannot be that this should be denied thee.
This one has never his last evening seen,
>> But by his folly was so near to it
>> That very little time was there to turn.   60
As I have said, I unto him was sent
>> To rescue him, and other way was none
>> Than this to which I have myself betaken.

Canto I: Dante kneeling before Statius

I've shown him all the people of perdition,
    And now those spirits I intend to show   65
    Who purge themselves beneath my guardianship.[22]
How I have brought him would be long to tell thee.
    Virtue descendeth from on high that aids me
    To lead him to behold thee and to hear thee.
Now may it please thee to vouchsafe his coming;   70
    He seeketh Liberty, which is so dear,[23]
    As knoweth he who life for her refuses.
Thou know'st it; since, for her, to thee not bitter
    Was death in Utica, where thou didst leave
    The vesture, that will shine so, the great day.[24]   75
By us the eternal edicts are not broken;
    Since this one lives, and Minos binds not me;[25]
    But of that circle I, where are the chaste
Eyes of thy Marcia,[26] who in looks still prays thee,
    O holy breast, to hold her as thine own;   80
    For her love, then, incline thyself to us.[27]
Permit us through thy sevenfold realm to go;
    I will take back this grace from thee to her,
    If to be mentioned there below thou deignest."
"Marcia so pleasing was unto mine eyes   85
    While I was on the other side," then said he,
    "That every grace she wished of me I granted;
Now that she dwells beyond the evil river,[28]
    She can no longer move me, by that law
    Which, when I issued forth from there, was made.   90
But if a Lady of Heaven do move and rule thee,
    As thou dost say, no flattery is needful;[29]
    Let it suffice thee that for her thou ask me.
Go, then, and see thou gird this one about
    With a smooth rush,[30] and that thou wash his face,   95
    So that thou cleanse away all stain therefrom,[31]
For 'twere not fitting that the eye o'ercast
    By any mist should go before the first
    Angel, who is of those of Paradise.

Canto I: Dante bows before the Angel Pilot

This little island round about its base   100
    Below there, yonder, where the willow beats it,
    Doth rushes bear upon its washy ooze;
No other plant that putteth forth the leaf,
    Or that doth indurate, can there have life,
    Because it yieldeth not unto the shocks.   105
Thereafter be not this way your return;
    The sun, which now is rising,[32] will direct you
    To take the mount[33] by easier ascent."
With this he vanished; and I raised me up[34]
    Without a word, and wholly drew myself   110
    Unto my Guide, and turned mine eyes to him.
And he began: "Son, follow thou my steps;
    Let us turn back, for on this side declines
    The plain unto its lower boundaries."
The dawn was vanquishing the matin hour   115
    Which fled before it, so that from afar
    I recognized the trembling of the sea.
Along the solitary plain we went[35]
    As one who unto the lost road returns,
    And till he finds it seems to go in vain.   120
As soon as we were come to where the dew
    Fights with the sun,[36] and, being in a part
    Where shadow falls, little evaporates,
Both of his hands upon the grass outspread
    In gentle manner did my Master place;   125
    Whence I, who of his action was aware,
Extended unto him my tearful cheeks;
    There did he make in me uncovered wholly
    That hue which Hell had covered up in me.[37]
Then came we down upon the desert shore[38]   130
    Which never yet saw navigate its waters
    Any that afterward had known return.
There he begirt me as the other pleased;[39]
    O marvellous! for even as he culled
    The humble plant,[40] such it sprang up again   135
Suddenly there where he uprooted it.

8

CANTO II

ALREADY had the sun the horizon reached[1]
    Whose circle of meridian covers o'er
    Jerusalem with its most lofty point,
And night that opposite to him revolves
    Was issuing forth from Ganges with the Scales   5
    That fall from out her hand when she exceedeth;[2]
So that the white and the vermilion cheeks
    Of beautiful Aurora,[3] where I was,
    By too great age were changing into orange.
We still were on the border of the sea,   10
    Like people who are thinking of their road,
    Who go in heart, and with the body stay;[4]
And lo! as when, upon the approach of morning,
    Through the gross vapors Mars grows fiery red[5]
    Down in the West upon the ocean floor,   15
Appeared to me—may I again behold it!—
    A light along the sea so swiftly coming,
    Its motion by no flight of wing is equalled;
From which when I a little had withdrawn
    Mine eyes, that I might question my Conductor,*   20
    Again I saw it brighter grown and larger.
Then on each side of it appeared to me
    I knew not what of white, and underneath it
    Little by little there came forth another.
My master yet had uttered not a word   25

*Leader, guide (in this case, Virgil).

While the first whiteness into wings unfolded;[6]
But when he clearly recognized the pilot,[7]
He cried: "Make haste, make haste to bow the knee!
Behold the Angel of God! fold thou thy hands!
Henceforward shalt thou see such officers!   30
See how he scorneth human arguments,
So that nor oar he wants, nor other sail
Than his own wings, between so distant shores.[8]
See how he holds them pointed up to heaven,
Fanning the air with the eternal pinions,   35
That do not moult themselves like mortal hair!"
Then as still nearer and more near us came
The Bird Divine, more radiant he appeared,
So that near by the eye could not endure him,
But down I cast it; and he came to shore   40
With a small vessel, very swift and light,[9]
So that the water swallowed naught thereof.[10]
Upon the stern stood the Celestial Pilot;
Beatitude seemed written in his face,[11]
And more than a hundred spirits sat within.   45
"*In exitu Israel de 'Ægypto!*"[12]
They chanted all together in one voice,
With whatso in that psalm[13] is after written.
Then made he sign of holy rood* upon them,
Whereat all cast themselves upon the shore,   50
And he departed swiftly as he came.
The throng which still remained there unfamiliar
Seemed with the place, all round about them gazing,
As one who in new matters makes essay.
On every side was darting forth the day   55
The sun, who had with his resplendent shafts
From the mid-heaven chased forth the Capricorn,[14]
When the new people lifted up their faces
Towards us, saying to us: "If ye know,
Show us the way to go unto the mountain."   60

*The Holy Cross, upon which Christ was crucified.

And answer made Virgilius: "Ye believe
    Perchance that we have knowledge of this place,
    But we are strangers[15] even as yourselves.
Just now we came, a little while before you,
    Another way, which was so rough and steep,   65
    That mounting will henceforth seem sport to us."
The souls who had, from seeing me draw breath,
    Become aware that I was still alive,
    Pallid in their astonishment became;
And as to messenger who bears the olive[16]   70
    The people throng to listen to the news,
    And no one shows himself afraid of crowding,
So at the sight of me stood motionless
    Those fortunate spirits, all of them, as if
    Oblivious to go and make them fair.[17]   75
One from among them[18] I saw coming forward,
    As to embrace me, with such great affection,
    That it incited me to do the like.
O empty shadows, save in aspect only!
    Three times[19] behind it did I clasp my hands,   80
    As oft returned with them to my own breast!
I think with wonder I depicted me;
    Whereat the shadow smiled[20] and backward drew;
    And I, pursuing it, pressed farther forward.
Gently it said that I should stay my steps;   85
    Then knew I who it was, and I entreated
    That it would stop awhile to speak with me.
It made reply to me: "Even as I loved thee
    In mortal body, so I love thee free;
    Therefore I stop; but wherefore goest thou?"   90
"My own Casella! to return once more
    There where I am, I make this journey,"[21] said I;
    "But how from thee has so much time been taken?"[22]
And he to me: "No outrage has been done me,
    If he who takes both when and whom he pleases   95
    Has many times denied to me this passage,
For of a righteous will his own is made.

He, sooth to say, for three months past has taken
    Whoever wished to enter with all peace;
Whence I, who now had turned unto that shore   100
    Where salt the waters of the Tiber grow,
    Benignantly by him have been received.
Unto that outlet now his wing is pointed,
    Because for evermore assemble there
    Those who tow'rds Acheron do not descend."[23]   105
And I: "If some new law take not from thee
    Memory or practice of the amorous song,
    Which used to quiet in me all my longings,
Thee may it please to comfort therewithal
    Somewhat this soul of mine, that with its body   110
    Hitherward coming is so much distressed."
"Love, that within my mind discourses with me,"[24]
    Forthwith began he so melodiously,
    The melody within me still is sounding.
My Master, and myself, and all that people   115
    Which with him were, appeared as satisfied
    As if naught else might touch the mind of any.
We all of us were motionless and attentive
    Unto his notes; and lo! the grave old man,
    Exclaiming: "What is this, ye laggard spirits?[25]   120
What negligence, what standing still is this?
    Run to the mountain to strip off the slough,[26]
    That lets not God be manifest to you."
Even as when, collecting grain or tares,
    The doves, together at their pasture met,   125
    Quiet, nor showing their accustomed pride,
If aught appear of which they are afraid,
    Upon a sudden leave their food alone,
    Because they are assailed by greater care;[27]
So that fresh company did I behold   130
    The song relinquish, and go tow'rds the hill,
    As one who goes, and knows not whitherward;
Nor was our own departure less in haste.[28]

CANTO III

*I*NASMUCH as the instantaneous flight
  Had scattered them asunder o'er the plain,
  Turned to the mountain whither* reason spurs us,[1]
I pressed me close unto my faithful comrade,
  And how without him had I kept my course?   5
  Who would have led me up along the mountain?
He seemed to me within himself remorseful;[2]
  O noble conscience, and without a stain,
  How sharp a sting is trivial fault to thee!
After his feet had laid aside the haste   10
  Which mars the dignity of every act,[3]
  My mind, that hitherto had been restrained,
Let loose its faculties as if delighted,
  And I my sight directed to the hill[4]
  That highest tow'rds the heaven uplifts itself.[5]   15
The sun, that in our rear was flaming red,
  Was broken in front of me into the figure
  Which had in me the stoppage of its rays;[6]
Unto one side I turned me, with the fear
  Of being left alone, when I beheld   20
  Only in front of me the ground obscured.[7]
"Why dost thou still mistrust?" my Comforter
  Began to say to me turned wholly round;
  "Dost thou not think me with thee, and that I
   guide thee?

*Where.

13

'Tis evening there already where is buried[8]   25
    The body within which I cast a shadow;
    'Tis from Brundusium ta'en, and Naples has it.
Now if in front of me no shadow fall,
    Marvel not[9] at it more than at the heavens,
    Because one ray impedeth not another.   30
To suffer torments, both of cold and heat,
    Bodies like this that Power provides, which wills
    That how it works be not unveiled to us.
Insane is he who hopeth that our reason
    Can traverse the illimitable way,   35
    Which the one Substance in three Persons follows!
Mortals, remain contented at the *Quia;*[10]
    For if ye had been able to see all,
    No need there were for Mary to give birth;
And ye have seen desiring without fruit,   40
    Those whose desire would have been quieted,
    Which evermore is given them for a grief.
I speak of Aristotle and of Plato,
    And others many";—and here he bowed his head,
    And more he said not, and remained disturbed.   45
We came meanwhile unto the mountain's foot;
    There so precipitate we found the rock,
    That nimble legs would there have been in vain.
'Twixt Lerici and Turbìa, the most desert,
    The most secluded pathway[11] is a stair   50
    Easy and open, if compared with that.
"Who knoweth now[12] upon which hand the hill
    Slopes down," my Master said, his footsteps staying,
    "So that who goeth without wings may mount?"
And while he held his eyes upon the ground   55
    Examining the nature of the path,
    And I was looking up around the rock,
On the left hand[13] appeared to me a throng
    Of souls, that moved their feet in our direction,
    And did not seem to move, they came so slowly.   60

Canto III: The Company of Souls upon the Cliff

"Lift up thine eyes," I to the Master said;
    "Behold, on this side, who will give us counsel,
    If thou of thine own self can have it not."
Then he looked at me, and with frank expression
    Replied: "Let us go there, for they come slowly,   65
    And thou be steadfast in thy hope, sweet son."
Still was that people as far off from us,
    After a thousand steps of ours I say,
    As a good thrower with his hand would reach,[14]
When they all crowded unto the hard masses   70
    Of the high bank, and motionless stood and close,
    As he stands still to look who goes in doubt.
"O happy dead! O spirits elect already!"[15]
    Virgilius made beginning, "by that peace
    Which I believe is waiting for you all,   75
Tell us upon what side the mountain slopes,
    So that the going up be possible,
    For to lose time irks him most who most knows."[16]
As sheep come issuing forth from out the fold
    By ones and twos and threes, and the others stand   80
    Timidly, holding down their eyes and nostrils,
And what the foremost does the others do,
    Huddling themselves against her, if she stop,
    Simple and quiet and the wherefore know not;
So moving to approach us thereupon   85
    I saw the leader of that fortunate flock,[17]
    Modest in face and dignified in gait.
As soon as those in the advance saw broken
    The light upon the ground at my right side,[18]
    So that from me the shadow reached the rock,   90
They stopped, and backward drew themselves somewhat;
    And all the others, who came after them,
    Not knowing why nor wherefore, did the same.
"Without your asking, I confess to you
    This is a human body which you see,
    Whereby the sunshine on the ground is cleft.   95

Marvel ye not thereat, but be persuaded
    That not without a power which comes from Heaven
    Doth he endeavor to surmount this wall."
The Master thus; and said those worthy people: 100
    "Return ye then, and enter in before us,"
    Making a signal with the back o' the hand.
And one of them began: "Whoe'er thou art,[19]
    Thus going turn thine eyes, consider well
    If e'er thou saw me in the other world."   105
I turned me tow'rds him, and looked at him closely;
    Blond was he, beautiful, and of noble aspect,
    But one of his eyebrows had a blow divided.
When with humility I had disclaimed
    E'er having seen him, "Now behold!" he said,   110
    And showed me high upon his breast a wound.
Then said he with a smile: "I am Manfredi,
    The grandson of the Emperess Costanza;[20]
    Therefore, when thou returnest, I beseech thee
Go to my daughter beautiful, the mother   115
    Of Sicily's honor and of Aragon's,[21]
    And the truth tell her, if aught else be told.
After I had my body lacerated
    By these two mortal stabs,[22] I gave myself
    Weeping to Him, who willingly doth pardon.[23]   120
Horrible my iniquities had been;
    But Infinite Goodness hath such ample arms,
    That it receives whatever turns to it.
Had but Cosenza's pastor, who in chase
    Of me was sent by Clement at that time,[24]   125
    In God read understandingly this page,[25]
The bones of my dead body still would be
    At the bridge-head, near unto Benevento,
    Under the safeguard of the heavy cairn.
Now the rain bathes and moveth them the wind,   130
    Beyond the realm,[26] almost beside the Verde,
    Where he transported them with tapers quenched.[27]

By malison of theirs is not so lost
    Eternal Love, that it cannot return,
    So long as hope has anything of green.[28]   135
True is it, who in contumacy[29] dies
    Of Holy Church, though penitent at last,
    Must wait upon the outside of this bank
Thirty times told the time that he has been
    In his presumption[30] unless such decree   140
    Shorter by means of righteous prayers[31] become.
See now if thou hast power to make me happy,
    By making known unto my good Costanza[32]
    How thou hast seen me, and this ban beside,
For those on earth can much advance us here."   145

CANTO IV

Whenever by delight or else by pain,
    That seizes any faculty of ours,
    Wholly to that the soul collects itself,
It seemeth that no other power it heeds;
    And this against that error is which thinks   5
    One soul above another kindles in us.
And hence, whenever aught is heard or seen
    Which keeps the soul intently bent upon it,
    Time passes on, and we perceive it not,
Because one faculty is that which listens,   10
    And other that which the soul keeps entire;
    This is as if in bonds, and that is free.
Of this I had experience positive
    In hearing and in gazing at that spirit;[1]
    For fifty full degrees uprisen was   15
The sun, and I had not perceived it,[2] when
    We came to where those souls with one accord
    Cried out unto us: "Here is what you ask."[3]
A greater opening ofttimes hedges up
    With but a little forkful of his thorns   20
    The villager, what time the grape imbrowns,[4]
Than was the passage-way through which ascended
    Only my Leader and myself behind him,
    After that company departed from us.
One climbs Sanleo and descends in Noli,   25
    And mounts the summit of Bismantova,[5]
    With feet alone; but here one needs must fly;

With the swift pinions and the plumes I say
    Of great desire, conducted after him
    Who gave me hope, and made a light for me.   30
We mounted upward through the rifted rock,
    And on each side the border pressed upon us,
    And feet and hands the ground beneath required.
When we were come upon the upper rim
    Of the high bank, out on the open slope,   35
    "My Master," said I, "what way shall we take?"
And he to me: "No step of thine descend;
    Still up the mount behind me win thy way,
    Till some sage escort shall appear to us."
The summit was so high it vanquished sight,   40
    And the hillside precipitous far more
    Than line from middle quadrant to the centre.[6]
Spent with fatigue was I, when I began:
    "O my sweet Father! turn thee and behold
    How I remain alone, unless thou stay!"[7]   45
"O son," he said, "up yonder drag thyself,"
    Pointing me to a terrace somewhat higher,
    Which on that side encircles all the hill.
These words of his so spurred me on, that I
    Strained every nerve, behind him scrambling up,   50
    Until the circle was beneath my feet.[8]
Thereon ourselves we seated both of us
    Turned to the East, from which we had ascended,
    For all men are delighted to look back.
To the low shores mine eyes I first directed,   55
    Then to the sun uplifted them, and wondered
    That on the left hand we were smitten by it.[9]
The Poet well perceived that I was wholly
    Bewildered at the chariot of the light,
    Where 'twixt us and the Aquilon[10] it entered.   60
Whereon he said to me: "If Castor and Pollux
    Were in the company of yonder mirror,
    That up and down conducteth with its light,

Canto IV: Dante follows Virgil up the Rugged Mountainside

Thou wouldst behold the zodiac's jagged wheel

    Revolving still more near unto the Bears,   65

    Unless it swerved aside from its old track.[11]

How that may be wouldst thou have power to think,

    Collected in thyself, imagine Zion

    Together with this mount on earth to stand,

So that they both one sole horizon have,   70

    And hemispheres diverse; whereby the road

    Which Phaeton, alas! knew not to drive,

Thou'lt see how of necessity must pass

    This on one side, when that upon the other,

    If thine intelligence right clearly heed."[12]   75

"Truly, my Master," said I, "never yet

    Saw I so clearly as I now discern,

    There where my wit appeared incompetent,

That the mid-circle of supernal motion,

    Which in some art is the Equator called,   80

    And aye remains between the Sun and Winter,

For reason which thou sayest, departeth hence

    Tow'rds the Septentrion, what time

      the Hebrews

    Beheld it tow'rds the region of the heat[13]

But, if it pleaseth thee, I fain would learn   85

    How far we have to go; for the hill rises

    Higher than eyes of mine have power to rise."

And he to me: "This mount is such, that ever

    At the beginning down below 'tis tiresome,

    And aye the more* one climbs, the less it hurts.   90

Therefore, when it shall seem so pleasant to thee,

    That going up shall be to thee as easy

    As going down the current in a boat,[14]

Then at this pathway's ending thou wilt be;

    There to repose thy panting breath expect;   95

    No more I answer; and this I know for true."

And as he finished uttering these words,

*All the more.

A voice close by us sounded: "Peradventure*
    Thou wilt have need of sitting down ere that."[15]
At sound thereof each one of us turned round,   100
    And saw upon the left hand a great rock,
    Which neither I nor he before had noticed.
Thither we drew; and there were persons there
    Who in the shadow stood behind the rock,
    As one through indolence is wont to stand.   105
And one of them, who seemed to me fatigued,
    Was sitting down, and both his knees embraced,
    Holding his face low down between them bowed.
"O my sweet Lord," I said, "do turn thine eye
    On him who shows himself more negligent   110
    Than even if Sloth herself his sister were."[16]
Then he turned round to us, and he gave heed,
    Just lifting up his eyes above his thigh,
    And said: "Now go thou up, for thou art valiant."[17]
Then knew I who he was;[18] and the distress,   115
    That still a little did my breathing quicken,
    My going to him hindered not; and after
I came to him he hardly raised his head,
    Saying: "Hast thou seen clearly how the sun
    O'er thy left shoulder drives his chariot?"[19]   120
His sluggish attitude and his curt words
    A little unto laughter moved my lips;[20]
    Then I began: "Belacqua, I grieve not
For thee henceforth; but tell me, wherefore seated
    In this place art thou? Waitest thou an escort?   125
    Or has thy usual habit seized upon thee?"[21]
And he: "O brother, what's the use of climbing?
    Since to my torment would not let me go
    The Angel of God, who sitteth at the gate.
First heaven must needs so long revolve me round   130
    Outside thereof, as in my life it did,
    Since the good sighs I to the end postponed,

*Perhaps.

Unless, e'er that,* some prayer may bring me aid
    Which rises from a heart that lives in grace;
    What profit others that in heaven are heard not?"[22]   135
Meanwhile the Poet was before me mounting,
    And saying: "Come now; see the sun has touched
    Meridian,[23] and from the shore the night
Covers already with her foot Morocco?"[24]

*Before that.

CANTO V

I HAD already from those shades[1] departed,
  And followed in the footsteps of my Guide,
  When from behind, pointing his finger at me,
One shouted: "See, it seems as if shone not
  The sunshine on the left of him below,[2]   5
  And like one living seems he to conduct him!"
Mine eyes I turned at utterance of these words,
  And saw them watching with astonishment
  But me, but me, and the light which was broken!
"Why doth thy mind so occupy itself,"   10
  The Master said, "that thou thy pace dost slacken?
  What matters it to thee what here is whispered?
Come after me, and let the people talk;
  Stand like a steadfast tower, that never wags
  Its top for all the blowing of the winds;   15
For evermore the man in whom is springing
  Thought upon thought, removes from him the mark,[3]
  Because the force of one the other weakens."
What could I say in answer but "I come"?
  I said it somewhat with that color tinged[4]   20
  Which makes a man of pardon sometimes worthy.
Meanwhile along the mountain-side across
  Came people in advance of us a little,
  Singing the Miserere[5] verse by verse.
When they became aware I gave no place   25
  For passage of the sunshine through my body,
  They changed their song into a long, hoarse "Oh!"[6]

And two of them, in form of messengers,
    Ran forth to meet us, and demanded of us,
    "Of your condition make us cognizant."   30
And said my Master: "Ye can go your way
    And carry back again to those who sent you,
    That this one's body is of very flesh.
If they stood still because they saw his shadow,
    As I suppose, enough is answered them;   35
    Him let them honor, it may profit them."[7]
Vapors enkindled saw I ne'er so swiftly
    At early nightfall cleave the air serene,
    Nor, at the set of sun, the clouds of August,
But upward they returned in briefer time,   40
    And, on arriving, with the others wheeled
    Tow'rds us, like troops that run without a rein.[8]
"This folk that presses unto us is great,
    And cometh to implore thee," said the Poet;
    "So still go onward, and in going listen."[9]   45
"O soul that goest to beatitude
    With the same members wherewith thou wast born,"
    Shouting they came, "a little stay thy steps,
Look, if thou e'er hast any of us seen,
    So that o'er yonder thou bear news of him;   50
    Ah, why dost thou go on? Ah, why not stay?[10]
Long since we all were slain by violence,[11]
    And sinners even to the latest hour;
    Then did a light from heaven admonish us,
So that, both penitent and pardoning, forth   55
    From life we issued reconciled to God,
    Who with desire to see Him stirs our hearts."
And I: "Although I gaze into your faces,
    No one I recognize; but if may please you
    Aught I have power to do, ye well-born spirits,[12]   60
Speak ye, and I will do it, by that peace
    Which, following the feet of such a Guide,
    From world to world makes itself sought by me."[13]

Canto V: The Body of Buonconte da Montefeltro in the Arno

And one began:[14] "Each one has confidence
    In thy good offices without an oath,   65
    Unless the I cannot cut off the I will;[15]
Whence I, who speak alone before the others,
    Pray thee, if ever thou dost see the land
    That 'twixt Romagna lies and that of Charles,[16]
Thou be so courteous to me of thy prayers   70
    In Fano,[17] that they pray for me devoutly,
    That I may purge away my grave offences.
From thence was I; but the deep wounds, through which
    Issued the blood wherein I had my seat,
    Where dealt me in bosom of the Antenori,[18]   75
There where I thought to be the most secure;
    'Twas he of Este had it done, who held me
    In hatred far beyond what justice willed.[19]
But if towards the Mira I had fled,[20]
    When I was overtaken at Oriaco,   80
    I still should be o'er yonder where men breathe.
I ran to the lagoon, and reeds and mire
    Did so entangle me that I fell, and saw there
    A lake made from my veins upon the ground."
Then said another: "Ah, be that desire   85
    Fulfilled that draws thee to the lofty mountain,
    As thou with pious pity aidest mine.
I was of Montefeltro, and am Buonconte;[21]
    Giovanna, nor none other cares for me;
    Hence among these I go with downcast front."[22]   90
And I to him: "What violence or what chance
    Led thee astray[23] so far from Campaldino,
    That never has thy sepulture been known?"
"Oh," he replied, "at Casentino's foot
    A river crosses named Archiano, born   95
    Above the Hermitage in Apennine.[24]
There where the name thereof becometh void
    Did I arrive, pierced through and through the throat,
    Fleeing on foot, and bloodying the plain;

There my sight lost I, and my utterance   100
     Did in the name of Mary end, and there
     I fell, and tenantless my flesh remained.
Truth will I speak, repeat it to the living;[25]
     God's Angel took me up, and he of hell
     Shouted:[26] 'O thou from heaven, why dost thou
         rob me?   105
Thou bearest away the eternal part of him,
     For one poor little tear,[27] that takes him from me;
     But with the rest,[28] I'll deal in other fashion!'
Well knowest thou how in the air is gathered
     That humid vapor which to water turns,[29]   110
     Soon as it rises where the cold doth grasp it.
He joined that evil will, which aye seeks evil,*
     To intellect, and moved the mist and wind
     By means of power, which his own nature gave;
Thereafter, when the day was spent, the valley   115
     From Pratomagno to the great yoke[30] covered
     With fog, and made the heaven above intent,
So that the pregnant air to water changed;
     Down fell the rain, and to the gullies came
     Whate'er of it earth tolerated not;   120
And as it mingled with the mighty torrents,
     Towards the royal river[31] with such speed
     It headlong rushed, that nothing held it back.
My frozen body near unto its outlet
     The robust Archian found, and into Arno   125
     Thrust it, and loosened from my breast the cross
I made of me,[32] when agony o'ercame me;
     It rolled me on the banks and on the bottom;
     Then with its booty covered and begirt me."
"Ah, when thou hast returned unto the world,   130
     And rested thee from thy long journeying,"
     After the second followed the third spirit,[33]

*All seeks evil.

"Do thou remember me who am the Pia;
    Siena made me, unmade me Maremma;[34]
      He knoweth it, who had encircled first,   135
Espousing me, my finger with his gem."

CANTO VI

WHENE'ER is broken up the game of Zara,[1]
    He who has lost remains behind despondent,
    The throws repeating, and in sadness learns;
The people with the other all depart;
    One goes in front, and one behind doth pluck him,   5
    And at his side one brings himself to mind;
He pauses not, and this and that one hears;
    They crowd no more to whom his hand he stretches,
    And from the throng he thus defends himself.
Even such was I in that dense multitude,   10
    Turning to them this way and that my face,
    And, promising, I freed myself therefrom.[2]
There was the Aretine,[3] who from the arms
    Untamed of Ghin di Tacco had his death,
    And he who fleeing from pursuit was drowned.[4]   15
There was imploring with his hands outstretched
    Frederick Novello,[5] and that one of Pisa
    Who made the good Marzucco seem so strong.[6]
I saw Count Orso;[7] and the soul divided
    By hatred and by envy from its body,[8]   20
    As it declared, and not for crime committed,
Pierre de la Brosse I say; and here provide
    While still on earth the Lady of Brabant,
    So that for this she be of no worse flock![9]
As soon as I was free from all those shades   25
    Who only prayed that some one else may pray,[10]
    So as to hasten their becoming holy,

Began I: "It appears that thou deniest,
    O light of mine, expressly in some text,
    That orison* can bend decree of Heaven;[11]   30
And ne'ertheless these people pray for this.
    Might then their expectation bootless† be?
    Or is to me thy saying not quite clear?"
And he to me: "My writing is explicit,
    And not fallacious is the hope of these,   35
    If with sane intellect 'tis well regarded;
For top of judgment doth not vail itself,
    Because the fire of love fulfils at once[12]
    What he must satisfy who here installs him.
And there, where I affirmed that proposition,   40
    Defect was not amended by a prayer.
    Because the prayer from God was separate.[13]
Verily, in so deep a questioning
    Do not decide, unless she tell it thee,[14]
    Who light 'twixt truth and intellect shall be.   45
I know not if thou understand; I speak
    Of Beatrice; her shalt thou see above,
    Smiling and happy, on this mountain's top."
And I: "Good Leader, let us make more haste,
    For I no longer tire me as before;   50
    And see, e'en‡ now the hill a shadow casts."
"We will go forward with this day," he answered,
    "As far as now is possible for us;
    But otherwise the fact is than thou thinkest.
Ere thou art up there, thou shalt see return   55
    Him, who now hides himself behind the hill,
    So that thou dost not interrupt his rays.[15]
But yonder there behold! a soul[16] that stationed
    All, all alone is looking hitherward;
    It will point out to us the quickest way."   60

*Prayer.
†Useless.
‡Even.

We came up unto it; O Lombard soul,[17]
    How lofty and disdainful thou didst bear thee,
    And grand and slow in moving of thine eyes!
Nothing whatever did it say to us,
    But let us go our way, eying us only   65
    After the manner of a couchant lion;[18]
Still near to it Virgilius drew, entreating
    That it would point us out the best ascent;
    And it replied not unto his demand,
But of our native land and of our life   70
    It questioned us; and the sweet Guide began:
    "Mantua,"[19]—and the shade, all in itself recluse,
Rose tow'rds him from the place where first it was,
    Saying: "O Mantuan, I am Sordello
    Of thine own land!" and one embraced the other.   75
Ah! servile Italy, grief's hostelry!
    A ship without a pilot in great tempest!
    No Lady thou of Provinces, but brothel![20]
That noble soul was so impatient, only
    At the sweet sound of his own native land,   80
    To make its citizens glad welcome there;
And now within thee are not without war
    Thy living ones, and one doth gnaw the other
    Of those whom one wall and one fosse* shut in![21]
Search, wretched one, all round about the shores   85
    Thy seaboard, and then look within thy bosom,
    If any part of thee enjoyeth peace!
What boots it,† that for thee Justinian
    The bridle mend, if empty be the saddle?[22]
    Withouten‡ this the shame would be the less.   90
Ah! people, thou that oughtest to be devout,
    And to let Cæsar sit upon the saddle,
    If well thou hearest what God teacheth thee,

---

*Moat or ditch around a walled and fortified city.
†What good or use is it?
‡Without.

Behold how fell this wild beast[23] has become,
    Being no longer by the spur corrected,   95
    Since thou hast laid thy hand upon the bridle.
O German Albert! who abandonest[24]
    Her that has grown recalcitrant and savage,
    And oughtest to bestride her saddle-bow,
May a just judgment[25] from the stars down fall   100
    Upon thy blood, and be it new and open,
    That thy successor may have fear thereof;
Because thy father and thyself have suffered,
    By greed of those transalpine lands distrained,
    The garden of the empire to be waste.   105
Come and behold[26] Montecchi and Cappelletti,
    Monaldi and Fillippeschi,[27] careless man!
    Those sad already, and these doubt-depressed!
Come, cruel one! come and behold the oppression
    Of thy nobility, and cure their wounds,   110
    And thou shalt see how safe is Santafiore![28]
Come and behold thy Rome, that is lamenting,
    Widowed, alone, and day and night exclaims,
    "My Cæsar, why hast thou forsaken me?"
Come and behold how loving are the people;   115
    And if for us no pity moveth thee,
    Come and be made ashamed of thy renown!
And if it lawful be, O Jove Supreme!
    Who upon earth for us wast crucified,[29]
    Are thy just eyes averted otherwhere?   120
Or preparation is't, that, in the abyss
    Of thine own counsel, for some good thou makest[30]
    From our perception utterly cut off?
For all the towns of Italy are full
    Of tyrants, and becometh a Marcellus[31]   125
    Each peasant churl* who plays the partisan!
My Florence![32] well mayst thou contented be

*Person of low birth.

With this digression, which concerns thee not,
    Thanks to thy people who such forethought take!
Many at heart have justice, but shoot slowly,   130
    That unadvised they come not to the bow,
    But on their very lips[33] thy people have it!
Many refuse to bear the common burden;
    But thy solicitous people answereth
    Without being asked, and crieth: "I submit."[34]   135
Now be thou joyful, for thou hast good reason;
    Thou affluent, thou in peace, thou full of wisdom![35]
    If I speak true, the event conceals it not.
Athens and Lacedæmon, they who made
    The ancient laws, and were so civilized,   140
    Made towards living well a little sign[36]
Compared with thee, who makest such fine-spun
    Provisions, that to middle of November
    Reaches not what thou in October spinnest.[37]
How oft, within the time of thy remembrance,   145
    Laws, money, offices, and usages
    Hast thou remodelled, and renewed thy members?
And if thou mind thee well, and see the light,
    Thou shalt behold thyself like a sick woman,
    Who cannot find repose upon her down,   150
But by her tossing wardeth off her pain.[38]

Canto VII: The Poet Sordello kneels before Virgil

CANTO VII

After the gracious and glad salutations
    Had three and four times been reiterated,
    Sordello backward drew and said, "Who are you?"[1]
"Or ever to this mountain were directed
    The souls deserving to ascend to God,   5
    My bones were buried by Octavian.[2]
I am Virgilius;[3] and for no crime else
    Did I lose heaven, than for not having faith";
    In this wise then my Leader made reply.
As one who suddenly before him sees   10
    Something whereat he marvels, who believes
    And yet does not, saying, "It is! it is not!"
So he appeared; and then bowed down his brow,
    And with humility returned towards him,
    And, where inferiors embrace, embraced him.   15
"O glory of the Latians, thou," he said,
    "Through whom our language showed what it could do,[4]
    O pride eternal of the place I came from,
What merit or what grace to me reveals thee?
    If I to hear thy words be worthy, tell me   20
    If thou dost come from Hell, and from what cloister."
"Through all the circles of the doleful realm,"
    Responded he, "have I come hitherward;
    Heaven's power impelled me, and with that I come.
I by not doing, not by doing, lost   25
    The sight of that high sun which thou desirest,[5]
    And which too late by me was recognized.

A place there is below not sad with torments,[6]
    But darkness only, where the lamentations
    Have not the sound of wailing, but are sighs.   30
There dwell I with the little innocents
    Snatched by the teeth of Death, or ever they
    Were from our human sinfulness exempt.
There dwell I among those who the three saintly
    Virtues[7] did not put on, and without vice   35
    The others knew[8] and followed all of them.
But if thou know and can, some indication
    Give us by which we may the sooner come
    Where Purgatory has its right beginning."[9]
He answered: "No fixed place has been assigned us;   40
    'Tis lawful for me to go up and round;
    So far as I can go, as guide I join thee.
But see already how the day declines,
    And to go up by night we are not able;[10]
    Therefore 'tis well to think of some fair sojourn.   45
Souls are there on the right hand here withdrawn;
    If thou permit me I will lead thee to them,
    And thou shalt know them not without delight."
"How is this?" was the answer; "should one wish
    To mount by night would he prevented be   50
    By others? or mayhap would not have power?"
And on the ground the good Sordello drew
    His finger, saying, "See, this line alone[11]
    Thou couldst not pass after the sun is gone;
Not that aught else would hindrance give, however,   55
    To going up, save the nocturnal darkness;
    This with the want of power the will perplexes.
We might indeed therewith return below,
    And, wandering, walk the hill-side round about,
    While the horizon holds the day imprisoned."   60
Thereon my Lord, as if in wonder, said:
    "Do thou conduct us thither, where thou sayest
    That we can take delight in tarrying."

Little had we withdrawn us from that place,
 When I perceived the mount was hollowed out[12]   65
 In fashion as the valleys here are hollowed.
"Thitherward," said that shade, "will we repair,
 Where of itself the hill-side makes a lap,
 And there for the new day will we await."
'Twixt hill and plain there was a winding path   70
 Which led us to the margin of that dell,
 Where dies the border more than half away.
Gold and fine silver, and scarlet and pearl-white,
 The Indian wood resplendent and serene,
 Fresh emerald the moment it is broken,   75
By herbage and by flowers within that hollow
 Planted, each one in color would be vanquished,
 As by its greater vanquished is the less.
Nor in that place had nature painted only,
 But of the sweetness of a thousand odors   80
 Made there a mingled fragrance and unknown.[13]
"*Salve Regina*,"[14] on the green and flowers
 There seated, singing, spirits I beheld,
 Which were not visible outside the valley.
"Before the scanty sun now seeks his nest,"   85
 Began the Mantuan who had led us thither,
 "Among them do not wish me to conduct you.
Better from off this ledge the acts and faces
 Of all of them will you discriminate,
 Than in the plain below received among them.   90
He who sits highest,[15] and the semblance bears
 Of having what he should have done neglected,
 And to the others' song moves not his lips,
Rudolph the Emperor[16] was, who had the power
 To heal the wounds that Italy have slain,   95
 So that through others slowly she revives.
The other, who in look doth comfort him,
 Governed the region where the water springs,
 The Moldau bears the Elbe, and Elbe the sea.

His name was Ottocar;[17] and in swaddling-clothes   100
    Far better he than bearded Winceslaus[18]
    His son, who feeds in luxury and ease.
And the small-nosed,[19] who close in council seems
    With him that has an aspect so benign,
    Died fleeing and disflowering the lily;   105
Look there, how he is beating at his breast!
    Behold the other one,[20] who for his cheek
    Sighing has made of his own palm a bed;
Father and father-in-law of France's Pest[21]
    Are they, and know his vicious life and lewd,   110
    And hence proceeds the grief that so doth
      pierce them.
He who appears so stalwart, and chimes in,
    Singing, with that one of the manly nose,[22]
    The cord of every valor wore begirt;
And if as King had after him remained   115
    The stripling[23] who in rear of him is sitting,
    Well had the valor passed from vase to vase,
Which cannot of the other heirs be said.
    Frederick and Jacomo possess the realms,
    But none the better heritage possesses.   120
Not oftentimes upriseth through the branches
    The probity of man;[24] and this He wills
    Who gives it, so that we may ask of Him.
Eke* to the large-nosed reach my words, no less
    Than to the other, Pier, who with him sings;   125
    Whence Provence and Apulia grieve already.
The plant is as inferior to its seed,[25]
    As more than Beatrice and Margaret
    Costanza[26] boasteth of her husband still.
Behold the monarch of the simple life,   130
    Harry of England, sitting there alone;
    He in his branches has a better issue.[27]

*Also.

He who the lowest on the ground among them
    Sits looking upward, is the Marquis William,
    For whose sake Alessandria and her war   135
Make Monferrat and Canavese weep."[28]

Canto VIII: The Angels putting the Serpent to Flight

CANTO VIII

'T was now the hour[1] that turneth back desire
    In those who sail the sea, and melts the heart,
    The day they've said to their sweet friends farewell,
And the new pilgrim[2] penetrates with love,
    If he doth hear from far away a bell   5
    That seemeth to deplore the dying day,
When I began to make of no avail
    My hearing, and to watch one of the souls[3]
    Uprisen, that begged attention with its hand.
It joined and lifted upward both its palms,   10
    Fixing its eyes upon the orient,[4]
    As if it said to God, "Naught else I care for."
"Te lucis ante"[5] so devoutly issued
    Forth from its mouth, and with such dulcet notes,
    It made me issue forth from my own mind.[6]   15
And then the others, sweetly and devoutly,
    Accompanied it through all the hymn entire,
    Having their eyes on the supernal wheels.[7]
Here, Reader,[8] fix thine eyes well on the truth,
    For now indeed so subtile is the veil,   20
    Surely to penetrate within is easy.
I saw that army of the gentle-born
    Thereafterward in silence upward gaze,
    As if in expectation, pale and humble;
And from on high come forth and down descend   25
    I saw two Angels with two flaming swords,
    Truncated and deprivëd of their points.

Green as the little leaflets just now born
    Their garments were, which, by their verdant pinions[9]
    Beaten and blown abroad, they trailed behind.   30
One just above us came to take his station,
    And one descended to the opposite bank,
    So that the people were contained between them.
Clearly in them discerned I the blond head;
    But in their faces was the eye bewildered,   35
    As faculty confounded by excess.[10]
"From Mary's bosom both of them have come,"[11]
    Sordello said, "as guardians of the valley
    Against the serpent, that will come anon."
Whereupon I, who knew not by what road,   40
    Turned round about, and closely drew myself,
    Utterly frozen, to the faithful shoulders.[12]
And once again Sordello: "Now descend we
    'Mid the grand shades, and we will speak to them;
    Right pleasant will it be for them to see you."   45
Only three steps I think that I descended,
    And was below, and saw one who was looking
    Only at me, as if he fain would know me.
Already now the air was growing dark,
    But not so that between his eyes and mine   50
    It did not show what it before locked up.[13]
Tow'rds me he moved, and I tow'rds him did move;
    Noble Judge Nino![14] how it me delighted,
    When I beheld thee not among the damned![15]
No greeting fair was left unsaid between us;   55
    Then asked he: "How long is it since thou camest
    O'er the far waters to the mountain's foot?"[16]
"Oh!" said I to him, "through the dismal places
    I came this morn; and am in the first life,
    Albeit the other, going thus, I gain."[17]   60
And on the instant my reply was heard,
    He and Sordello both shrank back from me,[18]
    Like people who are suddenly bewildered.

One to Virgilius, and the other turned
    To one who sat there, crying, "Up, Currado!   65
    Come and behold what God in grace has willed!"[19]
Then, turned to me: "By that especial grace
    Thou owest unto Him, who so conceals
    His own first wherefore, that it has no ford,[20]
When thou shalt be beyond the waters wide,   70
    Tell my Giovanna that she pray for me,
    Where answer to the innocent is made.[21]
I do not think her mother loves me more,
    Since she has laid aside her wimple white,[22]
    Which she, unhappy, needs must wish again.[23]   75
Through her full easily is comprehended
    How long in woman lasts the fire of love,
    If eye or touch do not relight it often.
So fair a hatchment* will not make for her
    The Viper marshalling the Milanese   80
    A-field, as would have made Gallura's Cock."[24]
In this wise spake he, with the stamp impressed
    Upon his aspect of that righteous zeal
    Which measurably burneth in the heart.
My greedy eyes still wandered up to heaven,   85
    Still to that point where slowest are the stars,
    Even as a wheel the nearest to its axle.[25]
And my Conductor: "Son, what dost thou gaze at
    Up there?" And I to him: "At those three torches[26]
    With which this hither pole is all on fire."   90
And he to me: "The four resplendent stars
    Thou sawest this morning are down yonder low,
    And these have mounted up to where those were."
As he was speaking, to himself Sordello
    Drew him, and said, "Lo there our Adversary!"[27]   95
    And pointed with his finger to look thither.
Upon the side on which the little valley

---

*Ornament, adornment.

No barrier hath, a serpent was; perchance
 The same which gave to Eve the bitter food.
'Twixt grass and flowers came on the evil streak,   100
 Turning at times its head about, and licking
 Its back like to a beast that smoothes itself.
I did not see, and therefore cannot say
 How the celestial falcons 'gan to move,
 But well I saw that they were both in motion.   105
Hearing the air cleft by their verdant wings,
 The serpent fled, and round the Angels wheeled,
 Up to their stations flying back alike.
The shade that to the Judge had near approached
 When he had called, throughout that whole assault   110
 Had not a moment loosed its gaze on me.[28]
"So may the light that leadeth thee on high
 Find in thine own free-will as much of wax
 As needful is up to the highest azure,"
Began it, "if some true intelligence   115
 Of Valdimagra or its neighborhood[29]
 Thou knowest, tell it me, who once was great there.
Currado Malaspina[30] was I called;
 I'm not the elder, but from him descended;
 To mine I bore the love which here refineth."   120
"O," said I unto him, "through your domains
 I never passed, but where is there a dwelling
 Throughout all Europe, where they are not
  known?
That fame, which doeth honor to your house,
 Proclaims its Signors and proclaims its land,   125
 So that he knows of them who ne'er was there.
And, as I hope for heaven, I swear to you
 Your honored family[31] in naught abates
 The glory of the purse and of the sword.
It is so privileged by use and nature,   130
 That though a guilty head misguide the world,
 Sole it goes right, and scorns the evil way."

And he: "Now go; for the sun shall not lie
    Seven times upon the pillow which the Ram
    With all his four feet covers and bestrides,   135
Before that such a courteous opinion
    Shall in the middle of thy head be nailed
    With greater nails than of another's speech,
Unless the course of justice standeth still."[32]

Canto IX: Dante, in a Dream, carried off by an Eagle

CANTO IX

$\mathcal{T}$HE concubine of old Tithonus[1] now
    Gleamed white upon the eastern balcony,
    Forth from the arms of her sweet paramour;
With gems[2] her forehead all relucent* was,
    Set in the shape of that cold animal   5
    Which with its tail[3] doth smite amain† the people,
And of the steps, with which she mounts, the Night
    Had taken two in that place where we were,
    And now the third was bending down its wings;[4]
When I, who something had of Adam in me,[5]   10
    Vanquished by sleep, upon the grass reclined,
    There where all five of us[6] already sat.
Just at the hour when her sad lay begins
    The little swallow, near unto the morning,
    Perchance in memory of her former woes,[7]   15
And when the mind of man, a wanderer
    More from the flesh, and less by thought imprisoned,[8]
    Almost prophetic in its visions is,
In dreams it seemed to me I saw suspended
    An eagle[9] in the sky, with plumes of gold,   20
    With wings wide open, and intent to stoop,
And this, it seemed to me, was where had been
    By Ganymede his kith and kin abandoned,
    When to the high consistory he was rapt.
I thought within myself, perchance he strikes   25

---

*Shining, reflecting.
†Among.

From habit only here, and from elsewhere
    Disdains to bear up any in his feet.
Then wheeling somewhat more, it seemed to me,
    Terrible as the lightning he descended,
    And snatched me upward even to the fire.   30
Therein it seemed that he and I were burning,
    And the imagined fire[10] did scorch me so,
    That of necessity my sleep was broken.
Not otherwise Achilles started up,
    Around him turning his awakened eyes,   35
    And knowing not the place in which he was,
What time from Chiron stealthily his mother
    Carried him sleeping in her arms to Scyros,
    Wherefrom the Greeks withdrew him
        afterwards,[11]
Than I upstarted, when from off my face   40
    Sleep fled away; and pallid I became,
    As doth the man who freezes with affright.*
Only my Comforter was at my side,
    And now the sun was more than two hours high,
    And turned towards the sea-shore was my face.[12]   45
"Be not intimidated," said my Lord,
    "Be reassured, for all is well with us;
    Do not restrain, but put forth all thy strength.
Thou hast at length arrived at Purgatory;
    See there the cliff that closes it around;   50
    See there the entrance, where it seems disjoined.
Whilom† at dawn, which doth precede the day,
    When inwardly thy spirit was asleep
    Upon the flowers that deck the land below,
There came a Lady and said: 'I am Lucìa;[13]   55
    Let me take this one up, who is asleep;
    So will I make his journey easier for him.'
Sordello and the other noble shapes

*Fear, terror.
†Formerly; in the past.

Remained; she took thee, and, as day grew bright,
    Upward she came, and I upon her footsteps.   60
She laid thee here; and first her beauteous eyes
    That open entrance pointed out to me;
    Then she and sleep together went away."
In guise of one whose doubts are reassured,
    And who to confidence his fear doth change,   65
    After the truth has been discovered to him,
So did I change; and when without disquiet
    My Leader saw me, up along the cliff
    He moved, and I behind him, tow'rd the height.
Reader, thou seest well how I exalt   70
    My theme, and therefore if with greater art
    I fortify it, marvel not thereat.[14]
Nearer approached we, and were in such place,
    That there, where first appeared to me a rift
    Like to a crevice that disparts a wall,   75
I saw a portal, and three stairs beneath,
    Diverse in color, to go up to it,
    And a gate-keeper, who yet spake no word.
And as I opened more and more mine eyes,
    I saw him seated on the highest stair,   80
    Such in the face that I endured it not.[15]
And in his hand he had a naked sword,
    Which so reflected back the sunbeams tow'rds us,
    That oft in vain I lifted up mine eyes.
"Tell it from where you are,[16] what is't you wish?"   85
    Began he to exclaim; "Where is the escort?
    Take heed your coming hither harm you not!"
"A Lady of Heaven,[17] with these things conversant,"
    My Master answered him, "but even now
    Said to us, 'Thither go; there is the portal.'"   90
"And may she speed your footsteps in all good,"
    Again began the courteous janitor;*
    "Come forward then unto these stairs of ours."[18]

*Gatekeeper.

Thither did we approach; and the first stair
    Was marble white, so polished and so smooth,   95
    I mirrored myself therein as I appear.
The second, tinct of deeper hue than perse,
    Was of a calcined and uneven stone,
    Cracked all asunder lengthwise and across.
The third, that uppermost rests massively,   100
    Porphyry seemed to me, as flaming red
    As blood that from a vein is spirting forth.
Both of his feet was holding upon this
    The Angel of God, upon the threshold seated,
    Which seemed to me a stone of diamond.[19]   105
Along the three stairs upward with good will
    Did my Conductor draw me, saying: "Ask
    Humbly that he the fastening may undo."[20]
Devoutly at the holy feet I cast me,
    For mercy's sake besought that he would open,   110
    But first upon my breast three times I smote.[21]
Seven P's[22] upon my forehead he described
    With the sword's point, and, "Take heed that thou wash
    These wounds, when thou shalt be within," he said.
Ashes, or earth that dry is excavated,   115
    Of the same color[23] were with his attire,
    And from beneath it he drew forth two keys[24]
One was of gold, and the other was of silver;
    First with the white, and after with the yellow,
    Plied he the door, so that I was content.   120
"Whenever faileth either of these keys
    So that it turn not rightly in the lock,"
    He said to us, "this entrance doth not open.
More precious one is, but the other needs
    More art and intellect ere it unlock,[25]   125
    For it is that which doth the knot unloose.
From Peter I have them; and he bade me err
    Rather in opening than in keeping shut,
    If people but fall down before my feet."

Then pushed the portals of the sacred door, 130
 Exclaiming: "Enter; but I give you warning
 That forth returns whoever looks behind."[26]
And when upon their hinges were turned round
 The swivels of that consecrated gate,
 Which are of metal, massive and sonorous, 135
Roared not so loud, nor so discordant seemed
 Tarpeia, when was ta'en from it the good
 Metellus, wherefore meagre it remained.[27]
At the first thunder-peal I turned attentive,
 And *"Te Deum laudamus"*[28] seemed to hear 140
 In voices mingled with sweet melody.
Exactly such an image rendered me
 That which I heard, as we are wont to catch,
 When people singing with the organ stand;[29]
For now we hear, and now hear not, the words. 145

Canto X: The Marble Sculptures portraying Pride

CANTO X

When we had crossed the threshold of the door
    Which the perverted love of souls disuses,[1]
    Because it makes the crooked way seem straight,
Re-echoing I heard it closed again;[2]
    And if I had turned back mine eyes upon it,   5
    What for my failing had been fit excuse?
We mounted upward through a rifted rock,[3]
    Which undulated to this side and that,
    Even as a wave receding and advancing
"Here it behoves us use a little art,"   10
    Began my Leader, "to adapt ourselves
    Now here, now there, to the receding side."
And this our footsteps so infrequent made,
    That sooner had the moon's decreasing disk[4]
    Regained its bed to sink again to rest,   15
Than we were forth from out that needle's eye;[5]
    But when we free and in the open were,
    There where the mountain backward piles itself,
I wearied out, and both of us uncertain[6]
    About our way, we stopped upon a plain   20
    More desolate than roads across the deserts.
From where its margin borders on the void,
    To foot of the high bank that ever rises,
    A human body three times told would measure;[7]
And far as eye of mine could wing its flight,   25
    Now on the left, and on the right flank now,
    The same this cornice did appear to me.

Thereon our feet had not been moved as yet,
>When I perceived the embankment round about,
>Which all right of ascent had interdicted,   30
To be of marble white, and so adorned
>With sculptures, that not only Polycletus,
>But Nature's self, had there been put to shame.[8]
The Angel,[9] who came down to earth with tidings
>Of peace, that had been wept for many a year,   35
>And opened Heaven from its long interdict,[10]
In front of us appeared so truthfully
>There sculptured in a gracious attitude,
>He did not seem an image that is silent.
One would have sworn that he was saying, *"Ave"*;[11]   40
>For she was there in effigy portrayed
>Who turned the key[12] to ope the exalted love,
And in her mien this language had impressed,
>*"Ecce ancilla Dei,"*[13] as distinctly
>As any figure stamps itself in wax.[14]   45
"Keep not thy mind upon one place alone,"
>The gentle Master said, who had me standing
>Upon that side where people have their hearts;[15]
Whereat I moved mine eyes, and I beheld
>In rear of Mary, and upon that side   50
>Where he was standing who conducted me,
Another story on the rock imposed;
>Wherefore I passed Virgilius and drew near,
>So that before mine eyes it might be set.
There sculptured in the self-same marble were   55
>The cart and oxen,[16] drawing the holy ark,
>Wherefore one dreads an office not appointed.
People appeared in front, and all of them
>In seven choirs divided, of two senses
>Made one say, "No," the other, "Yes, they sing."   60
Likewise unto the smoke of the frankincense,
>Which there was imaged forth, the eyes and nose
>Were in the yes and no discordant made.
Preceded there the vessel benedight,

Dancing with girded loins, the humble Psalmist,   65
    And more and less than King was he in this,
Opposite, represented at the window
    Of a great palace, Michal looked upon him,
    Even as a woman scornful and afflicted.
I moved my feet from where I had been standing,   70
    To examine near at hand another story,[17]
    Which after Michal glimmered white upon me.
There the high glory of the Roman Prince
    Was chronicled, whose great beneficence
    Moved Gregory[18] to his great victory;   75
'Tis of the Emperor Trajan I am speaking;
    And a poor widow at his bridle stood,
    In attitude of weeping and of grief.
Around about him seemed it thronged and full
    Of cavaliers, and the eagles in the gold   80
    Above them visibly in the wind were moving.
The wretched woman in the midst of these
    Seemed to be saying: "Give me vengeance, Lord,
    For my dead son, for whom my heart is breaking."
And he to answer her: "Now wait until   85
    I shall return." And she: "My Lord," like one
    In whom grief is impatient, "shouldst thou not
Return?" And he: "Who shall be where I am
    Will give it thee." And she: "Good deed of others
    What boots it* thee, if thou neglect thine own?"   90
Whence he: "Now comfort thee, for it behoves me
    That I discharge my duty ere I move;
    Justice so wills, and pity doth retain me."
He who on no new thing[19] has ever looked
    Was the creator of this visible language,   95
    Novel to us, for here it is not found.
While I delighted me in contemplating
    The images of such humility,[20]
    And dear to look on for their Maker's sake,

*What good or use is it?

"Behold, upon this side, but rare they make   100
    Their steps,"[21] the Poet murmured, "many people;
    These will direct us to the lofty stairs."
Mine eyes, that in beholding were intent
    To see new things, of which they curious are,
    In turning round towards him were not slow.   105
But still I wish not, Reader, thou shouldst swerve
    From thy good purposes, because thou hearest
    How God ordaineth that the debt be paid;
Attend not to the fashion of the torment,
    Think of what follows; think that at the worst   110
    It cannot reach beyond the mighty sentence.[22]
"Master," began I, "that which I behold
    Moving towards us seems to me not persons,
    And what I know not, so in sight I waver."
And he to me: "The grievous quality   115
    Of this their torment bows them so to earth,
    That my own eyes at first had strife with it;
But look there fixedly, and disentangle
    By sight what cometh underneath those stones;[23]
    Already canst thou see how each is stricken."[24]   120
O ye proud Christians! wretched, weary ones!
    Who, in the vision of the mind infirm,
    Confidence have in your backsliding steps,
Do ye not comprehend that we are worms,
    Born to bring forth the angelic butterfly   125
    That flieth unto judgment without screen?*
Wherefore your spirit doth it float on high?
    Like are ye unto insects undeveloped,
    Even as the worm in which formation fails![25]
As to sustain a ceiling or a roof,   130
    In place of corbel, oftentimes a figure[26]
    Is seen to join its knees unto its breast,
Which makes of the unreal real anguish
    Arise in him who sees it; fashioned thus

*Defense.

Beheld I those, when I had ta'en good heed.
True is it, they were more or less bent down,
    According as they more or less were laden;
    And he who had most patience[27] in his looks
Weeping did seem to say, "I can no more!"

CANTO XI

OUR Father,[1] thou who dwellest in the heavens,
 Not circumscribed, but from the greater love
 Thou bearest to the first effects on high,
Praised be thy name and thine omnipotence
 By every creature,[2] as befitting is   5
 To render thanks to thy sweet effluence.
Come unto us the peace of thy dominion,
 For unto it we cannot of ourselves,
 If it come not, with all our intellect.
Even as thine own Angels of their will   10
 Make sacrifice to thee, Hosanna singing,
 So may all men make sacrifice of theirs.
Give unto us this day our daily manna,[3]
 Withouten* which in this rough wilderness
 Backward goes he who toils most to advance.   15
And even as we the trespass we have suffered
 Pardon in one another, pardon thou
 Benignly, and regard not our desert.†
Our virtue, which is easily o'ercome,
 Put not to proof with the old Adversary,[4]   20
 But thou from him who spurs it so, deliver.
This last petition verily, dear Lord,
 Not for ourselves is made, who need it not,[5]
 But for their sake who have remained behind us."

*Without.
†Merit.

Thus for themselves and us good furtherance[6]   25
    Those shades imploring, went beneath a weight
    Like unto that of which we sometimes dream,[7]
Unequally in anguish round and round
    And weary all, upon that foremost cornice,
    Purging away the smoke-stains of the world.[8]   30
If there good words are always said for us,
    What may not here be said and done for them,
    By those who have a good root to their will?
Well may we help them wash away the marks
    That hence they carried, so that clean and light   35
    They may ascend unto the starry wheels![9]
"Ah! so may pity and justice you disburden
    Soon, that ye may have power to move the wing,
    That shall uplift you after your desire,
Show us on which hand tow'rd the stairs the way   40
    Is shortest, and if more than one the passes,
    Point us out that which least abruptly falls;[10]
For he who cometh with me, through the burden
    Of Adam's flesh[11] wherewith he is invested,
    Against his will is chary of his climbing."   45
The words of theirs which they returned to those
    That he whom I was following had spoken,
    It was not manifest from whom they came,[12]
But it was said: "To the right hand come with us
    Along the bank, and ye shall find a pass   50
    Possible for living person to ascend.
And were I not impeded by the stone,
    Which this proud neck of mine doth subjugate,
    Whence I am forced to hold my visage down,
Him, who still lives[13] and does not name himself,   55
    Would I regard, to see if I may know him
    And make him piteous unto this burden.
A Latian was I,[14] and born of a great Tuscan;
    Guglielmo Aldobrandeschi was my father;
    I know not if his name were ever with you.[15]   60

The ancient blood and deeds of gallantry
    Of my progenitors so arrogant made me
    That, thinking not upon the common mother,[16]
All men I held in scorn to such extent
    I died therefore,[17] as know the Sienese,   65
    And every child in Campagnatico.
I am Omberto; and not to me alone
    Has pride done harm, but all my kith and kin
    Has with it dragged into adversity.
And here must I this burden bear for it   70
    Till God be satisfied, since I did not
    Among the living, here among the dead."
Listening I downward bent[18] my countenance;
    And one of them, not this one who was speaking,
    Twisted himself beneath the weight that cramps him,   75
And looked at me, and knew me, and called out,
    Keeping his eyes laboriously fixed
    On me, who all bowed down was going with them.
"O," asked I him, "art thou not Oderisi,[19]
    Agobbio's honor, and honor of that art   80
    Which is in Paris called illuminating?"[20]
"Brother," said he, "more laughing are the leaves
    Touched by the brush of Franco Bolognese;[21]
    All his the honor now, and mine in part.
In sooth I had not been so courteous   85
    While I was living, for the great desire
    Of excellence, on which my heart was bent.
Here of such pride is paid the forfeiture;
    And yet I should not be here, were it not
    That, having power to sin, I turned to God.[22]   90
O thou vain glory of the human powers,
    How little green upon thy summit lingers,
    If 't be not followed by an age of grossness![23]
In painting Cimabue thought that he
    Should hold the field, now Giotto has the cry,[24]   95
    So that the other's fame is growing dim.

So has one Guido from the other taken[25]
    The glory of our tongue, and he perchance
    Is born,[26] who from the nest shall chase them both.
Naught is this mundane rumor but a breath   100
    Of wind, that comes now this way and now that,
    And changes name, because it changes side.
What fame shalt thou have more, if old peel off
    From thee thy flesh, than if thou hadst been dead
    Before thou left the *pappo* and the *dindi*,[27]   105
Ere pass a thousand years? which is a shorter
    Space to the eterne, than twinkling of an eye
    Unto the circle that in heaven wheels slowest.[28]
With him,[29] who takes so little of the road
    In front of me, all Tuscany resounded;   110
    And now he scarce is lisped of in Siena,
Where he was lord, what time was overthrown
    The Florentine delirium,[30] that superb
    Was at that day as now 'tis prostitute.
Your reputation is the color of grass   115
    Which comes and goes, and that discolors it
    By which it issues green from out the earth."
And I: "Thy true speech fills my heart with good
    Humility, and great tumor[31] thou assuagest;
    But who is he, of whom just now thou spakest?"   120
"That," he replied, "is Provenzan Salvani,
    And he is here because he had presumed
    To bring Siena all into his hands.
He has gone thus, and goeth without rest
    E'er since he died; such money renders back   125
    In payment he who is on earth too daring."
And I: "If every spirit who awaits
    The verge of life before that he repent,
    Remains below there and ascends not hither,[32]
(Unless good orison shall him bestead,)   130
    Until as much time as he lived be passed,
    How was the coming granted him in largess?"

"When he in greatest splendor lived," said he,
    "Freely upon the Campo of Siena,
    All shame being laid aside, he placed himself;   135
And there to draw his friend from the duress[33]
    Which in the prison-house of Charles he suffered,
    He brought himself to tremble in each vein.
I say no more, and know that I speak darkly;
    Yet little time shall pass before thy neighbors   140
    Will so demean themselves that thou canst gloss it.[34]
This action has released him from those confines."[35]

CANTO XII

ABREAST, like oxen going in a yoke,[1]
  I with that heavy-laden soul went on,
  As long as the sweet pedagogue permitted;
But when he said, "Leave him, and onward pass,
  For here 'tis good that with the sail and oars,   5
  As much as may be, each push on his barque";
Upright, as walking wills it, I redressed
  My person, notwithstanding that my thoughts
  Remained within me downcast and abated.[2]
I had moved on, and followed willingly   10
  The footsteps of my Master, and we both
  Already showed how light of foot we were,
When unto me he said: "Cast down thine eyes;
  'Twere well for thee, to alleviate the way,
  To look upon the bed beneath thy feet."[3]   15
As, that some memory there may be of them,
  Above the buried dead[4] their tombs in earth
  Bear sculptured on them what they were before;
Whence often there we weep for them afresh,
  From pricking of remembrance, which alone   20
  To the compassionate doth set its spur;
So saw I there, but of a better semblance
  In point of artifice, with fingers covered
  Whate'er as pathway from the mount projects.
I saw that one who was created noble[5]   25
  More than all other creatures, down from heaven
  Fall like a thunder-bolt upon one side.

I saw Briareus[6] smitten by the dart
    Celestial, lying on the other side,
    Heavy upon the earth by mortal frost.   30
I saw Thymbræus, Pallas saw, and Mars,[7]
    Still clad in armor round about their father,
    Gaze at the scattered members of the giants.
I saw, at foot of his great labor, Nimrod,
    As if bewildered,[8] looking at the people   35
    Who had been proud with him in Sennaar.
O Niobe![9] with what afflicted eyes
    Thee I beheld upon the pathway traced,
    Between thy seven and seven children slain!
O Saul![10] how fallen upon thy proper sword   40
    Didst thou appear there lifeless in Gilboa,
    That felt thereafter neither rain nor dew!
O mad Arachne![11] so I thee beheld
    E'en then half spider, sad upon the shreds
    Of fabric wrought in evil hour for thee!   45
O Rehoboam![12] no more seems to threaten
    Thine image there; but full of consternation
    A chariot bears it off, when none pursues!
Displayed moreo'er the adamantine pavement
    How unto his own mother made Alcmæon[13]   50
    Costly appear the luckless ornament;
Displayed how his own sons did throw themselves
    Upon Sennacherib[14] within the temple,
    And how, he being dead, they left him there;
Displayed the ruin and the cruel carnage   55
    That Tomyris[15] wrought, when she to Cyrus said,
    "Blood didst thou thirst for, and with blood I glut thee!"
Displayed how routed fled the Assyrians
    After that Holofernes[16] had been slain,
    And likewise the remainder of that slaughter.   60
I saw there Troy in ashes and in caverns;
    O Ilion! thee, how abject and debased,
    Displayed the image that is there discerned![17]

Canto XII: The Souls of the Proud, bearing Heavy Stones

Who e'er of pencil master was or stile,[18]
    That could portray the shades and traits which there   65
    Would cause each subtile genius to admire?
Dead seemed the dead, the living seemed alive;
    Better than I saw not who saw the truth,
    All that I trod upon while bowed I went.
Now wax ye proud, and on with looks uplifted,   70
    Ye sons of Eve,[19] and bow not down your faces
    So that ye may behold your evil ways!
More of the mount by us was now encompassed,
    And far more spent the circuit of the sun,
    Than had the mind preoccupied imagined,[20]   75
When he, who ever watchful in advance
    Was going on, began: "Lift up thy head,
    'Tis no more time to go thus meditating.
Lo there an Angel who is making haste
    To come towards us; lo, returning is   80
    From service of the day the sixth handmaiden.[21]
With reverence thine acts and looks adorn,
    So that he may delight to speed us upward;
    Think that this day will never dawn again."
I was familiar with his admonition   85
    Ever to lose no time; so on this theme
    He could not unto me speak covertly.
Towards us came the being beautiful
    Vested in white, and in his countenance
    Such as appears the tremulous morning star.[22]   90
His arms he opened, and opened then his wings;
    "Come," said he, "near at hand here are the steps,
    And easy from henceforth is the ascent."
At this announcement few are they who come!
    O human creatures, born to soar aloft,   95
    Why fall ye thus before a little wind?[23]
He led us on to where the rock was cleft;
    There smote upon my forehead with his wings,[24]
    Then a safe passage promised unto me.

Canto XII: Dante looking at the Spirit of Arachne

As on the right hand, to ascend the mount   100
    Where seated is the church that lordeth it
    O'er the well-guided, above Rubaconte,
The bold abruptness of the ascent is broken
    By stairways that were made there in the age
    When still were safe the ledger and the stave,   105
E'en thus attempered is the bank which falls
    Sheer downward from the second circle there;
    But on this side and that the high rock grazes.[25]
As we were turning thitherward our persons,
    "*Beati pauperes spiritu,*"[26] voices   110
    Sang in such wise that speech could tell it not.
Ah me! how different are these entrances
    From the Infernal! for with anthems here
    One enters, and below with wild laments.
We now were mounting up the sacred stairs,   115
    And it appeared to me by far more easy[27]
    Than on the plain it had appeared before.
Whence I: "My Master, say, what heavy thing
    Has been uplifted from me, so that hardly
    Aught of fatigue is felt by me in walking?"   120
He answered: "When the P's which have remained
    Still on thy face almost obliterate
    Shall wholly, as the first is, be erased,
Thy feet will be so vanquished by good will,
    That not alone they shall not feel fatigue,   125
    But urging up will be to them delight."
Then did I even as they do who are going
    With something on the head to them unknown,
    Unless the signs of others make them doubt,
Wherefore the hand to ascertain is helpful,   130
    And seeks and finds, and doth fulfil the office
    Which cannot be accomplished by the sight;
And with the fingers of the right hand spread
    I found but six the letters,[28] that had carved
    Upon my temples he who bore the keys;   135
Upon beholding which my Leader smiled.

CANTO XIII

WE were upon the summit of the stairs,
  Where for the second time is cut away
  The mountain, which ascending shriveth* all.[1]
There in like manner doth a cornice bind
  The hill all round about, as does the first,   5
  Save that its arc more suddenly is curved.[2]
Shade is there none, nor sculpture[3] that appears;
  So seems the bank, and so the road seems smooth,
  With but the livid color of the stone.[4]
"If to inquire we wait for people here,"   10
  The Poet said, "I fear that peradventure
  Too much delay will our election have."
Then steadfast on the sun his eyes he fixed,
  Made his right side the centre of his motion,
  And turned the left part of himself about.[5]   15
"O thou sweet light! with trust in whom I enter
  Upon this novel journey, do thou lead us,"
  Said he, "as one within here should be led.
Thou warmest the world, thou shinest over it;
  If other reason prompt not otherwise,   20
  Thy rays should evermore our leaders be!"
As much as here is counted for a mile,
  So much already there had we advanced
  In little time, by dint of ready will;
And tow'rds us there were heard to fly, albeit   25

*Absolves.

71

They were not visible, spirits uttering[6]
    Unto Love's table courteous invitations.
The first voice that passed onward in its flight,
    "*Vinum non habent*,"[7] said in accents loud,
    And went reiterating it behind us.   30
And ere it wholly grew inaudible
    Because of distance, passed another, crying,
    "I am Orestes!"[8] and it also stayed not.
"O," said I, "Father, these, what voices are they?"
    And even as I asked, behold the third,   35
    Saying: "Love those from whom ye have had evil!"[9]
And the good Master said: "This circle scourges
    The sin of envy, and on that account
    Are drawn from love the lashes of the scourge.
The bridle of another sound shall be;[10]   40
    I think that thou wilt hear it, as I judge,
    Before thou comest to the Pass of Pardon.
But fix thine eyes athwart* the air right steadfast,
    And people thou wilt see before us sitting,
    And each one close against the cliff is seated."   45
Then wider than at first mine eyes I opened;
    I looked before me, and saw shades with mantles[11]
    Not from the color of the stone diverse.
And when we were a little farther onward,
    I heard a cry of, "Mary, pray for us!"   50
    A cry of, "Michael, Peter, and All Saints!"[12]
I do not think there walketh still on earth
    A man so hard, that he would not be pierced
    With pity at what afterward I saw.
For when I had approached so near to them   55
    That manifest to me their acts became,
    Drained was I at the eyes by heavy grief.
Covered with sackcloth vile they seemed to me,
    And one sustained the other with his shoulder,
    And all of them were by the bank sustained.   60

*Through.

Canto XIII: The Souls of the Envious

Thus do the blind, in want of livelihood,
>   Stand at the doors of churches asking alms,
>   And one upon another leans his head,
So that in others pity soon may rise,
>   Not only at the accent of their words,   65
>   But at their aspect, which no less implores.
And as unto the blind the sun comes not,
>   So to the shades, of whom just now I spake,
>   Heaven's light will not be bounteous of itself;
For all their lids an iron wire transpierces,   70
>   And sews them up, as to a sparhawk* wild
>   Is done, because it will not quiet stay.[13]
To me it seemed, in passing, to do outrage,
>   Seeing the others without being seen;
>   Wherefore I turned me to my counsel sage.   75
Well knew he what the mute one wished to say,[14]
>   And therefore waited not for my demand,
>   But said: "Speak, and be brief, and to the point."
I had Virgilius upon that side
>   Of the embankment from which one may fall,   80
>   Since by no border 'tis engarlanded;[15]
Upon the other side of me I had
>   The shades devout, who through the horrible seam
>   Pressed out the tears[16] so that they bathed their cheeks.
To them I turned me, and, "O people, certain,"   85
>   Began I, "of beholding the high light,
>   Which your desire has solely in its care,
So may grace speedily dissolve the scum
>   Upon your consciences,[17] that limpidly
>   Through them descend the river of the mind,   90
Tell me, for dear 'twill be to me and gracious,
>   If any soul among you here is Latian,†
>   And 'twill perchance be good for him I learn it."

*Small hawk.
†Italian.

"O brother mine, each one is citizen
    Of one true city;[18] but thy meaning is,   95
    Who may have lived in Italy a pilgrim."
By way of answer this I seemed to hear
    A little farther on than where I stood,
    Whereat I made myself still nearer heard.
Among the rest I saw a shade that waited   100
    In aspect, and should any one ask how,
    Its chin it lifted upward like a blind man.[19]
"Spirits," I said, "who stoopest to ascend,
    If thou art he who did reply to me,
    Make thyself known to me by place or name."   105
"Sienese was I," it replied, "and with
    The others here recleanse[20] my guilty life,
    Weeping to Him to lend himself to us.
Sapient I was not, although I Sapìa[21]
    Was called, and I was at another's harm   110
    More happy far than at my own good fortune.
And that thou mayst not think that I deceive thee,
    Hear if I was as foolish as I tell thee.
    The arc already of my years descending,
My fellow-citizens near unto Colle[22]   115
    Were joined in battle with their adversaries,
    And I was praying God for what he willed.
Routed were they, and turned into the bitter
    Passes of flight; and I, the chase beholding,
    A joy received unequalled by all others;   120
So that I lifted upward my bold face
    Crying to God, 'Henceforth I fear thee not,'
    As did the blackbird at the little sunshine.[23]
Peace I desired with God at the extreme
    Of my existence, and as yet would not   125
    My debt have been by penitence discharged,
Had it not been that in remembrance held me[24]
    Pier Pettignano[25] in his holy prayers,
    Who out of charity was grieved for me.

But who art thou, that into our conditions   130
    Questioning goest, and hast thine eyes unbound
    As I believe, and breathing dost discourse?"
"Mine eyes,"[26] I said, "will yet be here ta'en from me,
    But for short space; for small is the offence
    Committed by their being turned with envy.   135
Far greater is the fear, wherein suspended
    My soul is, of the torment underneath,
    For even now the load down there weighs on me."
And she to me: "Who led thee, then, among us
    Up here, if to return below thou thinkest?"   140
    And I: "He who is with me, and speaks not;
And living am I; therefore ask of me,
    Spirit elect, if thou wouldst have me move
    O'er yonder yet my mortal feet for thee."
"O, this is such a novel thing to hear,"   145
    She answered, "that great sign it is God loves thee;
    Therefore with prayer of thine sometimes assist me.
And I implore, by what thou most desirest,
    If e'er thou treadest the soil of Tuscany,
    Well with my kindred reinstate my fame.[27]   150
Them wilt thou see among that people vain
    Who hope in Talamone, and will lose there
    More hope than in discovering the Diana;
But there still more the admirals will lose."[28]

CANTO XIV

W_{HO} is this one[1] that goes about our mountain,
    Or ever Death has given him power of flight,
    And opes his eyes and shuts them at his will?"
"I know not who, but know he's not alone;
    Ask him thyself, for thou art nearer to him,   5
    And gently, so that he may speak, accost him."
Thus did two spirits, leaning tow'rds each other,
    Discourse about me there on the right hand;
    Then held supine[2] their faces to address me.
And said the one: "O soul, that, fastened still   10
    Within the body, tow'rds the heaven art going,
    For charity console us, and declare
Whence comest and who art thou; for thou mak'st us
    As much to marvel at this grace of thine
    As must a thing that never yet has been."   15
And I: "Through midst of Tuscany there wanders
    A streamlet that is born in Falterona,[3]
    And not a hundred miles of course suffice it;
From thereupon do I this body bring.
    To tell you who I am were speech in vain,   20
    Because my name as yet makes no great noise."[4]
"If well thy meaning I can penetrate
    With intellect of mine," then answered me
    He who first spake, "thou speakest of the Arno."
And said the other to him: "Why concealed   25
    This one the appellation of that river,
    Even as a man doth of things horrible?"

And thus the shade that questioned was of this
    Himself acquitted: "I know not; but truly
    'Tis fit the name of such a valley perish;   30
For from its fountain-head (where is so pregnant*
    The Alpine mountain whence is cleft Peloro[5]
    That in few places it that mark surpasses)
To where it yields itself in restoration
    Of what the heaven doth of the sea dry up,[6]   35
    Whence have the rivers that which goes with them,
Virtue is like an enemy avoided
    By all, as is a serpent, through misfortune
    Of place, or through bad habit that impels them;
On which account have so transformed their nature   40
    The dwellers in that miserable valley,
    It seems that Circe had them in her pasture.[7]
'Mid ugly swine,[8] of acorns worthier
    Than other food for human use created,
    It first directeth its impoverished way.   45
Curs findeth it thereafter, coming downward,
    More snarling than their puissance demands,
    And turns from them disdainfully its muzzle.[9]
It goes on falling, and the more it grows,
    The more it finds the dogs becoming wolves,   50
    This maledict† and misadventurous ditch.[10]
Descended then through many a hollow gulf,
    It finds the foxes so replete with fraud,[11]
    They fear no cunning that may master them.
Nor will I cease because another[12] hears me;   55
    And well 'twill be for him, if still he mind him
    Of what a truthful spirit to me unravels.
Thy grandson I behold, who doth become
    A hunter of those wolves upon the bank
    Of the wild stream, and terrifies them all.   60

---

*Abundant with waters.
†Cursed.

He sells their flesh, it being yet alive;
 Thereafter slaughters them like ancient beeves;
 Many of life, himself of praise, deprives.
Blood-stained he issues from the dismal forest;
 He leaves it such, a thousand years from now   65
 In its primeval state 'tis not re-wooded."[13]
As at the announcement of impending ills
 The face of him who listens is disturbed,
 From whate'er side the peril seize upon him;
So I beheld that other soul, which stood   70
 Turned round to listen, grow disturbed and sad,[14]
 When it had gathered to itself the word.
The speech of one and aspect of the other
 Had me desirous made to know their names,
 And question mixed with prayers I made thereof,   75
Whereat the spirit which first spake to me
 Began again: "Thou wishest I should bring me me
 To do for thee what thou'lt not do for me;[15]
But since God willeth that in thee shine forth
 Such grace of his, I'll not be chary with thee;   80
 Know, then, that I Guido del Duca am.[16]
My blood was so with envy set on fire,
 That if I had beheld a man make merry,
 Thou wouldst have seen me sprinkled o'er with pallor.
From my own sowing such the straw I reap![17]   85
 O human race! why dost thou set thy heart
 Where interdict of partnership must be?[18]
This is Renier,[19] this is the boast and honor
 Of the house of Calboli, where no one since
 Has made himself the heir of his desert.   90
And not alone his blood is made devoid,
 'Twixt Po and mount, and sea-shore and the Reno,[20]
 Of good required for truth and for diversion;
For all within these boundaries is full
 Of venomous roots, so that too tardily   95
 By cultivation now would they diminish.[21]

Where is good Lizio,[22] and Arrigo Manardi,
    Pier Traversaro, and Guido di Carpigna,
    O Romagnuoli into bastards turned?
When in Bologna will a Fabbro rise?   100
    When in Faenza a Bernardin di Fosco,
    The noble scion of ignoble seed?
Be not astonished, Tuscan, if I weep,
    When I remember, with Guido da Prata,
    Ugolin d' Azzo, who was living with us,   105
Frederick Tignoso and his company,
    The house of Traversara, and th' Anastagi,
    And one race and the other is extinct;
The dames and cavaliers,[23] the toils and ease
    That filled our souls with love and courtesy,   110
    There where the hearts have so malicious grown!
O Brettinoro! why dost thou not flee,
    Seeing that all thy family is gone,
    And many people, not to be corrupted?
Bagnacaval does well in not begetting,   115
    And ill does Castrocaro, and Conio worse,
    In taking trouble to beget such Counts.[24]
Will do well the Pagani; when their Devil[25]
    Shall have departed; but not therefore pure
    Will testimony of them e'er remain.   120
O Ugolin de' Fantoli,[26] secure
    Thy name is, since no longer is awaited
    One who, degenerating, can obscure it!
But go now, Tuscan, for it now delights me
    To weep far better than it does to speak,   125
    So much has our discourse my mind distressed."[27]
We were aware that those beloved souls
    Heard us depart; therefore, by keeping silent,
    They made us of our pathway confident.[28]
When we became alone by going onward,   130
    Thunder, when it doth cleave the air, appeared
    A voice,[29] that counter to us came, exclaiming:

"Shall slay me whosoever findeth me!"[30]
    And fled as the reverberation dies
    If suddenly the cloud asunder bursts.   135
As soon as hearing had a truce from this,[31]
    Behold another, with so great a crash,
    That it resembled thunderings following fast:
"I am Aglaurus,[32] who became a stone!"
    And then, to press myself close to the Poet,   140
    I backward, and not forward,[33] took a step.
Already on all sides the air was quiet;
    And said he to me: "That was the hard curb
    That ought to hold a man within his bounds;
But you take in the bait so that the hook   145
    Of the old Adversary draws you to him,
    And hence availeth little curb or call.[34]
The heavens are calling you, and wheel around you,
    Displaying to you their eternal beauties,
    And still your eye is looking on the ground;[35]   150
Whence He, who all discerns, chastises you."

Canto XV: Dante's Vision of the Stoning of St. Stephen

CANTO XV

As much as 'twixt the close of the third hour
   And dawn of day appeareth of that sphere
   Which aye in fashion of a child is playing,
So much it now appeared, towards the night,
   Was of his course remaining to the sun;   5
   There it was evening, and 'twas midnight here;[1]
And the rays smote the middle of our faces,
   Because by us the mount was so encircled,
   That straight towards the west we now were going;
When I perceived my forehead overpowered   10
   Beneath the splendor far more than at first,
   And stupor were to me the things unknown;
Whereat towards the summit of my brow
   I raised my hands, and made myself the visor
   Which the excessive glare diminishes.   15
As when from off the water, or a mirror,
   The sunbeam leaps unto the opposite side,
   Ascending upward in the selfsame measure
That it descends, and deviates as far
   From falling of a stone in line direct,[2]   20
   (As demonstrate experiment and art,)
So it appeared to me that by a light
   Refracted there before me I was smitten;
   On which account my sight was swift to flee.
"What is that, Father sweet, from which I cannot   25
   So fully screen my sight that it avail me,"
   Said I, "and seems towards us to be moving?"
"Marvel thou not, if dazzle thee as yet

The family of heaven," he answered me;
   "An angel 'tis, who comes to invite us upward.   30
Soon will it be, that to behold these things
   Shall not be grievous, but delightful to thee[3]
   As much as nature fashioned thee to feel."
When we had reached the Angel benedight,*
   With joyful voice he said: "Here enter in   35
   To stairway far less steep than are the others."[4]
We mounting were, already thence departed,
   And *"Beati misericordes"* was
   Behind us sung, "Rejoice, thou that o'ercomest!"[5]
My master and myself, we two alone   40
   Were going upward, and I thought, in going,
   Some profit to acquire from words of his;
And I to him directed me, thus asking:
   "What did the spirit of Romagna mean,
   Mentioning interdict and partnership?"[6]   45
Whence he to me: "Of his own greatest failing
   He knows the harm; and therefore wonder not
   If he reprove us, that we less may rue it.
Because are thither pointed your desires
   Where by companionship each share is lessened,   50
   Envy doth ply the bellows to your sighs.[7]
But if the love of the supernal sphere[8]
   Should upwardly direct your aspiration,
   There would not be that fear within your breast;
For there, as much the more as one says *Our*,   55
   So much the more of good each one possesses,
   And more of charity in that cloister burns."
"I am more hungering to be satisfied,"
   I said, "than if I had before been silent,
   And more of doubt within my mind I gather.   60
How can it be, that boon distributed
   The more possessors can more wealthy make
   Therein, than if by few it be possessed?"[9]

*Blessed (from the Italian word *benedetto*).

84

And he to me: "Because thou fixest still
    Thy mind entirely upon earthly things,   65
    Thou pluckest darkness from the very light.
That goodness infinite and ineffable
    Which is above there, runneth unto love,
    As to a lucid body comes the sunbeam.[10]
So much it gives itself as it finds ardor,   70
    So that as far as charity extends,
    O'er it increases the eternal valor.
And the more people thitherward aspire,
    More are there to love well, and more they
        love there,
    And, as a mirror, one reflects the other.   75
And if my reasoning appease thee not,
    Thou shalt see Beatrice; and she will fully
    Take from thee this and every other longing.[11]
Endeavor, then, that soon may be extinct,
    As are the two already,[12] the five wounds   80
    That close themselves again by being painful."
Even as I wished to say, "Thou dost appease me,"
    I saw that I had reached another circle,
    So that my eager eyes made me keep silence.
There it appeared to me that in a vision   85
    Ecstatic on a sudden I was rapt,[13]
    And in a temple many persons saw;
And at the door a woman, with the sweet
    Behavior of a mother, saying: "Son,
    Why in this manner hast thou dealt with us?   90
Lo, sorrowing, thy father and myself
    Were seeking for thee";—and as here she ceased,
    That which appeared at first had disappeared.[14]
Then I beheld another with those waters
    Adown her cheeks which grief distils whenever   95
    From great disdain of others it is born,
And saying: "If of that city thou art lord,
    For whose name was such strife among the gods,
    And whence doth every science scintillate,

Avenge thyself on those audacious arms 100
    That clasped our daughter, O Pisistratus";
    And the lord seemed to me benign and mild
To answer her with aspect temperate:
    "What shall we do to those who wish us ill,
    If he who loves us be by us condemned?"[15] 105
Then saw I people hot in fire of wrath,
    With stones a young man slaying, clamorously
    Still crying to each other, "Kill him! kill him!"
And him I saw bow down, because of death
    That weighed already on him, to the earth, 110
    But of his eyes made ever gates to heaven,
Imploring the high Lord, in so great strife,
    That he would pardon those his persecutors,
    With such an aspect as unlocks compassion.[16]
Soon as my soul had outwardly returned 115
    To things external to it which are true
    Did I my not false errors recognize.[17]
My Leader, who could see me bear myself
    Like to a man that rouses him from sleep,
    Exclaimed: "What ails thee, that thou canst not stand? 120
But hast been coming more than half a league
    Veiling thine eyes, and with thy legs entangled,
    In guise of one whom wine or sleep subdues?"[18]
"O my sweet Father, if thou listen to me,
    I'll tell thee," said I, "what appeared to me, 125
    When thus from me my legs were ta'en away."
And he: "If thou shouldst have a hundred masks
    Upon thy face, from me would not be shut
    Thy cogitations, howsoever small.[19]
What thou hast seen was that thou mayst not fail 130
    To ope thy heart unto the waters of peace,
    Which from the eternal fountain are diffused.
I did not ask, 'What ails thee?' as he does
    Who only looketh with the eyes that see not
    When of the soul bereft the body lies, 135

But asked it to give vigor to thy feet;[20]
      Thus must we needs urge on the sluggards, slow
      To use their wakefulness when it returns."
We passed along, athwart* the twilight peering[21]
      Forward as far as ever eye could stretch   140
      Against the sunbeams serotine† and lucent;
And lo! by slow degrees a smoke approached[22]
      In our direction, sombre as the night,
      Nor was there place to hide one's self therefrom.
This of our eyes and the pure air bereft us.‡   145

*Counter to.
†Late, of the evening (almost a direct translation from the Italian *serotini*).
‡Took away from us.

Canto XVI: Marco Lombardo follows the Poets through the Smoke

CANTO XVI

DARKNESS of hell,[1] and of a night deprived
Of every planet under a poor sky,
As much as may be tenebrous with cloud,
Ne'er made unto my sight so thick a veil,
As did that smoke which there enveloped us, 5
Nor to the feeling of so rough a texture;
For not an eye it suffered to stay open;[2]
Whereat mine escort, faithful and sagacious,
Drew near to me and offered me his shoulder.
E'en as a blind man goes behind his guide, 10
Lest he should wander, or should strike against
Aught that may harm or peradventure kill him,
So went I through the bitter and foul air,
Listening unto my Leader, who said only,
"Look that from me thou be not separated." 15
Voices I heard, and every one appeared
To supplicate for peace and misericord*
The Lamb of God who takes away our sins.
Still "*Agnus Dei*" their exordium was;[3]
One word there was in all, and metre one, 20
So that all harmony appeared among them.[4]
"Master," I said, "are spirits those I hear?"
And he to me: "Thou apprehendest truly,
And they the knot of anger[5] go unloosing."
"Now who art thou, that cleavest through our smoke, 25

*Mercy, pity.

And art discoursing of us even as though
Thou didst by calends still divide the time?"[6]
After this manner by a voice[7] was spoken;
Whereon my Master said: "Do thou reply,
And ask if on this side the way go upward."   30
And I: "O creature that dost cleanse thyself
To return beautiful to Him who made thee,
Thou shalt hear marvels[8] if thou follow me."
"Thee will I follow far as is allowed me,"
He answered; "and if smoke prevent our seeing,   35
Hearing shall keep us joined instead thereof."
Thereon began I: "With that swathing band
Which death unwindeth am I going upward,
And hither came I through the infernal anguish.[9]
And if God in his grace has me infolded,   40
So that he wills that I behold his court
By method wholly out of modern usage,[10]
Conceal not from me who ere death thou wast,
But tell it me, and tell me if I go
Right for the pass, and be thy words our escort."   45
"Lombard was I, and I was Marco called;[11]
The world I knew, and loved that excellence,
At which has each one now unbent his bow.[12]
For mounting upward, thou art going right."
Thus he made answer, and subjoined:* "I pray thee   50
To pray for me when thou shalt be above."
And I to him: "My faith I pledge to thee
To do what thou dost ask me; but am bursting
Inly with doubt, unless I rid me of it.
First it was simple, and is now made double   55
By thy opinion,[13] which makes certain to me,
Here and elsewhere, that which I couple with it.
The world forsooth is utterly deserted
By every virtue, as thou tellest me,
And with iniquity is big and covered;   60

*Added.

But I beseech thee point me out the cause,
 That I may see it, and to others show it;
 For one in the heavens, and here below one puts it."[14]
A sigh profound, that grief forced into Ai![15]
 He first sent forth, and then began he: "Brother,   65
 The world is blind, and sooth thou comest from it![16]
Ye who are living every cause refer
 Still upward to the heavens, as if all things
 They of necessity moved with themselves.
If this were so, in you would be destroyed   70
 Free will, nor any justice would there be
 In having joy for good, or grief for evil.
The heavens your movements do initiate,
 I say not all; but granting that I say it,
 Light has been given you for good and evil,   75
And free volition; which, if some fatigue
 In the first battles with the heavens it suffers,
 Afterwards conquers all, if well 'tis nurtured.
To greater force and to a better nature,[17]
 Though free, ye subject are, and that creates   80
 The mind in you the heavens have not in charge.
Hence, if the present world doth go astray,
 In you the cause is, be it sought in you;
 And I therein will now be thy true spy.[18]
Forth from the hand of Him, who fondles it   85
 Before it is, like to a little girl
 Weeping and laughing in her childish sport,
Issues the simple soul, that nothing knows,
 Save that, proceeding from a joyous Maker,
 Gladly it turns to that which gives it pleasure.   90
Of trivial good at first it takes the savor;
 Is cheated by it, and runs after it,
 If guide or rein turn not aside its love.[19]
Hence it behoved laws[20] for a rein to place,
 Behoved a king to have, who at the least   95
 Of the true city should discern the tower.
The laws exist,[21] but who sets hand to them?

No one; because the shepherd who precedes
    Can ruminate, but cleaveth not the hoof;[22]
Wherefore the people that perceives its guide   100
    Strike only at the good for which it hankers,
    Feeds upon that, and farther seeketh not.[23]
Clearly canst thou perceive that evil guidance
    The cause is that has made the world depraved,
    And not that nature is corrupt in you.[24]   105
Rome, that reformed the world, accustomed was
    Two suns to have,[25] which one road and the other,
    Of God and of the world, made manifest.
One has the other quenched, and to the crosier
    The sword is joined, and ill beseemeth it   110
    That by main force one with the other go,
Because, being joined, one feareth not the other;
    If thou believe not, think upon the grain,
    For by its seed each herb is recognized.[26]
In the land laved* by Po and Adige,[27]   115
    Valor and courtesy used to be found,
    Before that Frederick had his controversy;[28]
Now in security can pass that way
    Whoever will abstain, through sense of shame,
    From speaking with the good, or drawing near them.   120
True, three old men are left,[29] in whom upbraids
    The ancient age the new, and late they deem it
    That God restore them to the better life:
Currado da Palazzo,[30] and good Gherardo,[31]
    And Guido da Castel, who better named is   125
    In fashion of the French, the simple Lombard:[32]
Say thou henceforward that the Church of Rome,
    Confounding in itself two governments,
    Falls in the mire, and soils itself and burden."[33]
"O Marco mine,"[34] I said, "thou reasonest well;   130
    And now discern I why the sons of Levi
    Have been excluded from the heritage.[35]

*Washed, watered.

But what Gherardo is it,[36] who, as sample
    Of a lost race, thou sayest has remained
    In reprobation of the barbarous age?"   135
"Either thy speech deceives me, or it tempts me,"
    He answered me; "for speaking Tuscan to me,
    It seems of good Gherardo naught thou knowest.
By other surname do I know him not,
    Unless I take it from his daughter Gaia.[37]   140
    May God be with you, for I come no farther.
Behold the dawn, that through the smoke rays out,
    Already whitening; and I must depart—
    Yonder the Angel is[38]—e'er he appear."
Thus did he speak, and would no farther hear me.   145

CANTO XVII

REMEMBER, Reader,[1] if e'er in the Alps
    A mist o'ertook thee, through which thou couldst see
    Not otherwise than through its membrane mole,[2]
How, when the vapors humid and condensed
    Begin to dissipate themselves, the sphere   5
    Of the sun feebly enters in among them,
And thy imagination will be swift
    In coming to perceive how I re-saw
    The sun at first, that was already setting.[3]
Thus, to the faithful footsteps of my Master   10
    Mating mine own, I issued from that cloud
    To rays already dead on the low shores.[4]
O thou, Imagination, that dost steal us
    So from without sometimes, that man perceives not,
    Although around may sound a thousand trumpets,[5]   15
Who moveth thee, if sense impel thee not?
    Moves thee a light, which in the heaven takes form,
    By self, or by a will that downward guides it.[6]
Of her impiety, who changed her form
    Into the bird that most delights in singing,   20
    In my imagining appeared the trace;
And hereupon my mind was so withdrawn
    Within itself, that from without there came
    Nothing that then might be received by it.[7]
Then rained within my lofty fantasy   25
    One crucified, disdainful and ferocious
    In countenance, and even thus was dying.
Around him were the great Ahasuerus,

Esther his wife, and the just Mordecai,
    Who was in word and action so entire.*[8]   30
And even as this image burst asunder
    Of its own self, in fashion of a bubble[9]
    In which the water it was made of fails,
There rose up in my vision a young maiden
    Bitterly weeping, and she said: "O queen,   35
    Why hast thou wished in anger to be naught?
Thou'st slain thyself, Lavinia not to lose;
    Now hast thou lost me; I am she who mourns,
    Mother, at thine ere at another's ruin."[10]
As sleep is broken, when upon a sudden   40
    New light strikes in upon the eyelids closed,
    And broken quivers e'er it dieth wholly,
So this imagining of mine fell down
    As soon as the effulgence† smote my face,
    Greater by far than what is in our wont.[11]   45
I turned me round to see where I might be,
    When said a voice, "Here is the passage up";
    Which from all other purposes removed me,
And made my wish so full of eagerness
    To look and see who was it that was speaking,   50
    It never rests till meeting face to face;[12]
But as before the sun,[13] which quells the sight,
    And in its own excess its figure veils,
    Even so my power was insufficient here.
"This is a spirit divine, who in the way   55
    Of going up directs us without asking,
    And who with his own light himself conceals.
He does with us as man doth with himself;
    For he who sees the need,[14] and waits the asking,
    Malignly leans already tow'rds denial.   60
Accord we now our feet to such inviting,
    Let us make haste to mount ere it grow dark;[15]
    For then we could not till the day return."

*Unified in both speech and deeds.
†Light.

Thus my Conductor said; and I and he
　　Together turned our footsteps to a stairway;　　　　　65
　　And I, as soon as the first step I reached,
Near me perceived a motion as of wings,
　　And fanning in the face,[16] and saying, "*Beati*
　　Pacifici, who are without ill anger."[17]
Already over us were so uplifted　　　　　70
　　The latest sunbeams, which the night pursues,
　　That upon many sides the stars appeared.
"O manhood mine, why dost thou vanish so?"
　　I said within myself; for I perceived
　　The vigor of my legs was put in truce.[18]　　　　　75
We at the point were where no more ascends[19]
　　The stairway upward, and were motionless,
　　Even as a ship, which at the shores arrives;
And I gave heed a little, if I might hear
　　Aught whatsoever in the circle new;　　　　　80
　　Then to my Master turned me round and said:
"Say, my sweet Father, what delinquency
　　Is purged here in the circle where we are?
　　Although our feet may pause, pause not thy speech."
And he to me: "The love of good, remiss[20]　　　　　85
　　In what it should have done, is here restored;
　　Here plied again the ill-belated oar;
But still more openly to understand,
　　Turn unto me thy mind, and thou shalt gather
　　Some profitable fruit from our delay.　　　　　90
Neither Creator nor a creature ever,
　　Son," he began, "was destitute of love
　　Natural or spiritual; and thou knowest it.
The natural was ever without error;
　　But err the other may by evil object,　　　　　95
　　Or by too much, or by too little vigor.[21]
While in the first it well directed is,
　　And in the second moderates itself,
　　It cannot be the cause of sinful pleasure;

But when to ill it turns, and, with more care   100
    Or lesser than it ought, runs after good,
     'Gainst the Creator works his own creation.
Hence thou mayst comprehend that love must be
    The seed within yourselves of every virtue,
     And every act that merits punishment.   105
Now inasmuch as never from the welfare
    Of its own subject can love turn its sight,
     From their own hatred all things are secure;
And since we cannot think of any being
    Standing alone, nor from the First divided,   110
     Of hating Him is all desire cut off.[22]
Hence if, discriminating, I judge well,
    The evil that one loves is of one's neighbor,
     And this is born in three modes in your clay.
There are, who, by abasement of their neighbor,   115
    Hope to excel, and therefore only long
     That from his greatness he may be cast down;
There are, who power, grace, honor, and renown
    Fear they may lose because another rises,
     Thence are so sad that the reverse they love;   120
And there are those whom injury seems to chafe,
    So that it makes them greedy for revenge,
     And such must needs shape out another's harm.[23]
This threefold love is wept for down below;
    Now of the other will I have thee hear,[24]   125
     That runneth after good with measure faulty.
Each one confusedly a good conceives
    Wherein the mind may rest, and longeth for it;
     Therefore to overtake it each one strives.
If languid love[25] to look on this attract you,   130
    Or in attaining unto it, this cornice,
     After just penitence,[26] torments you for it.
There's other good that does not make man happy;[27]
    'Tis not felicity, 'tis not the good
     Essence, of every good the fruit and root.   135

The love that yields itself too much to this
    Above us is lamented in three circles;
    But how tripartite it may be described,
I say not, that thou seek it for thyself."[28]

CANTO XVIII

$\mathcal{A}$N end had put unto his reasoning
    The lofty Teacher, and attent was looking
    Into my face, if I appeared content;
And I, whom a new thirst still goaded on,
    Without was mute, and within: "Perchance
    The too much questioning I make annoys him."[1]
But that true Father, who had comprehended
    The timid wish, that opened not itself,
    By speaking gave me hardihood to speak.
Whence I: "My sight is, Master, vivified
    So in thy light, that clearly I discern
    Whate'er thy speech importeth or describes.
Therefore I thee entreat, sweet Father dear,
    To teach me love,[2] to which thou dost refer
    Every good action and its contrary."
"Direct," he said, "towards me the keen eyes
    Of intellect, and clear will be to thee
    The error of the blind, who would be leaders.
The soul, which is created apt to love,
    Is mobile unto everything that pleases,
    Soon as by pleasure she is waked to action.
Your apprehension from some real thing[3]
    An image draws, and in yourselves displays it,
    So that it makes the soul turn unto it.
And if, when turned, towards it she incline,
    Love is that inclination;[4] it is nature,
    Which is by pleasure bound in you anew.
Then even as the fire doth upward move

5

10

15

20

25

By its own form, which to ascend is born,
    Where longest in its matter it endures,   30
So comes the captive soul into desire,[5]
    Which is a motion spiritual, and ne'er rests
    Until she doth enjoy the thing beloved.
Now may apparent be to thee how hidden
    The truth is from those people, who aver   35
    All love is in itself a laudable thing;[6]
Because its matter may perchance appear
    Aye to be good; but yet not each impression
    Is good, albeit good may be the wax."[7]
"Thy words, and my sequacious intellect,"   40
    I answered him, "have love revealed to me;
    But that has made me more impregned* with doubt;
For if love from without be offered us,
    And with another foot the soul go not,
    If right or wrong she go, 'tis not her merit."[8]   45
And he to me: "What reason seeth here,
    Myself can tell thee; beyond that await
    For Beatrice, since 'tis a work of faith.[9]
Every substantial form, that segregate
    From matter is, and with it is united,   50
    Specific power has in itself collected,
Which without act is not perceptible,
    Nor shows itself except by its effect,
    As life does in a plant by the green leaves.[10]
But still, whence cometh the intelligence   55
    Of the first notions, man is ignorant,
    And the affection for the first allurements,[11]
Which are in you as instinct in the bee
    To make its honey;[12] and this first desire
    Merit of praise or blame containeth not.   60
Now, that to this all others may be gathered,
    Innate within you is the power that counsels,
    And it should keep the threshold of assent.[13]

*Pregnant.

Canto XVIII: The Multitude of the Slothful

This is the principle, from which is taken
    Occasion of desert in you, according
    As good and guilty loves it takes and winnows.[14]
Those who, in reasoning, to the bottom went,
    Were of this innate liberty aware,
    Therefore bequeathed they Ethics to the world.[15]
Supposing, then, that from necessity
    Springs every love that is within you kindled,
    Within yourselves the power is to restrain it.[16]
The noble virtue[17] Beatrice understands
    By the free will; and therefore see that thou
    Bear it in mind, if she should speak of it."
The moon, belated almost unto midnight,
    Now made the stars appear to us more rare,
    Formed like a bucket, that is all ablaze,
And counter to the heavens ran through those paths
    Which the sun sets aflame, when he of Rome
    Sees it 'twixt Sardes and Corsicans go down;[18]
And that patrician shade, for whom is named
    Pietola more than any Mantuan town,[19]
    Had laid aside the burden of my lading;
Whence I, who reason manifest and plain
    In answer to my questions had received,
    Stood like a man in drowsy revery.[20]
But taken from me was this drowsiness
    Suddenly by a people,[21] that behind
    Our backs already had come round to us.
And as, of old, Ismenus and Asopus
    Beside them saw at night the rush and throng,
    If but the Thebans were in need of Bacchus,
So they along that circle curve their step,[22]
    From what I saw of those approaching us,
    Who by good-will and righteous love are ridden.
Full soon they were upon us, because running
    Moved onward all that mighty multitude,
    And two in the advance cried out, lamenting,

65

70

75

80

85

90

95

"Mary in haste unto the mountain ran,   100
    And Cæasar, that he might subdue Ilerda,
    Thrust at Marseilles, and then ran into Spain."[23]
"Quick! quick! so that the time may not be lost
    By little love!" forthwith the others cried,
    "For ardor in well-doing freshens grace!"[24]   105
"O folk, in whom an eager fervor now
    Supplies perhaps delay and negligence
    Put by you in well-doing, through lukewarmness,[25]
This one who lives, and truly I lie not,
    Would fain go up, if but the sun relight us;   110
    So tell us where the passage nearest is."
These were the words of him who was my Guide;
    And some one of those spirits said: "Come on
    Behind us, and the opening shalt thou find;
So full of longing are we to move onward,   115
    That stay we cannot; therefore pardon us,
    If thou for churlishness our justice take.
I was San Zeno's Abbot at Verona,
    Under the empire of good Barbarossa,
    Of whom still sorrowing Milan holds discourse;[26]   120
And he has one foot in the grave already,
    Who shall erelong lament that monastery,
    And sorry be for having there had power,
Because his son, in his whole body sick,
    And worse in mind, and who was evil-born,   125
    He put into the place of its true pastor."[27]
If more he said, or silent was, I know not,
    He had already passed so far beyond us;[28]
    But this I heard, and to retain it pleased me.
And he who was in every need my succor   130
    Said: "Turn thee hitherward; see two of them
    Come fastening upon slothfulness their teeth."[29]
In rear of all they shouted: "Sooner were
    The people dead to whom the sea was opened,
    Than their inheritors the Jordan saw;[30]   135

And those who the fatigue did not endure
    Unto the issue, with Anchises' son,
    Themselves to life withouten* glory offered."[31]
Then when from us so separated were
    Those shades, that they no longer could be seen,   140
    Within me a new thought did entrance find,
Whence others many and diverse were born;
    And so I lapsed from one into another,
    That in a reverie mine eyes I closed,
And meditation into dream transmuted.[32]   145

*Without.

CANTO XIX

*I*T was the hour when the diurnal* heat
    No more can warm the coldness of the moon,
    Vanquished by earth, or peradventure Saturn,
When geomancers their Fortuna Major
    See in the orient before the dawn   5
    Rise by a path that long remains not dim,[1]
There came to me in dreams a stammering woman,[2]
    Squint in her eyes, and in her feet distorted,
    With hands dissevered,† and of sallow hue.‡
I looked at her; and as the sun restores   10
    The frigid members, which the night benumbs,
    Even thus my gaze[3] did render voluble
Her tongue, and made her all erect thereafter
    In little while, and the lost countenance
    As love desires it so in her did color.   15
When in this wise she had her speech unloosed,
    She 'gan to sing so, that with difficulty
    Could I have turned my thoughts away from her.
"I am," she sang, "I am the Siren sweet
    Who mariners amid the main unman,   20
    So full am I of pleasantness to hear.
I drew Ulysses from his wandering way[4]
    Unto my song, and he who dwells with me
    Seldom departs, so wholly I content him."

*Of the day.
†Maimed, crippled.
‡Pale, yellowish.

Her mouth was not yet closed again, before   25
    Appeared a Lady saintly and alert[5]
    Close at my side to put her to confusion.
"Virgilius, O Virgilius! who is this?"
    Sternly she said; and he was drawing near
    With eyes still fixed upon that modest one.   30
She seized the other and in front laid open,
    Rending her garments, and her belly showed me;
    This waked me with the stench that issued from it.[6]
I turned mine eyes, and good Virgilius said:
    "At least thrice have I called thee;[7] rise and come;   35
    Find we the opening by which thou mayst enter."
I rose; and full already of high day
    Were all the circles of the Sacred Mountain,
    And with the new sun at our back we went.
Following behind him, I my forehead bore   40
    Like unto one who has it laden with thought,
    Who makes himself the half arch of a bridge,[8]
When I heard say, "Come, here the passage is,"[9]
    Spoken in a manner gentle and benign,
    Such as we hear not in this mortal region.   45
With open wings, which of a swan appeared,
    Upward he turned us who thus spake to us,
    Between the two walls of the solid granite.
He moved his pinions afterwards and fanned us,[10]
    Affirming those *qui lugent* to be blessed,[11]   50
    For they shall have their souls with comfort filled.
"What aileth thee, that aye to earth* thou gazest?"
    To me my Guide began to say, we both
    Somewhat beyond the Angel having mounted.
And I: "With such misgiving makes me go   55
    A vision new, which bends me to itself,
    So that I cannot from the thought withdraw me."[12]

*Down to the ground.

Canto XIX: Virgil reproves Dante for gazing downward

"Didst thou behold," he said, "that old enchantress,
     Who sole above us henceforth is lamented?[13]
     Didst thou behold how man is freed from her?   60
Suffice it thee, and smite earth with thy heels,
     Thine eyes lift upward to the lure, that whirls
     The Eternal King with revolutions vast."
Even as the hawk, that first his feet surveys,
     Then turns him to the call and stretches forward,   65
     Through the desire of food that draws him thither,
Such I became, and such, as far as cleaves
     The rock to give a way to him who mounts,
     Went on to where the circling doth begin.[14]
On the fifth circle when I had come forth,   70
     People I saw upon it who were weeping,
     Stretched prone upon the ground, all downward turned.[15]
"*Adhæsit pavimento anima mea,*"
     I heard them say with sighings so profound,
     That hardly could the words be understood.[16]   75
"O ye elect of God, whose sufferings
     Justice and Hope both render less severe,
     Direct ye us towards the high ascents."
"If ye are come secure from this prostration,[17]
     And wish to find the way most speedily,   80
     Let your right hands be evermore outside."[18]
Thus did the Poet ask, and thus was answered
     By them somewhat in front of us; whence I
     In what was spoken divined the rest concealed,[19]
And unto my Lord's eyes mine eyes I turned;   85
     Whence he assented with a cheerful sign
     To what the sight of my desire implored.
When of myself I could dispose at will,
     Above that creature did I draw myself,
     Whose words before had caused me to take note,   90
Saying: "O Spirit, in whom weeping ripens
     That without which to God we cannot turn,[20]
     Suspend awhile for me thy greater care.

Who wast thou, and why are your backs turned upwards,
    Tell me, and if thou wouldst that I procure thee   95
    Anything there whence living I departed."[21]
And he to me: "Wherefore our backs the heaven
    Turns to itself, know shalt thou; but beforehand
    Scias quod ego fui successor Petri.[22]
Between Siestri and Chiaveri descends   100
    A river beautiful, and of its name
    The title of my blood its summit makes.[23]
A month and little more essayed I how
    Weighs the great cloak on him from mire who keeps it;
    For all the other burdens seem a feather.   105
Tardy, ah woe is me! was my conversion;
    But when the Roman Shepherd I was made,
    Then I discovered life to be a lie.[24]
I saw that there the heart was not at rest,
    Nor farther in that life could one ascend;[25]   110
    Whereby the love of this was kindled in me.
Until that time a wretched soul and parted
    From God was I, and wholly avaricious;
    Now, as thou seest, I here am punished for it.
What avarice does is here made manifest   115
    In the purgation of these souls converted,
    And no more bitter pain the Mountain has.
Even as our eye did not uplift itself
    Aloft, being fastened upon earthly things,
    So justice here has merged it in the earth.[26]   120
As avarice had extinguished our affection
    For every good, whereby was action lost,
    So justice here doth hold us in restraint,
Bound and imprisoned by the feet and hands;
    And so long as it pleases the just Lord   125
    Shall we remain immovable and prostrate."
I on my knees had fallen,[27] and wished to speak;
    But even as I began, and he was 'ware,
    Only by listening, of my reverence,

"What cause," he said, "has downward bent thee thus?"   130
    And I to him: "For your own dignity,
    Standing, my conscience stung me with remorse."[28]
"Straighten thy legs, and upward raise thee, brother,"
    He answered: "Err not, fellow-servant am I[29]
    With thee and with the others to one power.   135
If e'er that holy, evangelic sound,
    Which sayeth *neque nubent*,[30] thou hast heard,
    Well canst thou see why in this wise I speak.
Now go; no longer will I have thee linger,
    Because thy stay doth incommode my weeping,   140
    With which I ripen[31] that which thou hast said.
On earth[32] I have a grandchild named Alagia,
    Good in herself, unless indeed our house
    Malevolent may make her by example,[33]
And she alone remains to me on earth."   145

CANTO XX

*I*LL strives the will against a better will;
　　Therefore, to pleasure him, against my pleasure
　　I drew the sponge not saturate from the water.[1]
Onward I moved, and onward moved my Leader,
　　Through vacant places, skirting still the rock,　　　　5
　　As on a wall close to the battlements;
For they that through their eyes pour drop by drop
　　The malady which all the world pervades,
　　On the other side too near the verge approach.[2]
Accursed mayst thou be, thou old she-wolf,[3]　　　　10
　　That more than all the other beasts hast prey,
　　Because of hunger infinitely hollow!
O heaven, in whose gyrations some appear
　　To think conditions here below are changed,
　　When will he come through whom she shall depart?[4]　　15
Onward we went with footsteps slow and scarce,[5]
　　And I attentive to the shades I heard
　　Piteously weeping and bemoaning them;
And I by peradventure heard "Sweet Mary!"[6]
　　Uttered in front of us amid the weeping　　　　20
　　Even as a woman does who is in child-birth;
And in continuance: "How poor thou wast
　　Is manifested by that hostelry
　　Where thou didst lay thy sacred burden down."
Thereafterward I heard: "O good Fabricius,[7]　　　　25
　　Virtue with poverty didst thou prefer
　　To the possession of great wealth with vice."

So pleasurable were these words to me
  That I drew farther onward to have knowledge
  Touching that spirit whence they seemed to come   30
He furthermore was speaking of the largess
  Which Nicholas unto the maidens gave,[8]
  In order to conduct their youth to honor.
"O soul that dost so excellently speak,
  Tell me who wast thou," said I, "and why only   35
  Thou dost renew these praises well deserved?
Not without recompense shall be thy word,[9]
  If I return to finish the short journey
  Of that life which is flying to its end."
And he: "I'll tell thee, not for any comfort   40
  I may expect from earth, but that so much
  Grace shines in thee or ever thou art dead.[10]
I was the root of that malignant plant[11]
  Which overshadows all the Christian world,
  So that good fruit is seldom gathered from it;   45
But if Douay and Ghent and Lille and Bruges
  Had power,[12] soon vengeance would be taken on it;
  And this I pray of Him who judges all.
Hugh Capet was I called upon the earth;
  From me were born the Louises and Philips,[13]   50
  By whom in later days has France been governed.
I was the son of a Parisian butcher,
  What time the ancient kings had perished all,
  Excepting one, contrite in cloth of gray.[14]
I found me grasping in my hands the rein   55
  Of the realm's government, and so great power
  Of new acquest, and so with friends abounding,
That to the widowed diadem promoted
  The head of mine own offspring was, from whom
  The consecrated bones of these began.   60
So long as the great dowry of Provence[15]
  Out of my blood took not the sense of shame,
  'Twas little worth, but still it did no harm.

Canto XX: The Souls of the Avaricious

Then it began with falsehood and with force
    Its rapine; and thereafter, for amends, 65
    Took Ponthieu, Normandy, and Gascony.
Charles came to Italy, and for amends
    A victim made of Conradin, and then
    Thrust Thomas back to heaven, for amends.
A time I see, not very distant now,[16] 70
    Which draweth forth another Charles from
        France,
    The better to make known both him and his.
Unarmed he goes, and only with the lance
    That Judas jousted with; and that he thrusts
    So that he makes the paunch of Florence burst. 75
He thence not land, but sin and infamy,
    Shall gain, so much more grievous to himself
    As the more light such damage he accounts.
The other, now gone forth, ta'en in his ship,
    See I his daughter sell,[17] and chaffer for her 80
    As corsairs do with other female slaves.
What more, O Avarice, canst thou do to us,
    Since thou my blood so to thyself hast drawn,
    It careth not for its own proper flesh?
That less may seem the future ill and past, 85
    I see the flower-de-luce Alagna enter,
    And Christ in his own Vicar captive made.[18]
I see him yet another time derided;
    I see renewed the vinegar and gall,
    And between living thieves I see him slain. 90
I see the modern Pilate[19] so relentless,
    This does not sate him, but without decretal
    He to the temple bears his sordid sails![20]
When, O my Lord! shall I be joyful made
    By looking on the vengeance[21] which, concealed, 95
    Makes sweet thine anger in thy secrecy?
What I was saying[22] of that only bride
    Of the Holy Ghost, and which occasioned thee
    To turn towards me for some commentary,

So long has been ordained to all our prayers   100
    As the day lasts; but when the night comes on,
    Contrary sound we take instead thereof.[23]
At that time we repeat Pygmalion,
    Of whom a traitor, thief, and parricide
    Made his insatiable desire of gold;[24]   105
And the misery of avaricious Midas,[25]
    That followed his inordinate demand,
    At which forevermore one needs must laugh.[26]
The foolish Achan each one then records,
    And how he stole the spoils; so that the wrath   110
    Of Joshua still appears to sting him here.[27]
Then we accuse Sapphira with her husband,[28]
    We laud the hoof-beats Heliodorus[29] had,
    And the whole mount in infamy encircles
Polymnestor who murdered Polydorus.[30]   115
    Here finally is cried: 'O Crassus, tell us,
    For thou dost know, what is the taste of gold?'[31]
Sometimes we speak, one loud, another low,
    According to desire of speech, that spurs us
    To greater now and now to lesser pace.   120
But in the good that here by day is talked of,
    Erewhile* alone I was not; yet near by
    No other person lifted up his voice."[32]
From him already we departed were,
    And made endeavor to o'ercome the road[33]   125
    As much as was permitted to our power,
When I perceived, like something that is falling,
    The mountain tremble,[34] whence a chill seized
        on me,
    As seizes him who to his death is going.
Certes† so violently shook not Delos,[35]   130
    Before Latona made her nest therein
    To give birth to the two eyes of the heaven.

*A while before, some time ago.
†Certainly, surely.

Then upon all sides there began a cry,
    Such that the Master drew himself towards me,
    Saying, "Fear not,[36] while I am guiding thee."   135
"Gloria in excelsis Deo,"[37] all
    Were saying, from what near I comprehended,
    Where it was possible to hear the cry.
We paused immovable and in suspense,
    Even as the shepherds who first heard that song,[38]   140
    Until the trembling ceased, and it was finished.
Then we resumed again our holy path,
    Watching the shades that lay upon the ground,
    Already turned to their accustomed plaint.
No ignorance ever with so great a strife   145
    Had rendered me importunate to know,
    If erreth not in this my memory,
As meditating then I seemed to have;
    Neither from haste to question did I dare,
    Nor of myself I there could aught perceive;   150
So I went onward timorous and thoughtful.[39]

CANTO XXI

$\mathcal{T}$HE natural thirst,[1] that ne'er is satisfied
    Excepting with the water for whose grace
    The woman of Samaria besought,[2]
Put me in travail, and haste goaded me
    Along the encumbered path behind my Leader,   5
    And I was pitying that righteous vengeance.[3]
And lo! in the same manner as Luke writeth
    That Christ appeared to two upon the way[4]
    From the sepulchral cave already risen,
A shade appeared to us, and came behind us,   10
    Down gazing on the prostrate multitude,
    Nor were we ware of it, until it spake,
Saying, "My brothers, may God give you peace!"
    We turned us suddenly, and Virgilius rendered
    To him the countersign thereto conforming,[5]   15
Thereon began he: "In the blessed council,
    Thee may the court veracious place in peace,
    That me doth banish in eternal exile!"[6]
"How," said he, and the while we went with speed,
    "If ye are shades whom God deigns not on high,   20
    Who up his stairs so far has guided you?"
And said my Teacher: "If thou note the marks[7]
    Which this one bears, and which the Angel traces,
    Well shalt thou see he with the good must reign.
But because she who spinneth day and night[8]   25
    For him had not yet drawn the distaff off,
    Which Clotho lays for each one and compacts,

His soul, which is thy sister and my own,[9]
    In coming upwards could not come alone,
    By reason that it sees not in our fashion.   30
Whence I was drawn from out the ample throat
    Of Hell[10] to be his guide, and I shall guide him
    As far on as my school[11] has power to lead.
But tell us, if thou knowest, why such a shudder
    Erewhile the mountain gave, and why together   35
    All seemed to cry, as far as its moist feet?"[12]
In asking he so hit the very eye
    Of my desire, that merely with the hope
    My thirst became the less unsatisfied.
"Naught is there," he began,[13] "that without order   40
    May the religion of the mountain feel,
    Nor aught that may be foreign to its custom.
Free is it here from every permutation;[14]
    What from itself heaven in itself receiveth
    Can be of this the cause, and naught beside;   45
Because that neither rain, nor hail, nor snow,
    Nor dew, nor hoar-frost any higher falls
    Than the short, little stairway of three steps.[15]
Dense clouds do not appear, nor rarefied,
    Nor coruscation, nor the daughter of Thaumas,[16]   50
    That often upon earth her region shifts;
No arid vapor[17] any farther rises
    Than to the top of the three steps I spake of,
    Whereon the Vicar of Peter[18] has his feet.
Lower down perchance it trembles less or more,   55
    But, for the wind that in the earth is hidden
    I know not how, up here it never trembled.
It trembles here, whenever any soul
    Feels itself pure, so that it soars, or moves
    To mount aloft, and such a cry attends it.   60
Of purity the will alone gives proof,
    Which, being wholly free to change its convent,
    Takes by surprise the soul, and helps it fly.

First it wills well; but the desire permits not,
    Which divine justice with the self-same will   65
    There was to sin, upon the torment sets.
And I, who have been lying in this pain
    Five hundred years and more,[19] but just now felt
    A free volition for a better seat.[20]
Therefore thou heardst the earthquake, and the pious   70
    Spirits along the mountain rendering praise
    Unto the Lord, that soon he speed them upwards."
So said he to him; and since we enjoy
    As much in drinking as the thirst is great,
    I could not say how much it did me good.   75
And the wise Leader: "Now I see the net
    That snares you here, and how ye are set free,
    Why the earth quakes, and wherefore ye rejoice.
Now who thou wast he pleased that I may know;
    And why so many centuries thou hast here   80
    Been lying, let me gather from thy words."
"In days when the good Titus,[21] with the aid
    Of the supremest King, avenged the wounds
    Whence issued forth the blood by Judas sold,
Under the name that most endures and honors,   85
    Was I on earth," that spirit made reply,
    "Greatly renowned, but not with faith as yet.
My vocal spirit was so sweet, that Rome
    Me, a Thoulousian, drew unto herself,
    Where I deserved to deck my brows with myrtle.   90
Statius the people name me still on earth;
    I sang of Thebes, and then of great Achilles;
    But on the way fell with my second burden.
The seeds unto my ardor were the sparks
    Of that celestial flame which heated me,   95
    Whereby more than a thousand have been fired;
Of the Æneid speak I, which to me
    A mother was, and was my nurse in song;
    Without this weighed I not a drachma's weight.

And to have lived upon the earth what time   100
    Virgilius lived, I would accept one sun
    More than I must err issuing from my ban."[22]
These words towards me made Virgilius turn
    With looks that in their silence said, "Be silent!"[23]
    But yet the power that wills cannot do all things;   105
For tears and laughter are such pursuivants*
    Unto the passion from which each springs forth,
    In the most truthful least the will they follow.
I only smiled, as one who gives the wink;[24]
    Whereat the shade was silent, and it gazed   110
    Into mine eyes, where most expression dwells;
And, "As thou well mayst consummate a labor
    So great," it said, "why did thy face just now
    Display to me the lightning of a smile?"
Now am I caught on this side and on that;[25]   115
    One keeps me silent, one to speak conjures me,
    Wherefore I sigh, and I am understood.
"Speak," said my Master, "and be not afraid
    Of speaking, but speak out, and say to him
    What he demands with such solicitude."   120
Whence I: "Thou peradventure marvellest,
    O antique spirit, at the smile I gave;
    But I will have more wonder seize upon thee.
This one, who guides on high these eyes of mine,
    Is that Virgilius,[26] from whom thou didst learn   125
    To sing aloud of men and of the Gods.
If other cause thou to my smile imputedst,
    Abandon it as false, and trust it was
    Those words which thou hast spoken
        concerning him."
Already he was stooping to embrace   130
    My Teacher's feet; but he said to him: "Brother,
    Do not;[27] for shade thou art, and shade beholdest."

*Follow so closely.

And he uprising: "Now canst thou the sum
    Of love which warms me to thee comprehend,
    When this our vanity I disremember,   135
Treating a shadow as substantial thing."[28]

CANTO XXII

ALREADY was the Angel left behind us,
    The Angel who to the sixth round had turned us,[1]
    Having erased one mark from off my face;
And those who have in justice their desire
    Had said to us, *"Beati,"* in their voices,   5
    With *"sitio,"*[2] and without more ended it.
And I, more light[3] than through the other passes,
    Went onward so, that without any labor
    I followed upward the swift-footed spirits;
When thus Virgilius began: "The love   10
    Kindled by virtue aye* another kindles,[4]
    Provided outwardly its flame appear.
Hence from the hour that Juvenal descended[5]
    Among us into the infernal Limbo,
    Who made apparent to me thy affection,   15
My kindliness towards thee was as great
    As ever bound one to an unseen person,
    So that these stairs will now seem short to me.
But tell me, and forgive me as a friend,
    If too great confidence let loose the rein,   20
    And as a friend now hold discourse with me;
How was it possible within thy breast
    For avarice to find place,[6] 'mid so much wisdom
    As thou wast filled with by thy diligence?"
These words excited Statius at first   25

*Always.

Somewhat to laughter;[7] afterward he answered:
"Each word of thine is love's dear sign to me.
Verily oftentimes do things appear
    Which give fallacious matter to our doubts,
    Instead of the true causes which are hidden!   30
Thy question shows me thy belief to be
    That I was niggard in the other life,
    It may be from the circle where I was;
Therefore know thou that avarice was removed
    Too far from me;[8] and this extravagance   35
    Thousands of lunar periods have punished.
And were it not that I my thoughts uplifted,
    When I the passage heard where thou exclaimest,
    As if indignant, unto human nature,
'To what impellest thou not, O cursed hunger   40
    Of gold, the appetite of mortal men?'[9]
    Revolving I should feel the dismal joustings.[10]
Then I perceived the hands could spread too wide
    Their wings in spending, and repented me
    As well of that as of my other sins;   45
How many with shorn hair[11] shall rise again
    Because of ignorance, which from this sin
    Cuts off repentance[12] living and in death!
And know that the transgression which rebuts
    By direct opposition any sin   50
    Together with it here its verdure dries.[13]
Therefore if I have been among that folk
    Which mourns its avarice, to purify me,
    For its opposite has this befallen me."
"Now when thou sangest the relentless weapons   55
    Of the twofold affliction of Jocasta,"[14]
    The singer of the Songs Bucolic said,[15]
"From that which Clio[16] there with thee preludes,
    It does not seem[17] that yet had made thee faithful
    That faith without which no good works suffice.[18]   60
If this be so, what candles or what sun

      Scattered thy darkness so that thou didst trim
      Thy sails behind the Fisherman thereafter?"[19]
And he to him: "Thou first directedst me
      Towards Parnassus, in its grots to drink,   65
      And first concerning God didst me enlighten.[20]
Thou didst as he who walketh in the night,
      Who bears his light behind,[21] which helps
      him not,
      But maketh wise the persons after him,
When thou didst say: 'The age renews itself,   70
      Justice returns, and man's primeval time,
      And a new progeny descends from heaven.[22]
Through thee I Poet was, through thee a Christian;[23]
      But that thou better see what I design,
      To color it will I extend my hand.   75
Already was the world in every part
      Pregnant with the true creed, disseminated
      By messengers of the eternal kingdom;
And thy assertion, spoken of above,
      With the new preachers was in unison;   80
      Whence I to visit them the custom took.[24]
Then they became so holy in my sight,
      That, when Domitian persecuted them,[25]
      Not without tears of mine were their laments;
And all the while that I on earth remained,   85
      Them I befriended, and their upright customs
      Made me disparage all the other sects.
And ere I led the Greeks unto the rivers
      Of Thebes, in poetry, I was baptized,[26]
      But out of fear was covertly a Christian,   90
For a long time professing paganism;
      And this lukewarmness caused me the fourth circle
      To circuit round more than four centuries.[27]
Thou, therefore, who hast raised the covering
      That hid from me the good of which I speak,   95
      While in ascending we have time to spare,
Tell me, in what place is our friend Terentius,

Cæcilius, Plautus, Varro, if thou knowest;[28]
    Tell me if they are damned, and in what alley."
"These, Persius and myself, and others many,"   100
    Replied my Leader, "with that Grecian are
    Whom more than all the rest the Muses suckled,
In the first circle of the prison blind;[29]
    Ofttimes we of the mountain hold discourse
    Which hath our nurses[30] ever with itself.   105
Euripides is with us, Antiphon,
    Simonides, Agatho, and many other
    Greeks who of old their brows with laurel decked.
There some of thine own people may be seen,
    Antigone, Deiphile and Argìa,   110
    And there Ismene mournful as of old.
There she is seen who pointed out Langìa;
    There is Tiresias' daughter, and there Thetis,
    And there Deidamia with her sisters."[31]
Silent already were the poets both,   115
    Attent once more in looking round about,
    From the ascent and from the walls released;[32]
And four handmaidens of the day already
    Were left behind, and at the pole the fifth
    Was pointing upward still its burning horn,[33]   120
What time my Guide: "I think that tow'rds the edge
    Our dexter* shoulders it behoves us turn,
    Circling the mount as we are wont to do."[34]
Thus in that region custom was our guide;
    And we resumed our way with less suspicion   125
    For the assenting of that worthy soul.
They in advance went on, and I alone
    Behind them, and I listened to their speech,
    Which gave me lessons in the art of song.[35]
But soon their sweet discourses interrupted   130
    A tree which midway in the road we found,
    With apples sweet and grateful to the smell.

*Right.

And even as a fir-tree tapers upward
    From bough to bough, so downwardly did that;
    I think in order that no one might climb it.[36]   135
On that side where our pathway was enclosed
    Fell from the lofty rock a limpid water,
    And spread itself abroad upon the leaves.
The Poets twain unto the tree drew near,
    And from among the foliage a voice   140
    Cried: "Of this food ye shall have scarcity."[37]
Then said: "More thoughtful Mary was of making
    The marriage feast complete and honorable,
    Than of her mouth which now for you responds;[38]
And for their drink the ancient Roman women   145
    With water were content;[39] and Daniel
    Disparaged food,[40] and understanding won.
The primal age was beautiful as gold;
    Acorns it made with hunger savorous,[41]
    And nectar every rivulet with thirst.   150
Honey and locusts were the aliments
    That fed the Baptist in the wilderness;[42]
    Whence he is glorious, and so magnified
As by the Evangel is revealed to you."

CANTO XXIII

$\mathcal{T}$HE while among the verdant leaves mine eyes
  I riveted, as he is wont to do
  Who wastes his life pursuing little birds,[1]
My more than Father said unto me: "Son,
  Come now; because the time that is ordained us   5
  More usefully should be apportioned out."
I turned my face and no less soon my steps
  Unto the Sages,[2] who were speaking so
  They made the going of no cost to me;
And lo! were heard a song and a lament,   10
  "*Labia mea, Domine,*"[3] in fashion
  Such that delight and dolence* it brought forth.
"O my sweet Father, what is this I hear?"
  Began I; and he answered: "Shades that go
  Perhaps the knot unloosing of their debt."[4]   15
In the same way that thoughtful pilgrims do,[5]
  Who, unknown people on the road o'ertaking,
  Turn themselves round to them, and do not stop,
Even thus, behind us with a swifter motion
  Coming and passing onward, gazed upon us   20
  A crowd of spirits silent and devout.
Each in his eyes was dark and cavernous,
  Pallid in face, and so emaciate
  That from the bones the skin did shape itself.
I do not think that so to merest rind   25

*Sorrow.

Could Erisichthon have been withered up
   By famine,[6] when most fear he had of it.
Thinking within myself I said: "Behold,
   This is the folk who lost Jerusalem,
   When Mary made a prey of her own son."[7]   30
Their sockets were like rings without the gems;[8]
   Whoever in the face of men reads *omo*[9]
   Might well in these have recognized the *m*.
Who would believe the odor of an apple,
   Begetting longing, could consume them so,   35
   And that of water, without knowing how?
I still was wondering what so famished them,
   For the occasion not yet manifest
   Of their emaciation and sad squalor;
And lo! from out the hollow of his head   40
   His eyes a shade turned on me, and looked
      keenly;
   Then cried aloud: "What grace to me is this?"[10]
Never should I have known him by his look;
   But in his voice was evident to me
   That which his aspect had suppressed within it.   45
This spark within me wholly re-enkindled
   My recognition of his altered face,
   And I recalled the features of Forese.[11]
"Ah, do not look at this dry leprosy,"
   Entreated he, "which doth my skin discolor,   50
   Nor at default of flesh that I may have;
But tell me truth of thee, and who are those
   Two souls, that yonder make for thee an escort;
   Do not delay in speaking unto me."
"That face of thine, which dead I once bewept,   55
   Gives me for weeping now no lesser grief,"
   I answered him, "beholding it so changed!
But tell me, for God's sake, what thus denudes you?[12]
   Make me not speak while I am marvelling,
   For ill speaks he who's full of other longings."   60

Canto XXIII: Dante recognizes the Soul of Forese

And he to me: "From the eternal council[13]
    Falls power into the water and the tree
    Behind us left, whereby I grow so thin.
All of this people who lamenting sing,
    For following beyond measure appetite   65
    In hunger and thirst are here re-sanctified.
Desire to eat and drink enkindles in us
    The scent that issues from the apple-tree,
    And from the spray that sprinkles o'er the
        verdure;
And not a single time alone,[14] this ground   70
    Encircling, is renewed our pain,—
    I say our pain, and ought to say our solace,—
For the same wish doth lead us to the tree
    Which led the Christ rejoicing to say *Eli*,
    When with his veins he liberated us."[15]   75
And I to him: "Forese, from that day
    When for a better life thou changedst worlds,
    Up to this time five years have not rolled round.
If sooner were the power exhausted in thee
    Of sinning more, than thee the hour surprised   80
    Of that good sorrow which to God reweds us,
How hast thou come up hitherward already?
    I thought to find thee down there underneath,
    Where time for time doth restitution make."[16]
And he to me: "Thus speedily has led me   85
    To drink of the sweet wormwood of these torments,
    My Nella with her overflowing tears;
She with her prayers devout and with her sighs
    Has drawn me from the coast where one awaits,
    And from the other circles set me free.[17]   90
So much more dear and pleasing is to God
    My little widow, whom so much I loved,
    As in good works she is the more alone;
For the Barbagia of Sardinia
    By far more modest in its women is   95
    Than the Barbagia I have left her in.[18]

O brother sweet, what wilt thou have me say?
    A future time is in my sight already,
    To which this hour will not be very old,
When from the pulpit shall be interdicted   100
    To the unblushing womankind of Florence
    To go about displaying breast and paps.[19]
What savages were e'er, what Saracens,
    Who stood in need, to make them covered go,
    Of spiritual or other discipline?   105
But if the shameless women were assured
    Of what swift Heaven prepares for them, already
    Wide open would they have their mouths to howl;
For if my foresight here deceive me not,
    They shall be sad ere he has bearded cheeks[20]   110
    Who now is hushed to sleep with lullaby.
O brother, now no longer hide thee from me;
    See that not only I, but all these people
    Are gazing there, where thou dost veil the sun."[21]
Whence I to him: "If thou bring back to mind   115
    What thou with me hast been and I with thee,
    The present memory will be grievous still.[22]
Out of that life he turned me back who goes
    In front of me, two days agone when round
    The sister of him yonder[23] showed herself,"   120
And to the sun I pointed. "Through the deep
    Night of the truly dead has this one[24] led me,
    With this true flesh, that follows after him.
Thence his encouragements have led me up,
    Ascending and still circling round the mount   125
    That you doth straighten, whom the world made crooked.[25]
He says that he will bear me company,
    Till I shall be where Beatrice will be;[26]
    There it behoves me to remain without him.
This is Virgilius, who thus says to me,"   130
    And him I pointed at; "the other is[27]
    That shade for whom just now shook every slope
Your realm, that from itself discharges him."

Canto XXIV: The Souls of the Gluttonous

CANTO XXIV

Nor speech the going, nor the going that
    Slackened; but talking we went bravely on,
    Even as a vessel urged by a good wind.
And shadows, that appeared things doubly dead,
    From out the sepulchres of their eyes betrayed   5
    Wonder at me, aware that I was living.
And I, continuing my colloquy,
    Said: "Peradventure* he goes up more slowly[1]
    Than he would do, for other people's sake.
But tell me, if thou knowest, where is Piccarda;[2]   10
    Tell me if any one of note I see
    Among this folk that gazes at me so."
"My sister, who, 'twixt beautiful and good,
    I know not which was more, triumphs rejoicing
    Already in her crown on high Olympus."[3]   15
So said he first, and then: " 'Tis not forbidden
    To name each other here, so milked away
    Is our resemblance by our dieting.
This," pointing with his finger, "is Buonagiunta,
    Buonagiunta of Lucca;[4] and that face   20
    Beyond him there, more peaked than the others,
Has held the holy Church within his arms;
    From Tours was he, and purges by his fasting
    Bolsena's eels and the Vernaccia wine."[5]
He named me many others one by one;   25

*Perhaps.

And all contented seemed at being named,[6]
   So that for this I saw not one dark look.
I saw for hunger bite the empty air
   Ubaldin dalla Pila, and Boniface,[7]
   Who with his crook had pastured many people.[8]   30
I saw Messer Marchese, who had leisure
   Once at Forlì for drinking with less dryness,[9]
   And he was one who ne'er felt satisfied.
But as he does who scans, and then doth prize
   One more than others, did I him of Lucca,[10]   35
   Who seemed to take most cognizance of me.
He murmured, and I know not what Gentucca[11]
   From that place heard I, where he felt the wound
   Of justice, that doth macerate them so.
"O soul," I said, "that seemest so desirous   40
   To speak with me, do so that I may hear thee,
   And with thy speech appease thyself and me."
"A maid is born, and wears not yet the veil,"
   Began he, "who to thee shall pleasant make
   My city, howsoever men may blame it.[12]   45
Thou shalt go on thy way with this prevision;
   If by my murmuring thou hast been deceived,
   True things hereafter will declare it to thee.
But say if him I here behold, who forth
   Evoked the new-invented rhymes, beginning,   50
   Ladies, that have intelligence of love?"[13]
And I to him: "One am I,[14] who, whenever
   Love doth inspire me, note, and in that measure
   Which he within me dictates, singing go."
"O brother, now I see," he said, "the knot[15]   55
   Which me, the Notary, and Guittone held
   Short of the sweet new style that now I hear.[16]
I do perceive full clearly how your pens[17]
   Go closely following after him who dictates,
   Which with our own forsooth came not to pass;   60
And he who sets himself to go beyond,

No difference sees from one style to another";
      And as if satisfied, he held his peace.
Even as the birds, that winter tow'rds the Nile,
      Sometimes into a phalanx form themselves,   65
      Then fly in greater haste, and go in file;[18]
In such wise all the people who were there,
      Turning their faces, hurried on their steps,
      Both by their leanness and their wishes light.
And as a man, who weary is with trotting,   70
      Lets his companions onward go, and walks,
      Until he vents the panting of his chest;
So did Forese let the holy flock
      Pass by, and came with me behind it, saying,
      "When will it be that I again shall see thee?"   75
"How long," I answered, "I may live, I know not;
      Yet my return will not so speedy be,
      But I shall sooner in desire arrive;[19]
Because the place where I was set to live
      From day to day of good is more depleted,   80
      And unto dismal ruin seems ordained."
"Now go," he said, "for him most guilty of it
      At a beast's tail behold I dragged along
      Towards the valley where is no repentance.
Faster at every step the beast is going,   85
      Increasing evermore until it smites him,
      And leaves the body vilely mutilated.[20]
Not long those wheels shall turn,"[21] and he uplifted
      His eyes to heaven, "ere shall be clear to thee
      That which my speech no farther can declare.   90
Now stay behind; because the time so precious
      Is in this kingdom, that I lose too much
      By coming onward thus abreast with thee."
As sometimes issues forth upon a gallop
      A cavalier from out a troop that ride,   95
      And seeks the honor of the first encounter,
So he with greater strides departed from us;

And on the road remained I with those two,[22]
    Who were such mighty marshals of the world.
And when before us he had gone so far   100
    Mine eyes became to him such pursuivants*
    As was my understanding to his words,[23]
Appeared to me with laden and living boughs
    Another apple-tree,[24] and not far distant,
    From having but just then turned thitherward.   105
People I saw beneath it lift their hands,
    And cry I know not what towards the leaves,
    Like little children eager and deluded,
Who pray, and he they pray to doth not answer,
    But, to make very keen their appetite,   110
    Holds their desire aloft, and hides it not.
Then they departed as if undeceived;
    And now we came unto the mighty tree
    Which prayers and tears so manifold refuses.
"Pass farther onward without drawing near;   115
    The tree of which Eve ate is higher up,
    And out of that one has this tree been raised."
Thus said I know not who among the branches;
    Whereat Virgilius, Statius, and myself
    Went crowding forward on the side that rises.   120
"Be mindful," said he, "of the accursed ones
    Formed of the cloud-rack, who inebriate
    Combated Theseus with their double breasts;[25]
And of the Jews who showed them soft in drinking,[26]
    Whence Gideon would not have them for companions,   125
    When he tow'rds Midian the hills descended."
Thus, closely pressed to one of the two borders,[27]
    On passed we, hearing sins of gluttony,
    Followed forsooth by miserable gains;
Then set at large upon the lonely road,   130
    A thousand steps and more we onward went,
    In contemplation, each without a word,

*Followers.

"What go ye thinking thus, ye three alone?"[28]
    Said suddenly a voice, whereat I started
    As terrified and timid beasts are wont.   135
I raised my head to see who this might be,
    And never in a furnace was there seen
    Metals or glass so lucent and so red
As one I saw who said "If it may please you
    To mount aloft, here it behoves you turn;   140
    This way goes he who goeth after peace."
His aspect had bereft me of my sight,
    So that I turned me back unto my Teachers,
    Like one who goeth as his hearing guides him.
And as, the harbinger of early dawn,   145
    The air of May doth move and breathe out fragrance,
    Impregnate all with herbage and with flowers,
So did I feel a breeze strike[29] in the midst
    My front, and felt the moving of the plumes
    That breathed around an odor of ambrosia;   150
And heard it said: "Blessed are they whom grace
    So much illumines, that the love of taste
    Excites not in their breasts too great desire,
Hungering at all times so far as is just."[30]

XXV: The Sinners passing through the Fire

CANTO XXV

*N*ow was it the ascent no hindrance brooked,
  Because the sun had his meridian circle
  To Taurus left, and night to Scorpio;[1]
Wherefore as doth a man who tarries not,
  But goes his way, whate'er to him appear,   5
  If of necessity the sting transfix him,
In this wise did we enter through the gap,
  Taking the stairway, one before the other,[2]
  Which by its narrowness divides the climbers.
And as the little stork that lifts its wing   10
  With a desire to fly, and does not venture
  To leave the nest, and lets it downward droop,
Even such was I, with the desire of asking
  Kindled and quenched, unto the motion coming
  He makes who doth address himself to speak.   15
Not for our pace, though rapid it might be,
  My father sweet forbore, but said: "Let fly
  The bow of speech[3] thou to the barb hast drawn."
With confidence I opened then my mouth,
  And I began: "How can one meagre grow   20
  There where the need of nutriment applies not?"[4]
"If thou wouldst call to mind how Meleager
  Was wasted by the wasting of a brand,[5]
  This would not," said he, "be to thee so sour;[6]
And wouldst thou think how at each tremulous motion   25
  Trembles within a mirror your own image;[7]
  That which seems hard would mellow seem to thee.
But that thou mayst content thee in thy wish

Lo Statius here;[8] and him I call and pray
    He now will be the healer of thy wounds."   30
"If I unfold to him the eternal vengeance,"
    Responded Statius, "where thou present art,
    Be my excuse that I can naught deny thee."[9]
Then he began: "Son, if these words of mine
    Thy mind doth contemplate and doth receive,   35
    They'll be thy light unto the How thou sayest.
The perfect blood, which never is drunk up[10]
    Into the thirsty veins, and which remaineth
    Like food that from the table thou removest,
Takes in the heart for all the human members   40
    Virtue informative,[11] as being that
    Which to be changed to them goes through the veins.
Again digest, descends it where 'tis better
    Silent to be than say;[12] and then drops thence
    Upon another's blood in natural vase.   45
There one together with the other mingles,[13]
    One to be passive meant, the other active[14]
    By reason of the perfect place it springs from;
And being conjoined, begins to operate,
    Coagulating first, then vivifying   50
    What for its matter it had made consistent.
The active virtue, being made a soul
    As of a plant, (in so far different,
    This on the way is, that arrived already,)
Then works so much, that now it moves and feels   55
    Like a sea-fungus, and then undertakes
    To organize the powers whose seed it is.[15]
Now, Son, dilates and now distends itself
    The virtue from the generator's heart,
    Where nature is intent on all the members.   60
But how from animal it man becomes
    Thou dost not see as yet; this is a point
    Which made a wiser man than thou once err
So far, that in his doctrine separate
    He made the soul from possible intellect,[16]   65

For he no organ saw by this assumed.
Open thy breast unto the truth that's coming,
And know that, just as soon as in the fœtus
The articulation of the brain is perfect,
The primal Motor turns to it well pleased   70
At so great art of nature, and inspires
A spirit new with virtue all replete,
Which what it finds there active doth attract
Into its substance, and becomes one soul,
Which lives, and feels, and on itself revolves.   75
And that thou less may wonder at my word,
Behold the sun's heat, which becometh wine,
Joined to the juice that from the vine distils.[17]
Whenever Lachesis has no more thread,[18]
It separates from the flesh, and virtually   80
Bears with itself the human and divine;
The other faculties are voiceless all;[19]
The memory, the intelligence, and the will
In action far more vigorous than before.[20]
Without a pause it falleth of itself   85
In marvellous way on one shore or the other;[21]
There of its roads it first is cognizant.
Soon as the place there circumscribeth it,
The virtue informative rays round about,
As, and as much as, in the living members.   90
And even as the air, when full of rain,
By alien rays that are therein reflected,
With divers colors shows itself adorned,
So there the neighboring air doth shape itself[22]
Into that form which doth impress upon it   95
Virtually the soul that has stood still.
And then in manner of the little flame,
Which followeth the fire where'er it shifts,
After the spirit followeth its new form.
Since afterwards it takes from this its semblance,   100
It is called shade; and thence it organizes
Thereafter every sense, even to the sight.

Thence is it that we speak, and thence we laugh;
    Thence is it that we form the tears and sighs,
    That on the mountain thou mayhap hast heard.   105
According as impress us our desires
    And other affections, so the shade is shaped,
    And this is cause of what thou wonderest at."
And now unto the last of all the circles[23]
    Had we arrived, and to the right hand turned,   110
    And were attentive to another care.
There the embankment shoots forth flames of fire,
    And upward doth the cornice breathe a blast
    That drives them back, and from itself sequesters.
Hence we must needs go on the open side,[24]   115
    And one by one; and I did fear the fire
    On this side, and on that the falling down.
My Leader said: "Along this place one ought
    To keep upon the eyes a tightened rein,
    Seeing that one so easily might err."   120
"*Summæ Deus clementiæ*,"[25] in the bosom
    Of the great burning chanted then I heard,
    Which made me no less eager to turn round;
And spirits saw I walking through the flame;
    Wherefore I looked, to my own steps and theirs   125
    Apportioning my sight from time to time.
After the close which to that hymn is made,
    Aloud they shouted, "*Virum non cognosco*";[26]
    Then recommenced the hymn with voices low.
This also ended, cried they: "To the wood   130
    Diana ran, and drove forth Helice
    Therefrom, who had of Venus felt the poison."[27]
Then to their song returned they; then the wives
    They shouted, and the husbands who were chaste,[28]
    As virtue and the marriage vow imposes.   135
And I believe that them this mode suffices,
    For all the time the fire is burning them;
    With such care is it needful, and such food,
That the last wound of all should be closed up.[29]

CANTO XXVI

While on the brink thus one before the other
    We went upon our way, oft the good Master
    Said: "Take thou heed! suffice it that I warn thee."
On the right shoulder[1] smote me now the sun,
    That, raying out, already the whole west   5
    Changed from its azure aspect into white.
And with my shadow did I make the flame
    Appear more red; and even to such a sign
    Shades saw I many, as they went, give heed.
This was the cause that gave them a beginning   10
    To speak of me; and to themselves began they
    To say: "That seems not a factitious body!"[2]
Then towards me, as far as they could come,
    Came certain of them, always with regard
    Not to step forth where they would not be burned.[3]   15
"O thou who goest, not from being slower
    But reverent perhaps, behind the others,
    Answer me, who in thirst and fire am burning.
Nor to me only is thine answer needful;
    For all of these have greater thirst for it   20
    Than for cold water Ethiop or Indian.[4]
Tell us how is it that thou makest thyself
    A wall unto the sun, as if thou hadst not
    Entered as yet into the net of death."
Thus one of them addressed me,[5] and I straight   25
    Should have revealed myself, were I not bent
    On other novelty that then appeared.

For through the middle of the burning road
    There came a people face to face with these,
    Which held me in suspense with gazing at them.   30
There see I hastening upon either side
    Each of the shades, and kissing one another[6]
    Without a pause, content with brief salute.
Thus in the middle of their brown battalions
    Muzzle to muzzle one ant meets another   35
    Perchance to spy their journey or their fortune.
No sooner is the friendly greeting ended,
    Or ever the first footstep passes onward,
    Each one endeavors to outcry the other;
The new-come people: "Sodom and Gomorrah!"[7]   40
    The rest: "Into the cow Pasiphae enters,
    So that the bull unto her lust may run!"[8]
Then as the cranes, that no Riphæan mountains
    Might fly in part, and part towards the sands,
    These of the frost, those of the sun avoidant,[9]   45
One folk is going, and the other coming,
    And weeping they return to their first songs,
    And to the cry that most befitteth them;[10]
And close to me approached, even as before,
    The very same who had entreated me,   50
    Attent to listen in their countenance.
I, who their inclination twice had seen,
    Began: "O souls secure in the possession,
    Whene'er it may be, of a state of peace,
Neither unripe nor ripened have remained   55
    My members upon earth, but here are with me
    With their own blood and their articulations.
I go up here to be no longer blind;
    A Lady is above,[11] who wins this grace,
    Whereby the mortal through your world I bring.   60
But as your greatest longing satisfied
    May soon become, so that the Heaven may house you
    Which full of love is, and most amply spreads,[12]

Tell me, that I again in books may write it,
  Who are you, and what is this multitude   65
  Which goes upon its way behind your backs?"
Not otherwise with wonder is bewildered[13]
  The mountaineer, and staring round is dumb,
  When rough and rustic to the town he goes,
Than every shade became in its appearance;   70
  But when they of their stupor were disburdened,
  Which in high hearts is quickly quieted,
"Blessed be thou, who of our border-lands,"
  He recommended who first had questioned us,[14]
  "Experience freightest for a better life.   75
The folk that comes not with us have offended
  In that for which once Cæsar, triumphing,
  Heard himself called in contumely, 'Queen.'
Therefore they separate, exclaiming, 'Sodom!'
  Themselves reproving, even as thou hast heard,   80
  And add unto their burning by their shame.[15]
Our own transgression was hermaphrodite;
  But because we observed not human law,
  Following like unto beasts our appetite,[16]
In our opprobrium by us is read,   85
  When we part company, the name of her
  Who bestialized herself in bestial wood.[17]
Now knowest thou our acts, and what our crime was;
  Wouldst thou perchance by name know who we are,
  There is not time to tell, nor could I do it.   90
Thy wish to know me shall in sooth be granted;
  I'm Guido Guinicelli,[18] and now purge me,
  Having repented ere the hour extreme."
The same that in the sadness of Lycurgus[19]
  Two sons became, their mother re-beholding,   95
  Such I became, but rise not to such height,
The moment I heard name himself the father
  Of me and of my betters,[20] who had ever
  Practised the sweet and gracious rhymes of love;   99

And without speech and hearing thoughtfully
    For a long time I went, beholding him,
    Nor for the fire did I approach him nearer.[21]
When I was fed with looking, utterly
    Myself I offered ready for his service,
    With affirmation that compels belief.   105
And he to me: "Thou leavest footprints such
    In me, from what I hear, and so distinct,
    Lethe[22] cannot efface them, nor make dim.
But if thy words just now the truth have sworn,
    Tell me what is the cause why thou displayest   110
    In word and look that dear thou holdest me?"
And I to him: "Those dulcet lays of yours
    Which, long as shall endure our modern fashion,
    Shall make forever dear their very ink!"
"O brother," said he, "he whom I point out,   115
    And here he pointed at a spirit in front,
    "Was of the mother tongue a better smith.[23]
Verses of love and proses of romance,
    He mastered all; and let the idiots talk,
    Who think the Lemosin[24] surpasses him.   120
To clamor more than truth they turn their faces,
    And in this way establish their opinion,
    Ere art or reason has by them been heard.
Thus many ancients with Guittone did,[25]
    From cry to cry still giving him applause,   125
    Until the truth has conquered with most persons.
Now, if thou hast such ample privilege
    'Tis granted thee to go unto the cloister
    Wherein is Christ the abbot[26] of the college,
To him repeat for me a Paternoster,*   130
    So far as needful to us of this world,
    Where power of sinning is no longer ours."

*An "Our Father" (the prayer).

Then, to give place perchance to one behind,
    Whom he had near, he vanished in the fire
    As fish in water going to the bottom.   135
I moved a little tow'rds him pointed out,
    And said that to his name my own desire
    An honorable place was making ready.
He of his own free will began to say:
    Tan m' abellis vostre cortes deman,[27]   140
    Que jeu nom' puesc ni vueill a vos cobrire;
Jeu sui Arnaut, que plor e vai chantan;
    Consiros vei la passada folor,
    E vei jauzen lo jorn qu' esper denan.
Ara vus prec per aquella valor,   145
    Que vus condus al som de la scalina,
    *Sovenga vus a temprar ma dolor.**
Then hid him in the fire that purifies them.

---

*So pleases me your courteous demand.
    I cannot and I will not hide me from you.
I am Arnaut, who weep and singing go;
    Contrite I see the folly of the past,
    And joyous see the hoped-for day before me.
Therefore do I implore you, by that power
    Which guides you to the summit of the stairs,
    Be mindful to assuage my suffering!

CANTO XXVII

As when he vibrates forth his earliest rays,
　　In regions where his Maker shed his blood,
　　(The Ebro falling under lofty Libra,
And waters in the Ganges burnt with noon,)
　　So stood the Sun;[1] hence was the day departing,　　　　5
　　When the glad Angel of God appeared to us.[2]
Outside the flame he stood upon the verge,*
　　And chanted forth, *"Beati mundo corde,"*[3]
　　In voice by far more living than our own.
Then: "No one farther goes,[4] souls sanctified,　　　　10
　　If first the fire bite not; within it enter,
　　And be not deaf unto the song beyond."
When we were close beside him thus he said;
　　Wherefore e'en† such became I, when I heard him,
　　As he is who is put into the grave.　　　　15
Upon my claspëd hands I straightened me,
　　Scanning the fire, and vividly recalling
　　The human bodies I had once seen burned.[5]
Towards me turned themselves my good Conductors,‡
　　And unto me Virgilius said: "My son,　　　　20
　　Here may indeed be torment, but not death.
Remember thee, remember! and if I
　　On Geryon have safely guided thee,[6]
　　What shall I do now I am nearer God?

*The edge.
†Then.
‡Guides.

Believe for certain, shouldst thou stand a full   25
    Millennium in the bosom of this flame,
    It could not make thee bald a single hair.
And if perchance thou think that I deceive thee,
    Draw near to it, and put it to the proof[7]
    With thine own hands upon thy garment's hem.   30
Now lay aside, now lay aside all fear,
    Turn hitherward, and onward come securely";
    And I still motionless, and 'gainst my conscience!
Seeing me stand still motionless and stubborn,
    Somewhat disturbed he said: "Now look thou, Son,   35
    'Twixt Beatrice and thee there is this wall."[8]
As at the name of Thisbe oped his lids
    The dying Pyramus, and gazed upon her,
    What time the mulberry became vermilion,
Even thus, my obduracy being softened,[9]   40
    I turned to my wise Guide, hearing the name
    That in my memory evermore is welling.
Whereat he wagged his head, and said: "How now?
    Shall we stay on this side?" then smiled as one
    Does at a child who's vanquished by an apple.   45
Then into the fire in front of me he entered,
    Beseeching Statius to come after me,[10]
    Who a long way before divided us.
When I was in it, into molten glass
    I would have cast me to refresh myself,   50
    So without measure was the burning there!
And my sweet Father, to encourage me,
    Discoursing still of Beatrice went on,
    Saying: "Her eyes I seem to see already!"[11]
A voice, that on the other side was singing,   55
    Directed us, and we, attent alone
    On that, came forth where the ascent began.
"Venite, benedicti Patris mei,"[12]
    Sounded within a splendor, which was there
    Such it o'ercame me, and I could not look.   60

"The sun departs," it added, "and night cometh;
    Tarry ye not, but onward urge your steps,
    So long as yet the west becomes not dark."
Straight forward through the rock the path ascended
    In such a way that I cut off the rays   65
    Before me of the sun, that now was low.
And of few stairs we yet had made assay,*
    Ere by the vanished shadow the sun's setting
    Behind us wet perceived, I and my Sages.
And ere in all its parts immeasurable   70
    The horizon of one aspect had become,
    And Night her boundless dispensation held,
Each of us of a stair had made his bed;
    Because the nature of the mount took from us
    The power of climbing, more than the delight.   75
Even as in ruminating passive grow
    The goats, who have been swift and venturesome
    Upon the mountain-tops ere they were fed,
Hushed in the shadow, while the sun is hot,
    Watched by the herdsman, who upon his staff   80
    Is leaning, and in leaning tendeth them;
And as the shepherd, lodging out of doors,
    Passes the night beside his quiet flock,
    Watching that no wild beast may scatter it,
Such at that hour were we, all three of us,   85
    I like the goat, and like the herdsmen they,
    Begirt on this side and on that by rocks.
Little could there be seen of things without;
    But through that little I beheld the stars
    More luminous and larger than their wont.   90
Thus ruminating, and beholding these,
    Sleep seized upon me,—sleep, that oftentimes
    Before a deed is done has tidings of it.
It was the hour, I think, when from the East

*Tried.

First on the mountain Citherea beamed,   95
    Who with the fire of love seems always burning;
Youthful and beautiful in dreams[13] methought
    I saw a lady walking in a meadow,
    Gathering flowers; and singing she was saying:
"Know whosoever may my name demand   100
    That I am Leah, and go moving round
    My beauteous hands to make myself a garland.
To please me at the mirror, here I deck me,
    But never doth my sister Rachel leave
    Her looking-glass, and sitteth all day long.   105
To see her beauteous eyes as eager is she,
    As I am to adorn me with my hands;
    Her, seeing, and me, doing satisfies."[14]
And now before the antelucan* splendors
    That unto pilgrims the more grateful rise,   110
    As, home-returning, less remote they lodge,
The darkness fled away on every side,
    And slumber with it; whereupon I rose,
    Seeing already the great Masters risen.
"That apple sweet,[15] which through so many branches   115
    The care of mortals goeth in pursuit of,
    To-day shall put in peace thy hungerings."
Speaking to me, Virgilius of such words
    As these made use; and never were there gifts
    That could in pleasantness compare with these.   120
Such longing upon longing came upon me
    To be above, that at each step thereafter
    For flight I felt in me the pinions growing.
When underneath us was the stairway all
    Run o'er, and we were on the highest step,   125
    Virgilius fastened upon me his eyes,
And said: "The temporal fire and the eternal,
    Son, thou hast seen, and to a place art come
    Where of myself no farther I discern.

*Pre-dawn.

By intellect and art I here have brought thee;[16]   130
  Take thine own pleasure for thy guide henceforth;
  Beyond the steep ways and the narrow art thou.
Behold the sun, that shines upon thy forehead;
  Behold the grass, the flowerets, and the shrubs
  Which of itself alone this land produces.   135
Until rejoicing come the beauteous eyes
  Which weeping caused me to come unto thee,
  Thou canst sit down, and thou canst walk among them.
Expect no more or word or sign from me;
  Free and upright and sound is thy freewill,   140
  And error were it not to do its bidding;
Thee o'er thyself I therefore crown and mitre!"[17]

CANTO XXVIII

*E*AGER already to search in and round,
  The heavenly forest, dense and living-green,
  Which tempered to the eyes the new-born day,[1]
Withouten* more delay I left the bank,
  Taking the level country slowly, slowly   5
  Over the soil that everywhere breathes fragrance.
A softly-breathing air, that no mutation
  Had in itself, upon the forehead smote me
  No heavier blow than of a gentle wind,
Whereat the branches, lightly tremulous,   10
  Did all of them bow downward toward that side[2]
  Where its first shadow casts the Holy Mountain;
Yet not from their upright direction swayed,
  So that the little birds upon their tops
  Should leave the practice of each art of theirs;   15
But with full ravishment the hours of prime,
  Singing, received they in the midst of leaves,
  That ever bore a burden to their rhymes,
Such as from branch to branch goes gathering on
  Through the pine forest on the shore of
   Chiassi,[3]
  When Eolus unlooses the Sirocco.[4]   20
Already my slow steps had carried me
  Into the ancient wood so far, that I
  Could not perceive where I had entered it.

*Without.

153

And lo! my further course a stream cut off,[5]   25
    Which tow'rd the left hand with its little waves
    Bent down the grass that on its margin grew.
All waters that on earth most limpid are
    Would seem to have within themselves some mixture
    Compared with that which nothing doth conceal,   30
Although it moves on with a brown, brown current
    Under the shade perpetual, that never
    Ray of the sun lets in, nor of the moon.
With feet I stayed, and with mine eyes I passed
    Beyond the rivulet, to look upon   35
    The great variety of the fresh may.
And there appeared to me (even as appears
    Suddenly something that doth turn aside
    Through very wonder every other thought)
A lady all alone,[6] who went along   40
    Singing and culling floweret after floweret,
    With which her pathway was all painted over.
"Ah, beauteous lady,[7] who in rays of love
    Dost warm thyself, if I may trust to looks,
    Which the heart's witnesses are wont to be,   45
May the desire come unto thee to draw
    Near to this river's bank," I said to her,
    "So much that I may hear what thou art singing.
Thou makest me remember where and what
    Proserpina[8] that moment was when lost   50
    Her mother her, and she herself the Spring."
As turns herself, with feet together pressed
    And to the ground, a lady who is dancing,
    And hardly puts one foot before the other,
On the vermilion and the yellow flowerets   55
    She turned towards me, not in other wise
    Than maiden who her modest eyes cast down;
And my entreaties made to be content,
    So near approaching, that the dulcet sound
    Came unto me together with its meaning.[9]   60

XXVIII: Dante, Virgil and Statius in the Ancient Forest

As soon as she was where the grasses are
  Bathed by the waters of the beauteous river,
  To lift her eyes she granted me the boon.
I do not think there shone so great a light
  Under the lids of Venus, when transfixed   65
  By her own son,[10] beyond his usual custom!
Erect upon the other bank she smiled,
  Bearing full many colors in her hands,
  Which that high land produces without seed.
Apart three paces did the river make us;   70
  But Hellespont, where Xerxes passed across,[11]
  (A curb still to all human arrogance,)
More hatred from Leander did not suffer
  For rolling between Sestos and Abydos,[12]
  Than that from me, because it oped* not then.[13] 75
"Ye are new-comers;[14] and because I smile,"
  Began she, "peradventure, in this place
  Elect to human nature for its nest,[15]
Some apprehension keeps you marvelling;
  But the psalm *Delectasti*[16] giveth light   80
  Which has the power to uncloud your intellect.
And thou who foremost art, and didst entreat me,
  Speak, if thou wouldst hear more; for I came ready
  To all thy questionings, as far as needful."
"The water," said I, "and the forest's sound,   85
  Are combating within me my new faith
  In something which I heard opposed to this."[17]
Whence she: "I will relate how from its cause
  Proceedeth that which maketh thee to wonder,
  And purge away the cloud that smites upon thee. 90
The Good Supreme, sole in itself delighting,
  Created man good, and this goodly place
  Gave him as hansel† of eternal peace.

---

*Opened.
†Gift made as a token for good luck.

By his default short while he sojourned here;
    By his default to weeping and to toil[18]   95
    He changed his innocent laughter and sweet play.
That the disturbance which below is made
    By exhalations of the land and water,
    (Which far as may be follow after heat,)
Might not upon mankind wage any war,   100
    This mount ascended tow'rds the heaven so high,
    And is exempt,[19] from there where it is locked.
Now since the universal atmosphere
    Turns in a circuit with the primal motion[20]
    Unless the circle is broken on some side,   105
Upon this height, that all is disengaged
    In living ether, doth this motion strike
    And make the forest sound, for it is dense;
And so much power the stricken plant possesses
    That with its virtue it impregns the air,   110
    And this, revolving, scatters it around;
And yonder earth, according as 'tis worthy
    In self or in its clime, conceives and bears
    Of divers qualities the divers trees;
It should not seem a marvel then on earth,   115
    This being heard, whenever any plant
    Without seed manifest there taketh root.
And thou must know, this holy table-land
    In which thou art is full of every seed,
    And fruit has in it never gathered there.[21]   120
The water which thou seest springs not from vein
    Restored by vapor that the cold condenses,
    Like to a stream that gains or loses breath;
But issues from a fountain safe and certain,
    Which by the will of God as much regains   125
    As it discharges, open on two sides.
Upon this side with virtue it descends,
    Which takes away all memory of sin;
    On that, of every good deed done restores it.

Here Lethe, as upon the other side   130
    Eunoë, it is called;[22] and worketh not
    If first on either side it be not tasted.
This every other savor doth transcend;
    And notwithstanding slaked so far may be
    Thy thirst, that I reveal to thee no more,   135
I'll give thee a corollary still in grace,
    Nor think my speech will be to thee less dear.
    If it spread out beyond my promise to thee.
Those who in ancient times have feigned in song
    The Age of Gold[23] and its felicity,   140
    Dreamed of this place perhaps upon Parnassus.
Here was the human race in innocence;
    Here evermore was Spring, and every fruit;
    This is the nectar of which each one speaks."
Then backward did I turn me wholly round   145
    Unto my Poets, and saw that with a smile
    They had been listening to these closing words;
Then to the beautiful lady turned mine eyes.

CANTO XXIX

*S*INGING like unto an enamoured lady
  She, with the ending of her words, continued:
  "Beati quorum tecta sunt peccata."[1]
And even as Nymphs, that wandered all alone
  Among the sylvan shadows, sedulous   5
  One to avoid and one to see the sun,
She then against the stream moved onward, going
  Along the bank, and I abreast of her,
  Her little steps with little steps attending.
Between her steps and mine were not a hundred,   10
  When equally the margins gave a turn,
  In such a way, that to the East I faced.
Nor even thus our way continued far
  Before the lady wholly turned herself
  Unto me, saying, "Brother, look and listen!"   15
And lo! a sudden lustre ran across
  On every side athwart the spacious forest,
  Such that it made me doubt if it were
   lightning.
But since the lightning ceases as it comes,
  And that continuing brightened more and more, 20
  Within my thought I said, "What thing is this?"
And a delicious melody there ran
  Along the luminous air, whence holy zeal
  Made me rebuke the hardihood* of Eve;

---

*Daring, presumptuousness.

For there were earth and heaven obedient were,   25
    The woman only, and but just created,
    Could not endure to stay 'neath any veil;
Underneath which had she devoutly stayed,
    I sooner should have tasted those delights
    Ineffable, and for a longer time.[2]   30
While 'mid such manifold first-fruits I walked
    Of the eternal pleasure all enrapt,
    And still solicitous of more delights,
In front of us like an enkindled fire
    Became the air beneath the verdant boughs,   35
    And the sweet sound as singing now was heard.
O Virgins sacrosanct! if ever hunger,
    Vigils, or cold for you I have endured,
    The occasion spurs me their reward to claim!
Now Helicon[3] must needs pour forth for me,   40
    And with her choir Urania must assist me,
    To put in verse things difficult to think.[4]
A little farther on, seven trees of gold
    In semblance the long spade still intervening
    Between ourselves and them did counterfeit;   45
But when I had approached so near to them
    The common object, which the sense deceives,
    Lost not by distance any of its marks,
The faculty that lends discourse to reason
    Did apprehend that they were candlesticks,   50
    And in the voices of the song "Hosanna!"[5]
Above them flamed the harness beautiful,[6]
    Far brighter than the moon in the serene
    Of midnight, at the middle of her month.
I turned me round, with admiration filled,   55
    To good Virgilius, and he answered me
    With visage no less full of wonderment.[7]
Then back I turned my face to those high things,
    Which moved themselves towards us so sedately,
    They had been distanced by new-wedded brides.   60

Canto XXIX: The Elders in the Mystic Procession

The lady chid* me: "Why dost thou burn only
    So with affection for the living lights,
    And dost not look at what comes after them?"
Then saw I people, as behind their leaders,
    Coming behind them, garmented in white,   65
    And such a whiteness never was on earth.
The water on my left flank was resplendent,
    And back to me reflected my left side,
    E'en as a mirror, if I looked therein.
When I upon my margin had such post   70
    That nothing but the stream divided us,
    Better to see I gave my steps repose;
And I beheld the flamelets onward go,
    Leaving behind themselves the air depicted,
    And they of trailing pennons† had the semblance,   75
So that it overhead remained distinct
    With sevenfold lists, all of them of the colors
    Whence the sun's bow is made, and
        Delia's girdle.[8]
These standards to the rearward longer were
    Than was my sight; and, as it seemed to me,   80
    Ten paces were the outermost apart.
Under so fair a heaven as I describe
    The four and twenty Elders, two by two,
    Came on incoronate with flower-de-luce.[9]
They all of them were singing: "Blessed thou[10]   85
    Among the daughters of Adam art, and blessed
    Forevermore shall be thy loveliness."
After the flowers and other tender grasses
    In front of me upon the other margin
    Were disencumbered of that race elect,   90
Even as in heaven star followeth after star,
    There came close after them four animals,
    Incoronate each one with verdant leaf.

*Scolded, chided.
†Pennants.

Plumed with six wings[11] was every one of them,
  The plumage full of eyes; the eyes of Argus[12]   95
  If they were living would be such as these.
Reader![13] to trace their forms no more I waste
  My rhymes; for other spendings press me so,
  That I in this cannot be prodigal.
But read Ezekiel, who depicteth them   100
  As he beheld them from the region cold
  Coming with cloud, with whirlwind, and with fire;
And such as thou shalt find them in his pages,
  Such were they here; saving that in their plumage
  John is with me, and differeth from him.[14]   105
The interval between these four contained
  A chariot triumphal on two wheels,
  Which by a Griffin's neck came drawn along;
And upward he extended both his wings
  Between the middle list and three and three,   110
  So that he injured none by cleaving it.[15]
So high they rose that they were lost to sight;
  His limbs were gold, so far as he was bird,
  And white the others with vermilion mingled.
Not only Rome with no such splendid car   115
  E'er gladdened Africanus, or Augustus,
  But poor to it that of the Sun would be,—
That of the Sun,[16] which swerving was burnt up
  At the importunate orison of Earth,
  When Jove was so mysteriously just.   120
Three maidens at the right wheel[17] in a circle
  Came onward dancing; one so very red
  That in the fire she hardly had been noted.
The second was as if her flesh and bones
  Had all been fashioned out of emerald;   125
  The third appeared as snow but newly fallen.
And now they seemed conducted by the white,
  Now by the red, and from the song of her
  The others took their step, or slow or swift.
Upon the left hand four made holiday   130

Vested in purple,[18] following the measure
    Of one of them with three eyes in her head.
In rear of all the group here treated of
    Two old men I beheld, unlike in habit,
    But like in gait, each dignified and grave.   135
One showed himself as one of the disciples
    Of that supreme Hippocrates;[19] whom nature
    Made for the animals she holds most dear;
Contrary care the other manifested,
    With sword so shining and so sharp,[20] it caused   140
    Terror to me on this side of the river.
Thereafter four I saw of humble aspect,[21]
    And behind all an aged man alone
    Walking in sleep[22] with countenance acute.
And like the foremost company these seven   145
    Were habited; yet of the flower-de-luce
    Nor garland round about the head they wore,
But of the rose, and other flowers vermilion;
    At little distance would the sight have sworn
    That all were in a flame above their brows.   150
And when the car was opposite to me
    Thunder was heard;[23] and all that folk august
    Seemed to have further progress interdicted,
There with the vanward ensigns standing still.

CANTO XXX

WHEN the Septentrion of the highest heaven[1]
    (Which never either setting knew or rising,
    Nor veil of other cloud than that of sin,
And which made every one therein aware
    Of his own duty, as the lower makes   5
    Whoever turns the helm to come to port)
Motionless halted, the veracious people,
    That came at first between it and the Griffin,
    Turned themselves to the car, as to their peace.[2]
And one of them, as if by Heaven commissioned,   10
    Singing, *"Veni, sponsa, de Libano"*[3]
    Shouted three times, and all the others after.
Even as the Blessed at the final summons
    Shall rise up[4] quickened each one from his cavern,
    Uplifting light the reinvested flesh,   15
So upon that celestial chariot
    A hundred rose *ad vocem tanti senis,*[5]
    Ministers and messengers of life eternal.
They all were saying, *"Benedictus qui venis,"*[6]
    And, scattering flowers above and round about,   20
    "Manibus o date lilia plenis."[7]
Ere now have I beheld,[8] as day began,
    The eastern hemisphere all tinged with rose,
    And the other heaven with fair serene adorned;
And the sun's face, uprising, overshadowed   25
    So that by tempering influence of vapors
    For a long interval the eye sustained it;
Thus in the bosom of a cloud of flowers

Which from those hands angelical ascended,
    And downward fell again inside and out,   30
Over her snow-white veil with olive cinct*
    Appeared a lady under a green mantle,
    Vested in color of the living flame.
And my own spirit, that already now
    So long a time had been,⁹ that in her presence   35
    Trembling with awe it had not stood abashed,
Without more knowledge having by mine eyes,
    Through occult virtue that from her proceeded
    Of ancient love the mighty influence felt.
As soon as on my vision smote the power   40
    Sublime, that had already pierced me through
    Ere from my boyhood I had yet come forth,
To the left hand I turned with that reliance
    With which the little child runs to his mother,
    When he has fear, or when he is afflicted,   45
To say unto Virgilius: "Not a drachm†
    Of blood remains in me, that dost not tremble;
    I know the traces of the ancient flame."¹⁰
But us Virgilius of himself deprived
    Had left, Virgilius, sweetest of all fathers,   50
    Virgilius, to whom I for safety gave me:
Nor whatsoever lost the ancient mother
    Availed my cheeks now purified from dew,
    That weeping they should not again be darkened.
"Dante,¹¹ because Virgilius has departed   55
    Do not weep yet, do not weep yet awhile;
    For by another sword thou need'st must weep."
E'en as an admiral, who on poop and prow
    Comes to behold the people that are working
    In other ships, and cheers them to well-doing,   60
Upon the left hand border of the car,
    When at the sound I turned of my own name,
    Which of necessity is here recorded,

*An olive garland.
†Dram; small portion.

XXX: Beatrice appears among Angels

I saw the Lady,[12] who erewhile appeared
    Veiled underneath the angelic festival, 65
    Direct her eyes to me across the river.
Although the veil, that from her head descended,
    Encircled with the foliage of Minerva,[13]
    Did not permit her to appear distinctly,
In attitude still royally majestic 70
    Continued she, like unto one who speaks,
    And keeps his warmest utterance in reserve:
"Look at me well; in sooth* I'm Beatrice!
    How didst thou deign to come unto the
       Mountain? 74
    Didst thou not know that man is happy here?"
Mine eyes fell downward into the clear fountain,
    But, seeing myself therein, I sought the grass,
    So great a shame did weigh my forehead down.
As to the son the mother seems superb,[14]
    So she appeared to me; for somewhat bitter 80
    Tasteth the savor of severe compassion.
Silent became she, and the Angels sang
    Suddenly, *"In te, Domine, speravi"*:
    But beyond *pedes meos* did not pass.[15]
Even as the snow among the living rafters† 85
    Upon the back of Italy‡ congeals,
    Blown on and drifted by Sclavonian§ winds,
And then, dissolving, trickles through itself
    Whene'er the land that loses shadow| breathes,
    So that it seems a fire that melts a taper; 90
E'en thus was I without a tear or sigh,
    Before the song of those who sing forever
    After the music of the eternal spheres.

*In truth, really.
†Trees, which will become beams.
‡The Apennine mountain chain.
§From Slavonia.
|Africa; no shadows are cast when the sun is directly overhead.

But when I heard in their sweet melodies
    Compassion for me, more than had they said,   95
    "O wherefore, lady, dost thou thus consume him?"
The ice, that was about my heart congealed,
    To air and water changed, and in my anguish
    Through mouth and eyes came gushing from my breast.
She, on the right-hand border of the car   100
    Still firmly standing, to those holy beings
    Thus her discourse directed afterwards:
"Ye keep your watch[16] in the eternal day,
    So that nor night nor sleep can steal from you
    One step the ages make upon their path;   105
Therefore my answer is with greater care,
    That he may hear me who is weeping yonder,
    So that the sin and dole be of one measure.
Not only by the work of those great wheels,
    That destine every seed unto some end,   110
    According as the stars are in conjunction,
But by the largess of celestial graces,[17]
    Which have such lofty vapors for their rain
    That near to them our sight approaches not,
Such had this man become in his new life[18]   115
    Potentially, that every righteous habit
    Would have made admirable proof in him;
But so much more malignant and more savage
    Becomes the land untilled and with bad seed,
    The more good earthly vigor it possesses.   120
Some time did I sustain him with my look;
    Revealing unto him my youthful eyes,
    I led him with me turned in the right way.
As soon as ever of my second age[19]
    I was upon the threshold and changed life,   125
    Himself from me he took and gave to others.[20]
When from the flesh to spirit I ascended,
    And beauty and virtue were in me increased,
    I was to him less dear and less delightful;

And into ways untrue[21] he turned his steps,   130
    Pursuing the false images of good,
    That never any promises fulfil;
Nor prayer for inspiration me availed,
    By means of which in dreams[22] and otherwise
    I called him back, so little did he heed them.   135
So low he fell, that all appliances
    For his salvation were already short,
    Save showing him the people of perdition.
For this I visited the gates of death,
    And unto him, who so far up has led him,[23]   140
    My intercessions were with weeping borne.
God's lofty fiat would be violated,
    If Lethe should be passed, and if such viands
    Should tasted be, withouten any scot*
Of penitence,[24] that gushes forth in tears."   145

*Payment.

CANTO XXXI

O thou who art beyond the sacred river,"[1]
　　Turning to me the point of her discourse,
　　That edgewise even had seemed to me so keen,
She recommenced, continuing without pause,
　　"Say, say if this be true; to such a charge,　　　　5
　　Thy own confession[2] needs must be conjoined."
My faculties were in so great confusion,
　　That the voice moved, but sooner was extinct
　　Than by its organs it was set at large.
Awhile she waited; then she said: "What thinkest?　　10
　　Answer me; for the mournful memories
　　In thee not yet are by the waters injured."
Confusion and dismay together mingled
　　Forced such a Yes![3] from out my mouth, that sight
　　Was needful to the understanding of it.　　　　15
Even as a cross-bow breaks, when 'tis discharged,
　　Too tensely drawn the bowstring and the bow,
　　And with less force the arrow hits the mark,
So I gave way beneath that heavy burden,
　　Outpouring in a torrent tears and sighs,　　　　20
　　And the voice flagged upon its passage forth.
Whence she to me: "In those desires of mine
　　Which led thee to the loving of that good,
　　Beyond which there is nothing to aspire to,
What trenches lying traverse or what chains　　　　25
　　Didst thou discover, that of passing onward
　　Thou shouldst have thus despoiled thee of the hope?

And what allurements or what vantages
    Upon the forehead of the others showed,
    That thou shouldst turn thy footsteps unto them?" 30
After the heaving of a bitter sigh,
    Hardly had I the voice to make response,
    And with fatigue my lips did fashion it.
Weeping I said: "The things that present were
    With their false pleasure turned aside my steps,[4] 35
    Soon as your countenance concealed itself."
And she: "Shouldst thou be silent, or deny
    What thou confessest, not less manifest
    Would be thy fault, by such a Judge 'tis known.
But when from one's own cheeks comes bursting forth 40
    The accusal of the sin, in our tribunal
    Against the edge the wheel doth turn itself.[5]
But still, that thou mayst feel a greater shame
    For thy transgression, and another time
    Hearing the Sirens[6] thou mayst be more strong, 45
Cast down the seed of weeping and attend;
    So shalt thou hear, how in an opposite way
    My buried flesh should have directed thee.
Never to thee presented art or nature
    Pleasure so great as the fair limbs wherein 50
    I was enclosed, which scattered are in earth.
And if the highest pleasure thus did fail thee
    By reason of my death, what mortal thing
    Should then have drawn thee into its desire?
Thou oughtest verily at the first shaft 55
    Of things fallacious to have risen up
    To follow me, who was no longer such.
Thou oughtest not to have stooped thy pinions downward
    To wait for further blows, or little girl,[7]
    Or other vanity of such brief use. 60
The callow birdlet waits for two or three,
    But to the eyes of those already fledged,
    In vain the net is spread or shaft is shot."

Canto XXXI: Dante submerged in the River Lethë

Even as children silent in their shame
  Stand listening with their eyes upon the ground,   65
  And conscious of their fault, and penitent;
So was I standing; and she said: "If thou
  In hearing sufferest pain, lift up thy beard[8]
  And thou shalt feel a greater pain in seeing."
With less resistance is a robust holm*   70
  Uprooted, either by a native wind
  Or else by that from regions of Iarbas,[9]
Than I upraised at her command my chin;
  And when she by the beard the face demanded,
  Well I perceived the venom of her meaning.   75
And as my countenance was lifted up,
  Mine eye perceived those creatures beautiful
  Had rested from the strewing of the flowers;
And, still but little reassured, mine eyes
  Saw Beatrice turned round[10] towards the monster,   80
  That is one person only in two natures.
Beneath her veil, beyond the margent green,
  She seemed to me far more her ancient self
  To excel, than others here, when she was here.[11]
So pricked me then the thorn of penitence,   85
  That of all other things the one which turned me
  Most to its love became the most my foe.
Such self-conviction stung me at the heart
  O'erpowered I fell,[12] and what I then became
  She knoweth who had furnished me the cause.   90
Then, when the heart restored my outward sense,
  The lady I had found alone,[13] above me
  I saw, and she was saying, "Hold me, hold me."
Up to my throat she in the stream had drawn me,
  And, dragging me behind her, she was moving   95
  Upon the water lightly as a shuttle.[14]
When I was near unto the blessed shore,
  "Asperges me,"[15] I heard so sweetly sung,

*An oak tree.

Remember it I cannot, much less write it.
The beautiful lady opened wide her arms,   100
    Embraced my head, and plunged me underneath,[16]
    Where I was forced to swallow of the water.
Then forth she drew me, and all dripping brought
    Into the dance of the four beautiful,
    And each one with her arm did cover me.   105
"We here are Nymphs, and in the Heaven are stars;
    Ere Beatrice descended to the world,
    We as her handmaids were appointed her.
We'll lead thee to her eyes; but for the pleasant
    Light that within them is, shall sharpen thine   110
    The three beyond, who more profoundly look."
Thus singing they began; and afterwards
    Unto the Griffin's breast they led me with them,
    Where Beatrice was standing, turned towards us.
"See that thou dost not spare thine eyes," they said;   115
    "Before the emeralds have we stationed thee,
    Whence Love aforetime drew for thee his weapons."
A thousand longings, hotter than the flame,
    Fastened mine eyes upon those eyes relucent,
    That still upon the Griffin steadfast stayed.[17]   120
As in a glass the sun, not otherwise
    Within them was the twofold monster shining,
    Now with the one, now with the other nature.
Think, Reader,[18] if within myself I marvelled,
    When I beheld the thing itself stand still,   125
    And in its image it transformed itself.
While with amazement filled and jubilant,
    My soul was tasting of the food, that while
    It satisfies us makes us hunger for it,
Themselves revealing of the highest rank   130
    In bearing, did the other three advance,
    Singing to their angelic saraband.[19]
"Turn, Beatrice, O turn thy holy eyes,"
    Such was their song, "unto thy faithful one,
    Who has to see thee ta'en so many steps.   135

In grace do us the grace that thou unveil
    Thy face to him, so that he may discern
    The second beauty[20] which thou dost conceal."
O splendor of the living light eternal![21]
    Who underneath the shadow of Parnassus   140
    Has grown so pale, or drunk so at its cistern,
He would not seem to have his mind encumbered
    Striving to paint thee as thou didst appear,
    Where the harmonious heaven o'ershadowed thee,
When in the open air thou didst unveil?   145

CANTO XXXII

*S*o steadfast and attentive were mine eyes
    In satisfying their decennial thirst,[1]
    That all my other senses were extinct,
And upon this side and on that they had
    Walls of indifference, so the holy smile   5
    Drew them unto itself with the old net;
When forcibly my sight was turned away
    Towards my left hand by those goddesses,
    Because I heard from them a "Too intently!"[2]
And that condition of the sight which is   10
    In eyes but lately smitten by the sun
    Bereft me of my vision some short while;
But to the less when sight re-shaped itself,
    I say the less in reference to the greater
    Splendor from which perforce I had withdrawn,   15
I saw upon its right wing wheeled about
    The glorious host, returning with the sun
    And with the sevenfold flames upon
        their faces.
As underneath its shields, to save itself,
    A squadron turns, and with its banner wheels,   20
    Before the whole thereof can change its front,
That soldiery of the celestial kingdom
    Which marched in the advance had wholly
        passed us
    Before the chariot had turned its pole.[3]
Then to the wheels the maidens turned themselves,   25

177

And the Griffin moved its burden benedight,*
    But so that not a feather of him fluttered.
The lady fair who drew me through the ford[4]
    Followed with Statius[5] and myself the wheel
    Which made its orbit with the lesser arc.   30
So passing through the lofty forest, vacant
    By fault of her who in the serpent trusted,[6]
    Angelic music made our steps keep time.
Perchance as great a space had in three flights
    An arrow loosened from the string o'erpassed,   35
    As we had moved when Beatrice descended.[7]
I heard them murmur all together, "Adam!"
    Then circled they about a tree despoiled
    Of blooms and other leafage[8] on each bough.
Its tresses, which so much the more dilate   40
    As higher they ascend, had been by Indians
    Among their forests marvelled at for height.
"Blessed art thou, O Griffin, who dost not
    Pluck[9] with thy beak these branches sweet to taste,
    Since appetite by this was turned to evil."   45
After this fashion round the tree robust
    The others shouted; and the twofold creature:
    "Thus is preserved the seed of all the just."[10]
And turning to the pole which he had dragged,
    He drew it close beneath the widowed bough,   50
    And what was of it unto it left bound.[11]
In the same manner as our trees (when downward
    Falls the great light, with that together mingled
    Which after the celestial Lasca shines)[12]
Begin to swell, and then renew themselves,   55
    Each one with its own color, ere the Sun
    Harness his steeds beneath another star:
Less than of rose and more than violet
    A hue disclosing, was renewed the tree[13]
    That had erewhile its boughs so desolate.   60

*Blessed.

XXXII: The Harlot and the Giant in the Chariot

I never heard, nor here below is sung,
    The hymn which afterward that people sang,
    Nor did I bear the melody throughout.
Had I the power to paint how fell asleep
    Those eyes compassionless, of Syrinx hearing,   65
    Those eyes to which more watching cost so dear,
Even as a painter who from model paints
    I would portray how I was lulled asleep;
    He may, who well can picture drowsihood.[14]
Therefore I pass to what time I awoke,   70
    And say a splendor rent from me the veil
    Of slumber, and a calling: "Rise, what dost thou?"[15]
As to behold the apple-tree in blossom
    Which makes the Angels greedy for its fruit,
    And keeps perpetual bridals in the Heaven,   75
Peter and John and James conducted were,[16]
    And, overcome, recovered at the word
    By which still greater slumbers have been broken,
And saw their school diminished by the loss
    Not only of Elias, but of Moses,   80
    And the apparel of their Master changed;[17]
So I revived, and saw that piteous one[18]
    Above me standing, who had been conductress
    Aforetime of my steps beside the river,
And all in doubt I said, "Where's Beatrice?"   85
    And she: "Behold her seated underneath
    The leafage new, upon the root of it.
Behold the company that circles her;
    The rest behind the Griffin are ascending
    With more melodious song, and more profound."   90
And if her speech were more diffuse I know not,
    Because already in my sight was she
    Who from the hearing of aught else had shut me.
Alone she sat upon the very earth,
    Left there as guardian of the chariot   95
    Which I had seen the biform monster fasten.

Encircling her, a cloister made themselves
  The seven Nymphs, with those lights in their hands
  Which are secure from Aquilon and Auster.[19]
"Short while shalt thou be here a forester,[20]   100
  And thou shalt be with me forevermore
  A citizen of that Rome where Christ is Roman.[21]
Therefore, for that world's good which liveth ill,
  Fix on the car thine eyes, and what thou seest,
  Having returned to earth, take heed thou write."[22]   105
Thus Beatrice; and I, who at the feet
  Of her commandments all devoted was,
  My mind and eyes directed where she willed.
Never descended with so swift a motion
  Fire from a heavy cloud, when it is raining   110
  From out the region which is most remote,
As I beheld the bird of Jove[23] descend
  Down through the tree, rending away the bark,
  As well as blossoms and the foliage new,
And he with all his might the chariot smote,   115
  Whereat it reeled, like vessel in a tempest
  Tossed by the waves, now starboard and now larboard.
Thereafter saw I leap into the body
  Of the triumphal vehicle a Fox,
  That seemed unfed with any wholesome food.   120
But for his hideous sins upbraiding him,
  My Lady put him to as swift a flight[24]
  As such a fleshless skeleton could bear.
Then by the way that it before had come,
  Into the chariot's chest I saw the Eagle   125
  Descend,[25] and leave it feathered with his plumes.
And such as issues from a heart that mourns,
  A voice from Heaven there issued, and it said:
  "My little bark, how badly art thou freighted!"
Methought, then, that the earth did yawn between 130
  Both wheels, and I saw rise from it a Dragon,[26]
  Who through the chariot upward fixed his tail,

And as a wasp that draweth back its sting,
    Drawing unto himself his tail malign,
    Drew out the floor, and went his way rejoicing.   135
That which remained behind, even as with grass
    A fertile region, with the feathers, offered
    Perhaps with pure intention and benign,
Reclothed itself,[27] and with them were reclothed
    The pole and both the wheels so speedily,   140
    A sigh doth longer keep the lips apart.
Transfigured thus the holy edifice
    Thrust forward heads upon the parts of it,
    Three on the pole and one at either corner.
The first were horned like oxen; but the four   145
    Had but a single horn upon the forehead;
    A monster such had never yet been seen![28]
Firm as a rock upon a mountain high,
    Seated upon it, there appeared to me
    A shameless whore,[29] with eyes swift glancing round,   150
And, as if not to have her taken from him,
    Upright beside her I beheld a giant;
    And even and anon they kissed each other.
But because she her wanton, roving eye
    Turned upon me,[30] her angry paramour   155
    Did scourge her from her head unto her feet.
Then full of jealousy, and fierce with wrath,
    He loosed the monster, and across the forest
    Dragged it so far, he made of that alone
A shield unto the whore and the strange beast.   160

CANTO XXXIII

$\mathcal{D}$EUS, *venerunt gentes,"*[1] alternating
    Now three, now four, melodious psalmody
    The maidens in the midst of tears began;
And Beatrice, compassionate and sighing,
    Listened to them with such a countenance,   5
    That scarce more changed was Mary at
        the cross.
But when the other virgins place had given
    For her to speak, uprisen to her feet
    With color as of fire, she made response:
"Modicum, et non videbitis me;[2]   10
    Et iterum, my sisters predilect,*
    Modicum, et vos videbitis me."
Then all the seven in front of her she placed;
    And after her, by beckoning only, moved
    Me and the lady and the sage who stayed.[3]   15
So she moved onward; and I do not think
    That her tenth step was placed upon the
        ground,
    When with her eyes upon mine eyes she smote,
And with a tranquil aspect, "Come more quickly,"
    To me she said, "that, if I speak with thee,   20
    To listen to me thou mayst be well placed."
As soon as I was with her as I should be,
    She said to me: "Why, brother,[4] dost thou not
    Venture to question now, in coming with me?"

*Dearly beloved.

183

As unto those who are too reverential, 25
    Speaking in presence of superiors,
    Who drag no living utterance to their teeth,
It me befell, that without perfect sound
    Began I: "My necessity, Madonna,
    You know,[5] and that which thereunto is good." 30
And she to me: "Of fear and bashfulness
    Henceforward I will have thee strip thyself,
    So that thou speak no more as one who dreams.
Know that the vessel which the serpent broke
    Was, and is not;[6] but let him who is guilty 35
    Think that God's vengeance does not fear a sop.[7]
Without an heir[8] shall not forever be
    The Eagle that left his plumes upon the car,
    Whence it became a monster, then a prey;
For verily I see, and hence narrate it, 40
    The stars already near to bring the time,[9]
    From every hindrance safe, and every bar,
Within which a Five-hundred, Ten, and Five,[10]
    One sent from God, shall slay the thievish woman
    And that some giant who is sinning with her. 45
And peradventure my dark utterance,
    Like Themis and the Sphinx,[11] may less persuade thee,
    Since, in their mode, it clouds the intellect;
But soon the facts shall be the Naiades
    Who shall this difficult enigma solve, 50
    Without destruction of the flocks and harvests.[12]
Note thou; and even as by me are uttered
    These words, so teach them unto those who live
    That life which is a running unto death;
And bear in mind, whene'er thou writest them, 55
    Not to conceal what thou hast seen the plant,[13]
    That twice already has been pillaged here.
Whoever pillages or shatters it,
    With blasphemy of deed offendeth God,
    Who made it holy for his use alone. 60

XXXIII: Dante drinks of the River Eunoë

For biting that, in pain and in desire
    Five thousand years and more the first-born soul
    Craved Him,[14] who punished in himself the bite.
Thy genius slumbers, if it deem it not
    For special reason so pre-eminent   65
    In height, and so inverted in its summit.
And if thy vain imaginings had not been
    Water of Elsa round about thy mind,[15]
    And Pyramus to the mulberry,[16] their pleasure,
Thou by so many circumstances only   70
    The justice of the interdict of God[17]
    Morally in the tree wouldst recognize.
But since I see thee in thine intellect
    Converted into stone and stained with sin,
    So that the light of my discourse doth daze thee,   75
I will too, if not written, at last painted,
    Thou bear it back within thee, for the reason
    That cinct with palm the pilgrim's staff[18] is borne."
And I: "As by a signet is the wax
    Which does not change the figure stamped upon it,   80
    My brain is now imprinted by yourself.
But wherefore so beyond my power of sight
    Soars your desirable discourse, that aye
    The more I strive, so much the more I lose it?"[19]
"That thou mayst recognize," she said, "the school   85
    Which thou hast followed,[20] and mayst see how far
    Its doctrine follows after my discourse,
And mayst behold your path from the divine
    Distant as far as separated is
    From earth the heaven that highest hastens on."[21]   90
Whence her I answered: "I do not remember
    That ever I estranged myself from you,
    Nor have I conscience of it that reproves me."
"And if thou art not able to remember,"
    Smiling she answered, "recollect thee now   95
    That thou this very day hast drunk of Lethe;

And if from smoke a fire may be inferred,
　　Such an oblivion clearly demonstrates[22]
　　Some error in thy will elsewhere intent.
Truly from this time forward shall my words　　　　　100
　　Be naked,[23] so far as is befitting
　　To lay them open unto thy rude gaze."
And more coruscant and with slower steps
　　The sun was holding the meridian circle,
　　Which, with the point of view, shifts here and there,[24]　　105
When halted (as he cometh to a halt,
　　Who goes before a squadron as its escort,
　　If something new he find upon his way)
The maidens seven[25] at a dark shadow's edge,
　　Such as, beneath green leaves and branches black,　　　110
　　The Alp upon its frigid border wears.
In front of them the Tigris and Euphrates[26]
　　Methought I saw forth issue from one fountain,
　　And slowly part, like friends, from one another.
"O light, O glory of the human race![27]　　　　　115
　　What stream is this which here unfolds itself
　　From out one source, and from itself withdraws?"
For such a prayer, 'twas said unto me, "Pray
　　Matilda[28] that she tell thee"; and here answered,
　　As one does who doth free himself from blame,　　　　120
The beautiful lady: "This and other things
　　Were told to him by me; and sure I am
　　The water of Lethe has not hid them from him."
And Beatrice: "Perhaps a greater care,
　　Which oftentimes our memory takes away,　　　　　125
　　Has made the vision of his mind obscure.
But Eunoë behold, that yonder rises;
　　Lead him to it, and, as thou art accustomed,[29]
　　Revive again the half-dead virtue in him."
Like gentle soul, that maketh no excuse,　　　　　130
　　But makes its own will of another's will
　　As soon as by a sign it is disclosed,

Even so, when she had taken hold of me,
     The beautiful lady moved, and unto Statius[30]
     Said, in her womanly manner, "Come with him."   135
If, Reader,[31] I possessed a longer space
     For writing it, I yet would sing in part
     Of the sweet draught that ne'er would satiate me;
But inasmuch as full are all the leaves
     Made ready for this second canticle,   140
     The curb of art no farther lets me go.
From the most holy water I returned
     Regenerate, in the manner of new trees
     That are renewed with a new foliage,
Pure and disposed to mount unto the stars.[32]   145

Endnotes

In the notes to this edition of Purgatorio *all quotations from the Bible are from the King James Version.*

CANTO I

1. (p. 3) *To run o'er better waters . . . a sea so cruel:* In Dante's opening tercet, the sea journey is a metaphor for Dante the Pilgrim's journey, as well as a metaphor for Dante the Poet's composition of the poem. The "little vessel of my genius" strikes a humble tone in keeping with the theme of humility in *Purgatorio*, but by the time Dante reaches Paradise, this "little vessel" will become a much larger and imposing ship (*Paradiso* II: 1–15). Hell is here described as "a sea so cruel."

2. (p. 3) *that second kingdom . . . becometh worthy:* Dante defines Purgatory here as the "second kingdom," the first kingdom being Hell. (For a discussion of Dante's conception of Purgatory, see the "Introduction" to this edition of *Purgatorio*.)

3. (p. 3) *dead Poesy here rise again:* While some readers of *Purgatorio* believe that Dante's reference to "dead Poesy" refers to the vanished splendor of classical poetry that is being revived by Dante's genius, most commentators gloss the line to mean that "dead Poesy" refers to the descriptions of the damned souls in Dante's *Inferno*. In keeping with the theme of Easter Sunday (the Pilgrim and Virgil are about to enter the realm of the afterlife, where souls are being purged of all sin before advancing to Paradise), the original Italian text employs the verb *resurga* ("rise again"), which underlines the central event of Christianity, the Resurrection of Christ.

4. (p. 3) *O holy Muses:* In *Inferno*, Dante the Poet followed the tradition of epic poetry established by Homer and Virgil and invoked the muses twice (*Inferno* II: 7–9 and XXXII: 10). Here, his third invocation

includes the adjective "holy," in keeping with the elevated theme of salvation that now occupies Dante the Poet. Later in *The Divine Comedy*, in *Paradiso* I: 13, Dante will call upon Apollo for poetic inspiration.

5. (p. 3) *here Calliope:* Dante calls for Calliope, a muse who presided over epic poetry, to be especially influential upon his verse. In doing so, he refers to the singing contest between the muses and the nine daughters of Pierus, a Macedonian ruler who gave his offspring the names of the muses, a fact that no doubt accounted for their later presumption when they challenged their nine namesakes to a singing contest. Calliope represented the muses in the contest and sang of Ceres and Prosperina—of planting, birth, and rebirth. On the contrary, the King's daughters (collectively referred to as the Pierides) sang of pride, describing the same battle of the giants against the gods that Dante mentions in *Inferno* (XIV: 43–72 and XXXI: 44–45, 91–96). Dante identifies himself with Calliope and his verse with her topic of humility, again befitting the setting of *Purgatorio*, where humility becomes the grand theme. Dante found the description of the singing contest in Ovid's *Metamorphoses* V: 294–678.

6. (p. 3) *the miserable magpies:* Because of their presumption, the Pierides were punished by being transformed into magpies, birds identified with constant cackling and larceny.

7. (p. 3) *they despaired of pardon:* When the Pierides were told that they had lost the singing contest, they began to revile the muses and thus revealed their unrepentant nature (the exact opposite of the contrite nature common to the souls being purged in this "second kingdom").

8. (p. 3) *the oriental sapphire:* The most precious kind of sapphire is that from the Orient and is sky-blue. After being in skyless Hell, Dante the Pilgrim in Purgatory is constantly aware of the heavens, and the increasing sense of light underlines the eventual goal of purification. Here, the reflected azure color from Venus provides the blue light.

9. (p. 3) *Of the pure air, as far as the first circle:* The air between the lunar sphere and earth would be cloudless, serene, and pure. Some commentators take the "first circle" to mean the heaven of the moon, while others (probably more correctly) take the reference to mean simply the horizon, since it is the one that can be immediately perceived by the naked eye.

10. (p. 3) *from the dead air:* That is, from Hell.

11. (p. 3) *The beauteous planet . . . Veiling the Fishes that were in her escort:* Venus is the beauteous planet that inspires the emotion of love, as Dante explains in *Il Convivio* (*The Banquet*) II: v: 13–14. With his reference to the Fishes (Pisces), Dante states that Venus is the morning star in conjunction with Pisces. According to the passage of time calculated from a reading of *Inferno*, Dante the Pilgrim descended into Hell on Good Friday and now stands on the threshold of Purgatory on the early morning of Easter Sunday, April 10, 1300. More than a century ago, Dante scholars discovered that on this date in 1300 Venus was actually the evening star, not the morning star, and that it was in conjunction with Aries (the Ram), not Pisces (the Fishes). The discrepancy between Dante's statement and these calculations has been explained in various ways. Dante probably found the calculations of the positions of the various heavenly bodies in a contemporary work—the *Almanach*, by Prophacius Judaeus (c.1236–1304)—but this source defined Venus as a morning star in 1301 rather than 1300. Thus, Dante the Poet either misread the information (a distinct possibility); or, he willfully changed the information because he wanted his journey to the Afterlife to take place on 1300 for all sorts of symbolic and religious reasons (the most likely explanation for a poem in which the poet takes artistic liberties with science, theology, and philosophy); or, the journey described in the poem actually took place in 1301 (the least likely hypothesis).

12. (p. 3) *To the right hand I turned:* To observe Venus, Dante must face east. When he turns to the right to look upon "the other pole" (the South Pole, for those who, like Dante, inhabit the Northern Hemisphere), he is facing south.

13. (p. 3) *four stars / Ne'er seen before save by the primal people:* Here Dante invents the existence of four stars that, except by Dante the Pilgrim, have not been observed since the time of Adam and Eve (the "primal people"—in the original Italian, the *prima gente*). Although some readers of the poem (including Longfellow in his commentary to this passage) identify these stars with the Southern Cross, it would have been virtually impossible for Dante to have known of the existence of this constellation. It makes more sense to consider the stars as celestial representations of the four cardinal or pagan virtues: prudence, temperance,

justice, and fortitude. Adam and Eve could have seen these stars because, when they inhabited the Garden of Eden, they were on top of the Mountain of Purgatory, at the foot of which Dante the Pilgrim now stands. After the Fall, the "primal people" were expelled from the Garden and, along with the rest of the human race, were forced to inhabit the lands opposite the Earthly Paradise. For Dante this would have meant the Northern Hemisphere, where the stars of the southern sky were not visible.

14. (p. 3) *widowed site:* Because Adam, Eve, and their descendants were deprived of the sight of these four stars, they may be said to have been "widowed" of these heavenly bodies.

15. (p. 4) *to the other pole, / There where the Wain had disappeared already:* Turning toward the left and facing the North Pole, the Pilgrim notes that the constellation of the Wain (which means "cart" or "wagon"; the constellation is known variously as the Big Dipper, the Big Bear, or Ursa Major) is now below the northern horizon.

16. (p. 4) *an old man alone:* Cato of Utica (Marcus Porcius Cato, surnamed Uticensis, 95–46 B.C.), a Roman Stoic famous for his rigid morality, sided with Pompey Caesar in 49 B.C. After the defeat of Pompey at Pharsalus, Cato continued to fight in North Africa until only the city of Utica held out against Caesar. Rather than surrender to a man he considered to be a tyrant, Cato committed suicide after spending much of the night reading Plato's *Phaedo* on the immortality of the soul. Dante once again confounds his reader, placing a pagan, a suicide, and a bitter opponent of Caesar in Purgatory rather than in Hell with such characters as the suicide Pier della Vigna or Brutus and Cassius, the murderers of Julius Caesar. Dante praises Cato in *De Monarchia (Monarchy)* II: v: 15–17 and *Il Convivio* IV: xxviii: 13–19. It seems clear that he considers Cato to be the personification of a love for liberty, a parallel to the search for spiritual freedom by the souls being purged in Purgatory. Dante's sources for Cato were probably Cicero's *De Officiis* I: cxii and Lucan's *Pharsalia* II: 234–391 and IX: 253–618. For the modern reader, it should not be too difficult to accept Cato of Utica as the guardian of the repentant souls who arrive to be purged if we can also accept another virtuous pagan, Virgil, as the heaven-sent guide for Dante the Pilgrim.

17. (p. 4) *a double list:* In two strands or tresses Dante follows

Lucan's *Pharsalia* II: 372–376 in recounting how Cato refused to cut his beard or hair because of the outbreak of civil war in Rome.

18. (p. 4) *his countenance with light:* Cato's face shines with the rays of the four stars as if the sun were shining on his face. Dante probably considered Cato to be the personification of the four cardinal virtues that the stars represent.

19. (p. 4) *"the blind river . . . from the eternal prison":* In *Inferno* XXXIV: 127–132, Dante the Poet describes a place that "not by sight is known, but by the sound / Of a small rivulet"—a small stream that is never identified by name but which many scholars identify as the river Lethe. Dante the Pilgrim and Virgil had followed the course of this stream out of Hell to the lower slope of the Mountain of Purgatory. Because it flows through a dark passageway, it is here described as "blind." It is clear that Cato takes the two travelers as escapees from Hell, "the eternal prison."

20. (p. 4) *"Who guided you? . . . The laws of the abyss, are they thus broken?":* Note that Cato's questions are entirely different in tone from those that the various demons of Hell addressed to the travelers in *Inferno*, underlining the very different tone of this canticle. (Dante calls each of the three divisions of his poem—*Inferno*, *Purgatorio*, and *Paradiso*—a *cantica*, or "canticle.") Since no other souls have ever traveled the path Dante the Pilgrim and Virgil have trod, Cato is naturally wondering if the "house rules" of Purgatory have been changed without his knowledge.

21. (p. 4) *"I came not of myself ":* Virgil's answer to Cato recalls Dante's response to Cavalcante in *Inferno* X: 61, in which he uses the same phrase. There, Dante had referred to Virgil; now Virgil refers to Beatrice, "A Lady from Heaven" (l. 53). (For the details of how Beatrice descended from heaven and sought the Roman poet out in Limbo to assist the Pilgrim in the dark wood, see *Inferno* II: 52–74.) In Virgil's highly rhetorical conversation with Cato, it is important to note how drastically his remarks differ from the often angry and indignant words he directed to the demons in Hell.

22. (p. 6) *"beneath my guardianship":* Virgil's statement here makes it clear that Cato serves as the guardian of the entire Mountain of Purgatory—and not just the limited territory that makes up the vestibule of the Antepurgatory.

23. (p. 6) *"He seeketh Liberty, which is so dear":* Virgil affirms that liberty or freedom—in the case of Dante the Pilgrim's journey, freedom from sin—is the goal of the journey in this realm of the afterlife.

24. (p. 6) *"The vesture, that will shine so, the great day"*: Here Virgil tells Cato that his suicide in Utica, a city in North Africa that was the last bastion of the forces opposing Julius Caesar, will result in his ultimate salvation. His body ("the vesture") will join the general resurrection of the souls who are saved at the Last Judgment and will be particularly glorious.

25. (p. 6) *"Minos binds not me"*: Since Virgil has been sent with the virtuous pagans to Limbo, he is not subject to the jurisdiction of Minos, the infernal judge (see *Inferno* V: 4–15 for a description of how he treats the damned souls who come before him in Hell).

26. (p. 6) *"Eyes of thy Marcia"*: Marcia, Cato's second wife, is mentioned in *Inferno* IV: 128 as one of the virtuous pagans in Limbo.

27. (p. 6) *"For her love, then, incline thyself to us"*: Virgil uses the fact that he resides in the same realm as Cato's ex-wife Marcia to convince Cato to allow them safe passage through the seven parts of Purgatory (l. 82). He promises Cato that in return for passage, he will speak well to Marcia about him.

28. (p. 6) *"the evil river"*: The reference is to the Acheron, one of the five rivers of Hades (see *Inferno* III: 70–81 and XIV: 116).

29. (p. 6) *"no flattery is needful"*: Cato's response to Virgil is a gentle rebuke, for while Marcia may well have pleased Cato before his death, he is now among the blessed souls that anticipate ultimate salvation after the Last Judgment, and as a result, he is now quite beyond the secular appeal of Virgil's rhetorical flourishes.

30. (p. 6) *"a smooth rush"*: This rush, or reed, replaces the cord that Dante had tied around his waist in Hell and that Virgil instructed him to remove in order to signal Geryon in *Inferno* XVI: 106–114. If the cord was meant to give the Pilgrim confidence, the reed stands for the proper humility that he must now display in this very different realm of the afterlife.

31. (p. 6) *"cleanse away all stain therefrom"*: The grimy stains of Hell need to be removed from the Pilgrim's face before he is ready to confront the heavenly guardian figures that he will encounter on his journey.

32. (p. 8) *"The sun, which now is rising"*: It is dawn on the morning of Easter Sunday, 1300.

33. (p. 8) *"the mount":* The reference is to the Mountain of Purgatory.

34. (p. 8) *With this he vanished; and I raised me up:* Cato disappears mysteriously and suddenly, and the Pilgrim finally ceases to kneel as he had been ordered to do by Virgil in l. 51.

35. (p. 8) *Along the solitary plain we went:* The reader should remember that in *Inferno* I: 91–93, the Pilgrim was obliged to take not the direct path up the mountain, the foot of which he reached in the opening lines of the poem (*Inferno* I: 13). Rather, he took the roundabout path through Hell before he could ascend the mountain—that is, before Dante could ascend the mountain, he had to be girded with the reed of humility.

36. (p. 8) *to where the dew / Fights with the sun:* Because of a gentle, moist sea breeze, the dew (a traditional symbol of God's grace, reminding us daily of Christian baptism) takes longer to evaporate in the sun's warmth.

37. (p. 8) *my tearful cheeks; . . . That hue which Hell had covered up in me:* Before Dante can visit Purgatory, the sympathetic tears that he shed in various places in Hell when gazing upon the horrible punishments of the damned must be removed (as well as any sympathy for those rightly condemned souls). Misplaced sympathy for the damned was one of the Pilgrim's moral failings that had to be corrected during his journey through Hell.

38. (p. 8) *the desert shore:* Continuing the image of "the solitary plain" of l. 118, Dante recalls the "desert slope" of *Inferno* I: 29, underlining the fact that no other human being ever returned to describe the journey that the Pilgrim is undertaking. It must also be remembered that in *Inferno* XXVI: 133, Ulysses spied the Mountain of Purgatory from afar before his ship was destroyed in a storm. In short, the Pilgrim's journey remains dangerous and fraught with uncertainty if he is heading toward a place where one of classical antiquity's cleverest warriors met his doom.

39. (p. 8) *as the other pleased:* This is probably a reference to Cato but also, possibly by extension, to God. In *Inferno* XXVI: 141, a similar statement refers to the Divine Will ("as pleased Another").

40. (p. 8) *The humble plant:* Once again, Dante the Poet alludes to an important episode in the *Aeneid* of Virgil (VI: 135–144). The Sybil informs Aeneas that he must pluck a golden bough to carry with him as he visits the Underworld. As soon as he takes the bough, another springs up to take its place. In *Inferno* II: 32, the Pilgrim told Virgil that he was neither Aeneas nor Saint Paul. But after his journey through Hell, Dante the Pilgrim is, in fact, prepared to retrace the steps of Aeneas and the piety that the Pilgrim requires is like the piety that characterized Virgil's epic hero. On this noble note, the prologue canto ends.

CANTO II

1. (p. 9) *Already had the sun the horizon reached:* The Poet opens this canto by telling us, by extremely complicated and learned means, that it is dawn. The concept of time has no real meaning in either Hell or Paradise, but in Purgatory time and its passage are constant preoccupations. Dante's geography differs substantially from our own. For him, Jerusalem (the site of the Crucifixion) is the center of the world and Purgatory (the antipodes) is directly opposite it. For Dante, just west of Spain at the Pillars of Hercules lies the westernmost point of the hemisphere, while the easternmost point for him is represented by the mouth of the Ganges River in India. Dante believed that Jerusalem, the Pillars of Hercules, the Ganges, and Purgatory shared a common horizon. The horizon of a location on earth may be described by a circle that is perpendicular to that point's meridian circle (the meridian circle is a circle passing through the point and the north and south poles). Bear in mind that Dante also believed that earth and not the sun was at the center of the universe and that the sun moved on a line from the Ganges through Jerusalem to the Pillars of Hercules and then to Purgatory. As Jerusalem and Purgatory are on opposite sides of earth, 180 degrees from each other, there is a twelve-hour difference between them. When the canto opens, it is dawn, or 6:00 A.M., in Purgatory and therefore sunset, or 6:00 P.M., in Jerusalem, noon at the Pillars of Hercules, and midnight in the Ganges. It is also important to understand that for Dante the Mountain of Purgatory is the only land in the southern hemisphere and that all the land that exists on earth is contained in one half of the northern hemisphere.

2. (p. 9) *from Ganges with the Scales / That fall from out her hand when she exceedeth:* The Poet explains that when the sun is in the constellation

Aries, the night revolving directly opposite the sun is in Libra ("the Scales"). The night holds the Scales in her hand (meaning that the constellation is visible). The Scales fall from the hand of night (that is, are no longer visible) when night becomes longer ("when she exceedeth") than the day after the autumnal equinox.

3. (p. 9) *Of beautiful Aurora:* The reference is to Dawn, whose white and vermilion cheeks in the eastern sky become increasingly orange and older with the ascent of the sun in the sky.

4. (p. 9) *Like people . . . Who go in heart, and with the body stay:* The Pilgrim is ready to begin the journey but uncertain as to which direction to take. As many commentators note, the restless heart is the spiritual condition that is required of a pilgrim, since such restlessness can be resolved only in God.

5. (p. 9) *Mars grows fiery red:* According to Dante's own *Il Convivio* II: xiii: 21, Mars reddened when it set and was seen through its vapors. The Poet employs this heavenly body to create his first epic simile in *Purgatorio*. Note that the Pilgrim looks west to view Mars, the direction any Tuscan would be accustomed to gaze in order to view the sea.

6. (pp. 9–10) *A light . . . into wings unfolded:* In ll. 17–26, the light increases in intensity until it materializes into the two wings and apparel of an angel.

7. (p. 10) *the pilot:* The Italian word employed by the Poet is *galeotto*. Technically, a *galeotto* is a sailor who rows on a galley, but Dante expands the word's meaning in Italian to include "guide" or "pilot." In *Inferno* VIII: 17, the Poet employs the word to describe the boatman of the River Styx, Phlegyas. In *Inferno* V: 137, Francesca da Rimini uses the word metaphorically to describe the book she read that led her into lustful sin.

8. (p. 10) *"between so distant shores":* As will become clearer in l. 110, the angel quickly travels the distance from the shore at Ostia (Rome's ancient seaport) to the Mountain of Purgatory with no other means except his wings ("he scorneth human arguments," l. 31, meaning the angel disdained any human means of transportation, such as oars or sails). Commentators point toward the fate of Ulysses in *Inferno* to explicate this passage in *Purgatorio*. It takes Ulysses more than five months to cover the same distance the angel covers in no time at all,

and while the angel uses his wings instead of sails and oars, Ulysses "of the oars made wings for our mad flight" (*Inferno* XXVI: 125). A more obvious comparison between this "Bird Divine" (l. 38) and "Celestial Pilot" (l. 43) and a corresponding figure in Hell is Charon, "the ferryman of the livid fen" (*Inferno* III: 98), who delivers the damned souls across the River Acheron to Hell.

9. (p. 10) *a small vessel, very swift and light:* In *Inferno* III: 93 Charon realizes that Dante is a living human being and not one of the souls of the damned. He foretells the Pilgrim's eventual salvation and journey to Purgatory, stating that he will travel there with "a lighter vessel."

10. (p. 10) *the water swallowed naught thereof:* In *Inferno* VIII: 28–30, the boat in which Phlegyas ferries souls across the River Styx draws no water, since the souls of the dead are weightless. Here again, a boat carrying souls draws no water.

11. (p. 10) *Beatitude seemed written in his face:* Scholars have debated the meaning of this line, since there are variants in the manuscripts: *Tal che parea beato per iscripto,* meaning that the angel had blessedness written on his face; or *tal che faria beato pur descripto,* meaning that the angel would make blessed anyone who saw him or heard him described. Longfellow accepts the first and more traditional reading, even though the most influential edition of Dante's poem in the twentieth century (that edited by Giorgio Petrocchi) privileges the second and less convincing reading.

12. (p. 10) *"In exitu Israel de 'Ægypto!":* The passengers in the angel's boat are singing Psalm 114 in the Bible, which describes the exodus of the Israelites from Egypt: "When Israel went out of Egypt." Dante provides only the first line, but it is clear from the text (l. 48) that the souls sing the entire text. The song is appropriate, since the day is Easter and the Christian Easter derives from the Jewish Passover holiday. Just as the people of Israel were delivered from bondage in Egypt, so, too, will the penitent who are about to undergo purification be delivered from the bondage of sin. In Dante's *Epistolam X ad Canem Grandem della Scala* (*The Letter to Cangrande*), in which he discusses a fourfold interpretation of his poem, he declares that *The Divine Comedy* has several senses: the literal sense; the allegorical or mystical sense; the moral sense; and the analogical sense. To demonstrate what he means, the poet cites this precise line: "Now if we look at the letter alone,

what is signified to us is the departure of the sons of Israel from Egypt during the time of Moses; if at the allegory, what is signified to us is our redemption through Christ; if at the moral sense, what is signified to us is the conversion of the soul from the sorrow and misery of sin to the state of grace; if at the analogical, what is signified to us is the departure of the sanctified soul from bondage to the corruption of this world into the freedom of eternal glory" (quoted in Robert S. Haller, ed., *Literary Criticism of Dante Alighieri*, Lincoln: University of Nebraska Press, 1973, p. 99; see "For Further Reading"). Some recent scholars have questioned Dante's authorship of this work (for a discussion of this problem, see Robert Hollander's *Dante's Epistle to Cangrande*, Ann Arbor: University of Michigan Press, 1993).

13. (p. 10) *They chanted . . . that psalm:* This is the first of many instances of singing in *Purgatorio*, often based upon Church liturgy. The psalm the Poet cites (see note 12, above) was usually sung at vespers on Sundays, and it is precisely vespers in Jerusalem when the Pilgrim hears the singing.

14. (p. 10) *The sun . . . chased forth the Capricorn:* The sun, personified implicitly in the person of Apollo the archer, is above the horizon and therefore casts its rays about; as the sun is in Aries, its rays strike the constellation Capricorn, moving it down the sky from the "mid-heaven."

15. (p. 11) *"But we are strangers":* In the original Italian, the word the Poet employs for "strangers" is *peregrin*, which means strangers, travelers in a foreign land, and—most importantly—pilgrims. Technically, only the protagonist Dante and the newly arrived souls in Purgatory can be described as making a true pilgrimage. It is also interesting that although Virgil is supposed to be the Pilgrim's guide, he claims he is as lost as are the new arrivals.

16. (p. 11) *And as to messenger who bears the olive:* The second epic simile in *Purgatorio* underlines an ancient custom, still alive in Dante's times: A messenger bearing good news carried an olive branch.

17. (p. 11) *to go and make them fair:* The souls about to be purified are so astonished at seeing a live human being in the Afterlife that they momentarily forget to cleanse themselves. Cato will soon (ll. 120–123) rebuke them for their lapse.

18. (p. 11) *One from among them:* In l. 91, this figure is identified as

Casella, a musician friend of Dante's from either Florence or Pistoia, a nearby Tuscan city. Casella apparently set some of Dante's poetry to music, and his historical existence is authenticated by several period manuscripts.

19. (p. 11) *O empty shadows, save in aspect only! / Three times:* Forgetting that the souls in Purgatory are spirits rather than physical beings, the Pilgrim attempts in vain to embrace his old friend. The meaning of "empty shadows" will become clearer in *Purgatorio* XXV: 79–108, where Statius explains how the "aerial body" of a dead soul is produced. The three futile embraces recall Virgil's *Aeneid* II: 792–794 and VI: 700–702.

20. (p. 11) *the shadow smiled:* We realize now that we are in an entirely different realm in Purgatory, one where (in contrast to Hell) its inhabitants smile, for they live in assurance of future salvation.

21. (p. 11) *"to return once more / There where I am, I make this journey":* In *Inferno* III: 91–93, Charon implies that the Pilgrim will achieve salvation and pass through Purgatory after his death. Here, the Pilgrim declares that his unusual journey through the afterlife is made for his future salvation and is a guarantee of that salvation.

22. (p. 11) *"But how from thee has so much time been taken?":* The Pilgrim's puzzled question implies that Casella has died some time before but only now is arriving in Purgatory.

23. (pp. 11–12) *"No outrage has been done me . . . Those who tow'rds Acheron do not descend":* Casella explains that the angel boatman ("he who takes both when and whom he pleases," l. 95) would not select him for passage for three months (l. 98). During that time, Casella was delayed near Ostia at the mouth of the Tiber (l. 101), the spot that Dante invents as the location where souls passing to Purgatory gather for their passage. Some scholars believe that Dante gives this power of selection to the angel to imitate Virgil's boatman Charon in the *Aeneid* (VI: 313–316).

24. (p. 12) "Love, that within my mind discourses with me": Casella courteously responds to the Pilgrim's request to sing a song, something that used to quiet his "longings." The very fact that the Pilgrim refers to such worries in his past implies that his own purgation still has far to go. The song Casella selects to sing is *Amor che ne la mente mi ragiona,* which Dante wrote roughly a decade before the date of the Pilgrim's journey in 1300. Dante placed the song in book III of his *Il*

Convivio, an unfinished work probably composed after 1300; there, it is interpreted allegorically as being in praise of Lady Philosophy. In *Il Convivio*, Lady Philosophy is said to have replaced Beatrice in the Poet's affections, and given the important role of Beatrice in *The Divine Comedy* (she is literally the one who will bring about Dante's salvation and cause his journey through the afterlife), the choice of this song is, to say the least, puzzling. Further on, in *Purgatorio* XXIV: 51, Bonagiunta da Lucca will quote the opening line of the most famous poem from Dante's *La Vita Nuova* (*The New Life*): *Donne ch'avete intelletto d'amore* ("Ladies, that have intelligence of love"). In *Paradiso* VIII: 37, the historical figure Charles Martel cites "you who move the third heaven by understanding," the first line in the first *canzone* in book II of *Il Convivio*. Clearly, Dante Alighieri was not afraid to praise his own work, even in the afterlife.

25. (p. 12) *the grave old man . . . "What is this, ye laggard spirits?"*: Cato of Utica appears here just as suddenly as he disappears in canto I, to rebuke the souls for their momentary distraction with Casella's music (and Dante's poetry). For a brief time these distractions have taken their minds off their intended goal—God.

26. (p. 12) *"strip off the slough"*: In the original Italian text, the "slough" is *lo scoglio*, the dead skin that a serpent sheds. This is a perfect image for a penitent sinner who must put away the mistakes of the past and be purified in Purgatory.

27. (p. 12) *Even as when . . . assailed by greater care:* The beautiful simile that concludes canto II compares the effects of Cato's rebuke to the flight of birds that, disturbed during feeding, allow fear to overcome their hunger.

28. (p. 12) *Nor was our own departure less in haste:* The Pilgrim and Virgil, along with the chastised souls, hastily depart on their journey through Purgatory.

CANTO III

1. (p. 13) *whither reason spurs us:* Here "reason" must be understood as justice, particularly divine justice. As Virgil and the Pilgrim come to their senses, they must turn to their true task.

2. (p. 13) *within himself remorseful:* Virgil feels remorse, not because of Cato's rebuke, but rather because he recognizes that he has lingered

too long on the journey. Cato's rebuke would not really apply to Virgil, since he is not undergoing purgation as the souls are.

3. (p. 13) *laid aside the haste / Which mars the dignity of every act:* While Virgil realizes that he should not have lingered, he does not discard the habitual dignity or solemnity that characterizes all his words and actions.

4. (p. 13) *my sight directed to the hill:* Now concentrating on the business at hand without mental distractions, the Pilgrim finally gazes up at the Mountain of Purgatory, the same mountain he was unable to climb in Hell (*Inferno* I: 13–15).

5. (p. 13) *tow'rds the heaven uplifts itself:* In the original Italian, the verb "uplifts" is a word Dante invents: *si dislaga* ("to unlake oneself"). In this case, the mountain "unlakes itself" from the sea that surrounds it, or emerges from the water.

6. (p. 13) *The sun ... stoppage of its rays:* Virgil and the Pilgrim have turned toward the mountain and are thus facing west, causing the recently risen sun to shine on their backs. This blocks its rays and creates a "figure," or shadow.

7. (p. 13) *with the fear / Of being left alone ... Only in front of me the ground obscured:* In Hell, as a living being, the Pilgrim's body had weight, but there was little light for him to cast a shadow. In Purgatory, light exists, but now the Pilgrim is momentarily frightened because the shadow forms in front of only him and not Virgil, causing him to think for an instant that he has been abandoned.

8. (p. 14) *'Tis evening there already where is buried:* Virgil now realizes that it is time to answer the Pilgrim's unverbalized questions about his own fate and points out that it is evening now at the place where he was buried. In 19 B.C., the Emperor Augustus had Virgil's body transferred from Brindisi (the Brundusium of l. 27) to Naples. As Italy is halfway between Jerusalem and the Pillars of Hercules, the time in Naples at the moment Virgil is speaking is approximately 3:00 to 6:00 P.M.

9. (p. 14) *Marvel not:* Virgil warns the Pilgrim not to expect a clear understanding of the laws of the afterlife through reason alone. Souls in Hell and Purgatory suffer pain even though they have no physical bodies. Virgil's lengthy speech to the Pilgrim on the limitations of reason is a stumbling block for any interpretation of *The Divine Comedy* that posits Virgil as the symbol of human reason:

With the insight that comes from his experience after death, the Roman poet realizes the futility of attempting to understand such mysteries as the Trinity (l. 36) with human reason alone. More information on the diaphanous nature of the bodies of the dead in Hell and Purgatory will be provided by Statius in *Purgatorio* XXV: 34–108.

10. (p. 14) *Mortals, remain contented at the* Quia: In scholastic terminology, *quia* refers to things that can be demonstrated by their effects alone, whereas the more important *quid* is that which can be demonstrated by a final cause. Basically, Virgil says that humans should simply be content with accepting things and not ask questions. Pagan philosophers such as Aristotle and Plato (l. 43) searched in vain for the truth (the *quid*), following the innate human desire to know, because they lived before the Christian era (before the birth of Jesus to Mary, l. 38), when the ability to know God (and therefore the truth) first became possible for humanity. Virgil recognizes that like the great virtuous pagans, he, too, is forever condemned to long hopelessly for the truth.

11. (p. 14) *'Twixt Lerici and Turbìa . . . most secluded pathway:* These two towns are on a stretch of the Mediterranean coastline of northern Italy where mountains descend extremely sharply to the sea; in Dante's times this region was considered to be an extremely difficult place to travel.

12. (p. 14) *"Who knoweth now":* Virgil knew his way around Hell because he was the author of the *Aeneid*, the great epic poem chronicling a journey there. As the Poet points out in *Inferno* IX: 23–24, Virgil was once conjured up in Hell by Erictho, the sorceress (Dante's source is Lucan's *Pharsalia* VI). But Virgil is now at a loss to determine how to proceed through this mysterious territory, Antepurgatory. While he stares down at the ground, attempting to use the very reason he has just criticized as being insufficient for answering the important questions, the Pilgrim looks up (the direction he intends to climb) and sees a group of people approaching.

13. (p. 14) *On the left hand:* As Virgil and the Pilgrim proceeded through Hell, they usually turned to the left. They continue this practice out of habit, but it will eventually become clear that the correct way to go round the Mountain of Purgatory is to the right.

14. (p. 16) *Still was that people as far off . . . As a good thrower with his hand would reach:* The souls are only a stone's throw away, but they are moving so incredibly slowly that even after a "thousand steps" that have taken hours to complete, they still have this stone's throw distance to cover. The souls are surprised at the sight of Virgil and the Pilgrim, for the pair is not traveling toward the right, which is the proper direction to climb the Mountain of Purgatory.

15. (p. 16) *"O happy dead! O spirits elect already!":* Unlike many of the conversations in Hell, which were not courteous, Virgil's tone follows the formal conventions of rhetorical greetings. Note that Virgil underlines the fact that these spirits, unlike him, are already destined for salvation.

16. (p. 16) *"For to lose time irks him most who most knows":* After Cato's rebuke over the delay listening to Casella's song at the end of canto II, Virgil has learned not to tarry.

17. (p. 16) *As sheep . . . that fortunate flock:* The thrust of this important simile, comparing the group of souls to humble sheep, is upon their humility and by implication their faith that stands against reliance upon human reason ("Simple and quiet and the wherefore know not," l. 84). The image of the people of God as a flock of sheep with God or Jesus tending to them is one that is omnipresent in Holy Scripture. Their slow movement, meekness, and sense of shame capture perfectly the attitude of those Christians who, as l. 37 recommends, "remain contented at the *Quia.*"

18. (p. 16) *The light upon the ground at my right side:* The Pilgrim and Virgil first faced the mountain, and then turned to the left to go toward the group of sheeplike souls. Now the sun is on the Pilgrim's left side and his shadow falls toward the wall of the mountain on his right. The souls are amazed that the Pilgrim's body casts a shadow, for they are not yet aware that he is mortal.

19. (p. 17) *"Whoe'er thou art":* This courteous address to the Pilgrim comes from a soul who identifies himself in l. 112 as Manfredi (c.1232–1266), the natural son of Emperor Frederick II. He identifies himself, however, not as Frederick's son but as the grandson of Empress Constance, the wife of the Emperor Henry VI. When Frederick died in 1250, Manfredi was appointed regent of the kingdom on behalf of his half-brother Conrad IV, and when Conrad died in 1254,

Manfredi again became regent, this time for Conrad's son Conradin, who was then only a young boy. In 1258, hearing a rumor of Conradin's death, the Sicilian nobles convinced Manfredi to assume the throne. But Pope Urban offered the throne instead to Louis IX of France and then to Louis's brother, Charles of Anjou. Charles came to Italy with an army and at the battle of Benevento on February 26, 1266, defeated Manfredi's army (composed of Saracens and Germans as well as Italians) and killed Manfredi. Charles refused Manfredi Christian burial because he had been excommunicated, but he placed the body near the Benevento bridge and had his army file past, each soldier dropping a stone on the grave. Later Pope Clement IV had Manfredi's body dug up and flung on the banks of the River Verde. Dante places Manfredi's father, Frederick II, among the heretics in Hell (*Inferno* X: 119) because he was thought to be an epicurean who had too many dealings with the Muslim infidels of the Middle East. In contrast to the souls of Hell, who frequently sought to hide their identity, Manfredi, confident in the hope of future salvation, smiles at the Pilgrim (l. 112) and answers most courteously.

20. (p. 17) *"The grandson of the Emperess Costanza"*: Constance (1154–1198) was the daughter of Roger II, king of Naples and Sicily, and wife of Henry VI; Frederick II was her son. She will also appear in *Paradiso* III: 118.

21. (p. 17) *"my daughter . . . Of Sicily's honor and of Aragon's"*: Manfredi married Beatrice of Savoy and named his daughter after his grandmother, Constance. The young Constance (Constanza) married Pedro III of Aragon in 1262 and died in 1302. Her sons include Alfonso (king of Aragon, 1285–1291); James (king of Sicily, 1285–1295 and king of Aragon, 1291–1327); and Frederick (king of Sicily, 1296–1327). Because Constance sired several sons who ruled in both Sicily and Aragon, Dante describes her as the "honor" of both regions.

22. (p. 17) *"my body lacerated / By these two mortal stabs"*: According to Dante's description, Manfredi received two fatal wounds at Benevento, one on his head (l. 108) and another on his breast (l. 111). It is important to remember that in portraying Christian martyrs, artists often depicted the wounds that caused their deaths.

23. (p. 17) *"willingly doth pardon"*: Manfredi was excommunicated by two popes, Alexander IV in 1258 and Urban IV in 1261, and it must

have surprised Dante's readers to discover that an excommunicant could receive God's forgiveness. But surely this is no more surprising than seeing Cato, a virtuous pagan who died without salvation, serving as the guardian of the Antepurgatory. Manfredi begged for forgiveness in his dying breath (something the sinners in Hell never did), and as a result of God's infinite grace, he was saved.

24. (p. 17) *"Cosenza's pastor ... sent by Clement at that time"*: Pope Clement IV ordered the archbishop of the town of Cosenza in Calabria to disinter Manfredi's body and cast it out of papal territory. This explains why his body is not still under the cairn formed by the stones dropped on the corpse by the troops of the victorious Charles of Anjou near Benevento. (See note 19 to this canto.)

25. (p. 17) *"this page"*: Commentators have argued over the meaning of the original Italian text. The Italian word *faccia*, which Longfellow translates here as "page," usually means "face"; while some commentators may accept this literal meaning, Longfellow and most others more correctly believe the word refers to the face of a page of the Bible in which God's mercy is discussed. The crucial point is that the Archbishop of Cosenza, as well as the Pope, failed to consider the all-embracing nature of God's mercy and forgiveness in hounding Manfredi even after the death of his mortal body. As the Poet has repeatedly shown in *Inferno*, he is not afraid to criticize ecclesiastical leaders, including the pope, for their shortcomings and their failures to appreciate the true meaning of Christian principles.

26. (p. 17) *"the realm"*: The *regno* ("realm") was the term used in Dante's time to refer to the southern part of Italy, including the kingdom of Naples down to and including Sicily.

27. (p. 17) *"beside the Verde ... with tapers quenched"*: Denied the favor of burial even in unconsecrated ground, Manfredi's body was abandoned to the harsh elements of rain and wind near the River Verde ("Green"), now called the River Liri. When heretics or excommunicants were buried, the mortuary tapers that generally accompanied burial were quenched, and they were turned upside down to symbolize the death of their souls.

28. (p. 18) *"By malison of theirs is not so lost ... So long as hope has anything of green"*: No curse (*malison*), even one pronounced by a pope, can

prevent God's mercy from saving a sinner who is repentant, so long as hope is alive (or "has anything of green," the traditional color of hope for Dante's culture). Thus, the fact that Manfredi's body was cast out of papal territory near the River Verde ("Green") was a sign of his future salvation.

29. (p. 18) *"in contumacy"*: Contumacy involves rejection of and disobedience to Church authority, resulting in the loss of the sacraments and therefore one's connection with God. Manfredi, who's been excommunicated, is clearly one of the contumacious, who are now identified as the first group of the late repentant. The slowness of the movements of this group, evident in l. 60, can be explained as a symbolic reference to their negligence, lateness, and disobedience to the Church from which they were cast out.

30. (p. 18) *"Thirty times . . . In his presumption"*: Dante invents the notion that the late repentants ("penitent at last," l. 137) must be delayed thirty times the period of time of their "presumption"—their separation from religion. Commentators have speculated that Dante derived the idea of the delay from Virgil's *Aeneid* (VI: 325–330), where Charon rejects the unburied souls of the dead for a hundred years. The specific number thirty may be a reference to the early Christian practice of saying prayers for the dead for thirty days after their demise.

31. (p. 18) *"righteous prayers"*: Dante affirms the belief that the prayers of those in a state of grace on earth may intercede on behalf of the souls in Purgatory. This theme of intercession becomes one of the central tenets of the entire canticle.

32. (p. 18) *"my good Costanza"*: Manfredi wants the Pilgrim to return to the world to report that he is, indeed, in Purgatory and that he requires the intercession of his loved ones to help him advance toward salvation. Costanza (Constance) is Manfredi's daughter, who died in 1302, and who is mentioned earlier in this canto, ll. 115–116.

CANTO IV

1. (p. 19) *Whenever by delight . . . in gazing at that spirit:* In this long opening passage Dante refutes Plato's notion that man has three souls rather than a single soul. He follows Aristotle, who argued that a single soul possesses three powers, and this notion in turn was forwarded by Thomas Aquinas, who advocated a single soul (thus following Christian dogma) with three different virtues or powers. The Poet presents the Pilgrim's distraction during his conversation with Manfredi as proof of the soul's unity. If there were three souls, it would be possible to note the passage of time without being distracted by a conversation, but in the Pilgrim's case, the power or faculty or virtue (depending on the terminology) that is absorbed in looking and listening pays no attention to the power or faculty or virtue that observes the passing of time.

2. (p. 19) *For fifty full degrees uprisen was ... I had not perceived it:* The Pilgrim has been so absorbed in his conversation that he has failed to notice that the sun has moved 50 degrees since sunrise. Since the sun moves in its daily rotation around the earth 15 degrees each hour, approximately three hours and twenty minutes have passed since the Pilgrim observed the arrival of the souls in the angel's boat. Since the sun rose on Easter 1300 around 6:00 A.M., it is now about 9:20 A.M.

3. (p. 19) *"Here is what you ask":* Virgil now finally receives the answer to his question of *Purgatorio* III: 76–77: "Tell us upon what side the mountain slopes, / So that the going up be possible." This return to business after the interruptions and digressions with Casella and Manfredi serve to remind the Pilgrim (and the reader) that the journey must not be delayed.

4. (p. 19) *A greater opening ... The villager, what time the grape imbrowns:* The Poet compares the very small opening that the Pilgrim and Virgil must pass through to the tiny openings in hedgerows filled with thorns that peasants employ to guard their grapes from thieves. The idea of the narrow passageway to salvation is a scriptural notion, most clearly expressed in Matthew 7: 13–14: "Enter ye in at the strait gate. . . ." The phrase "what time the grape imbrowns" echos the notion of the ripening grapes Jesus uses in his parables in Matthew 20: 1–16 and 21: 33–41 to refer to the Judgment Day.

5. (p. 19) *Sanleo ... Noli ... Bismantova:* To objectify the narrow nature of the passageway required to climb farther, the Poet refers to three places in Italy that are extremely inaccessible: San Leo, a town in the Romagna located high on a mountaintop; Noli, on the Gulf of Genoa in Liguria, a spot that can be reached only after a sharp descent from the rugged mountains behind it; and Bismantova, a tiny town in

Emilia south of Reggio, approachable only by a very steep pathway. Some editors of Dante's poem believe the original Italian text followed by Longfellow—*montasi su Bismantova in cacume*—should read *montasi su Bismantova 'n Cacume*, or "climb above Bismantova and Cacume," interpreting the line to refer to Cacume (a mountain peak near Anagni) rather than the summit over the town of Bismantova. Like other contemporary translators, Longfellow prefers to translate the phrase *in cacume* as "summit."

6. (p. 20) *Than line from middle quadrant to the centre:* Here the Poet means to say that the mountain slopes ever steeper than the 45-degree angle that is formed by a line drawn from the center of a circle to the middle of one of its quadrants. A quadrant is one-quarter of a circle's circumference.

7. (p. 20) *"unless thou stay!":* The Pilgrim is exhausted at the physical activity required in climbing up the mountain—after all, he has a body with physical weight—and he asks Virgil to "stay" his steps, or to slow down.

8. (p. 20) *Strained every nerve . . . Until the circle was beneath my feet:* Crawling up to the ledge above on his hands and knees (we know this is how he moves forward from the original Italian text, which utilizes the verb *carpando* that Longfellow has rendered neatly as "scrambling"), the Pilgrim finally reaches the ledge that circles the mountain. From his vantage point "on that side," though, it is not possible to see that the ledge "encircles all the hill" (l. 48).

9. (p. 20) *we seated both of us / Turned to the East . . . That on the left hand we were smitten by it:* After the tremendous effort of pulling themselves up the ledge, the Pilgrim and Virgil do what all mountain climbers do after a difficult ascent: They stop and gaze at the ground they have covered. They look down upon the beach where the sun has arisen in the east, and the Pilgrim wonders why the sun strikes him on the left as it rises to the north.

10. (p. 20) *Aquilon:* This is the north wind.

11. (pp. 20–22) *"If Castor and Pollux . . . from its old track":* The Pilgrim is accustomed to the positions of the heavenly bodies in the northern hemisphere and expects to find the sun in the south. In ll. 61–66, Virgil explains in metaphors that are extremely difficult for contemporary readers to follow that if Castor and Pollux (stars in

Gemini) were accompanied by the mirror (the sun), you would see the "zodiac's jagged wheel" (line 64, meaning the sun itself) closer to the constellations of the Bears, and therefore farther to the north. The reader is expected to recall that the sun is in Aries between March 21 and April 20 and in Gemini from May 21 through June 21. Longfellow's translation of the passage in l. 64 as "the zodiac's jagged wheel" (the original Italian reads *il Zodiaco rubecchio*, literally "the reddened, or flaming, Zodiac") shows his erudition, for in his note to the line, he points out that Dante's first commentator, Iacopo della Lana (c.1278–1358), defined the word *rubecchio* as not meaning only "red" or "ruddy" (the rendering most contemporary translators employ) for Iacopo noted that, in Tuscany, the word referred to an indented mill-wheel, something that Dante might well employ to represent the wheels on Apollo's chariot (the sun). Always the subtle poet and translator, Longfellow opts for the concrete image, not the adjectival modifier.

12. (p. 22) *"How that may be . . . right clearly heed":* Virgil tells the Pilgrim to imagine that Zion (Jerusalem) and Purgatory share the same horizon (the equator) and are on exactly opposite sides of earth. The reader has already encountered this kind of information in *Purgatorio* II: 1–9. In the northern hemisphere, the sun traveling from Jerusalem appears to move from left to right, and on the contrary, in the southern hemisphere the sun traveling from Jerusalem appears to move from right to left. The road that Phaeton did not know how to drive (ll. 71–72) refers to a story in Ovid's *Metamorphoses* II, also mentioned in *Inferno* XVII: 107. Apollo, the charioteer of the sun, allowed his son, Phaeton, to drive the chariot, but Phaeton lost control and Zeus was forced to kill him with a thunderbolt to save both heaven and earth. Phaeton's mad race across the sky created the stars of the Milky Way.

13. (p. 22) *"Truly, my Master . . . tow'rds the region of the heat":* The "midcircle of supernal motion" (l. 79), or the middle circle of celestial motion as the heavenly spheres revolve, is the celestial equator. The Pilgrim's complicated summation of the information he has gleaned from Virgil means the following. The celestial equator lies between the sun and the hemisphere in which winter reigns. Since Virgil has just explained how Jerusalem (Zion) and Purgatory are antipodal, the celestial equator always lies north of Purgatory ("tow'rds the Septentrion,"

l. 83); the Hebrews before the Diaspora saw it in the south (the "region of the heat," l. 84).

14. (p. 22) *"the more one climbs, the less it hurts . . . As going down the current in a boat":* Contrary to the experience of climbing mountains in the normal world, on the Mountain of Purgatory, as one goes higher, the ascent becomes easier. The climb is most difficult at the beginning, and this is appropriate, since the souls making the journey of purgation are heading toward a reward.

15. (p. 23) *A voice close by us sounded . . . "Thou wilt have need of sitting down ere that":* This figure is Belacqua, not identified until l. 123. He was apparently a maker of musical instruments and one of Dante's friends. Anonimo Fiorentino, the author of a commentary on Dante that dates from the fourteenth to the early fifteenth century, describes Belacqua as extremely lazy, a trait for which Dante often criticized him. The commentary reports a witty exchange between Belacqua and Dante: After Belacqua noted that Aristotle believed sitting quietly increased one's intelligence, Dante retorted that if sitting still made one wise, Belacqua was the wisest man who ever lived! Belacqua's sarcastic remark to the pair undercuts the erudite discussion of Virgil and the Pilgrim. Belacqua is a figure who had immense appeal for Samuel Beckett, the great twentieth-century existentialist novelist and dramatist of the absurd. Belacqua provides the name of the Irish writer's anti-heroic protagonist in his novels *Dream of Fair to Middling Women* and *More Pricks than Kicks.* Moreover, Dante's indolent, lethargic character Belacqua may well be the inspiration for any number of Beckett's absurdist figures in plays, who are constantly waiting, as in *Waiting for Godot.*

16. (p. 23) *"more negligent / Than even if Sloth herself his sister were":* Belacqua's posture makes him appear to the Pilgrim as the very brother of his metaphorical sister, the personified image of Sloth.

17. (p. 23) *"Now go thou up, for thou art valiant":* As in his interruption in ll. 98–99, Belacqua's second remark is curt, that of a man almost too indolent to compose several sentences in greeting an old friend. This second address mocks the Pilgrim (note that he really does not engage Virgil at all), but his tone is still affectionate.

18. (p. 23) *Then knew I who he was:* Belacqua's mocking and lazy tone of voice alone causes the Pilgrim to recognize with whom he is speaking (but the reader still is not yet given his name).

19. (p. 23) *"Hast thou seen clearly how the sun . . . drives his chariot?"*: Belacqua's third remark to the Pilgrim mocks the erudition contained in Virgil's explanation and the Pilgrim's reply. Even though Belacqua has overheard Virgil's discourse, he hardly bothers to look up at his visitors.

20. (p. 23) *laughter moved my lips*: After Dante the Pilgrim's harrowing experiences in Hell, the reader finally sees him smile.

21. (p. 23) *"Belacqua, I grieve not / For thee henceforth . . . upon thee?"*: Because the Pilgrim discovers Belacqua in Purgatory, he no longer frets about the condition of his mortal soul. Yet he teases his old friend, asking him why he has regressed to the indolent habits of his earthly existence. The Pilgrim mentions grieving for his friend, underscoring the fact that Belacqua passed away only recently.

22. (pp. 23–24) *"O brother, what's the use of climbing? . . . What profit others that in heaven are heard not?"*: Belacqua's final remark to the Pilgrim is completely in character, for he reveals that he will be denied entrance at the Gate of Purgatory by the angel guarding it for as long a time as the heavens revolved around him during his lifetime because he postponed his repentance until the very last moments of his existence. Only the prayers of those living in grace (and not the prayers of "others"—the prayers from those who are not in this state, l. 135) can shorten his period of waiting.

23. (p. 24) *"the sun has touched / Meridian"*: It is high noon, and therefore two and a half hours have passed since the Pilgrim and Virgil spoke with Manfredi.

24. (p. 24) *"the night / Covers already with her foot Morocco"*: Morocco here refers to Gibraltar, or the Pillars of Hercules, where it is around dusk or 6:00 P.M.

CANTO V

1. (p. 25) *from those shades*: That is, from Belacqua and the other negligent and indolent sinners undergoing purification.

2. (p. 25) *"The sunshine on the left of him below"*: The Pilgrim is now climbing up the slope of the mountain and is facing west with his shadow falling to the left. Once again, the souls of Purgatory note that as a living being, the Pilgrim casts a shadow while they cannot.

3. (p. 25) *"removes from him the mark"*: By this, Dante means to say that a man continuously thinking new thoughts puts the attainment

of his goal (his "mark," or target) ever further away. In other words, chaotic reasoning never hits its mark.

4. (p. 25) *that color tinged:* That is, the reddish color of blushing from shame.

5. (p. 25) *the Miserere: Miserere* ("have mercy") is the opening of the biblical Psalm 51, a prayer that begs God for forgiveness and asks for purification. This is an appropriate verse for those in Purgatory. As will become clearer as the poem unfolds, different groups of souls in Antepurgatory and Purgatory are associated with particular prayers. The exceptions are the first two groups in Antepurgatory the Pilgrim has already met: the excommunicated and the indolent or negligent.

6. (p. 25) *I gave no place / For passage of the sunshine through my body . . . a long, hoarse "Oh!":* Once again, souls note the corporeal nature of Dante's appearance, which parallels a similar reaction in *Purgatorio* II: 69.

7. (p. 26) *"it may profit them":* Since the Pilgrim is still alive, he may return to earth and ask the friends and relatives of the souls to pray for their purgation. This will hasten their passage into the upper reaches of Purgatory proper and their exit from Antepurgatory.

8. (p. 26) *Vapors enkindled . . . like troops that run without a rein:* The two messengers who carry the news to the waiting souls are as quick as meteors or lightning ("vapors enkindled") that cleave through the summer sky. Upon hearing the news, the entire group races toward the Pilgrim as rapidly as a cavalry troop with their horses out of control.

9. (p. 26) *"So still go onward, and in going listen":* Earlier Virgil had urged the Pilgrim not to tarry (and therefore not to imitate those in Antepurgatory who had tarried in various ways). Now he encourages the Pilgrim to listen, provided he continues his progress onward and upward.

10. (p. 26) *"o'er yonder . . . why not stay?":* "O'er yonder" refers to the world of the living. The Pilgrim is following Virgil's advice and refuses to stop to speak.

11. (p. 26) *"we all were slain by violence":* These souls are now positively identified as people who were sinners until the very end of their lives but who, at the last possible moment before they were slain by violent means, obtained forgiveness.

12. (p. 26) *"ye well-born spirits":* They are "well-born" because they are destined to be saved after purification. Those condemned to Hell

are, in contrast, called "evil-born" spirits (*Inferno* V: 7; XVIII: 76; and XXX: 48).

13. (p. 26) *"by that peace . . . From world to world makes itself sought by me"*: The Pilgrim swears to assist the spirits, invoking that which is most dear to him ("that peace"). Attaining this peace is a goal that inspires the Pilgrim with desire for itself ("makes itself sought by me") just as God provides the souls with the desire to see Him. The reference to "from world to world" (l. 63) must refer to the different realms of the afterlife through which the Pilgrim is traveling toward God.

14. (p. 28) *And one began:* This unnamed figure has been identified from the information he provides about his past life as Jacopo del Cassero, a nobleman from Fano who served as the *podestà* (executive administrative officer) of the city of Bologna in 1296 and ran afoul of the nobleman Azzo VIII d'Este there. In 1298, while Jacopo was heading to Milan via the River Brenta, Azzo had him stabbled near Oriaco, and he bled to death among the lagoons.

15. (p. 28) *"Unless the I cannot cut off the I will"*: That is, unless impotence or inability does not inhibit, or "cut off," the will.

16. (p. 28) *"That 'twixt Romagna lies and that of Charles"*: The land described is in the Marches of Italy, between Romagna in the north and the kingdom of Charles of Anjou to the south.

17. (p. 28) *"Fano"*: In Dante's time, this town on the Adriatic coast between Pesaro and Ancona was ruled by the Malatesta family of Rimini.

18. (p. 28) *"in bosom of the Antenori"*: The place Jacopo describes is in Paduan territory, referred to as Antenori because, according to legend, Padua was founded by the descendants of the Trojan Antenor, the son of King Priam who supposedly betrayed Troy to the Greeks. In *Inferno* XXXII: 88, Dante refers to Antenora, a section of the bottommost part of Cocytus that is named after Antenor and where treachery to country or party is punished. Just as Antenor betrayed the Trojans, his descendants betrayed Jacopo to the assassins sent by Azzo to kill him.

19. (p. 28) *"In hatred far beyond what justice willed"*: Jacopo apparently angered Azzo by opposing him politically and by speaking very badly about him, but having Jacopo assassinated was disproportionate to these wrongs. Note that implicit in this reasoned discussion of Azzo's

vengeance is Jacopo's forgiveness of the crime, a precondition for repentance and purgation.

20. (p. 28) *"if towards the Mira I had fled"*: Jacopo believes that if he had fled from his assassins toward La Mira, a small town on the banks of the River Brenta between Padua and Venice, he might have escaped.

21. (p. 28) *"I was of Montefeltro, and am Buonconte"*: This imposing figure identifies himself as being of the Montefeltro family. He is Buonconte da Montefeltro, son of Guido da Montefeltro, whom the Poet encounters in *Inferno* XXVII: 19–132. Like his father, Buonconte was a Ghibelline; he led the Ghibellines of Arezzo against the Florentine Guelphs at the battle of Campaldino in 1289, in which Dante is thought to have participated on the side of the Guelphs. The Ghibellines were soundly defeated, Buonconte was killed, and his body was never located on the battlefield.

22. (p. 28) *"Giovanna, nor none other cares for me . . . I go with downcast front"*: Apparently neither Buonconte's wife, Giovanna, nor his relatives or children are praying for his soul's salvation from Purgatory, causing Buonconte to hang his head in shame.

23. (p. 28) *"What violence or what chance / Led thee astray"*: As one of the Guelph soldiers in the army opposing Buonconte's Ghibellines, the Pilgrim must have thought it strange that the leader of the defeated army disappeared bodily in the course of the conflict. He wonders if Buonconte's body disappeared by a deliberate act of violence or simply by accident. Note that the Pilgrim has no rancor against his former enemy, and this attitude is appropriate for someone who is undergoing purgation himself.

24. (p. 28) *"at Casentino's foot . . . in Apennine"*: Satisfying the Pilgrim's curiosity, Buonconte informs him that he arrived wounded at the foot of the Casentino, an area that covers the upper valley of the River Arno and reaches as far as the slopes of the Apennines. The river called Archiano is formed in the Apennines above the Hermitage (monastery) of Camaldoli. Buonconte ended his life at the point where the Archiano flows into the River Arno and essentially disappears ("There where the name thereof becometh void," l. 97).

25. (p. 29) *"in the name of Mary end . . . repeat it to the living"*: Bleeding to death with his throat cut and without his horse, Buonconte's last words were to invoke Mary, an act that guaranteed his salvation. Once again, unlike the souls condemned to perdition in Hell, the souls of Purgatory want the living to know their fate and to pray for them (l. 103).

26. (p. 29) *"God's Angel took me up, and he of hell / Shouted"*: The Poet wants the reader to recall how, in *Inferno* XXVII: 112–120, a similar struggle for the soul of Guido da Montefeltro, Buonconte's father, ends quite differently when a black cherubim carries Guido's soul off to Hell. Even though Buonconte waited until the very last moment of his life to repent, he did so sincerely. It was commonly believed in Dante's day that angels and devils contended for the souls of the dead, pronouncing, in effect, a final judgment upon them.

27. (p. 29) *"'For one poor little tear'"*: In spite of the devil's attempt to minimize the contrition of Buonconte, it was this single tear that testified to Buonconte's sincere repentance.

28. (p. 29) *"'with the rest'"*: "The rest" is Buonconte's dead body, and ll. 109–129 make clear that the devil, in a fit of pique over losing Guido's soul, takes his anger out on these corporal remains.

29. (p. 29) *"Well knowest thou . . . which to water turns"*: Buonconte reminds the Pilgrim that he himself in *Il Convivio* IV: xviii: 4 describes the process of condensation, in which water is produced when moist air becomes cold.

30. (p. 29) *"the valley / From Pratomagno to the great yoke"*: The region Buonconte describes extends from the mountain ridge of Pratomagno that forms the southwest portion of the Casentino to the "great yoke," or main ridge, of the Apennines.

31. (p. 29) *"the royal river"*: The River Arno was then commonly called a "royal" river, because it flowed into the sea.

32. (p. 29) *"loosened from my breast the cross / I made of me"*: During his last moments, Buonconte folds his arms upon his breast in the sign of the cross, another symbol of his contrition.

33. (p. 29) *After the second followed the third spirit:* We now realize that a third soul is speaking to the Pilgrim, interrupting (but politely) his conversation with Buonconte.

34. (p. 30) *"Do thou remember me who am the Pia; / Siena made me, unmade me Maremma"*: In two of Dante's most famous lines in *The Divine Comedy*, we are introduced to this woman succinctly and swiftly. Imitated by T. S. Eliot in his 1922 poem *The Waste Land* ("Highbury bore

me "), these lines actually tell the reader very little that can be documented historically about the character. For years, she was identified with a certain Sienese woman, Pia Tolomei, who married Nello Pannocchieschi from the Maremma area, a swampy territory in southwestern Tuscany. Early commentators argued that she was murdered by her husband (one suggests she was thrown out of a window). More recent commentators are hesitant to identify this character with Pia Tolomei, but there is no doubt that she was murdered; that this murder took place in the Maremma; and that she refers to herself as *la Pia* in the original, employing the article with her first name—this not only gives her speech an intimate, familiar tone but also suggests that she may also serve as a representation of Pity itself. The last two lines of the canto underline the fact that her husband, who gave her a ring as the sign of his betrothal and knew about her death, may well have caused it himself. Whatever the historical identity of Pia might be, there is little doubt that Dante meant his reader to contrast her character to that of a woman who died in an adulterous affair in a parallel canto in the first canticle of his poem: Francesca da Rimini of *Inferno* V. Unlike Francesca, who overwhelms the Pilgrim with a self-serving story about her death, Pia is so considerate that she asks the Pilgrim only to remember her after he has rested from his long journey through the Afterlife (l. 131).

CANTO VI

1. (p. 31) *the game of Zara:* Dante's reference to a game of chance (*zara* means "hazard" or "chance") introduces the theme of how chance plays such an important role in our lives. Zara, the game Dante mentions, involved two players and three dice, and the players would call out a number before they cast the dice. Certain numbers with a cast of three dice would be more probable than others, while other numbers would have less probability of coming up. Thus, the game of Zara was not completely unlike the modern game of craps. Clearly the Pilgrim is being compared to the winner of such a game, but who is the losing player in the game? It has been suggested that this could be a reference to Virgil, since he seems to have missed out on salvation and is trapped (albeit comfortably) in Limbo, while other virtuous pagans, such as Cato earlier and Statius later, are treated quite differently.

At any rate, the interjection of the role of chance by this simile raises some troubling questions about how human fate is decided.

2. (p. 31) *promising, I freed myself therefrom:* Just as the winner at the game of chance distributes some of his winnings to disperse the crowd of well-wishers, so, too, does the Pilgrim promise the souls that he will ask their loved ones to pray for their quick transfer to Purgatory proper.

3. (p. 31) *the Aretine:* An Aretine is a citizen of the Tuscan city of Arezzo, and the reference is to Benincasa da Laterina, a judge from this city who sentenced a relative of the famous highwayman Ghin (Ghino) di Tacco (l. 39) to death. In revenge, Ghino murdered him in the office of the papal auditor in Rome. Early commentators said Laterina was beheaded in the presence of another of Dante's least favorite individuals, Pope Boniface VIII. On the contrary, Giovanni Boccaccio describes Ghino di Tacco quite favorably in *The Decameron* X: 2.

4. (p. 31) *he who fleeing from pursuit was drowned:* The earliest commentators on Dante identified this unnamed figure as Guccio de' Tarlati, a Ghibelline who lived in the Arezzo district and who perished in battle (perhaps at Campaldino) while attacking Guelph forces from Arezzo. Dante's line in the original Italian (*correndo in caccia*) can mean either hunting or being hunted, so there is some question as to whether he was advancing or retreating from those who eventually put him to death. Longfellow opts for the later interpretation ("fleeing from pursuit").

5. (p. 31) *Frederick Novello:* This member of the Conti Guidi family from the Casentino area was killed between 1289 and 1291 while fighting some of the Guelph forces from Arezzo.

6. (p. 31) *that one of Pisa . . . the good Marzucco seem so strong:* This Pisan has been identified as the son of Messer Marzucco degli Scornigiani. Marzucco's son was murdered around 1287 by Count Ugolino during the internecine strife in the city of Pisa (see *Inferno* XXXIII). Early commentators explained the phrase "seem so strong" by the fact that rather than avenging his son's death, Marzucco showed his fortitude by forgiving, rather than by seeking vengeance.

7. (p. 31) *Count Orso:* Orso, the son of Napoleone dell'Acerbia, was murdered by his cousin Alberto. Alberto's father, Alexander, and Napoleone killed each other over their inheritance, and both have

already been mentioned as traitors against family in Caina (*Inferno* XXXII: 55–58). This is yet another link to the first canticle and shows a parallel but ultimately different fate: Two brothers from one generation end in Hell, while one of their sons reaches Antepurgatory.

8. (p. 31) *the soul divided / By hatred and by envy from its body:* Pierre de la Brosse (named specifically in l. 22), chamberlain of King Phillip III of France, was hanged in 1278 because of accusations brought against him by Queen Marie of Brabant of the Netherlands (l. 23).

9. (p. 31) *of no worse flock!:* Since Marie of Brabant lived until 1321 (she and Dante died the same year), she could have read *Purgatorio*. If she had, she would have seen this warning to her that she should repent for having caused Pierre de la Brosse's execution and avoid ending in Hell with a "flock" far worse than Pierre's companions in Antepurgatory.

10. (p. 31) *that some one else may pray:* Over and over again in *Purgatorio*, the Pilgrim emphasizes the fact that the souls being purified ask only that they be remembered in the prayers of their friends and relatives who are still alive so that their time in Purgatory may be abbreviated.

11. (p. 32) *"That orison can bend decree of Heaven":* While stressing the intercessory power of prayer to assist the souls in Purgatory, the Pilgrim now wonders if one of Virgil's own verses (*Aeneid* VI: 337–383) argues that prayers do not possess the power to bend divine law. In that poem, Aeneas encounters the shade of the drowned ship's pilot Palinurus, who prays that his body be carried across the River Styx but is denied burial by the Sibyl, who declares that prayers cannot move heaven's decrees. In the Christian dispensation (interpreted by the medieval Catholic Church), prayers work miracles for the dead departed.

12. (p. 32) *"sane intellect . . . fire of love fulfils at once":* Virgil informs the Pilgrim that his words in the *Aeneid* and Christian practice with intercessory prayer are not in conflict. When proper reason ("sane intellect") considers the matter, the reasoning is obvious. God's judgment is the summit ("top," l. 37) of authority and need not concern itself with the question, since "the fire of love" is sufficient to cancel the sinner's debts almost instantly ("at once").

13. (p. 32) *"Because the prayer from God was separate":* This statement makes clear that the prayer of Pallinurus, the character in question in the *Aeneid*, was ineffective because he was a pagan and died before

Christ's redemption made purification from sin possible. In *Paradiso* XXXII: 82, Dante also makes it clear that God's grace was removed from mankind during the pagan period and was restored only by the sacrifice of Christ on the Cross.

14. (p. 32) *"Do not decide, unless she tell it thee":* Virgil warns the Pilgrim that such profound matters as the intercessory power of prayer should be taken up with the true authority, Beatrice (named later in l. 47) who is responsible for sending him to guide Dante through most of the afterlife. Even though he is a virtuous pagan, Virgil can grasp only a limited understanding of complicated Christian theological questions. Virgil calls Beatrice a light between the truth and the intellect (l. 45), and only she will be able to answer all of the Pilgrim's weighty theological questions.

15. (p. 32) *"thou dost not interrupt his rays":* Virgil and the Pilgrim are now climbing up the eastern side of the mountain in the early afternoon. Since that part of the mountain is in shadow, the Pilgrim's body no longer casts a shadow or, as the souls always remark, no longer interrupts the son's rays.

16. (p. 32) *"there behold! a soul":* Line 74 will reveal this soul to be Sordello, a poet born near Virgil's native city of Mantua, Italy, around 1200. An Italian troubadour who composed a number of lyrics in Provençal rather than Italian, Sordello composed a famous lament for the death of Blacatz in which he condemns the defects of several secular rulers of the time. This fact may account for Dante's choice of Sordello to point out the group of princes in upcoming canto VII. Sordello stands "all alone" (l. 59) and not in a group of like souls waiting for passage out of Antepurgatory, underlining his importance to the narrative. The fact that he has been "stationed" there (l. 58) implies that he has a function in this part of Antepurgatory. Although Dante honors Sordello by placing him in this position of importance, in *De Vulgari Eloquentia* (*On Eloquence in the Vernacular Tongue*) I: xv: 2 he criticizes Sordello for abandoning the Italian vernacular in his poetry, something that Dante never did.

17. (p. 33) *O Lombard soul:* The emotional tone of the Poet's apostrophe in praise of Sordello prepares the reader for the even more emotional and angry tone of the Poet's attacks against his native Italy (ll. 85–151).

18. (p. 33) *a couchant lion:* Sordello is described as lofty or stately and disdainful, a characteristic calculated to remind us of the noble spirits in Limbo (*Inferno* IV: 112–114). Most commentators link the comparison of Sordello with a couching lion to the Bible, *Genesis* 49: 9, where Judah is described in this fashion.

19. (p. 33) *"Mantua":* When Virgil mentions the name of his native city he provokes a dramatic change in Sordello's aloof and self-absorbed manner. Sordello's reply (ll. 74–75) and his subsequent embrace of Virgil will provoke a dramatic interruption in the flow of the poem, as Dante the Poet interjects his most famous and bitter invective against his native Italy for having rejected the rule of an emperor as, he believes, God intended. It is interesting that Sordello recognizes Virgil the Mantuan, not Virgil the epic poet.

20. (p. 33) *Ah! servile Italy, grief's hostelry! . . . but brothel:* The Poet's invective takes up the rest of canto VI, an extraordinary amount of space for this subject. Formerly the ruler of vast territories, Italy is now nothing but a harlot, is without an emperor ("a ship without a pilot," l. 77), and is the hostel, or receptacle, of grief and tribulation.

21. (p. 33) *one doth gnaw the other / Of those whom one wall and one fosse shut in!:* The moving sign of fraternal affection underlined in the embrace between Sordello and Virgil ("and one embraced the other," l. 75) is now contrasted to the internecine strife plaguing Italian cities and tearing them apart ("and one doth gnaw the other"). In reading the image of two inhabitants of a single city chewing each other apart, it is difficult not to recall the terrifying picture of Ugolino's punishment in *Inferno* XXXII: 127–132. Dante here defines the geographical boundaries of a medieval Italian city as the political space set off by a city wall and a moat ("fosse") around it.

22. (p. 33) *Justinian / The bridle mend, if empty be the saddle?:* Justinian, emperor of Constantinople from 527 to 565, was responsible for the collection of several codices of laws known under the general title of the *Corpus juris civilis*; it was basically the body of Roman law that passed to medieval Europe. This body of laws served as the "bridle" to lawlessness in Italy but only if a just emperor applied them (without such an emperor, Italy is riderless).

23. (p. 34) *this wild beast:* This beast is Italy, a riderless horse without the bridle of Roman law and the leadership of an imperial figure.

24. (p. 34) *O German Albert! who abandonest:* Albert I of Austria, son of Rudolf I of Hapsburg, was elected Holy Roman Emperor in 1298 but never received an Italian coronation, even though Pope Boniface VII recognized his election in 1303. He was assassinated by his nephew in 1308 before he could reorganize Italy's chaotic political situation. Dante thus felt that Albert had abdicated his role.

25. (p. 34) *May a just judgment:* The Poet writes from the perspective of the year 1300, and here he seems to predict either Albert's assassination or the death of Albert's son and heir in 1307. His successor (l. 102) would be Henry VII, who ruled from 1308 to 1313, but the fiction of the poem taking place in 1300 precludes the Poet from providing a precise name here.

26. (p. 34) *Come and behold:* The Poet now sarcastically invites Albert to see for himself the sad condition of Italy.

27. (p. 34) *Montecchi and Cappelletti, / Monaldi and Fillippeschi:* The Cappelletti family of Cremona headed an anti-imperial faction of Guelphs who opposed the pro-imperial Ghibelline faction headed by the Montecchi or Monticoli family. The Monaldis were Guelphs of the city of Orvieto who opposed a similar Ghibelline faction, the Fillippeschi family. By the time Dante wrote these verses, all four families were in decline, testimony to the destructive results of such civil strife in Italian communes. The literary treatments of the struggles of these four families in Italian works by Masuccio Salernitano, Luigi da Porto, and Matteo Bandello ultimately provided the source material for Shakespeare's *Romeo and Juliet* and that play's famous description of the Montague and Capulet families.

28. (p. 34) *Santafiore!:* This small town in Sienese territory had been ruled from the ninth to the thirteenth century by the counts of Santafiore, the Aldobrandeschi family. By the year 1300, the time of the poem's action, much of this territory had been seized by the Guelphs of Siena. In *Purgatorio* XI: 55–72, the reader will encounter Omberto Aldobrandeschi, one of this famous clan.

29. (p. 34) *O Jove Supreme! . . . for us wast crucified:* The Poet refers to the crucified Christ with a pagan equivalent.

30. (p. 34) *for some good thou makest:* The Poet wonders if perhaps God has some secret plan ("From our perception utterly cut off,"

l. 123) that will redeem Italy in much the same way that Christ has redeemed mankind.

31. (p. 34) *Marcellus:* A number of Roman consuls were named Marcellus, and all were opponents of Julius Caesar. Dante most likely is referring here to Marcus Claudius Marcellus, the "verbose Marcellus" that Lucan mentions in *Pharsalia* I: 313. He was consul in 51 B.C., was pardoned by Caesar upon the advice of the Roman senate (the subject of Cicero's *Pro Marcello*), and was later murdered in Greece. The Poet means here that every miserable peasant thinks himself a Roman rebel like Marcellus and turns against the Holy Roman Emperor, just as Marcellus sided with Pompey against Julius Caesar. Rebels against the imperial ideal are thus identified with base-born peasants ("Each peasant churl," l. 126).

32. (p. 34) *My Florence!:* Dante's invective against strife-torn Italy really warms up when he finally turns to his native city of Florence and attacks its government and its citizens.

33. (p. 35) *on their very lips:* Dante feels Florentines pay only lip service to Justice.

34. (p. 35) *"I submit":* Dante implies sarcastically that Florentines seek office only when they can profit from it.

35. (p. 35) *Now be thou joyful . . . thou full of wisdom!:* Dante contrasts Florentine prosperity with Italy's civil disorder.

36. (p. 35) *a little sign:* Here Dante mocks Florence's claims to be the inheritor of the civic and cultural traditions of ancient Athens and Sparta (the "Lacedæmon" of l. 139).

37. (p. 35) *Reaches not what thou in October spinnest:* Florence's laws are so changeable that legislation passed in October does not last until November. Dante's own personal tragedy and exile may come into play here, since it was the political upheavals between October and November of 1301 that ultimately resulted in the downfall of the White Guelphs and Dante's exile from his native city. Line 147 ("and renewed thy members") may refer to the practice of "renewing" the government's members by alternately exiling and recalling from exile opposing political factions.

38. (p. 35) *like a sick woman . . . wardeth off her pain:* In one of Dante's most famous political metaphors, he compares the restless, strife-torn city of Florence to the tossing and turnings of a sick woman upon her bed ("her down," l. 150). It is possible that this image has been suggested by a passage in Augustine's *Confessions* VI: 16, where Augustine tosses and turns on a hard and uncomfortable bed before his conversion as his soul struggles to find peace.

CANTO VII

1. (p. 37) *"Who are you?"*: Sordello employs a plural verb in the Italian when he asks this question, as he is addressing what he thinks are two shades. When he learns of Virgil's identity, he loses interest momentarily in the Pilgrim.

2. (p. 37) *"Octavian"*: Augustus, the first Roman emperor (63 B.C.–A.D. 14), was originally named Gaius Octavius. He was responsible for the bringing the body of Virgil from Brindisi to Naples in 19 B.C.

3. (p. 37) *"I am Virgilius"*: Note that Virgil answers only for himself, even though Sordello asked who both these travelers in Antepurgatory were.

4. (p. 37) *"glory of the Latians ... Through whom our language showed what it could do"*: Sordello salutes Virgil as the glory of the Latians (meaning not the Latins but the Italians). This statement underscores the fact that the language of ancient Rome was the forerunner of modern Romance languages, including the Provençal in which Sordello wrote and the Italian that Dante employed.

5. (p. 37) *"that high sun which thou desirest"*: God is pictured as the sun, the goal that all souls in Purgatory seek, but that souls such as Virgil's in Limbo cannot hope to attain.

6. (p. 38) *"A place there is below not sad with torments"*: Virgil now describes Limbo, where he dwells with the innocent children who died without sin and the virtuous pagan writers. He tells Sordello that he has traveled through all the circles of Hell to reach the place where he now stands, fortified by "Heaven's power" (l. 24).

7. (p. 38) *"the three saintly / Virtues"*: The reference is to the three Christian, or theological, virtues of faith, hope, and charity (or love).

8. (p. 38) *"The others knew"*: While the virtuous pagans could not know the Christian virtues before Christ's redemption of mankind, they did know and practice the four cardinal virtues: justice, prudence,

temperance, and courage. These pagan virtues had insufficient power to earn them their redemption.

9. (p. 38) *"Where Purgatory has its right beginning":* That is, where Antepurgatory ends and Purgatory proper begins.

10. (p. 38) *"No fixed place . . . by night we are not able":* Sordello provides the travelers and the reader with important information about Antepurgatory: The souls there have no fixed place but wander around, not unlike the pagans in Limbo, and they are not allowed to move around by night, forcing them to rest when the sun sets.

11. (p. 38) *"this line alone":* Sordello draws a line with his finger above the travelers on the slope. As he makes clear in ll. 55–57, not only does the lack of sunlight make it difficult to progress after sundown, but darkness also seems to symbolize the impotence of the will without the light of God's grace. Sordello therefore proposes that the two travelers return to stroll around the hillside of the slope of Purgatory.

12. (p. 39) *the mount was hollowed out:* Sordello takes the Pilgrim and Virgil to what modern critics call the Valley of the Princes.

13. (p. 39) *Gold and fine silver . . . a mingled fragrance and unknown:* The Valley of the Princes is framed as a traditional "pleasance" or *locus amoenus,* a conventional image of natural beauty in classical and medieval literature. However, the colors are such that the materials described are not mere grass and flowers but precious stones, pigments, metals, and dyes. The "Indian wood" of l. 74 has been interpreted as either ebony (somewhat unlikely, given the other bright colors here), or this term could actually refer to two different objects and "Indian" and "wood" should be separated by a comma. By itself, "Indian" (*indaco* in Italian) would be the dye indigo; "wood" (*legno*) might actually refer to *lignus* in Latin, a bright purple gem. The "scarlet" of l. 73 (in the original Italian, *cocco*) may be cochineal, a bright red substance made from dried insects. Basically, the picture of Nature here is even brighter and more resplendent than a true natural setting; it resembles an illuminated manuscript or a medieval altarpiece, fresco, or window created by craftsmen or painters. In like manner, the perfumes are mingled and produce such a sweet smell that the fragrances are "unknown."

14. (p. 39) *"Salve Regina":* In the Church liturgy, this particular song to the Virgin Mary ("Hail, Queen") was usually sung at

Compline (at dusk or just after dark), an appropriate time for the souls in the Valley of the Princes to be singing such a song. The text of the song is concerned with both pilgrimage and exile, which is also appropriate, since the souls in the valley are waiting for purification and entrance into heaven.

15. (p. 39) *"He who sits highest"*: Sordello (ll. 91–136) now begins his presentation of the various princes below the travelers in the Valley. In l. 92, "Of having what he should have done neglected," he reminds us that the people gathered here, like all those we have encountered so far in Antepurgatory, have been negligent in some way.

16. (p. 39) *"Rudolph the Emperor"*: Rudolf of Hapsburg (1218–1291, Holy Roman Emperor from 1273 until his death), was the father of the "German Albert" of *Purgatorio* VI: 91–117, who neglected affairs in Italy to tend to business in Germany.

17. (pp. 39–40) *"The other . . . was Ottocar"*: Ottocar, or Otakar II, was king of Bohemia from 1253 until 1278, when he was killed in battle with Rudolf of Hapsburg near Vienna. Now the two men reside together in the Valley of the Princes. In the region Otakar governed, the River Moldau flows through Prague and enters the River Elbe, which then flows through Germany into the North Sea (ll. 98–99).

18. (p. 40) *"Winceslaus"*: After Otakar's death, his son Wenceslas II made peace with Rudolf and ruled Bohemia from 1278 to 1305.

19. (p. 40) *"the small-nosed"*: The reference is to Philip III the Bold, who was born in 1245 and ruled France from 1270 until his death in 1285. Philip was king when the French lost Sicily during the Sicilian Vespers in 1282; he died later at the siege of Perpignan, during which time his army retreated and thus "died fleeing and disflowering the lily," the symbol of France (l. 105).

20. (p. 40) *"With him that has an aspect so benign . . . the other one"*: The references are to Henry I, king of Navarre from 1270 to 1274.

21. (p. 40) *France's Pest*: Philip IV the Fair, king of France between 1285 and 1314, was the son of Philip III the Bold and married Joan, the daughter of Henry I. Dante attacks Philip IV without mentioning his name in *Purgatorio* XX: 85–96, XXXII: 148–160, and XXXIII: 34–45, and in *Paradiso* XIX: 118–120. Philip was responsible for a number of important events, including the imprisonment of Pope Boniface VIII, the persecution of the Order of the Knights Templar, and the transfer of the papacy from Rome to Avignon that began the Babylonian Captivity of the Church.

22. (p. 40) *"He who appears so stalwart . . . with that one of the manly nose":* The first figure is Peter III, king of Aragon from 1276 to 1285, who assumed control of Sicily after the Sicilian Vespers of 1282 drove the French from that island. The figure with the "manly nose" is his adversary Charles I, also known as Charles of Anjou (1226–1285), who defeated Manfredi at the battle of Benevento in 1266 (Dante refers to the battle and Manfredi in cantos III and IV). Again two enemies in life are now reconciled in death. The "cord" of l. 114 perhaps refers to the belt that a new knight took on to symbolize his virtues and good deeds.

23. (p. 40) *"The stripling":* The reference is probably to Peter III's youngest son, Pedro, who died before he came to power. Peter had three other sons: Alfonso III, who reigned as king of Aragon for six years (1285–1291); James II of Aragon, who ruled Sicily from 1285 to 1296, then became king of Aragon after Alfonso's death in 1291; and Frederick II, who was king of Sicily from 1296 to 1337. As Dante says in ll. 117–120, the sons who inherited power did not have the talents of their father.

24. (p. 40) *"Not oftentimes upriseth through the branches / The probity of man":* Dante affirms that merit or character comes not from heredity but from God, and only God may be beseeched for such qualities. Note that in Dante's day, genealogical trees were drawn with upraised branches (this is why Dante writes "upriseth") rather than with branches heading downward.

25. (p. 40) *"the large-nosed . . . inferior to its seed":* The "large-nosed" is Charles of Anjou and Pier, "who with him sings," is Peter III. Provence and Apulia grieve together (l. 126) because both passed under the rule of Charles of Anjou's son Charles II, who became king of both areas when his father died in 1285 but who was a prisoner at the time in Spain and was released and crowned only in 1289. He died in 1309. Dante also mentions Charles II in *Paradiso* XIX: 127–129. Dante is making the point that in both the cases of Charles of Anjou and of Peter III, the seed (the father) is superior to the plant (the son) that hatches from it.

26. (p. 40) *"Beatrice and Margaret / Costanza":* Beatrice of Provence and Margaret of Burgundy both were married to Charles I of Anjou, while Costanza was the wife of Peter III of Aragon. The confusing lines here point to one central fact—that parents are unable to produce decent offspring. The general comparison of wives to husbands to sons should be read more or less as follows: The sons (the plants) are inferior to the fathers (the seeds) to the same extent as Costanza boasts of her husband Peter more than both Margaret and Beatrice boast of their husband (Charles I of Anjou). Scholars generally consider this passage to be one of Dante's least successful comparisons.

27. (p. 40) *"Harry of England . . . has a better issue":* Sordello attacked Harry (Henry III, 1216–1272) as good-for-nothing in his lament for Blacatz (see note 16, canto VI), but here Dante the Poet commends the good qualities of his son Edward I, the "better issue."

28. (p. 41) *"the Marquis William . . . Make Monferrat and Canavese weep":* William VII, marquis of Monferrato and Canavese, was captured by the townspeople of Alessandria in Piedmont in 1290, locked in an iron cage, and displayed to the public until his death in 1292. His son declared war against the city, and this conflict devastated the territories of the marquis, making the land "weep."

CANTO VIII

1. (p. 43) *now the hour:* It is now the hour of dusk and of Compline, the time of day in the Church liturgy when the *Te lucis ante* of l. 13 was usually sung (see also note 5 to this canto). The bell deploring "the dying day" (ll. 5–6) would be the bell signaling the arrival of Compline.

2. (p. 43) *the new pilgrim:* Dante uses "new" in the sense that this pilgrim far from home is still homesick and not yet accustomed to being in a strange land.

3. (p. 43) *one of the souls:* The soul who calls the others to attention with a hand gesture is never identified, but its function is that of a priest directing a church service, since the souls sing a song from the liturgy.

4. (p. 43) *upon the orient:* The traditional position for prayer in Dante's time was to stand, facing east (because Christ and the sunrise were associated with each other), with raised, clasped hands.

5. (p. 43) "Te lucis ante": As we learn in l. 17, Dante expected his reader to know this famous Compline song in its entirety. Its first line *Te lucis ante terminum* ("To you before the end of day") fits the time of the singing, and the fact that the other souls join in with the unidentified soul who directs reminds us of the chanting of monks. The song is a prayer for protection from nighttime fears, fantasies, and sexual transgressions in the form of evil dreams. We shall eventually learn that the souls actually cannot sleep in Antepurgatory (unlike the Pilgrim), and thus they cannot dream or be tempted by prurient fantasies. But the song is still relevant for them, since as souls waiting for purgation, they can imitate Christians on earth who perform the same liturgical prayers.

6. (p. 43) *from my own mind:* The Pilgrim is caught up in a rapture of ecstasy as he listens to the song, but unlike his reaction to Casella's song in *Purgatorio* II, his reaction here is appropriate.

7. (p. 43) *the supernal wheels:* That is, the revolving spheres of the heavens.

8. (p. 43) *Here, Reader:* This is the first of seven addresses by the Poet to the reader in *Purgatorio*. The others are to be found in the following cantos: IX: 70–72; X: 106–111; XVII: 1–9; XXIX: 97–105; XXXI: 124–126; and XXXIII: 136–141. In this instance, the Poet invites us to go beyond the literal level of his poem to the figurative or allegorical level, especially since he claims that the veil covering the "truth" is so transparent that to penetrate to the hidden message is simple. It has been suggested that the arrival of the two angels sent to guard the Valley of the Princes (l. 26) may be linked to *Inferno* IX, where an angel arrives to open the Gates of Dis.

9. (pp. 43–44) *two Angels . . . by their verdant pinions:* In the Bible, Genesis 3: 24, Cherubim with flaming swords are sent to guard the Garden of Eden after the Fall. Various interpretations have been given for the description of the blunted swords (l. 27): They may be blunted because the enemy (represented by the serpent that will soon appear) has already been conquered (by Christ's redemption); they may be blunted because they are ineffective during the evening, when everything in Antepurgatory seems to stop; or they may be blunted because God's Mercy tempers His righteous Justice. The angels are dressed in green because in Dante's culture, green was the color of Hope, here a reference to the hope of Salvation in Christ.

10. (p. 44) *As faculty confounded by excess:* The Pilgrim can make out the blond color of the angels' hair but cannot discern the details of their faces, so excessively beautiful are they.

11. (p. 44) *"From Mary's bosom both of them have come":* The mercy of the Virgin Mary, commonly associated with Eve (the original human being whose transgression with a serpent caused humanity's expulsion from the Garden of Eden), has sent the angels. In *Paradiso* XXXII: 4–6, we encounter a vision of the Virgin Mary with Eve seated nearby, the two figures finally reconciled. The link of these two key figures in Christian history may also be seen, at least in Italy, by the suggestion in the Latin rosary's first words, *Ave Maria* ("Hail, Mary"): The word "Ave" may be transformed to the Italian word for Eve ("Eva") by re-arranging the letters in a simple fashion. Most translators render the Italian word *grembo* as "bosom"; literally, it means "lap" and implies "womb," suggesting Mary's role in giving birth to Christ.

12. (p. 44) *Utterly frozen, to the frozen shoulders:* Here, as in *Inferno* XXXIV: 22–24 when the Pilgrim first encounters Satan, the Pilgrim is frightened because he does not know which way the serpent (obviously a symbol of Satan, as it was in the Garden of Eden) will approach. The "faithful shoulders" belong to the Pilgrim's guide, Virgil.

13. (p. 44) *But not so that . . . before locked up:* The darkening air has until now obscured the Pilgrim's features and those of the soul who stares at him, but as they approach more closely, they are able to recognize each other with the bit of light that remains.

14. (p. 44) *Noble Judge Nino!:* Nino Visconti of Pisa, grandson of the Count Ugolino rendered famous by *Inferno* XXXIII, died in 1296. He was a Guelph and shared power in Pisa with his grandfather but was eventually betrayed by Count Ugolino and forced to flee the city after the count supported the Ghibelline faction. Dante could have known him personally during the time he spent in Florence. This figure provides yet another example of how linked characters in Dante's poem often meet different fates after death.

15. (p. 44) *not among the damned!:* The Pilgrim has no reason to believe that Nino is an inveterate sinner, but in general, he is surprised to discover that anyone has been saved or destined for purification.

16. (p. 44) *"How long is it . . . / O'er the far waters to the mountain's foot?":* Without sufficient light to see that Dante casts a shadow, Nino

mistakenly believes that the Pilgrim is a soul who has arrived on the angelic boat of *Purgatorio* II: 41–45.

17. (p. 44) *"am in the first life, . . . the other, going thus, I gain":* The Pilgrim refers to the fact that he is alive still as being in "the first life," and defines the second, or "other," life—eternal life in heaven—as the purpose of his journey through the afterlife.

18. (p. 44) *He and Sordello both shrank back from me:* For the first time, Sordello realizes that the Pilgrim is alive, and Nino Visconti simultaneously comes to the same realization.

19. (p. 45) *"Up, Currado . . . grace has willed!":* Nino Visconti turns to Currado Malaspina, who will be identified specifically in l. 118 of the canto, and invites him to view the Pilgrim as an example of God's inexplicable grace.

20. (p. 45) *"no ford":* God's purposes are so mysterious and so unfathomable that, metaphorically, they are like a river with no discernible crossing, or ford. Human reason cannot completely understand God's reasons. As in *Purgatorio* III: 37, Nino Visconti is willing to accept the *quia*.

21. (p. 45) *"Tell my Giovanna . . . to the innocent is made":* Born about 1291, Giovanni was Nino Visconti's daughter by Beatrice d'Este. Like the other souls in Purgatory, Nino asks only that the Pilgrim remind his loved ones to pray for him, since those prayers will shorten his time in purification; the prayers of the innocent, such as his young daughter (then around nine years of age), are especially effective.

22. (p. 45) *"laid aside her wimple white":* Wearing white bands on a black veil would be the traditional sign of mourning for a woman in Dante's day. This reference concerns the widowed Beatrice d'Este, who married Galeazzo Visconti in June of 1300, thus laying aside her mourning clothes, "her wimple white." But since Beatrice's marriage to Galeazzo took place in June, *after* the imagined date of the Pilgrim's journey in the poem, Dante must be saying that Beatrice d'Este did not actually remove this sign of mourning but only contemplated doing so. Dante the Poet is far too accurate a writer to make a mistake of chronology.

23. (p. 45) *"needs must wish again":* Here there seems to be no question that the soul is predicting hard times for his former wife, since he says she shall have use of her widow's weeds quite soon. In fact,

Galeazzo Visconti was driven from Milan in 1302, only two years after the couple's marriage, and he died in poverty. Beatrice was not able to return to Milan until much later, with the return of his son Azzo to power, and she died in that city in 1334.

24. (p. 45) *"So fair a hatchment . . . as would have made Gallura's Cock"*: The heraldic device of the Visconti family of Milan was a blue serpent devouring a red Saracen. That of the Visconti branch of Pisa, to which Nino belonged, was a cock, or rooster. Gallura was a town in Sardinia ruled by Nino's branch of the Visconti family. Thus, Nino Visconti is stating that the Milanese symbol would not have made such a fine decoration for Beatrice (perhaps on her tomb) as his own family symbol would have done.

25. (p. 45) *My greedy eyes . . . the nearest to its axle:* The Pilgrim interrupts Nino Visconti's family tale with a gaze toward the heavens and toward the Antarctic, or southern pole. Here the stars revolve the slowest, just as the part of a wheel nearest its axle seems to move more slowly than the outermost parts of the wheel.

26. (p. 45) *"those three torches"*: Most commentators agree that these three new stars represent the theological virtues (faith, hope, and charity, or love) just as the "four resplendent stars" (l. 91) that were earlier mentioned in *Purgatorio* I: 25 as "flamelets" represent the four cardinal virtues identified with pagan antiquity. The replacement of the Christian stars for the pagan stars has obvious symbolic implications here, since Christian virtues superseded pagan virtues with the advent of the Christian era.

27. (p. 45) *"Lo there our Adversary!"*: The appearance of Satan, or Lucifer, in the guise of the serpent, recalls his role in the Expulsion from the Garden of Eden (l. 99).

28. (p. 46) *not a moment loosed its gaze on me:* Although the Pilgrim has been engrossed in watching the dramatic arrival of the serpent and the counterattack of the two angels, the shade soon to be identified as Currado Malaspina (l. 118) has never moved his glance away from the Pilgrim. This underlines the fact that the event the Pilgrim sees as a dramatic threat is in reality a kind of performance that the soon-to-be-purified souls in the Valley of the Princes observe each evening. No doubt it reminds them of God's grace that has saved them from

original sin (the Fall) caused by the serpent's temptation of Eve, our first mother.

29. (p. 46) *"Valdimagra or its neighborhood"*: The Malaspina family ruled the valley of the River Magra (Valdimagra) and had an estate there called Villafranca.

30. (p. 46) *"Currado Malaspina"*: Currado II, son of Federico I, marquis of Villafranca, and grandson of Currado I, "the elder" of l. 119, was a Ghibelline who died around 1294. Giovanni Boccaccio makes him and his daughter Spina characters in *The Decameron* II: 6.

31. (p. 46) *"Your honored family"*: Dante praises the Malaspina family in ll. 121–129, no doubt because he received hospitality from this noble clan in 1306, when he was in exile.

32. (p. 47) *"for the sun shall not lie . . . course of justice standeth still"*: Currado tells the Pilgrim that the sun will not return to the constellation of the Ram (Aries) seven times (seven years) before Dante will personally experience the hospitality of the Malaspina family. Given that the fictional date of the Pilgrim's journey is 1300, in less than seven years the historical Dante will find indeed himself in exile at the Malaspina's doorstep, in 1306. The proof of this hospitality will be "nailed" in the Pilgrim's head with greater "nails" (actual experience) than the verbal reports ("another's speech," l. 138) of this family's famous hospitality. This prophecy cannot be altered because the course of justice—in this case, the course of future events as ordained by God—cannot be stopped or altered unless by God Himself.

CANTO IX

1. (p. 49) *The concubine of old Tithonus*: Based on mythical references from Virgil's *Aeneid* VI: 584–585 and his *Georgics* I: 446–447, Dante retells the legend of Aurora, the goddess of dawn, who fell in love with Tithonus, a Trojan prince, and who asked the gods to grant him immortality but neglected to ask for immortal youth as well. Consequently, he grew ever older as she rose each day from his bed to greet the dawn.

2. (p. 49) *gems*: This is a reference to a zodiacal sign; the "gems" are the stars in a constellation.

3. (p. 49) *with its tail*: This is probably a reference to the constellation of Scorpio.

4. (p. 49) *its wings:* Metaphorically, Dante implies that the night has feet measuring the hours and wings that do the same thing. Thus, two hours have passed since sunset, and a third is about to end. This would make the time about 8:30 to 9:00 P.M.

5. (p. 49) *something had of Adam in me:* Like Adam, the Pilgrim has an earthly body that requires sleep and is mortal.

6. (p. 49) *all five of us:* The five are the Pilgrim, Virgil, Sordello, Nino Visconti, and Currado Malaspina.

7. (p. 49) *of her former woes:* A shift in time takes place here, for the swallow begins to sing early in the morning just before dawn. This timing underlines the fact that the dream the Pilgrim will have is prophetic, since it was generally held that dreams in the early morning hours could tell the future. Here Dante alludes to Ovid's *Metamorphoses* VI: 412–674 and the misfortunes of Philomela, who was raped by her sister Procne's husband, Tereus. Procne avenged herself on her husband by feeding his son to him in a meal. Before Tereus could slay the two women, the gods turned all three into birds. Ovid's version notes only that Tereus became a hoopoe. Tradition following Ovid recounted that Procne became the nightingale and Philomela a swallow, the account Dante accepts here. Later, in *Purgatorio* XVII: 19–21, he refers to Procne as a nightingale and presents her as one of three examples of wrath.

8. (p. 49) *less by thought imprisoned:* Freed from ties to the body in sleep, the mind may receive the truth of prophetic visions.

9. (p. 49) *An eagle:* In his dream, the Pilgrim imagines he is being carried off by Jove, as Ganymede was carried off by Jove in the shape of an eagle to become the cupbearer to the gods. We later discover (in l. 55) that in reality, Saint Lucy is carrying the Pilgrim up the mountain while he is asleep in her arms. This dream marks the transition from Antepurgatory to Purgatory.

10. (p. 50) *the imagined fire:* In his dream, the Pilgrim anticipates the fire through which he and all purified souls must pass in canto XXVII to enter the Earthly Paradise.

11. (p. 50) *Not otherwise Achilles started up . . . Greeks withdrew him afterwards:* The Pilgrim now compares his wakening to that of Achilles as described by Statius in the *Achilleid* I: 247–250, when his mother Thetis takes him in his sleep from his tutor, the centaur Chiron, to the island

of Scyros, where Ulysses and Diomedes (Diomed) eventually involve him in the war against Troy that will result in his death. Chiron has already appeared in *Inferno* XII: 71, and Ulysses and Diomedes have appeared as false counselors in *Inferno* XXVI: 56.

12. (p. 50) *was my face:* The Pilgrim now faces east with the morning (8:00 A.M.) sun in his face on Easter Monday.

13. (p. 50) *"'I am Lucìa'":* Saint Lucy of Syracuse (the patron saint of those afflicted with eye ailments) first appeared in *Inferno* II: 97. The Pilgrim's dream was filled with allusions to classical figures who experienced rape, violence, and ultimately death, while Virgil's explanation of the reality of what he dreamed provides a far more benign and Christian explanation for his dream.

14. (p. 51) *Reader . . . marvel not thereat:* In the Poet's second address to the reader, he warns his audience that he is about to employ a more eloquent treatment of even loftier subject matter.

15. (p. 51) *Such in the face that I endured it not:* So resplendent is the angel's face that the Pilgrim could not bear its glance.

16. (p. 51) *"Tell it from where you are":* Like Cato in *Purgatorio* I, the angel challenges the two travelers in much the way a military sentinel would, warning them to stop in their tracks and answer his questions.

17. (p. 51) *"A Lady of Heaven":* That is, Saint Lucy.

18. (p. 51) *"these stairs of ours":* The significance of the three stairs described in ll. 94–102 have caused much controversy, but essentially they represent the three stages involved in the absolution from sin—contrition, confession, and penance. The specific descriptions of the steps have occasioned various interpretations: The white marble acts as a mirror to encourage self-reflection; the purple ("perse") hue of the second step probably refers to the sinner's recognition of his "broken" sinlessless; and the blood-red color probably refers to the saving blood of Christ in the Eucharist. Interestingly enough, there is no mention of the intercession of a priest in this process, suggesting that Dante's view of absolution may have contained elements of unorthodox thinking.

19. (p. 52) *a stone of diamond:* The angel sits upon an adamantine threshold, and when we learn later in l. 127 that the angel has received from Saint Peter the guardianship of this portal, the words of Matthew 16: 18 in the Bible immediately come to mind: "Thou art Peter, and upon this rock I will build my church."

20. (p. 52) *"Ask humbly that he the fastening may undo":* We have learned in *Purgatorio* I: 133–136 that Dante donned the rush of humility before ascending the mountain.

21. (p. 52) *three times I smote:* In the act of contrition, worshipers of Dante's day would have struck their breasts, pronouncing the Latin words *mea culpa, mea culpa, mea maxima culpa.*

22. (p. 52) *Seven P's:* P is from the Latin *peccatum* ("sin"). Each of the seven deadly sins will be purged in Purgatory before souls are prepared to enter the kingdom of heaven.

23. (p. 52) *Ashes . . . Of the same color:* The angel is dressed in ashen-gray garments, the color (like that of earth) associated with penitence, humility, and also with Ash Wednesday, the beginning of Lent, the period of time spent in repentance before Easter.

24. (p. 52) *two keys:* These are the two keys mentioned by Christ in the Bible, Matthew 16: 18–19. He gives them to Saint Peter as the source of papal authority, with the power to bind and unbind in heaven and on earth.

25. (p. 52) *More precious one is, but the other needs / More art and intellect ere it unlock:* The more precious (golden/yellow) key may represent the power to absolve, while the less precious (silver/white) key may symbolize the knowledge the priest requires to perform the actual act of absolution. This explains why the silver key is tried first, for the priest may err in his judgment and the door will not unlock. However, God prefers a generous priest to one who is hesitant to forgive, "err / Rather in opening than in keeping shut" (ll. 127–128).

26. (p. 53) *"forth returns whoever looks behind":* Here the angel refers to the classical story of Orpheus, who rescued Eurydice from the Underworld but lost her when he turned around to look at her. This is also a reference to the biblical account in Genesis 19: 26 of Lot's wife, who looked back at the destruction of Sodom and Gomorrah and turned into a pillar of salt.

27. (p. 53) *And when upon their hinges . . . it remained:* This learned simile refers to the loud, grating sound the doors of the Roman treasury on the Tarpeian Rock of the Capitol in Rome made when Julius Caesar crossed the Rubicon in 49 B.C. and looted the treasury, in spite of the efforts of Metellus the tribune (one of Pompey's allies) to prevent this. Dante found this story in Lucan, *Pharsalia* III: 153–168.

28. (p. 53) "Te Deum laudamus": "We praise Thee, O God," a famous hymn in Dante's times, was perhaps first sung during the baptism of Saint Augustine by Saint Ambrose.

29. (p. 53) *Exactly such an image rendered me ... with the organ stand:* Even though the grating of a metal door might seem to produce a harsh, rather than sweet, sound, the Pilgrim states that his mind is divided between the "thunder-peal" (l. 139) of the doors and the meaning of the words that are being sung, just as it is sometimes difficult to understand the meaning of the words in a hymn accompanied by loud organ music. In Dante's time, major cathedrals were just beginning to be equipped with organs.

CANTO X

1. (p. 55) *the perverted love of souls disuses:* Dante believes that love is the force behind all human action, and that the threshold of Purgatory is infrequently used ("disuses," l. 2) because most humans pervert the object of their love and end as sinners, following the crooked way that always seems to be the easiest path. Significantly, in *Inferno* V: 20, Dante describes the doorway into Hell as extremely wide ("the portal's amplitude"), while he characterizes this path by its narrow width.

2. (p. 55) *I heard it closed again:* The Pilgrim knows by sound only that the portal to Purgatory has closed behind him and his guide. He heeds the warning of the angel not to look back or be disqualified from entering Purgatory.

3. (p. 55) *a rifted rock:* The path is actually an undulating, zigzag way through a rocky cleft.

4. (p. 55) *the moon's decreasing disk:* In *Inferno* XX: 127, the Poet noted that the moon was full on Thursday evening. Now, on Monday morning, it is about several hours after sunrise, since in *Purgatorio* IX: 44 the Pilgrim awakes before the gate just after 8 A.M., when the sun was more than two hours high. Thus, it should be around 9 A.M. now, and the moon is still visible in the sky.

5. (p. 55) *that needle's eye:* The travelers find themselves on a deserted ledge. That the space is described as a "needle's eye" reminds us of Christ's words to His disciples in the Bible, Matthew 19: 24: "It is easier for a camel to pass through the eye of a needle, than for a rich man to enter into the kingdom of God."

6. (p. 55) *both of us uncertain:* Since Virgil has never traveled this path, he is as uncertain of his way as the Pilgrim is.

7. (p. 55) *three times told would measure:* The width of the terrace from the inner rock wall to the outer edge is about three times the length of a human body, between 15 and 18 feet.

8. (p. 56) *sculptures . . . put to shame:* In *Purgatorio,* one of Dante's main themes is the description of works of art—a technique known in Greek as *ekphrasis* and employed by both Homer and Virgil and other epic poets to great effect. In this terrace, the relief sculpture will illustrate examples of the virtue of humility. This divine art work puts to shame the great classical sculpture of Polycletus, a contemporary of Phidias (c.452–412 B.C.), whose works Dante had never seen but had read about in various sources (Aristotle, Cicero, Pliny, and Quintilian). Even Nature herself (l. 33) has been outdone by the divine artwork.

9. (p. 56) *The Angel:* The first relief sculpture represents the famous scene of the Annunciation, in which the Angel Gabriel tells the Virgin Mary that she will give birth to the Son of God.

10. (p. 56) *its long interdict:* Heaven had been closed to mankind from the Fall of Man and the expulsion from the Garden of Eden until the death of Christ.

11. (p. 56) *"Ave":* In Latin, this word means "Hail." It is Gabriel's first word to Mary in Luke 1: 28.

12. (p. 56) *turned the key:* By giving birth to Christ, Mary unlocked heaven for mortal sinners.

13. (p. 56) *"Ecce ancilla Dei":* This, in Latin, is Mary's humble reply to the Angel in Luke 1: 38: "Behold the handmaid of the Lord."

14. (p. 56) *as distinctly . . . in wax:* Even though there is no sound issuing forth from these mute sculptural images, the impression of the art is so perfect that Mary can be "seen" to be speaking, just as a seal makes an image upon hot wax.

15. (p. 56) *Upon that side where people have their hearts:* That is, on Virgil's left.

16. (p. 56) *The cart and oxen:* The second image of humility, described in lines 55–69, refers to the Bible, 2 Samuel 6: 14–23. It shows King David ("the humble Psalmist," l. 65) dancing before the ark of the covenant as he brings it into Jerusalem, while Michal (l. 68), King Saul's daughter, is angered by his dancing. "One dreads an office not appointed" (l. 57) refers to Uzzah, who was struck dead when he tried to steady the shaky ark to keep it from falling. In one of his Latin letters (*Epistolae* XI), Dante defends himself from a similar charge of interfering in Church affairs, declaring that while Uzzah touched the holy ark, Dante only wants to guide the oxen pulling the cart. The fact that David was unafraid to dance for joy, even revealing his naked body as a sign of his humility before God's will, makes him an exemplum of humility. The arrogance of Michal links her to its opposite vice; in fact, she was rendered sterile for her pride.

17. (p. 57) *another story:* in ll. 71–93: The third scene depicts a great act of humility by the Roman Emperor Trajan (ruled A.D. 98–117). Legend claims that on his way to battle Trajan stopped and answered the pleas of a widow who had lost her son in his service. The legend appears in a life of Saint Gregory written in the ninth century by John the Deacon and was often repeated in devotional literature and paintings.

18. (p. 57) *Gregory:* Saint Gregory the Great (born c.540; pope 590–604) was widely believed by legend to have recalled Trajan to life from Hell so that he might repent (this would be Gregory's "greatest victory," l. 75). Saint Thomas Aquinas even discusses this belief (*Summa theologica* II, Suppl. Q 71 a.5 ad 5), suggesting that Trajan's punishment might have been only postponed. But Dante will place Trajan's soul in Paradise (*Paradiso* XX: 43–45), just as in *Paradiso* XX he also places other pagans he considers virtuous—Virgil, Cato, Statius, and Ripheus—in locations in the afterlife that orthodox Christians would find objectionable or impossible.

19. (p. 57) *He who on no new thing:* The reference is to God, to whom nothing can be seen anew since He sees everything eternally and has created this "visible language" (l. 95), so marvelous that it causes the viewer, the Pilgrim, to hear mysteriously the words spoken in the mute marble scenes.

20. (p. 57) *images of such humility:* The presentation of the first three images on this terrace set up the system of presentation on the other terraces. First, the Pilgrim encounters examples of virtues that

are the opposite of the vice condemned and purified (these reliefs have portrayed examples of humility, the opposite of pride); then he will encounter examples of the vice itself (see *Purgatorio* XII: 25–63).

21. (p. 58) *"but rare they make / Their steps":* While the Pilgrim is caught up in admiring the artwork, his guide directs his attention to the slowly moving group of penitents, the proud.

22. (p. 58) *But still I wish not, Reader ... beyond the mighty sentence:* In this third address to his readers, the Poet reminds us that even though the punishments in Purgatory do not seem so different from those in Hell, the penitents do not suffer for eternity and eventually gain salvation.

23. (p. 58) *"what cometh underneath those stones":* Both Virgil and the Pilgrim have difficulty in distinguishing between the penitent souls and the massive stones they are forced to balance on their shoulders.

24. (p. 58) *"how each is stricken":* The penitents are beating their breasts as a sign of repentance, although it is not clear how they can do this and balance huge boulders on their shoulders. (See a further description of their shape in ll. 130–135.)

25. (p. 58) *we are worms ... in which formation fails!:* The Poet compares human beings to worms or caterpillars capable of becoming butterflies if they so will it. Clearly it is much easier to remain a worm than to be transformed into a butterfly—that is, it is much easier for man to sin than to be transformed by penitence into something more angelic. One question that arises from this presentation of a sin being purified is whether or not the Pilgrim himself recognizes his own guilt. Pride was the original sin, and the historical Dante was certainly never accused of great humility. But so far, the Pilgrim has only observed the suffering of others and has not experienced it himself.

26. (p. 58) *In place of corbel, oftentimes a figure:* Here Dante offers a realistic image to describe the proud. They resemble the corbels, or capitals, shaped like crouching figures, called telamones, that are very common in Romanesque and Gothic buildings. They seem to be straining to hold up the weight of the building, just as the penitent proud hold up their rocks with great difficulty.

27. (p. 59) *he who had most patience:* Even the most resigned of the sinners who are being purified of their pride suffer the maximum pain.

CANTO XI

1. (p. 60) *"Our Father":* In ll. 1–24 of this canto, the prayer uttered by the penitent proud is an expanded version of the two versions of the Lord's Prayer in the Bible, Matthew 6: 9–13 and Luke 11: 2–4.

2. (p. 60) *"Praised be thy name . . . By every creature":* This seems to be a reference to the famous prayer by Saint Francis of Assisi, the *Laudes creaturarum*, also known as the *Cantico di frate Sole* ("Canticle of Brother Sun").

3. (p. 60) *"our daily manna":* Dante has changed the "daily bread" of the Lord's Prayer in the Bible, Luke 11: 3, to "manna." Also in the Bible, in the Book of Exodus, manna is a symbol of God's grace that enables the Israelites to survive the journey out of Egypt. Dante underlines this link with his mention of the "rough wilderness" in l. 14.

4. (p. 60) *"the old Adversary":* The reference is to Satan. In *Purgatorio* VIII: 95, the serpent threatening the Valley of the Princes is called "Our Adversary."

5. (p. 60) *"Not for ourselves is made, who need it not":* Even though the penitent proud are being punished severely, they know that eventually they will be saved. Therefore, they humbly address their prayers to God not on their own behalf but for the sake of those who remain behind them on earth and who are still capable of repenting of their arrogance and pride before their deaths.

6. (p. 61) *good furtherance:* The word translated by Longfellow in this fashion is, in the original Italian, *ramogna*. Scholars have hotly disputed its precise meaning and origin; it may mean something like the valediction one extends to a traveler on his journey—Godspeed, good journey, good return, stay safe.

7. (p. 61) *of which we sometimes dream:* Here the Poet compares the stones weighing down the penitent proud to the sense of suffocation under an enormous weight that one may have in a dream.

8. (p. 61) *the smoke-stains of the world:* The thick mist of sin that must be purged away.

9. (p. 61) *a good root to their will . . . unto the starry wheels!:* Those whose wills are rooted in good are in a state of grace. Once again the Poet urges his readers to pray for the souls in Purgatory so that, cleaned and purified, they may pass through the spheres of the planets and fixed stars to be with God in the Empyrean.

10. (p. 61) *"Ah! so may pity and justice . . . Point us out that which least abruptly falls":* Virgil addresses the penitent proud to show the way to him and to the Pilgrim, appealing to their desire to complete their purgation so that their souls can take flight toward God.

11. (p. 61) *the burden / Of Adam's flesh:* Just as the penitent proud are crushed by weight, the Pilgrim bears the weight of mortality.

12. (p. 61) *not manifest from whom they came:* The response to Virgil's request for directions seems to come from no particular individual— perhaps appropriate for people trying to live down their arrogance in life.

13. (p. 61) *"Him, who still lives":* The reference is to the Pilgrim.

14. (p. 61) *"A Latian was I":* The speaker, identifying himself in l. 67 as Omberto Aldobrandeschi, says he is an Italian (in Longfellow's translation Latian usually means Italian, not Latin). Omberto was killed in 1259 while fighting against the Sienese Guelphs as he defended one of the Aldobrandeschi fortresses at Campagnatico (l. 66). He was the son of Guglielmo Aldobrandeschi (l. 59), count of Santafiore (a town previously mentioned in *Purgatorio* VI: 111).

15. (p. 61) *"were ever with you":* That is, were ever known to you (the address is to both Virgil and the Pilgrim).

16. (p. 62) *"the common mother":* Perhaps this is a reference to Eve, from whom all mankind is descended (and therefore none have any right to claim arrogant pride of birth over others) or to earth (in which case the lesson of humility is the same).

17. (p. 62) *"to such extent / I died therefore":* One account of Omberto's death has him surrounded by overwhelming odds and charging into the midst of his superior enemies, merely to show his contempt and scorn for them—a reflection of his arrogant pride of birth.

18. (p. 62) *Listening I downward bent:* As we shall subsequently learn in *Purgatorio* XIII: 136–138, Dante himself suffered from pride, and his bent position here is a tacit admission that he requires purgation of this sin in the Afterlife.

19. (p. 62) *"art thou not Oderisi":* Oderisi da Gubbio (d. 1299) was apparently an acquaintance of Dante's. Oderisi was the son of Guido da Gubbio (alternatively Agobbio), his last name referring to the town near Perugia in Umbria from which he and his family came. He was a manuscript illustrator who worked in Bologna and was allegedly hired by Pope Boniface VIII to illuminate papal manuscripts in the Vatican library in Rome. In the story of Giotto in his *Lives of the Artists*, Giorgio Vasari cites ll. 79–84 from this canto of *Purgatorio*.

20. (p. 62) *"in Paris called illuminating?"*: While the Italian word for illustrating manuscripts is *miniare* (a reference to *minio*, or cinnabar, a red pigment frequently used to color the pages of manuscripts), Dante's original Italian employs another term, *alluminare*. This verb is based upon the French term *enluminier* and stresses light rather than any particular color. Obviously, Oderisi must have studied the French style of manuscript illustration.

21. (p. 62) *"Franco Bolognese"*: Very little is known of this other illustrator except for the lines Dante has written here. Bolognese is primarily important because his contemporary fame in 1300 allows Oderisi to demonstrate the humility he has learned after years of false pride in his art, for he defers to the skill of Franco without hesitation.

22. (p. 62) *"And yet I should not be here . . . turned to God"*: Oderisi explains that he repented before he died, therefore shortening his time in Antepurgatory. If he died in 1299, as most scholars believe he did, he reached the first terrace, where the proud are purified, quite quickly.

23. (p. 62) *"How little green . . . an age of grossness!"*: Earthly fame endures for only a brief time, unless one's renowned life is followed by a period of ignorance and lack of achievement. In other words, an artist may remain famous only if no good artists succeed him.

24. (p. 62) *"In painting Cimabue . . . now Giotto has the cry"*: Florentine artist Giovanni Cimabue (c.1240–c.1302) broke out of the old Byzantine style and began the development of artistic realism in late medieval art. His pupil Giotto di Bondone (c.1266/67–1337) continued to develop pictorial realism in Italian fresco and altarpiece painting and was considered by Giorgio Vasari to be the greatest painter of his day. Dante may well have known Giotto personally. His verses here do not necessarily imply that he ranks Giotto above Cimabue, but clearly Cimabue was once the rage, and now Giotto is. The point the Poet makes is about the vainglory of earthy prominence, not necessarily a relative ranking of painting styles.

25. (p. 63) *"So has one Guido from the other taken"*: Now the Poet gives an example of how passing fame obscured the renown of successive

artists by citing the case of Guido Guinizzelli (c.1225–1276), whose fame in poetry was eclipsed by that of Guido Cavalcanti (1259–1300). Guido Cavalcanti has already been mentioned in *Inferno* X: 63, when the Pilgrim meets his father, Cavalcante de' Cavalcanti.

26. (p. 63) *"and he perchance / Is born"*: Now the Poet suggests that some poet and some artist now alive will steal both Guido Cavalcanti's literary renown from him and Giotto's artistic renown. Most commentators believe that the genius who might eclipse them is none other than Dante himself, an example of the very pride for which the penitents here are being purified. Fame, as the Poet remarks in ll. 100–101, is just a changeable wind, constantly blowing now this way, now that way.

27. (p. 63) *"the* pappo *and the* dindi"*: This is baby talk for bread (*pane*) and money (*denaro*). Lines 103–105 ask the rhetorical questions: Would you have more fame if you died at a ripe old age than if you died when you used baby talk? For that matter, what are ten centuries (a thousand years) to eternity but the "twinkling of an eye" (l. 107)? The point again is that fame is simply a passing, ephemeral thing.

28. (p. 63) *"the circle that in heaven wheels slowest"*: A thousand years is only the blink of an eye compared with the time required for the heaven of the fixed stars (the eighth heaven) to make one turn from west to east. It was calculated that this rotation moved at the speed of one degree per 100 years, so a total circle took 36,000 years.

29. (p. 63) *"With him"*: Line 121 will identify this figure that Oderisi points out to the Pilgrim as Provenzan Salvani (c.1220–1269), a Ghibelline from Siena who, after the victory of the Ghibellines over the Guelphs at the battle of Montaperti in 1260, advocated that the city of Florence be razed to the ground against what was the winning advice of Farinata degli Uberti not to do so (see *Inferno* X). Salvani was eventually taken prisoner by the Florentines and beheaded, and Dante uses him as an outstanding example of pride in political power.

30. (p. 63) *"The Florentine delirium"*: This is a reference to the battle of Montaperti.

31. (p. 63) *"great tumor"*: Pride was traditionally depicted as a swelling up, like that of a tumor.

32. (p. 63) *"Remains below there and ascends not hither"*: That is, remains below in Antepurgatory and not in Purgatory proper, where the

Pilgrim is now standing. In ll. 127–132, the Pilgrim wonders how it is possible that Provenzan died in 1269 and is already in Purgatory, when souls in Antepurgatory generally spent a time there equal to their lifespan. Since Provenzan was thirty-one years old, without prayer (the "good orison" of l. 130), the Pilgrim calculates that he should not yet have arrived. Oderisi's third speech (ll. 133–138) addresses this question.

33. (p. 64) *"Freely upon the Campo of Siena . . . to draw his friend from the duress"*: Oderisi recounts the story of how Provenzan humbled himself by begging in the Campo, the public square of Siena, to ransom a friend held by Charles of Anjou after his friend had been captured at the battle of Tagliacozzo. Thus, Provenzan had at least one moment in his life when he subdued his famous arrogance and humbled himself for a friend, and the act is now rewarded in Purgatory.

34. (p. 64) *"Yet little time shall pass . . . thou canst gloss it"*: Just as Provenzan humbled himself, Dante will have humility forced upon his own proud character when the Florentines exile him in a few years' time.

35. (p. 64) *"This action has released him from those confines"*: This line would seem to imply that because of his act of humility, Provenzan skipped Antepurgatory altogether.

CANTO XII

1. (p. 65) *Abreast, like oxen going in a yoke:* As Oderisi and the Pilgrim have been walking together, the Pilgrim has been bending low so that he can hear and see Oderisi better (therefore participating, in a sense, in Oderisi's punishment for pride). Dante may also use the image of oxen because they are generally reputed to be mild, humble animals.

2. (p. 65) *Upright, as walking wills it . . . downcast and abated:* When the Pilgrim resumes his normal position, his thoughts remain focused upon the punishments of pride. He obviously feels this sin relates to his own character, and the recognition weighs down upon him psychologically.

3. (p. 65) *"Cast down thine eyes . . . bed beneath thy feet"*: After encountering the positive examples of humility, Virgil now directs the Pilgrim to gaze upon the negative examples of pride that will be carved into the path ("the bed") upon which he is walking. Casting down one's eyes, in a person as proud as Dante must have been, would be an appropriate

attitude of humility. Virgil notes that walking in this location with downcast eyes also makes the Pilgrim's way easier and more secure ("to alleviate the way," l. 14).

4. (p. 65) *Above the buried dead:* It was common during the Middle Ages for important people to be buried under the floors of churches as close to the altars as possible. Paving stones carved on the floor recalled the honored dead to their friends and relatives, and here relief carvings on the path achieve the same effect. Like the carvings on the walls of the mountain the Pilgrim and Virgin encountered in canto XI, the divine art here surpasses normal human talent ("but of a better semblance / In point of artifice," ll. 22–23).

5. (p. 65) *one who was created noble:* The reference is to Satan, the most beautiful and important of the angels, who rebelled against God out of pride. The relief carvings in the floor contain thirteen examples of the sin of pride and its fatal consequences. In the original Italian, Dante creates an acrostic with ll. 25–63. The first letters of the first lines of the first four tercets begin with the letter V; the next four tercets begin with the letter O; the next four tercets begin with the letter M. These twelve tercets form the acrostic series that spell out VVVVOOOOMMMM, forming the Italian word *uomo* ("man"). In the last, or thirteenth, tercet, the three letters are all employed. Naturally, recreating this acrostic in the English translation would be virtually impossible.

6. (p. 66) *Briareus:* This giant who challenged the Olympian gods and was burned beneath Mount Etna for his troubles is a classical counterpart to the rebellious angel Lucifer. Dante has already mentioned him in *Inferno* XXXI: 98, but there Virgil prevented the Pilgrim from actually seeing Briareus.

7. (p. 66) *Thymbræus, Pallas saw, and Mars:* The three figures named here are not exemplary figures of pride but are three gods (Apollo, indicated by the epithet Thymbraeus; Minerva, by the epithet Pallas; and Mars) who observed the defeat of the giants that rebelled against the Olympian gods.

8. (p. 66) *Nimrod / As if bewildered:* Already mentioned in *Inferno* XXXI: 77–81, this figure (according to the Bible, Genesis 10: 8–10 and 11: 1–4) was instrumental in building the Tower of Babel on the plains of Shinar. He is "bewildered" (l. 35) because no one understands his language.

9. (p. 66) *O Niobe!:* The wife of Amphion, king of Thebes, boasted of being superior to Latona, because she had seven sons and seven daughters while Latona only had one son and one daughter. Those two, however, were special: Apollo and Diana. To punish Niobe's arrogant pride, Apollo killed the seven sons, while Diana did the same with the seven daughters. Niobe was turned to stone but continued to cry tears through her marble cheeks. Dante's source for this account is Ovid's *Metamorphoses* VI: 182–312.

10. (p. 66) *O Saul!:* Niobe's biblical counterpart is Saul, the first king of Israel whom Samuel deposed for disobeying God's command and who fell upon his sword in Gilboa out of pride rather than be captured by the victorious Philistines (see 1 Samuel 15 and 1 Samuel 31). No rain or dew fell on that spot because of David's subsequent curse on the place where Saul killed himself (see 2 Samuel 1: 21).

11. (p. 66) *O mad Arachne!:* Arachne presumptuously challenged Minerva to a weaving contest and apparently won, but Minerva destroyed her work, and Arachne tried to hang herself. Minerva loosened the rope and turned it into a web and Arachne into a spider. Dante's source is Ovid's *Metamorphoses* VI: 1–143.

12. (p. 66) *O Rehoboam!:* This son of Solomon was selected to become king of Israel but his pride caused ten of the twelve tribes of Israel to rebel, resulting in the death of his tax collector, Aduram. Rehoboam fled cowardly to Jerusalem without even being pursued. The story is told in the Bible, 1 Kings 12: 1–19.

13. (p. 66) *Alcmæon:* As reported in Statius' *Thebaid* IV: 187–213, the soothsayer Amphiaraus foresaw that he would die in the attack upon Thebes and concealed himself to avoid this fate. But his wife, Eriphyle, was bribed with a golden necklace ("the luckless ornament," l. 51) to reveal her husband's hiding place and Amphiaraus was forced to go to war, where he knew he would die. Before Amphiaraus left, he asked his son, Alcmaeon, to take revenge, and Alcmaeon eventually killed his mother. Since the necklace was fashioned by the god Vulcan, lusting after such a divine artifact was an act of pride. Dante mentions Alcmaeon again in *Paradiso* IV: 103–105 as an example of filial piety toward one's father.

14. (p. 66) *Sennacherib:* This king of Assyria (704–681 B.C.) made war upon the Israelites, mocking their god and faith. Sennacherib was

killed by two of his sons while worshiping. (See the Bible, 2 Kings 19: 35–37 and Isaiah 37: 36–38.)

15. (p. 66) *Tomyris:* After Cyrus (c.560 B.C.–529 B.C.), founder of the Persian Empire, killed the son of Tomyris, queen of the Scythians, Tomyris defeated his army. Cyrus was killed and then decapitated, his head placed into a container of human blood. Tomyris was reputed to urge Cyrus to drink his fill of the blood. Dante's sources are Paulus Orosius' *Historiae adversus paganos* II: vii: 6 and Herodotus' *The History* I: 112–114.

16. (p. 66) *Holofernes:* According to Judith 13: 1–20 in the Apocrypha of the Bible, Judith decapitated this Assyrian general because of his arrogance and his mockery of the Hebrew god. When his troops saw the severed head of their general, they fled in terror. The story of Judith and Holofernes later became a popular theme for artists that was particularly well expressed in a statue by Donatello as well as in subsequent Renaissance and Baroque paintings.

17. (p. 66) *Troy . . . discerned:* The final tercet mentioning Troy, or Ilion (l. 62), contains a summary of the acrostic, employing the three letters in a single tercet (see note 5 to this canto). Troy was considered to be an exemplum of overweening pride brought down to grief.

18. (p. 68) *of pencil master was or stile:* Here the Poet refers to a pencil used for sketches and a style (a sharp-pointed instrument) employed for engraving: The pencil provides shading for the work of art, while the style creates the images carved in relief.

19. (p. 68) *Now wax ye proud . . . Ye sons of Eve:* The Poet uses sarcasm to admonish the so-called "sons of Eve," by which he refers to all of humanity, meaning the opposite of what he says.

20. (p. 68) *the mind preoccupied imagined:* Absorbed by the sight of the floor carvings, the Pilgrim has lost track of the passage of time.

21. (p. 68) *the sixth handmaiden:* As Virgil notes the arrival of an angel who will eventually erase one of the seven *P*s on the Pilgrim's forehead and pronounce a benediction upon him, he also tells us the time of day by referring to the sixth hour of the day (noon) as "the sixth handmaiden." Since it was around 9:00 A.M. during the last time signal the reader received, in *Purgatorio* X: 13–16, some two to three hours have passed on this terrace of pride.

22. (p. 68) *the tremulous morning star:* That is, Venus.

23. (p. 68) *At this announcement . . . a little wind? :* There is some debate about who speaks in ll. 94–96: the Angel of Humility or the Poet? Longfellow's punctuation (as he places the quotation marks, the angel's remarks end at l. 93) implies that Dante the Poet and not the angel speaks here. Other modern commentators take the words to be spoken by the angel. We believe the passage makes more sense if it is construed as Longfellow reads it.

24. (p. 68) *smote upon my forehead with his wings:* In this manner, we learn subsequently (ll. 118–135) that the Angel of Humility has removed the *P* from the Pilgrim's forehead.

25. (p. 70) *As on the right hand . . . the high rock grazes:* In these lines, Dante compares the ascent to the next level of Purgatory to the climb up to the site of the church of San Miniato al Monte in Florence, reached by crossing the Rubaconte Bridge (now the Ponte alle Grazie) over the Arno. The Rubaconte Bridge was named after a city official, Rubaconte di Mandelli, who laid the first stone for it. The path Dante describes up to the church no longer exists, since those stairways were there only when Florence was well governed ("in the age / When still were safe the ledger and the stave," ll. 104–105). The reference to "the ledger and the stave" point to scandals among public officials who were corrupted to keep improper records and to use false measures, and Dante's contemporary readers would have immediately recognized these scandals. The ledger scandal involves the destruction of a page from the city's public records to cover up fraud, while the stave scandal notes how a public official tampered with the proper weights of salt to keep a stave of every bushel for himself and was beheaded for his crimes. The present stairway to San Miniato al Monte was built several centuries after the stairway described by Dante was removed.

26. (p. 70) "*Beati pauperes spiritu*": Beginning with l. 110, a version of a beatitude attributed to Jesus will be cited on each of the next six terraces ("Blessed are the poor in spirit," from the Bible, Matthew 5: 3, is the one that begins here). Appropriately, this beatitude praises the humble of spirit.

27. (p. 70) *far more easy:* Even though the Pilgrim continues to have corporeal weight, he now feels lighter after the purification of pride, which was associated with weight.

28. (p. 70) *I found but six the letters:* Because he is unable to see the

*P*s on his forehead, the Pilgrim learns only from Virgil's remarks in ll. 121–126 that one has been erased by the Angel of Humility. Virgil's remarks also imply that the removal of the *P* of pride has also caused the other *P*s to become fainter (l. 122), since pride is such an archetypal sin. The Pilgrim makes the kind of gesture that a child might make; he counts the remaining *P*s on his forehead as if he is a schoolboy counting numbers with his fingers. Such a humble metaphor is appropriate for a Poet whose overweening pride has been purified during the process of traveling through the first terrace of Purgatory.

CANTO XIII

1. (p. 71) *which ascending shriveth all:* The original Italian of l. 3 contains a verb, *dismalare,* that Dante probably invented to mean "dis-evil," or to distance one from evil.

2. (p. 71) *its arc more suddenly is curved:* As the mountain is ascended, each circular terrace becomes smaller (the mirror image of what occurs in Hell as one descends). Since the entire mountain has seven terraces cut out of it, it resembles a large circular stairway winding around a constantly narrowing peak.

3. (p. 71) *Shade is there none, nor sculpture:* The terrace is at first empty of any penitents, and no carvings are apparent.

4. (p. 71) *the livid color of the stone:* Not only are there no stone carvings here, but the color of the stone is not the white marble of the terrace of pride. Instead, the stone is "livid," the color of a bruise. This dark blue or purple color is associated with the sin purified in this terrace, envy.

5. (p. 71) *the left part of himself about:* Before uttering his prayer to the sun (ll. 16–21), Virgil turns toward the sun's light for guidance. Here, it seems that this request for guidance to the sun should be taken literally—as merely a request for light, since no one has yet turned up to assist the travelers on their way.

6. (p. 72) *spirits uttering:* Instead of carvings, on this terrace disembodied voices render audibly positive examples of the virtue of Generosity, or Charity, the opposite of envy.

7. (p. 72) "Vinum non habent": "They have no wine" is a line taken from the story of the marriage feast of Cana in the Bible, John 2: 3. Mary tells Jesus that there is no wine for the guests,

setting the stage for the miracle of turning the water into wine. It is appropriate that this first example of charity is associated with the Virgin.

8. (p. 72) *"I am Orestes!"*: The second example of the virtue of charity, as opposed to envy, is from classical antiquity (as usual, Dante combines biblical and classical examples). Orestes' friend Pylades declared that he was Orestes in order to save his friend from execution, according to the account Dante might have found in Cicero's *De Amicitia* VIII: 24 or his *De Finibus* V: xxii: 63. The speaker here might be Pylades and not Orestes, although the point of the story is that both friends declared "I am Orestes!"

9. (p. 72) *"Love those from whom ye have had evil!"*: This is a loose version of the admonition spoken by Jesus during the Sermon on the Mount, as reported in the Bible, Matthew 5: 44.

10. (p. 72) *"This circle scourges / The sin of envy . . . The bridle of another sound shall be"*: For the first time, Virgil identifies this terrace as that purifying the sin of envy. More important, he also explains something of how Purgatory works with the image of the "scourge," or whip, and the "bridle." The soul being purified is first encouraged to imitate the positive virtue first with the scourge, then discouraged from imitating negative vice with the bridle. Virgil correctly judges that the Pilgrim will hear the "bridle," or the negative illustrations, just before they reach the angel with the blessing at the Pass of Pardon before heading to the third terrace.

11. (p. 72) *shades with mantles:* Because the mantles worn by the penitent envious are very close in color to that of the rocks themselves, Virgil and the Pilgrim discern their shapes only with great difficulty.

12. (p. 72) *"Mary, pray for us!" . . . "Michael, Peter, and All Saints!"*: These words come from the Litany of the Saints, often recited around Easter.

13. (p. 72) *And as unto the blind . . . will not quiet stay:* The Poet first pictures the penitent envious with the sackcloth costumes typical of the beggars or mendicant orders of friars who are forced to beg alms at churches and who, like groups of blind men, assist each other to find their way. The comparison of the envious to blind men becomes appropriate when we learn of their punishment in l. 70. As they were incapable of appreciating the good fortune of others in life and looked at them in hopes of seeing them not do well, their eyes are sewn shut. Unlike the young hunting birds whose eyes are temporarily sewn shut with thread while they are taught docility by their trainers, the envious have their eyes shut with iron wire.

14. (p. 74) *Well knew he what the mute one wished to say:* Here Virgil reads the Pilgrim's mind (the Pilgrim is "the mute one") and grants permission to him to interrogate the souls he encounters. Virgil will not speak again until almost the end of the next canto, in *Purgatorio* XIV: 143.

15. (p. 74) *by no border 'tis engarlanded:* Virgil takes a position on Dante's right, toward the outside rim of the terrace where there is no guardrail, described here by the Poet as a garland. Virgil does so to protect the Pilgrim from a possible fall.

16. (p. 74) *through the horrible seam / Pressed out the tears:* Many commentators have noted that in Dante's time, the etymology of the word *invidia* ("envy") was explained by connection with sight, or *videre* ("to see"). The envious looked at others with the hope of not seeing them do well. Thus, following the system of punishments in Hell, the *contrapasso* (or as Longfellow translates the word, the "counterpoise") punishments in Purgatory are often reflections of the sin in some manner. They may mirror the actual sin or may establish an ironic contrast to that sin. Here, the eyes of the envious are sewn shut but not so tightly that their penitent tears cannot still flow. (For a discussion of this conception of *contrapasso*, see the "Introduction" [pp. xxxi–lxi and note 16 to *Inferno* XXVIII: 142, the specific line where the term "counterpoise" is first used] in the companion edition of Longfellow's *Inferno*, edited by Peter Bondanella, New York: Barnes & Noble, 2003.) It is important to remember that when the Pilgrim first sees the envious, he participates in their punishment by reacting with tears: "Drained was I at the eyes by heavy grief" (l. 57).

17. (p. 74) *"the scum / Upon your consciences":* In the Pilgrim's address to the envious, he asserts that their sin is a stain on their consciences and serves to block the passage of "the river of the mind," the River Lethe, that the Pilgrim has already encountered in *Inferno* XIV: 130–138. This river of forgetfulness becomes one of the two streams from which the Pilgrim must drink in the Earthly Paradise toward the end of this canticle. By wishing that the penitent envious may receive

God's grace speedily to dissolve the scum of sin from their consciences so the Lethe may flow more freely, the Pilgrim is simply saying that he hopes they will speedily reach the Earthly Paradise and complete their purification.

18. (p. 75) *"each one is citizen / Of one true city":* In Hell and even in Antepurgatory, the Pilgrim consistently sought out members of his own city or language group, and his encounters with these familiar figures were often filled with civic and patriotic references of a nationalistic character. Now, in Purgatory proper, the Pilgrim is rebuked by a yet-to-be-named soul being purified of envy who implicitly corrects this manner of thinking, stating that in Purgatory, souls are all citizens of one city. A citizen of Italy is redefined as only a temporary pilgrim in Italy, since such geographical, political, cultural, or linguistic definitions are now irrelevant.

19. (p. 75) *like a blind man:* The blind frequently raise their chins in order to hear better.

20. (p. 75) *"recleanse":* Longfellow accepts the original Italian word as *rimondo* ("recleansing" or "purifying"), while some contemporary editors of Dante's text after Longfellow maintain that the word should be *rimendo* ("mending" or "stitching up"), a choice that would be in keeping with the picture of eyes sewn shut that dominates the canto's imagery.

21. (p. 75) *"Sapient I was not, although I Sapìa":* Sapìa was a woman from Siena born around 1210, the aunt of Provenzan Salvani, mentioned in *Purgatorio* XI: 121–142. After the battle of Colle Val d'Elsa in 1269, where Provenzan was captured and decapitated by the victorious Florentine Guelphs and their allies, apparently Sapìa gave much of her wealth to a hospital that she and her husband founded in Siena in 1265. According to the story she tells about herself here, she hated her fellow citizens of Siena and was jealous of her nephew Provenzan's prominence to such an extent that she actually rejoiced in the sight of his death and her native city's defeat on the battlefield. Note the play on words with "sapient," meaning "wise," and the woman's name.

22. (p. 75) *"Colle":* Today called Colle di Val d'Elsa, this Tuscan town in the valley of the River Elsa near San Gimignano is about 15 miles from Siena. Sapìa was probably in a family castle near the plain on which the battle was fought.

23. (p. 75) *"Crying to God . . . As did the blackbird at the little sunshine"*: Earlier, in l. 117, Sapìa seems to have impiously linked her own desires to that of God's will; now she recalls that she was so glad to see the demise of her nephew and her fellow townspeople after the battle that she blasphemed, no longer caring about her salvation. Early commentators explained the reference to the blackbird and the first rays of sunshine after a cold winter by noting that the blackbird was reputed to be deathly afraid of cold but upon the first signs of good weather would cackle and act arrogantly, as if spring had arrived permanently. Basically, this is yet another image of the arrogance and foolishness of those being punished in Purgatory, one particularly appropriate after the report of Sapìa's impious outburst of envious joy.

24. (p. 75) *"Peace I desired . . . in remembrance held me"*: In spite of her sins, Sapìa turned to charitable work, such as leaving money to a hospital, in her old age to expiate her mortal sins. But she emphasizes that these good works would not have been sufficient to discharge her debt (l. 126) and advance her through Antepurgatory rapidly if it weren't for the prayers said on her behalf after her death.

25. (p. 75) *"Pier Pettignano"*: Literally, the name means Peter the Combseller; he was regarded as a holy hermit of the Franciscan Order. He died in 1289 and was subsequently venerated in Siena as a saint. Sapìa must have died before 1289, since she received the benefit of some years of intercessory prayers this figure offered for her salvation.

26. (p. 76) *"Mine eyes"*: In his reply to Sapìa's question about his purpose for being in Purgatory, the Pilgrim (and therefore the Poet) admits that he has been guilty of pride (l. 137 speaks of the "torment underneath"—that is, in the terrace of pride, below that of envy) and expects to spend a good deal of time being punished with the weight of those rocks. On the contrary, the Pilgrim maintains that his eyes have been very little affected by envy.

27. (p. 76) *"Well with my kindred reinstate my fame"*: Once again, as is typical in Purgatory, Sapìa encourages the Pilgrim to ask her relatives and loved ones to pray for her. She is particularly impressed by the special dispensation he has received to journey through the afterlife, as expressed in l. 146, "that great sign it is God loves thee."

28. (p. 76) *"Who hope in Talamone . . . the admirals will lose"*: Sapìa's final words to the Pilgrim contain references to two obscure events in Sienese civil life: In 1303 Siena, which is inland, purchased the seaport of Talamone, hoping to build a fleet to rival that of Genoa or Pisa, but this plan was foiled by silt in the harbor and the malaria-ridden territory surrounding the city. The Sienese also spent an enormous amount of money searching for an underground river they named Diana. Both projects were total failures. The final reference to admirals must surely be Sapìa's comic reference to the citizenry of Siena, who hope to be admirals with a fleet and a harbor that will never be built. Of course, this closing tercet raises the question of whether Sapìa continues to suffer from the envy for which she has been condemned, since the tone of her rebuke of the foolishness of her fellow citizens seems close to her joy over their defeat in battle reported earlier. But here, in spite of Sapìa's sharp tongue, it is more likely that her words are meant to serve as a warning to her fellow citizens to avoid the pitfalls that will result from their civic pride.

CANTO XIV

1. (p. 77) *"Who is this one":* This canto opens with two blind souls whose conversation with the Pilgrim occupies almost the entire canto, from here to l. 126. However, as there is no immediate identification of a change in speaker, the reader naturally assumes that Sapìa continues to speak. The identities of the Pilgrim's two new interlocutors remain unclear until l. 81 (Guido del Duca) and l. 88 (Rinier da Calboli). It is also clear from some of their remarks that they are still fighting the effects of envy. For example, in l. 1 they describe the Mountain of Purgatory as "our" mountain, and in l. 3 they both seem irritated that the Pilgrim passes through the terrace of pride with his eyes unsewn and "opes and shuts them at his will."

2. (p. 77) *held supine:* Again the blind and penitent envious raise up their faces to speak to the Pilgrim in an exaggerated fashion, trying to compensate for their lack of sight with this unnatural position.

3. (p. 77) *"A streamlet that is born in Falterona":* This peak in the Tuscan Apennines is the origin of the River Arno, which is so closely identified with the Tuscan towns of Arezzo, Florence, and Pisa.

4. (p. 77) *"my name as yet makes no great noise":* Although the Pilgrim

seems here to demonstrate that he has learned the lesson of humility in the first terrace, he also lets it be known that he expects to achieve great fame in the future.

5. (p. 78) *"The Alpine mountain whence is cleft Peloro":* Dante refers to the Apennines as a single mountain chain that extends from Mount Falterona in the north, where the Arno begins, to the northeastern end of Sicily, where the mountain called Pelorus was supposedly cut off, or "cleft," from the mainland when the Strait of Messina was formed.

6. (p. 78) *"To where it yields itself in restoration . . . dry up":* From the mountains to the sea near Pisa, the River Arno replaces with its waters the moisture the sun dries up, and in turn this moisture falls again into the mountains where the Arno begins. However, this process of natural restoration cannot be said to characterize the inhabitants near the river, for in ll. 37–54, Guido del Duca elaborates on the corrupt nature of them all.

7. (p. 78) *"Circe had them in her pasture":* In Homer's *Odyssey* X: 133–150, the daughter of Perse and Helios, god of the sun, enchanted men and turned them into animals. In Dante's view, the inhabitants of the Arno valley in Tuscany have all become brutish.

8. (p. 78) *"ugly swine":* This phrase probably refers to the castle of Porciano (the Italian of this line is *brutti porci*) in the Casentino district, where the Arno begins its journey. Members of the Conti Guidi family lived here (Guidoguerra, one of the Conti Guidi, is mentioned in *Inferno* XVI: 38, while three brothers of this clan are mentioned in *Inferno* XXX: 77). Dante expected his readers to recognize all the locations, which are today known largely for being mentioned in his poem.

9. (p. 78) *"Curs findeth it thereafter . . . disdainfully their muzzle":* Next in its downward journey, the Arno reaches the city of Arezzo, identified with dogs—the motto of the city referred to a small dog that could nevertheless capture a wild boar. Even so, the word Dante employs for "curs" is *botoli*, and early commentators associated the term with yapping dogs with little bite. The river then diverts toward Florence in the northwest, as if it desired to turn its "muzzle" away from the snarling (but powerless) curs of Arezzo.

10. (p. 78) *"the dogs becoming wolves . . . misadventurous ditch":* The yapping but ineffectual dogs of Arezzo now become ravenous wolves. This is Dante's way of denoting his fellow Florentines, famous for

their avaricious ways. Likewise, the river becomes a cursed ditch by the time it reaches his native city.

11. (p. 78) *"the foxes so replete with fraud"*: Dante associates the inhabitants of the city of Pisa with the wily behavior of the fox, concluding a virtual bestiary of Tuscans along the River Arno.

12. (p. 78) *"another hears me"*: This is probably a reference to the Pilgrim, but older commentators believed that Guido del Duca (as yet unnamed) was referring to Rinier da Calboli (also unnamed at this point).

13. (pp. 78–79) *"Thy grandson I behold . . . 'tis not re-wooded"*: Guido del Duca's prophecy concerns the grandson of Rinier, Fulcieri da Calboli, who became famous for his cruelty against the White Guelphs (Dante's party) and the Ghibellines while he was *podestà* of Florence, in 1302–1303. His actions resulted in the deaths or torture of many of his opponents. Florence is turned into a "dismal forest" (l. 64) as the result of Fulcieri's butchery, and the region will not be "re-wooded" for a thousand years. The *"dismal forest"* of l. 64 recalls the "forest dark" of *Inferno* I: 2, the image that opens *The Divine Comedy*.

14. (p. 79) *disturbed and sad:* As befits a penitent, Rinier is saddened by the prophecy of the atrocious crimes that will be committed by his grandson several years after the fictional date of 1300.

15. (p. 79) *"To do for thee what thou'lt not do for me"*: When asked for his identity, Guido del Duca reminds the Pilgrim that he has not given his own name.

16. (p. 79) *"I Guido del Duca am"*: Very little is known of this character, who derives his fame from mention in Dante's poem. Contemporary documents reveal some bare facts. Apparently he was from Ravenna and was a judge in Rimini in 1199; he appears to have been an ally of the Ghibelline Pier Traversaro (mentioned in l. 98) and was driven out of the town of Bertinoro by the Guelphs in 1218. He was still alive in 1249, as at least one document attests.

17. (p. 79) *"such the straw I reap"*: While Sapìa of canto XIII rejoiced in the misfortunes of others, Guido was envious of the good fortunes of others. As a result, and metaphorically, rather than reaping wheat (the result of brotherly charity), he reaped its opposite, straw. This biblical notion is best expressed by Saint Paul in Galatians 6: 8.

18. (p. 79) *"Where interdict of partnership must be"*: In this line, which means "Where sharing must be forbidden," Dante implies the use of

some legal terminology (*divieto di consorzio*) that forbade holding office at the same time with other family members. In *Purgatorio* XV: 44-45, the Pilgrim will ask for an explanation of these words, and Virgil will provide him with a long response in XV: 46–75.

19. (p. 79) *"This is Renier"*: Rinier da Calboli, a Guelph from the city of Forlì in the Romagna, was *podestà* of Faenza, Parma, and Ravenna. Involved in the complicated internecine struggles between Guelphs and Ghibellines in the Romagna, he seized and lost power several times until he was finally killed in 1296 while trying to recapture the city of Forlì. In 1276 Guido da Montefeltro (whom the Pilgrim encounters in *Inferno* XXVII) besieged his stronghold of Calboli and destroyed its castle.

20. (p. 79) *" 'Twixt Po and mount . . . and the Reno"*: This phrase describes the boundaries of Romagna: its boundaries are the River Reno, to the west of Bologna; the River Po, flowing into the Adriatic sea to the north, near Ravenna; the Adriatic itself, to the east; and the hills of the Apennines, to the south.

21. (p. 79) *"For all within these boundaries . . . now would they diminish"*: Guido now balances his attacks upon the evils he associates with Tuscany and embarks on listing many noble and chivalrous men from Romagna (ll. 97–111). They would probably have been well known in Dante's times, as they all lived between the last part of the twelfth century and the thirteenth century. However, all are dead at the time of the poem, and their demise marks the end of a noble era from the past. The noble garden referred to metaphorically as chivalrous Romagna here is now destroyed by "venomous roots."

22. (p. 80) *"Where is good Lizio"*: In lines 97–111, Guido lists the individuals he just mentioned. Lizio da Valbona was a Guelph who lived in the first part of the thirteenth century and fought with Rinier at Forlì. Arrigo Mainardi was a Ghibelline from Bertinoro who was apparently alive as late as 1228. These two figures are characters in Boccaccio's *The Decameron* V: 4, so they must have been relatively well known. Pier Traversaro (c.1145–1225) was a major Ghibelline from Ravenna and an ally of Guido del Duca, whose son Paolo became a Guelph. Guido di Carpigna died around 1283 and was a Guelph supporter and *podestà* of Ravenna in 1251. Fabbro is probably Fabbro de' Lambertazzi, a leader of the Bologna Ghibellines who died in 1259. Bernardin di Fosco

played an important role in the defense of Faenza against the Emperor Frederick II in 1240 but later may well have sided with the Ghibellines, since he was *podestà* of Pisa in 1248 and Siena in 1249. Bernardin was of very humble origin, as l. 102 implies. Of Guido da Prata there is little known, but he seems to have been involved with the politics of Ravenna in the first half of the thirteenth century. Ugolino d'Azzo was a member of the important Ubaldini family of Tuscany, other members of which are recalled in *Inferno* X: 120 (Cardinal Ottaviano degli Ubaldini); *Inferno* XXXIII: 14 (Archbishop Ruggieri degli Ubaldini); and later in *Purgatorio* XXIV: 29 (Ubaldino della Pila). Ugolino married the daughter of Provenzan Salvini (*Purgatorio* XI: 121). Frederick, or Federico, Tignoso was a nobleman of Rimini believed to have lived in the first half of the thirteenth century. "Tignoso" actually means "mangy," a nickname used as a term of endearment because of his blond hair. He had a reputation for generosity and hospitality. The Traversaro clan was a powerful Ghibelline family from Ravenna (its most important member was the Pier Traversaro, listed above), while the Anastagi was another Ghibelline family of Ravenna. By 1300, the time of the Pilgrim's journey, both families had virtually disappeared, as l. 108 asserts. Boccaccio includes members of both the Traversaro and the Anastagi families in a story in *The Decameron* V: 8.

23. (p. 80) *"The dames and the cavaliers":* This nostalgic passage commemorating a lost chivalric past was later imitated by Ludovico Ariosto (1474–1533) to begin his epic poem, *Orlando furioso*.

24. (p. 80) *"O Brettinoro . . . to beget such Counts!":* Interrupting the list of honorable men from the Romagna who have disappeared, Guido del Duca now lists four towns of the area. Brettinoro (today Bertinoro), located between Forlì and Cesena, was supposed to be famous for its hospitality, and since such hospitality has been abandoned, the town might just as well disappear. It was Guido's birthplace. Bagnacavallo, located between Imola and Ravenna, was the home of a powerful Ghibelline family, the Malvicini, but by 1300 that family was almost extinct. Castrocaro, near Forlì, was once a castle controlled by the Ghibelline counts of Castrocaro, but after 1300, it was controlled by the Guelph Ordelaffi family of Forlì. The counts of Conio owned this Guelph stronghold located near Imola, but the castle was apparently destroyed after 1295. Guido del Duca concludes that

such families would do well to discontinue procreation, since they have bred only offspring unworthy of their noble past.

25. (p. 80) *"the Pagani, when their Devil":* This Ghibelline family was from Faenza, and Dante focuses upon one of their clan, "their Devil," Maghinardo Pagano da Susinna. He died in 1302 and took part in the French occupation of Florence in November 1301 by Charles of Valois. In *Inferno* XXVII: 50, Guido da Montefeltro refers to this figure as the Lioncel ("little lion") of the white lair, since his coat of arms bore a blue lion on a white field. He was remarkable for supporting the Ghibellines in Romagna on one side of the Apennines and the Guelphs in Tuscany on the other side. Maghinardo Pagano da Susinna is the only figure still alive in 1300 when the Pilgrim hears Guido del Duca's diatribe about the long-gone, good old days in Romagna.

26. (p. 80) *Ugolin de' Fantoli:* Ugolino de' Fantolini was a Guelph who served as *podestà* of Faenza on several occasions and who died in 1278. Both of his sons died before 1300, so Guido can truly say that his family name cannot be soiled any further by unworthy descendants.

27. (p. 80) *"But go now, Tuscan . . . my mind distressed":* Just as the Pilgrim has very little good to say in *The Divine Comedy* about Florence or the Tuscans, Guido emphasizes that he, a Romagnol, has spoken badly about his own people.

28. (p. 80) *They made us of our pathway confident:* Guido and Rinier fall silent. The Pilgrim and Virgil interpret this to mean they are following the right path, since they would have expected one of the two to correct them if they had taken the wrong direction.

29. (p. 80) *Thunder . . . A voice:* The negative examples of envy being punished are presented as voices, just as they were in *Purgatorio* XIII: 25–27, but now the voice is a thunderclap.

30. (p. 81) *"Shall slay me whosoever findeth me!":* This is a version of the words uttered by Cain in the Bible, Genesis 4: 14, after the murder of Abel, but God marked Cain so that no one would harm him. Cain is the archetypal example of envy.

31. (p. 81) *As soon as hearing had a truce from this:* That is, as soon as the sound of thunder faded.

32. (p. 81) *"I am Aglaurus, who became a stone":* Another thunderclap introduces the second example of envy. Out of jealousy, Aglauros, the daughter of the king of Athens, attempted to thwart a meeting between her sister, Herse, and Mercury and was turned into stone as punishment. Ovid, *Metamorphoses* II: 798–833, is the source.

33. (p. 81) *I backward, and not forward:* Longfellow follows a text that reads *in dietro* ("backward") rather than the *in destro* ("to the right"). Virgil and the Pilgrim always move to the right in climbing up the Mountain of Purgatory.

34. (p. 81) *"That was the hard curb . . . or call":* In *Purgatorio* XIII: 40, Dante spoke of the "bridle" that reins in mankind, and now he mentions another analogy with riding a horse, the "hard curb," or rein, that is designed to restrain mankind with its bit. But as Virgil notes, men swallow the bait proffered by the "old Adversary," or Satan (l. 146), and swallow his hook, thus allowing Satan to reel them in. Neither the bridle or God's "call" is sufficient to prevent men from sin. In Italian, the technical term Dante employs for "call" is *richiamo*, a whistle used to recall a falcon (metaphorically understood as the human soul) back to its master (metaphorically understood as God). The falcon imagery sends the reader back to the image of the souls on the terrace of the envious who have their eyes stitched shut like newly caught falcons (*Purgatorio* XIII: 70–72). In *Purgatorio* XIII: 37–42, Virgil described the scourge or whip, promising the Pilgrim that the rein or bridle will be heard from later, as it is here with the voices illustrating the punishment of envy. The Poet will return to this imagery again in *Purgatorio* XIX: 62–69.

35. (p. 81) *"is looking on the ground":* In spite of mankind's ability to gaze upon the miraculous visions in the heavens, it continues to focus on terrestrial concerns.

CANTO XV

1. (p. 83) *As much as . . . and 'twas midnight here:* Lines 1–6 contain yet another circumlocution to tell the reader the time of day. Basically, the Poet informs us that it is midafternoon, 3:00 P.M., in Purgatory and midnight in Italy, where he is writing ("here").

2. (p. 83) *As when from off the water, or a mirror . . . From falling of a stone in line direct:* Dazzled by the light from the radiance of an angle, the Poet now describes in ll. 16–24 how the ray of light is refracted: The light ray falls down and bounces up and under the Pilgrim's hand (l. 14) that is shading his eyes, so that angle of reflection is equal to the angle of incidence.

3. (p. 84) *"Soon will it be . . . delightful to thee"*: Virgil promises the Pilgrim that he will eventually be able to gaze upon such celestial radiance from an angel without turning his eyes away.

4. (p. 84) *"stairway far less steep than are the others"*: Because the Pilgrim is gradually shedding the symbolic *P*s on his brow, indicative of the seven deadly sins that must be removed from any penitent soul before the ascent to the top of Purgatory, the stairway to the third terrace of wrath is less steep than that to pride and envy. The angel (called variously by commentators the Angel of Charity, of Mercy, or of Generosity) thus introduces the Pilgrim and Virgil to the terrace where humility, or meekness—the opposite of wrath—is displayed and then the vice of wrath is punished. Three ecstatic visions of meekness will eventually be displayed in canto XVI, followed by three examples of wrath punished in canto XVII. The delay in moving through these cantos is caused by a long conversation between the Pilgrim and Marco Lombardo in canto XVI.

5. (p. 84) *"Beati misericordes"*: The Latin text of the fifth beatitude from the Sermon on the Mount in the Bible, Matthew 5: 7, translates as "Blessed are the merciful." This line is followed by an Italian expression that Longfellow renders as "Rejoice, thou that o'ercomest!" that may reflect the conclusion of the beatitudes in Matthew 5: 12 or may also be a word of encouragement from the angel. If these words are spoken by the angel, they probably accompany the act of removing another *P* from the Pilgrim's brow. The reader learns that this has been done only in l. 80, where we finally discover that Dante now lacks the *P* of envy, just as the earlier *P* of pride had been removed by the touch of an angel's wing.

6. (p. 84) *"What did the spirit of Romagna mean, / Mentioning interdict and partnership?"*: The Pilgrim now asks Virgil for an explanation of the puzzling lines in *Purgatorio* XIV: 86–87 spoken by Guido del Duca, "O human race! why dost thou set thy heart / Where interdict of partnership must be?" Note in l. 42 that it is now the Pilgrim and not his guide who thinks about self-improvement during their journey and speaks of "some profit to acquire from words of his."

7. (p. 84) *"Because are thither pointed your desires . . . Envy doth ply the bellows to your sighs"*: Virgil basically argues that earthly goods cannot be enjoyed by sharing, because sharing lessens their value to mankind (the "you" implied in "your desires" [l. 49] is plural, referring to mankind in general). Basically, Dante believes in a zero-sum economic universe: One man's gain is another man's loss. Thus, men covet what others have and suffer when they see others thrive. Heavenly goods, it will be argued later, operate in exactly the opposite fashion, for they increase when shared with others. The bellows image points to the inflation of the chest in its breathing that is typical of such sins as pride or anger.

8. (p. 84) *"the supernal sphere"*: This is the Empyrean, the ninth heaven in the Ptolemaic universe outside the stars where God resides; it is the realm that makes the other heavens revolve. It is only there that sharing increases the value of goods (ll. 54–57), and it is only there that the fear of the good fortune and prosperity of others does not decrease one's happiness, since sharing increases the quantity of love.

9. (p. 84) *"How can it be . . . if by few it be possessed?"*: The Pilgrim's desire to learn is strong, but his capacity to grasp the meaning of Virgil's explanation remains weak. He is too much caught up in the earthly and essentially selfish view of possession.

10. (p. 85) *"As to a lucid body comes the sunbeam"*: Virgil implies that light attracts light or, perhaps more precisely, like attracts like.

11. (p. 85) *"Thou shall see Beatrice . . . this and every other longing"*: This is the third time Beatrice appears by name in *The Divine Comedy* (the first two mentions were in *Inferno* II: 70 and 103), and it is clear that Virgil believes she knows more about theology than he does. Lines such as these have often moved commentators to identify Virgil with human reason and Beatrice with theology.

12. (p. 85) *"As are the two already"*: Virgil advises the Pilgrim to concentrate upon removing the last five *P*s from his forehead, and it is this line that informs the reader that the second *P* has been removed by the angel (see note 5 to this canto).

13. (p. 85) *in a vision / Ecstatic on a sudden I was rapt:* When the Pilgrim visited the terrace of the proud, carvings presented the examples of humility and appealed to his sense of sight; in the terrace of the envious, disembodied voices presented examples of charity and appealed to his sense of hearing. Now inner visions that appeal to the Pilgrim's conscience on the terrace of the wrathful will present examples of meekness or gentleness (the Italian word is *mansuetudine*), the opposite of wrath or anger. The fact that the visions are described as "ecstatic"

and that the Pilgrim is "rapt," or in rapture, imply that he is literally transported out of his body to witness the visions in question.

14. (p. 85) *And at the door a woman . . . had disappeared:* The first vision (ll. 86–93) is that of the Virgin Mary accompanied by Joseph. As told in the Bible, Luke 2: 40–50, they find Jesus teaching in the temple and treat him as the twelve-year-old-child he is then and not the Son of God he will become: They scold him for sneaking off during the visit to Jerusalem during Passover.

15. (pp. 85–86) *Then I beheld another . . . "if he who loves us be by us condemned":* The second vision of gentleness (ll. 94–105) comes from an account by Valerius Maximus in his *Facta et dicta memorabilia* (5:1) and concerns the Athenian tyrant Peisistratus (sixth century B.C.) The tyrant's wife urged him to put to death a youth who was in love with their daughter and who had dared to kiss her in public. Peisistratus was reported to have asked what he should do with those who hated him if he were to put to death those who loved him. Line 98 refers to the myth of the naming of Athens: Both Athena and Poseidon wanted to name the city but the gods selected Athena, who had offered the olive tree as a gift, which was considered much more useful than Poseidon's gift of a spring. A version of this story is found in Ovid's *Metamorphoses* VI: 70–82.

16. (p. 86) *Then saw I people hot in fire of wrath . . . as unlocks compassion:* The third and final vision of gentleness (ll. 106–114) concerns the death of Saint Stephen, the first martyr (or protomartyr), as reported in the Bible, Acts 7: 54–59. Stephen was slain outside the gates of Jerusalem by Jews who believed he had blasphemed. While it seems easy to forgive Jesus and the youth in the first two visions Dante presents, it is difficult to forgive this wrathful crowd.

17. (p. 86) *Soon as my soul had outwardly returned . . . Did I my not false errors recognize:* Lines 115–117 tell us that since the Pilgrim did not witness these visions with his physical eyes, from the physical perspective they are "errors." But they are not "false," since they are true depictions of events and reflect a subjective inner reality that is as true to the soul as "things external" are from a physical perspective.

18. (p. 86) *"What ails thee . . . one whom wine or sleep subdues":* As usual, Virgil's task is to spur the Pilgrim on in his journey. The guide compares the effect of the Pilgrim's visions on him to a drunk or a person overcome by sleep.

19. (p. 86) *"from me would not be shut / Thy cogitations, howsoever small"*: Virgil seems to be claiming that he can read the Pilgrim's thoughts, but it is not clear here or anywhere else in *The Divine Comedy* that he can actually do so.

20. (p. 87) *"But asked it to give vigor to thy feet"*: Here Virgil reports that he understands the Pilgrim has experienced a series of visions, but now he must spur him on his journey once again.

21. (p. 87) *athwart the twilight peering*: It is now nearing 6:00 P.M., the hour of Vespers, and although Virgil and the Pilgrim have covered only "more than half a league" (l. 121), they have walked for approximately three hours (see ll. 1–6) since the canto opened.

22. (p. 87) *by slow degrees a smoke approached*: This black smoke will engulf the travelers and the penitents during the entire next canto and is a visual metaphor for anger and wrath.

CANTO XVI

1. (p. 89) *Darkness of hell*: The smoke of anger is so dense and bitter that for the first time in Purgatory, we are in a place that recalls Hell—a place with no light from either the moon or the stars.

2. (p. 89) *Nor to the feeling . . . For not an eye it suffered to stay open*: Presumably, the Pilgrim's eyes are forced shut by this acrid, deadly smoke that causes the skin to feel as if it were being scratched by a rough cloth from a garment (l. 6). The fact that the Pilgrim is forced to share the punishment of the penitent wrathful underscores his moral failures in this area as well, and he will participate in the purgation with the rest of the souls he encounters on this terrace. Virgil no doubt remembers the righteous indignation that the Pilgrim expressed in *Inferno* VIII: 37–42 when he attacked his enemy Philippo Argenti, an act of which Virgil approved. Virgil may recognize the thin line between righteous indignation and wrath or intemperance that exists in Dante's character.

3. (p. 89) *"Agnus Dei" their exordium was*: This prayer, part of the mass since the seventh century, consists of a single line repeated twice (*Agnus Dei, qui tollis peccati mundi, miserere nobis*, or "Lamb of God, who takest away the sins of the world, have mercy on us"), followed by a third line in which the last phrase *miserere nobis* is replaced by *dona nobis pacem* ("grant us peace"). As such, this is an appropriate prayer for the penitents of wrath.

4. (p. 89) *So that all harmony appeared among them:* Anger is a sin that separates and divides, so the emphasis here is upon unison and harmony, a fact that is underscored by the monotony of the prayer.

5. (p. 89) *the knot of anger:* In general, sin may be represented as a knot, because it binds human free will; the loosening of a knot provides an image for purgation. In Dante's original text, the Poet uses Latin and employs a technical theological term, *iracundia*, the equivalent of the Italian word *ira* ("anger") here.

6. (p. 90) *Thou didst by calends still divide the time?:* The yet-to-be identified speaker in the midst of the thick smoke is invisible to the Pilgrim, as the Pilgrim is invisible to him. But the speaker senses the Pilgrim is mortal and therefore that he tells time by the ordinary calendar and does not measure time as the penitents do. They tell time by the standards of eternity, since it is not the amount of time spent in Purgatory but rather the strength of their contrition that matters. According to the Roman calendar, the "calends" is the first day of each month.

7. (p. 90) *by a voice:* This voice will prove to be that of a man named Marco Lombardo (see note 11 to this canto).

8. (p. 90) *"Thou shalt hear marvels":* The Pilgrim offers the unidentified soul a reward if he will follow the two travelers. He is hoping for directions, as is made clear in l. 30, where Virgil requests that the Pilgrim ask "if on this side the way go upward."

9. (p. 90) *"With that swathing band ... infernal anguish":* This "swathing band," *fascia* in the original Italian, refers to the human body that separates from the soul after death. In general usage, the word refers to the swaddling clothes with which infants are wrapped. The "marvels" (l. 33) are now revealed to be the news that the Pilgrim is traveling as a mortal through the afterlife and that he has already passed from Hell ("came I through the infernal anguish").

10. (p. 90) *"By method wholly out of modern usage":* Here the Pilgrim is declaring that he has been the only mortal man to ascend to heaven

since Saint Paul did it centuries ago, as told in the Bible, 2 Corinthians 12: 1–7. (See also *Inferno* II: 32: "I not Aeneas am, I am not Paul.")

11. (p. 90) *"Lombard was I, and I was Marco called"*: Very little is known about this figure, and Dante's line doesn't offer much help: It leaves open the question of whether the soul is to be considered Marco, a man from Lombardy, or whether his actual name is Marco Lombardo. Some scholars identify him as a man from Venice, while others believe he was living in France and that the term "Lombard" in this line would simply mean that he came from Italy. (During Dante's times, Italians were often called Lombards outside of Italy.)

12. (p. 90) *"now unbent his bow"*: Marco declares that he sought excellence and virtue, but given the decadence of current times, no one any longer aims at such a lofty target.

13. (p. 90) *First it was simple, and is now made double / By thy opinion*: The Pilgrim is vexed by doubt, literally "bursting / Inly with doubt" (ll. 53–54). His first doubt was raised by the words of Guido del Duca in *Purgatorio* XIV: 37–53, where he heard that the entire valley of the River Arno was corrupted. His doubt is now doubled by Marco's assertion in ll. 47–48 that the entire world is totally corrupted.

14. (p. 91) *"For one in the heavens, and here below one puts it"*: The Pilgrim demands to know whether evil and corruption are caused by the influence of the stars or by causes within men themselves. This is a central question for Dante to resolve if he is to assert mankind's free will in accepting or rejecting God's grace and salvation.

15. (p. 91) *that grief forced into Ai!*: As a penitent guilty of wrath, it is appropriate that Marco's irritated or angry response should be repressed and forced into the sound "ai!" (*uhi* in Italian).

16. (p. 91) *"and sooth thou comest from it!"*: Marco informs the Pilgrim that if he asks such a question, he obviously comes from the world that is blind to the real causes of "iniquity" (l. 60). In other words, Marco is not terribly impressed by the Pilgrim's intelligence at this point.

17. (p. 91) *"Ye who are living . . . to a better nature"*: In ll. 67–129, Marco addresses a number of important philosophical and theological topics. In ll. 67–78, he reaffirms that the stars do not control everything. Otherwise men would not have free will (l. 71), nor would there be any purpose in rewarding good and punishing evil (l. 72). The stars do influence mankind and may initiate human actions, but they do not cause all of our actions (l. 74). The individual must struggle against the negative effects of the stars, since he has free will from God, and if "well 'tis nurtured" (l. 78), like a healthy plant, this will grow stronger. The "greater force" of l. 78 refers to the superior power of God, to whom man is ultimately subject.

18. (p. 91) *"Hence . . . true spy":* In the tercet of ll. 82–84, Marco concludes his first argument in defense of free will and announces that he will expand this argument ("will now be thy true spy").

19. (p. 91) *"Forth from the hand of Him . . . turn not aside its love":* Marco maintains in ll. 85–93 that God creates the individual souls in each human being as completely innocent but requiring guidance. The soul is a tabula rasa ("that nothing knows," l. 88) but is easily tempted to anything that gives it pleasure.

20. (p. 91) *"Hence it behoved laws":* Marco now returns in l. 94 to deal with the problem of moral leadership in the secular world. A king or ruler is required at least to see the "true city" of God (heaven) from afar and to provide "guide or rein" (l. 93) to help mankind make the proper choices to reach that city. The "true city" will eventually be defined in *Purgatorio* XXXII: 102: "that Rome where Christ is Roman."

21. (p. 91) *"The laws exist":* As noted in *Purgatorio* VI: 88–90, the Roman Emperor Justinian set up the laws necessary to govern mankind, but these laws are ignored because the Church prevents them from taking effect. Marco's political views are thus resolutely Ghibelline in ideology.

22. (p. 92) *"Can ruminate, but cleaveth not the hoof":* Jewish dietary laws outlined in the Bible, Leviticus 11: 3, permitted the consumption of animals that chewed their cuds and had cloven hooves. According to medieval allegorical interpretations of this passage, the cud-chewing refers to thoughtful pondering or meditation, while the cloven hoof symbolizes the making of distinctions. The shepherd of l. 98 is obviously the pope (at the time it was Dante's hated Boniface VIII). Marco seems to say here that while Boniface is capable of understanding the laws, he is incapable of keeping temporal and spiritual power separate (that is, he "cleaveth not the hoof"). This is not one of Dante's most felicitous metaphors.

23. (p. 92) *"Wherefore the people . . . and farther seeketh not":* Since the shepherd (the pastor or guide; in this case the pope) seeks only material goods, and the unguided flock is attracted to the same goods, the people follow his example like sheep.

24. (p. 92) *"And not that nature is corrupt in you":* Marco's argument concludes that human nature is not depraved but that worldly depravity is caused primarily by lack of temporal leadership, which the Church has corrupted.

25. (p. 92) *"Rome . . . / Two suns to have":* According to Marco, who is a mouthpiece for the Poet here, once Rome had two separate but equal powers—the two suns of pope and emperor. Thus, Marco rejects the contemporary argument in favor of papal supremacy that defined the pope as the sun and the emperor as the moon, receiving only reflected light from the sun. It is not entirely clear when this perfect balance between secular and temporal power actually existed, but it was probably before the Donation of Constantine in the fourth century that supposedly gave temporal power to the Church. Dante's views on this subject are set out in his Latin treatise *De Monarchia* (see especially III: 10), a book that was attacked by orthodox Catholic thinkers after his death and that remained on the Index of Prohibited Books for centuries thereafter.

26. (p. 92) *"think upon the grain . . . each herb is recognized":* Marco focuses upon the image of grain, reminding the Pilgrim of Jesus' remarks in the Sermon on the Mount, as told in the Bible, Matthew 7: 16–17. Every tree is known by its fruit, according to Jesus, just as each herb is recognized by its seed, according to Marco.

27. (p. 92) *"laved by Po and Adige":* This is a reference to the Lombardy region of Italy. Marco is adding another region to those that have already been mentioned as being lost to corruption: Tuscany, especially the valley of the River Arno, and the Romagna.

28. (p. 92) *"Before that Frederick had his controversy":* While Dante had questions about the personal life of Emperor Frederick II (1194–1250) and places him in the realm of the heretics in Hell (*Inferno* X: 119), he had quite different and positive ideas about him as a political ruler and a man of enormous culture. Frederick's "controversy" was his intense political struggle during his reign (1212–1250) with a succession of popes, from Honorius III and Gregory IX to Innocent IV. In

Dante's view, the Church caused this struggle by usurping temporal power away from the empire.

29. (p. 92) *"True, three old men are left"*: While Frederick II reigned, Lombardy and the area watered by the Adige and Po Rivers boasted gentility and social order, but now the laws have been so corrupted that only three honest men remain in the area; Marco names them in the following lines. In *Inferno* VI: 73, Ciacco told the Pilgrim that only two just men remained in Florence. He doesn't identify them, but perhaps he was referring to Dante and another individual.

30. (p. 92) *Currado da Palazzo*: A Guelph supporter from Brescia, Currado was *podestà* of Piacenza in 1288. According to one of Dante's earliest commentators, Currado lost both his hands in battle but continued to wave the battle standard with the stumps of his arms.

31. (p. 92) *"good Gherardo"*: Gherardo da Camino of Treviso (c.1240–1306) was an important Guelph leader who is cited as the paragon of nobility in Dante's *Il Convivio* IV: xiv: 12. His son, Rizzardo, will be mentioned in *Paradiso* IX: 49–51. It has been claimed that Dante enjoyed Gherardo's hospitality after his exile from Florence.

32. (p. 92) *"Guido da Castel . . . the simple Lombard"*: Also praised in Dante's *Il Convivio* IV: xvi:6, for his nobility, Guido was a Guelph from Reggio Emilia who was born in 1235 and was still alive in 1315. Dante probably received Guido's hospitality during his exile. The epithet "simple" is definitely employed here in praise of Guido. He was apparently known to the French as "the simple Lombard," either because of his famous hospitality to French travelers or to single him out from the rest of the Italians (all generally identified by the French as Lombards) because he was so much more honorable than the others of his nation.

33. (p. 92) *"Falls into the mire, and soils itself and burden"*: Marco Lombardo's long speech ends formally in ll. 127–129, concluding that the Roman Church has sunk completely into a search for material goods ("falls in the mire") by confusing temporal with spiritual power. In so doing, the Church not only besmirches her own spiritual tasks but also those associated with the temporal rule that she has taken on as an additional burden.

34. (p. 92) *"O Marco mine"*: Dante's intimate response to Marco Lombardo underscores that he is almost in total agreement with

this character's analysis of the relationship between the Church and the state in his times, a view that is essentially Ghibelline in nature.

35. (p. 92) *"the sons of Levi / Have been excluded from the heritage"*: In the Bible, Numbers 18: 20–24, the members of the tribe of Levi are appointed to be priests of the temple and allowed to receive tithes but not to own land in the Promised Land. Dante thus finds biblical support for his charge that the Church has corrupted itself by material possessions.

36. (p. 93) *"But what Gherardo is it"*: The Pilgrim seems to be unaware of the identity of "good Gherardo" of l. 124.

37. (p. 93) *"Unless I take it from his daughter Gaia"*: The Pilgrim's ignorance of Gherardo's identity allows Marco to repeat the theme of the "good old days" versus contemporary depravity by mentioning the man's daughter, Gaia. This raises the question of whether Gaia is offered as a positive or negative example, but given the context of Marco's other remarks, it would seem that the reference would have to be negative. Gaia seems to be another example of how offspring fail to continue the virtue of their parents.

38. (p. 93) *"Yonder the Angel is"*: This is the Angel of Meekness, who will eventually erase the third *P* from the Pilgrim's brow and pronounce another beatitude. Marco must turn back into the cloud of acrid smoke when he begins to discern the white rays of light that mark the boundary of this third terrace where wrath is punished.

CANTO XVII

1. (p. 94) *Remember, Reader:* This is the Poet's fourth address to the reader in *Purgatorio*. It appears in exactly the middle of the thirty-three cantos of *Purgatorio* and, therefore, in the center of the 100 cantos of *The Divine Comedy*. The general theme of canto XVII, that love is the force behind all human activity, thus receives central emphasis in the poem's overall structure.

2. (p. 94) *than through its membrane mole:* In Dante's time it was believed that the mole was blind. Here, though, the Poet maintains that the mole sees dimly through a membrane covering its eyes, just as the Pilgrim can barely see through the Alpine mist while climbing the mountain.

3. (p. 94) *that was already setting:* The time is now sunset of Easter Monday, the second day on the mountain.

4. (p. 94) *To rays already dead on the low shores:* As the sun sets below the horizon, it is already dark on the lower part of the mountain, but the rays still strike the higher regions.

5. (p. 94) *O thou, Imagination . . . may sound a thousand trumpets:* The Poet notes that a person can get so caught up in visions, the "Imagination," that he wouldn't take note of the blaring of "a thousand trumpets."

6. (p. 94) *Moves thee a light . . . a will that downward guides it:* The Poet offers two explanations for his inner visions: They are either influenced by the stars in heaven, or a will directs the vision "downward" (clearly a reference to God). The visions the Pilgrim experiences are those of this second type and therefore do not depend upon any sensory experience.

7. (p. 94) *Of her impiety . . . might be received by it:* The three visions of wrath that follow involve violence. The first vision (ll. 19–24) refers to the myth of Procne (see note 7 for *Purgatorio* IX), who was angered over her husband's rape of her sister Philomela and, in a fit of wrath, fed his son to him. According to Dante, who followed traditional versions of this story, she was then transformed into a nightingale and Philomela into a swallow. The original source, Ovid's *Metamorphoses* VI: 412–674, does not specify the type of bird identified with either Procne or Philomela. The "bird that most delights in singing" (l. 20) is the nightingale.

8. (pp. 94–95) *Then rained within my lofty fantasy . . . in word and action so entire:* The second vision (ll. 25–30) is taken from Esther 3–7, a biblical rather than a classical source. This is the story of Haman, the minister of Ahasuerus, king of Persia, who attempted to have the Jew Mordecai killed but was himself punished in the same manner he had planned for his victim. Haman's actions were inspired by his wrath. The Latin Vulgate Dante read referred to the method of execution as a cross (implied in l. 26, "one crucified"), but Haman was most probably executed on a form of gallows. Mordecai is described as complete in the integrity of both his speech and his deeds ("in word and action").

9. (p. 95) *in fashion of a bubble:* The image of Mordecai and Haman bursts like an ordinary bubble, giving place to the third vision.

10. (p. 95) *a young maiden . . . "another's ruin":* Lines 34–39 recall Virgil's *Aeneid* XII: 595–607, the story of Amata, the wife of Latinus and mother of Lavinia, who hangs herself when she falsely believes Turnus has been killed in battle. Amata fears that Lavinia would then marry Aeneas, a union she bitterly opposed. Dante's version of this story has Lavinia speaking and reproaching her mother for her suicide. "Another's ruin" refers to Amata's mistaken belief that Turnus has been killed. Since Dante believes that it was part of God's divine plan to found Rome with the Trojans of Aeneas, he would condemn any attempt by humans to thwart this providential pattern in history, such as Amata's opposition to a projected union of Aeneas and Lavinia.

11. (p. 95) *Greater by far than what is in our wont:* The light that interrupts the third vision is described as being even greater than the light of the sun. This light emanates from the Angel of Meekness.

12. (p. 95) *"so full of eagerness . . . It never rests till meeting face to face":* Although the Pilgrim is full of intense desire to see the angel, his desire is not fulfilled.

13. (p. 95) *But as before the sun:* The radiance of the Angel of Meekness obscures the Pilgrim's vision.

14. (p. 95) *For he who sees the need:* The angel anticipates the desire of the Pilgrim, just as charitable men anticipate the needs of others. In *De Beneficiis* III: i: 3, Seneca writes that the best policy is to anticipate the desires of others, since waiting to be asked predisposes one to denying such a request. Dante also echoes Seneca's idea in *Il Convivio* I: viii: 16.

15. (p. 95) *ere it grow dark:* As Sordello has explained in *Purgatorio* VII: 55–56, the travelers are not permitted to move ahead during the evening darkness in Purgatory.

16. (p. 96) *a motion as of wings, / And fanning in the face:* The Pilgrim does not see the wing of the angel that brushes the third *P* of wrath from his forehead, since the angel is hidden in his own radiance. He does, however, feel a caress of air on his face.

17. (p. 96) *"Beati Pacifici, who are without ill anger":* Dante takes the phrase "Blessed are the peacemakers" from the Bible, where it appears as one of the beatitudes in Matthew 5: 9. Note that the qualification "who are without ill anger" leaves open the possibility of righteous indignation, the good form of anger, but rejects the "ill anger" that is a kind of thirst for personal revenge. Saint Thomas Aquinas makes this scholastic distinction between *ira mala* ("bad anger") and *ira bona* ("good anger") in *Summa theologica* II-II, q. 158, a. 2, resp., and Dante must certainly have known this work.

18. (p. 96) *The vigor of my legs was put in truce:* As the sunlight disappears or, more accurately, mixes with the starlight in ll. 70–72, the Pilgrim's strength begins to fail after the day's journey. He describes this process as a truce being imposed upon his legs.

19. (p. 96) *We at the point were where no more ascends:* The pair has reached the top step on the stairway, and they are probably sitting with their backs against the wall of the fourth terrace. As we are about to ascend to the terrace of the slothful, it is appropriate that the Pilgrim's sudden feeling of exhaustion will resemble that of the slothful souls he will soon meet.

20. (p. 96) *"The love of good, remiss":* In answer to the Pilgrim's question about what sin is purified in the next terrace (l. 82–83), Virgil explains that sloth is caused by a deficiency of love for the good. In ll. 88–139 he analyzes the seven deadly sins purified on each of the seven terraces of Purgatory, claiming that wrongly directed forms of love lead to sin. Some sins, such as the three sins punished in the three lower terraces—pride, envy, and wrath—are defined by wrong goals and harm others. Other types of sins are directed toward a good goal but lack proper measure and are either insufficient or excessive—insufficient love is sloth, which is punished here on the fourth terrace; excessive love may be expressed as avarice, gluttony, or lust, which are punished on the last three terraces. Virgil's observations here are similar to his explanation of the complex system of Hell's punishments in *Inferno* XI, where he divides sins not according to the seven deadly sins but according to the somewhat puzzling categories of incontinence, violence, and fraud. (For a discussion of this infernal system, see the "Introduction" to the companion edition of Longfellow's *Inferno*, edited by Peter Bondanella, New York: Barnes & Noble, 2003.)

21. (p. 96) *"But err the other . . . or by too little vigor":* Dante believes

that mankind naturally desires the good but that free will allows mankind to err in the three ways cited in note 20, above.

22. (p. 97) *"And since we cannot think . . . is all desire cut off"*: Dante asserts that hatred of self and of God is impossible, even though the sins of suicide and blasphemy punished in Hell would seem to argue to the contrary.

23. (p. 97) *"The evil that one loves is of one's neighbor . . . needs shape out another's harm"*: Human immorality rests primarily upon hatred for other human beings that the Poet defines as a "threefold love" in l. 124, because the three categories of sin that define such behavior are pride (ll. 115–117); envy (ll. 118–120); and wrath (ll. 121–23). These are the three sins punished on the first three terraces, or "down below," as the Poet says in l. 124.

24. (p. 97) *"Now of the other will I have thee hear"*: The other four sins (sloth, avarice, gluttony, and lust) concern imperfect searches for the good, unlike the first three sins, which are characterized by an incorrect object of desire.

25. (p. 97) *"languid love"*: Virgil defines sloth as love that is "languid," because it fails to respond as energetically as possible to God's love. In Dante's time, sloth was a failing particularly associated with such groups as clerics or scholars and involved not physical but spiritual laziness, which in Dante's view was also an intellectual laziness.

26. (p. 97) *"After just penitence"*: The terrace of sloth purifies only those who have repented; those who have not repented of their sloth are in Hell.

27. (p. 97) *"There's other good that does not make man happy"*: These goods are the goals of the misdirected kinds of love punished in the three terraces above that of sloth: money (avarice); food (gluttony), and sex (lust). They cannot make men happy, because God is the true source of happiness, "of every good the fruit and root" (l. 135).

28. (p. 98) *"But how tripartite . . seek it for thyself"*: After so much detailed analysis of the system of the seven deadly sins and the physical terrace system on which they are purified in Purgatory, it is remarkable that Virgil now informs the Pilgrim that he will remain silent about any further details, since the Pilgrim must seek them out himself. Virgil's discourse on the system of Hell's punishments in *Inferno* XI was based primarily upon classical ideas, not Christian ones, and it is thus not surprising that he could have come up with the explanations for that system of punishments. However, the Poet never really explains how Virgil, a first-century B.C. pagan, could have learned so much about the seven deadly sins, since these Christian theories reflect scholastic and medieval theology with which Virgil would not be familiar.

CANTO XVIII

1. (p. 99) *"Perchance / The too much questioning I make annoys him"*: There is a hint of spiritual laziness or sloth in the Pilgrim's reluctance to ask more questions, another indication that he participates in the sins and purifications on the Mountain of Purgatory.

2. (p. 99) *"teach me love"*: The Pilgrim's request is actually more precise, since the Italian world employed by Dante is *dimonstrare*, a verb that implies a rigorous philosophical argument, one that might be made by a scholar (in l. 2, the Pilgrim calls Virgil "lofty Teacher"). In canto XVII, Virgil discussed rational love and its harmful effects, not natural love. Now the Pilgrim wants Virgil to elaborate, touching upon philosophical proofs of the psychology of love that so fascinated Dante's contemporaries.

3. (p. 99) *"Your apprehension from some real thing"*: The apprehensive faculty (which includes senses plus perception) draws an image from some real object and focuses upon that form.

4. (p. 99) *"Love is that inclination"*: When the perception inclines toward what it contemplates, that is love.

5. (p. 100) *"So comes the captive soul into desire"*: Just as fire is an example of natural desire and aspires to rise up, so the soul, by its natural inclination toward love, yearns for that which attracts it.

6. (p. 100) *"All love is in itself a laudable thing"*: Here Dante resolutely rejects the idea that all love is, in and of itself, a good thing. This doctrine may be attributed to the Epicureans, followers of the Greek philosopher Epicurus (341–270 B.C.), who believed that pleasure was the only good, but perhaps also to the poetry of Dante's time, including the lyric verse he wrote before *The Divine Comedy*.

7. (p. 100) *"albeit good may be the wax"*: This image of the seal and the wax that is stamped underscores the fact that while mankind is disposed to love, a bad seal may fix a bad imprint on essentially good

wax. As a result, some unworthy love object may induce the innately good instinct of love to go in an evil direction.

8. (p. 100) *"For if love . . . 'tis not her merit"*: The Pilgrim worries that if the object of desire begins with an external object that is internalized by the apprehensive faculty and that all forms of love begin with movements of love ("And with another foot the soul go not," l. 44), how can the soul be blamed or praised if it makes an incorrect or correct choice of love object? The proper Christian response to this question begins with the belief that man has free will to choose good or evil.

9. (p. 100) *"await / For Beatrice, since 'tis a work of faith"*: Virgil underlines the deficiencies of human reasoning, telling the Pilgrim that only Beatrice and faith can answer such a question as the paradox of free will.

10. (p. 100) *"Every substantial form . . . by the green leaves"*: "Substantial form" is a scholastic term for that which gives something its separate existence, which according to Saint Thomas Aquinas (*Summa theologica* I. q. 76, a. 4, resp.) is the intellectual soul in man. The substantial form of a plant, its life, is revealed by its "green leaves."

11. (p. 100) *"Of the first notions, man is ignorant . . . for the first allurements"*: Human beings cannot know how we understand the "first notions" on which all understanding is based (truth, falsity, etc.). The first allurements, or the things that become objects of desire, are just as impossible to understand, except insofar as the good is the ultimate object of desire.

12. (p. 100) *"To make its honey"*: The bee's desire to make honey is similar to man's own behavior, since it involves cognition and desire.

13. (p. 100) *"Innate within you is the power that counsels . . . threshold of assent"*: The "power that counsels" is reason, which must make distinctions between things that are morally good and things that are morally bad and therefore should be blocked at the "threshold of assent," or the doorway of the soul.

14. (p. 102) *"it takes and winnows"*: This image compares the operation of reason under free will to the act of separating wheat grains from chaff.

15. (p. 102) *"Those who, in reasoning, to the bottom went . . . bequeathed they Ethics to the world"*: The ancient philosophers, such as Aristotle and Plato,

went to the essence, or "bottom," of moral philosophy and advocated human free will. They thereby gave "Ethics to the world," since Ethics presuppose freedom of the will and human choice between good and evil. Determinism, on the other hand, basically negates the possibility of ethical choice.

16. (p. 102) *"Supposing, then, that from necessity . . . the power is to restrain it":* Even if we grant that necessity determines every sort of human love, free will nevertheless gives us the innate power to check immoral choices.

17. (p. 102) *"The noble virtue":* In *Paradiso* V: 19–24, Beatrice will argue that free will is God's most precious gift to mankind.

18. (p. 102) *The moon, belated almost unto midnight . . . 'twixt Sardes and Corsicans go down:* This is another of Dante's complicated announcements of the time that is virtually impossible for a contemporary reader to understand. It is near midnight and the moon has risen late; it is apparently following the same path taken by the sun when, from Rome, it is seen setting between Sardinia and Corsica.

19. (p. 102) *Pietola more than any Mantuan town:* This is a reference to the small town (called Andes in Roman times) near Mantua that was the birthplace of Virgil. As such, Pietola is more famous than any other town near Mantua.

20. (p. 102) *Stood like a man in drowsy revery:* The fact that Dante is sleepy on this terrace of the slothful underscores his own need for purification of this sin.

21. (p. 102) *by a people:* That is, the slothful.

22. (p. 102) *And as, of old, Ismenus and Asopus . . . curve their step:* Ismenus and Asopus are two rivers in and near ancient Thebes, in Greece. When Thebans needed rain, they raced about the riverbanks at night to invoke the assistance of Bacchus, and Dante compares this activity to that of the slothful, who now run in much the same manner around the curve of the terrace in which they are purified. Dante probably found this source in Statius' *Thebaid* IX, which refers to the two rivers and the Bacchic rites.

23. (p. 103) *"Mary in haste . . . and then ran into Spain":* Here the positive virtue is zeal (spiritual and temporal), the opposite of sloth. As usual, the first of the positive examples to be contrasted to the sin

being purified concerns the Virgin Mary. Dante mentions her haste to visit Elizabeth when, in the Bible, Luke 1: 39–56, she hears of the older woman's pregnancy with the child who will later become John the Baptist. The second example of zeal concerns Julius Caesar, who left Brutus in charge of part of his army besieging Marseilles and went on to the ancient town of Ilerda, modern Lérida in Spain. The classical source is probably Lucan's *Pharsalia* IV: 29–49.

24. (p. 103) *"Quick! quick! . . . freshens grace"*: In this terrace, the penitents do not offer a prayer as they do in other locations of Purgatory. But their brief cries, uttered almost breathlessly, underline both the definition of the vice of sloth ("by little love," l. 104) and that of its opposite virtue, zeal ("ardor," l. 105).

25. (p. 103) *"lukewarmness"*: Virgil provides yet another definition of sloth.

26. (p. 103) *"I was San Zeno's Abbot at Verona . . . still sorrowing Milan holds discourse"*: The church of San Zeno just outside the city of Verona was the location of a monastery, and its abbot in the time of Emperor Frederick Barbarossa (ruled 1152–1190) was a certain Gherardo II, who died in 1187. In 1162 Barbarossa destroyed the city of Milan.

27. (p. 103) *"And he has one foot in the grave already . . . true pastor"*: The reference is to Alberto della Scala, Lord of Verona, who in 1300 (the fictional date of the Pilgrim's journey to the Afterlife) had only one more year to live. Alberto appointed his "evil-born" (l. 125), or illegitimate, son, Giuseppe, to serve as abbot of the monastery, rather than an unnamed "true pastor," or a more legitimate abbot. Alberto's third illegitimate son, Cangrande della Scala, would be Dante's patron and host when the poet lived in Verona around 1314.

28. (p. 103) *He had already passed so far beyond us*: Alberto is so zealous to pursue his purification that he passes far ahead of the Pilgrim. If he does have more to say, it will not be possible to hear it.

29. (p. 103) *"fastening upon slothfulness their teeth"*: Two souls are so zealous in their rush toward purification that they figuratively "bite" *accidia*—that is, they attack sloth with their examples.

30. (p. 103) *"Sooner were . . . the Jordan saw"*: The first example of the sin of sloth is a biblical one and refers to the incident in Numbers 14: 1–39 in which the Hebrews are reluctant to cross the desert with

Moses after God had given them safe passage through the Red Sea. As a result, all but those who were born in the desert (except for Joshua and Caleb) were allowed to cross the Jordon.

31. (p. 104) *"And those who the fatigue . . . withouten glory offered":* The second example of sloth, a classical one, comes from Virgil's *Aeneid* V: 605–640 and concerns the followers of Aeneas who rebelled against the Trojan hero's leadership and elected to remain in Sicily.

32. (p. 104) *a new thought . . . into dream transmuted:* The Pilgrim's wandering thoughts that move from reverie to meditation to dream in l. 145 also reflect the same kind of moral laziness that constitutes the very sin punished on the terrace of Sloth. The last line of the canto prepares us for the Pilgrim's second dream, in canto XIX. The Pilgrim has three dreams in *Purgatorio*: in cantos IX, XIX, and XXVII.

CANTO XIX

1. (p. 105) *It was the hour . . . that long remains not dim:* Lines 1–6 provide another difficult Dantesque time check, telling the reader that it is shortly before dawn on Tuesday, the beginning of the Pilgrim's third day. Because the Pilgrim's dream takes place shortly before dawn, it is a prophetic one, as the one in canto IX was (see note 9 to that canto). In Dante's time, it was believed that the moon chilled earth and that Saturn had the same effect. According to Dante, at this time of day geomancers (diviners who tell the future by reading the random points arranged on a surface and matching them with configurations of stars) see Fortuna Major—a pattern created by the last stars in the constellation of Aquarius and the first stars of Pisces. This figure can best be seen at sunrise.

2. (p. 105) *There came to me in dreams a stammering woman:* Lines 7–33 present a strange dream of a *femmina balba* ("stammering woman"), whose ugliness is minutely described by the Pilgrim. We later learn from Virgil (ll. 59) who she is, since he says that she is purged "above us"—meaning in the three terraces above that of sloth that are devoted to avarice, gluttony, and lust.

3. (p. 105) *Even thus my gaze:* In Dante's dream, the woman who stammers has deformed hands and legs and is a sickly yellow color; she is transformed into a woman who speaks correctly, has straight limbs, and has the proper color desirable in a woman (probably either white or perhaps the color of a blush).

4. (p. 105) *"I am the Siren sweet . . . I drew Ulysses from his wandering way"*: The stammering woman, now transformed by Dante's dream, claims to be the siren who tempted Ulysses from his path homeward in the *Odyssey* XII: 39–200. But since Dante did not know Homer's work firsthand and read about him only in the works of other poets and philosophers, he does not realize that Ulysses actually resisted the siren's song by lashing himself to the mast of his ship.

5. (p. 106) *a Lady saintly and alert:* This figure has been identified in many ways—as Beatrice (surely not correct), as Saint Lucy, as Lady Philosophy, and as Grace. It is important to bear in mind that she is a figure in a dream, just as the stammering woman is a figure in a dream, so perhaps no specific identification is possible.

6. (p. 106) *She seized the other and in front laid open . . . with the stench that issued from it:* Longfellow translates the original Italian *L'altra prendea* as ("She seized"), believing that the verb refers to the saintly and alert Lady. Most contemporary translators take Virgil to be the subject of the verb and have him reveal the ugly and stinking reality beneath her garments. The smell of the woman's foul belly awakens the Pilgrim.

7. (p. 106) *"At least thrice have I called thee":* It is not surprising that on the terrace of sloth, the Pilgrim sleeps so soundly that it takes several calls from Virgil to awaken him from his dream. This is one more example of how the Pilgrim participates in the sins that are being purified in Purgatory.

8. (p. 106) *the half arch of a bridge:* After his strange dream, the Pilgrim is pensive and bent with thought, like the shape of a bridge's arch.

9. (p. 106) *"Come, here the passage is":* These words are spoken by the Angel of Zeal, who directs the Pilgrim to the proper path.

10. (p. 106) *and fanned us:* As in canto XVII: 67, when the *P* of wrath was removed by the caress of the Angel of Mercy, here the Angel of Zeal removes the *P* of sloth from the Pilgrim's forehead without any concrete gesture.

11. (p. 106) *Affirming those* qui lugent *to be blessed:* Qui lugent translates from the Latin as "who mourns." The biblical beatitude for this

terrace of sloth is from Matthew 5: 4, "Blessed are they that mourn: for they shall be comforted."

12. (p. 106) *"I cannot from the thought withdraw me"*: Even without the *P* of sloth on his brow, the Pilgrim still suffers from the effects of spiritual lethargy.

13. (p. 108) *Who sole above us henceforth is lamented? :* Virgil identifies the stammering woman as the symbol of the sins on the terraces "above us" to be purified. These are the sins of incontinence (the first section of sins punished in Hell): avarice, gluttony, and lust.

14. (p. 108) *Thine eyes lift upward to the lure . . . Went on to where the circling doth begin:* The Poet returns to imagery drawn from medieval falconry, which he also employs in *Inferno* XVII: 127–136 (a description of Geryon) and in *Purgatorio* XIV: 145–150. This imagery is quite complex. God ("The Eternal King") is now defined as the falconer, whose lure (in Italian *logoro*), or call, to the falcon is represented by the heavens that He whirls about our heads. The falcon's behavior is then compared to the Pilgrim's: The falcon first looks down to his bound feet but then eventually flies toward the call, carrying his quarry back to his master so that the bird will be fed. In like manner, the Pilgrim goes upward toward the passage in the rock to resume his circling path around the Mountain of Purgatory and, of course, travel toward his master.

15. (p. 108) *On the firth circle . . . all downward turned:* The Pilgrim arrives at the terrace of avarice and prodigality and immediately sees the penitent souls purging themselves, stretched out on the ground.

16. (p. 108) *"Adhaesit pavimento anima mea" . . . the words be understood:* This line is from the Bible, Psalms 119: 25, and translates from the Latin as "My soul cleaveth unto the dust." The penitent are hard to understand because they are speaking with their faces pressed upon the ground.

17. (p. 108) *"If ye are come secure from this prostration":* The unidentified penitent who speaks to the travelers here reveals one of the rules that govern behavior in Purgatory: Penitents do not necessarily have to spend time in purification at every level. If they are not guilty of a particular sin, they may pass through one terrace toward another that contains a sin connected to their own lives. The Pilgrim and Virgil are here taken for souls passing through to another level by the speaker, who in l. 99 will be identified as Pope Adrian V.

18. (p. 108) *"Let your right hands be evermore outside":* The two travelers are instructed to walk with their right sides toward the cliff of the terrace ("outside") and their left sides toward the inside of the mountain. They would therefore be walking counterclockwise up the mountain.

19. (p. 108) *In what was spoken divined the rest concealed:* The Pilgrim identifies the position of the speaker by hearing him, but he is not able to see his lips move.

20. (p. 108) *"whom weeping ripens / That without which to God we cannot turn":* There is no returning to God without purification first, and the process of purification is "ripened" like fruit by our tears.

21. (p. 109) *"Who wast thou . . . whence living I departed":* The Pilgrim asks the penitent soul three questions: what his identity is; why the souls are prostrate; and whether the souls want assistance back in the world of the living. The answers will take up most of the rest of the canto.

22. (p. 109) Scias quod ego fui successor Petri: The pentitent soul, who we will soon learn is Pope Adrian V, responds, "Know that I was a successor of Peter." Note that he replies in Latin, not in the Italian that Pope Nicholas III employed in *Inferno* XIX: 52–57 and 66–87.

23. (p. 109) *"Between Siestri and Chiaveri . . . its summit makes":* The penitent soul informs us that between the towns of Siestri and Chiaveri, coastal towns near Genoa, there is a river (the Lavagna) that has given his family its title. They would be the counts of Lavagna, the Fieschi family, and this identifies the soul as Ottobono Fieschi, who was elected pope on July 11, 1276, and died a month later on August 16, before he had the opportunity to be crowned. Ottobono had taken the name Adrian V.

24. (p. 109) *"A month and little more . . . I discovered life to be a lie":* Pope Adrian had little more than a month to contemplate the heaviness of the burden of the papacy. During that time, according to the Poet, he repented of his sin of avarice ("my conversion," l. 106) after realizing the vanity of the world's riches ("life to be a lie," l. 108).

25. (p. 109) *"Nor farther in that life could one ascend":* By being elected pope, Adrian had ascended to the highest office possible, and at the same time he realized the worthlessness of worldly goals. It is significant that this is the first pope the Pilgrim meets who will eventually be saved; the popes in *Inferno*, such as Nicholas III and Boniface VIII, are either damned or about to be damned.

26. (p. 109) *"So justice here has merged it in the earth":* Making clear the meaning of l. 115, "What avarice does is here made manifest," Adrian now explains the *contrapasso*, or counterpoise, involved in the punishment of avarice. Just as avaricious souls were too attached to earthly things, now they are virtually pinned to earth and rest immobile, so their punishment fits the sin perfectly. (For more on the notion of *contrapasso*, see note 16 to canto XIII.)

27. (p. 109) *I on my knees had fallen:* The Pilgrim kneels before Adrian to show his respect for the Pope's penitence; in the original Italian, he employs the formal *voi* in l. 131, a form of address the Pilgrim uses with very few characters in *The Divine Comedy*. Contrast the Pilgrim's attitude here with that when he addresses the damned Pope Nicholas III in *Inferno* XIX.

28. (p. 110) *"Standing, my conscience stung me with remorse":* Perhaps the Pilgrim is remorseful because of the very irreverent manner in which he treated the popes in *Inferno* XIX—not, as the line could also be interpreted, because of his righteous indignation over the sins of the individuals there, who just happened to be popes.

29. (p. 110) *"Straighten thy legs . . . fellow-servant am I":* Adrian's admonition to the Pilgrim to rise up may refer to the Bible, Revelation 19: 10. Here the angel tells John, who has fallen before his feet, to rise up and that they are "fellow-servants."

30. (p. 110) *"Which sayeth neque nubent":* This Latin term, which translates as "neither marry," is a reference to the Bible, Matthew 22: 24–30. Jesus is sarcastically asked which of seven brothers, each of whom in turn married the eldest brother's widow, would be joined with her after the resurrection. Jesus answers: "For in the resurrection, they neither marry, nor are given in marriage." Basically, Adrian is telling the Pilgrim that all such official titles, such as husband, wife, or even pope, will mean nothing in the afterlife.

31. (p. 110) *"With which I ripen":* Adrian refers back to the Pilgrim's remark of l. 91, "O Spirit, in whom weeping ripens."

32. (p. 110) *"On earth":* Adrian finally answers the third part of the Pilgrim's three questions in ll. 94–96, concerning what he might do

for the penitent soul. Adrian supplies him with the name of his niece (though Longfellow translates *nepote* as "grandchild"), Alagia Fieschi, who was the wife of Moroello Malaspina, one of Dante's friends.

33. (p. 110) *"Good in herself, unless indeed our house / Malevolent may make her by example":* This implies that the Fieschi family had a rather bad reputation. In *Purgatorio* XXIV: 29–30, we meet another member of the family, Bonifazio Fieschi, who is being purged of his gluttony, and one early Dante commentator declared that the women of the Fieschi family were basically little more than prostitutes. Since Dante was the guest of Moroello Malaspina in 1307 or 1308 and probably met Alagia, his host's wife, the Poet is probably paying off his debt to that family by favorable mention of this maligned woman.

CANTO XX

1. (p. 111) *Ill strives the will against a better will . . . I drew the sponge not saturate from the water:* The Pilgrim heeds Adrian's advice to pass on quickly and describes his reluctant parting from Adrian's presence as withdrawing a sponge not yet filled with liquid from the water.

2. (p. 111) *The malady which all the world pervades . . . the verge approach:* Although pride is generally considered to be the archetypal sin (especially since it was the sin of Satan), according to Saint Paul in the Bible, 1 Timothy 6: 10, avarice, or cupidity, is the "root of all evil." Just as the world is pervaded by avarice, the terrace is so covered with the souls of the penitent avaricious that there is little room to move. The two travelers must stay close to the inside wall of the mountain ("close to the battlements," l. 6) to avoid the crowd that piles up even to the edge of the precipice.

3. (p. 111) *thou old she-wolf:* Virgil now seems to identify the she-wolf (*lupa* in the original Italian) that the Pilgrim first encountered blocking his path in *Inferno* I: 49–54 as avarice. Apparently for Dante, this she-wolf accounts for more sins than those associated with either of the other two animals mentioned in *Inferno* I—more than either the *lonza* (Longfellow renders this word as "panther," but most modern translations use "leopard") or the *leone* (lion), symbols respectively of envy and pride.

4. (p. 111) *When will he come through whom she shall depart?* Dante

commentators have traditionally seen this as a reference to the grey-
hound (*veltro*) of *Inferno* I: 101, who will drive away avarice, personified
in the feminine form of the she-wolf. The line must certainly also re-
fer to some political leader of Dante's times, perhaps Cangrande della
Scala or Emperor Henry VII of Germany; Henry appointed Can-
grande the imperial vicar of Verona.

5. (p. 111) *with footsteps slow and scarce:* The travelers step carefully
out of respect for the penitents who are so crowded together.

6. (p. 111) *"Sweet Mary!":* A yet-to-be-identified voice cries out the
names of those who are renowned for their poverty, the opposite of
avarice, and describes the actions by which they set a positive example.
As has been the case on the other terraces, the first example concerns
the Virgin Mary, who gave birth to Jesus in an humble stable: "How
poor thou wast / Is manifested by that hostelry / Where thou didst
lay thy sacred burden down" (ll. 22–24). The voice will be identified in
l. 49 as that of Hugh Capet.

7. (p. 111) *"O good Fabricius":* The second illustration of poverty
concerns Caius Fabricius Lucinus, Roman consul in 282 and 278 B.C.,
who refused to accept bribes and died a pauper. He is mentioned by
Dante in *De Monarchia* II: v: 11, as well as by Virgil in the *Aeneid* VI:
843–844.

8. (p. 112) *the largess / Which Nicholas unto the maidens gave:* The third
case of generosity (like poverty, the opposite of avarice) is Saint
Nicholas, a bishop in Asia Minor during the fourth century under
Emperor Constantine. (He eventually also became known as Santa
Claus.) One legend about him recounts that to save three daughters of
an impoverished lord from being sold into prostitution, he provided
dowries of gold for each of them.

9. (p. 112) *"O soul . . . Not without recompense shall be thy word":* The
Pilgrim asks the unidentified soul two questions: what is the man's
identity (answered in l. 49) and why is only he crying out aloud the ex-
amples of poverty or generosity (answered in ll. 121–123). As usual, he
promises assistance through the intercession of the prayers of loved
ones if the soul responds.

10. (p. 112) *"I'll tell thee . . . Grace shines in thee or ever thou art dead":* The
soul says he is responding to the questions not because of the offer of

assistance, but because of the Divine Grace that shines in the Pilgrim even before he has died.

11. (p. 112) *"I was the root of that malignant plant"*: Dante's notions about the genealogy of the Capetian dynasty in France are shaky. Hugh I, duke of the Franks and often called Hugh the Great, died in 956. Louis V, the last of the Carolingian kings of France, died in 987. Upon his death, the son of Hugh I—Hugh II, generally known as Hugh Capet—ruled as king of France until 996. It was Hugh II who founded the Capetian dynasty and might be best described as "the root of that malignant plant." But Dante seems to conflate father and son; following popular tradition, the Florentine historian Giovanni Villani claims that Hugh I, not Hugh II, was the son of a butcher (see l. 52: "I was the son of a Parisian butcher"). It is easy to see how Dante might have confused the father with the son, or vice versa, and subsequent Dante scholars have argued for the identification of the speaker in this canto with both the father and his son. Dante would have disliked the policies of either individual, since the Capetian rulers were opposed to any re-establishment of the Roman Empire and frequently supported Florentine governments not to Dante's liking.

12. (p. 112) *"But if Douay and Ghent and Lille and Bruges / Had power"*: These Flemish cities rose up against the French in 1302; eventually the Flemish defeated the French at the battle of Courtrai in 1320.

13. (p. 112) *"From me were born the Louises and Philips"*: Some ten kings followed Hugh Capet to the throne of France between 996 and 1314: Eight of them were named either Louis or Philip, including the famous crusader king and saint, Louis IX (1226–1270) and Philip IV the Fair (1285–1314), one of Dante's most hated targets of invective (see *Inferno* XIX: 87; *Purgatorio* VII: 109–110, XX: 85–96, XXXII: 155–156, and XXXIII: 34–45; and *Paradiso* XIX: 118).

14. (p. 112) *"Excepting one, contrite in cloth of gray"*: The Poet seems to have confused Charles, duke of Lorraine, the last of the Carolingians, who was imprisoned by Hugh II, with Childeric III, the last of the Merovingians, who was deposed and sent to a monastery by Pepin the Short in 752.

15. (p. 112) *"the great dowry of Provence"*: Provence was annexed to the French monarchy with the marriage of Charles of Anjou (also

known as Charles I; brother of Louis IX of France) to Beatrice, daughter of Raymond Berenger IV of Provence in 1245. Lines 61–66 recount French imperialism and the annexation of Normandy from England in 1202 and both Ponthieu and Gascony from England in 1295. Lines 67–81 recount what incensed Dante even more, the invasion of Italy by various members of the French royal family and the general chaos that ensued. Charles of Anjou was responsible both for the defeat of Manfredi in 1266 at Benevento (see *Purgatorio* III: 118–129) and for the execution of Coradin, grandson of Frederick II, after the battle of Tagliacozzo in 1268 (see *Inferno* XXVIII: 17–18). Dante even repeats the untrue rumor that Charles was responsible for murdering Saint Thomas of Aquinas (l. 69).

16. (p. 114) *A time I see, not very distant now:* Hugh Capet's account of past history now moves to prophecy, since the fictional date of the Pilgrim's journey is 1300. Charles III, also known as Charles of Valois (1270–1325), was called into Italy by Pope Boniface VIII to make peace. According to Dante, Charles entered Florence unarmed except for treachery, "the lance / That Judas jousted with" of ll. 73–74, and with it he burst the "paunch" of the bloated and gluttonous city, l. 75. The capture resulted in the exile of the White Guelphs, including Dante. As l. 76 notes, Charles gained "not land, but sin and infamy" for his troubles, a reference to the fact that he later emerged from the Sicilian Vespers uprising (in which the Sicilians successfully revolted against French rule) with nothing, thereby earning the nickname Charles Sansterre (Charles "Landless").

17. (p. 114) *"The other . . . See I his daughter sell":* Charles II (c.1254–1309), son of Charles of Anjou and king of Naples, was captured by the Aragonese after the Sicilian Vespers, imprisoned on a ship between 1284 and 1287, and eventually forced to give his daughter into a marriage with Azzo VIII of Este in 1305 in return for a great deal of money. He was crowned king of Sicily but never gained control of it. The actions of this descendant of Hugh Capet—he sold his daughter for gain, "as corsairs do with other female slaves" (l. 81)—were exactly opposite those of Saint Nicholas, who gave dowries to the poor.

18. (p. 114) *"I see the flower-de-luce . . . And Christ in his own Vicar captive made":* Hugh Capet now describes the worst crime of his descendant King Philip IV the Fair. Excommunicated by Pope Boniface VIII for

his taxation of the clergy, Philip imprisoned the Pope in his palace in the town of Anagni (Dante refers to it as "Alagna" in l. 86). The reference to the "flower-de-luce," or fleur-de-lis, refers to the emblem of the French royal family.

19. (p. 114) *"I see the modern Pilate"*: In ll. 87–93, Dante compares the infamous attack on the pope at Anagni with the betrayal of Christ. Like Christ, Boniface was (metaphorically) forced to drink vinegar and gall, and like Christ he was slain (or at least the shock of the event eventually caused his death, in 1303) in the company of two living thieves, Philip's agent, William of Nogaret, and his Roman ally, Sciarra Colonna. Philip the Fair would be the modern Pilate who metaphorically washed his hands of his crime after the Pope died. Although Dante hated Pope Boniface and welcomes him into Hell even before his death (see *Inferno* XIX: 52–57), his negative judgment was upon the man, not the noble office he held.

20. (p. 114) *"This does not sate him . . . to the temple bears his sordid sails!"*: Dante also attacks Philip the Fair for destroying the Knights Templars, a religious order of knights founded during the Crusades; he did so in 1307 without papal consent ("decretal"). In 1312 Pope Clement V, the French puppet pope, officially decreed the end of the Templars, resulting in the burning of its grand master, Jacques de Molay, in Philip's presence. Philip's motivation in suppressing the Knights Templars was that of avarice—he wanted to take their great wealth for himself.

21. (p. 114) *"shall I be joyful made / By looking on the vengeance"*: Dante may well have intended this expressed wish for divine vengeance upon Philip the Fair to be a prophecy of things to come. Philip died in a hunting accident in 1314, and in *Paradiso* XIX: 118–120, the Poet expresses his satisfaction over Philip's ignoble demise after tangling with a wild boar.

22. (p. 114) *"What I was saying"*: Hugh Capet now answers the Pilgrim's earlier question of ll. 35–36: "why only / Thou doest renew these praises well deserved." In other words, why is he, alone, reciting the first set of examples of poverty and generosity?

23. (p. 115) *"As the day lasts . . . Contrary sound we take instead thereof"*: Hugh Capet informs the Pilgrim that the positive examples of poverty and generosity are proclaimed during the day and the negative examples of avarice at night. This practice seems to contradict the general

rule, elsewhere applied, that virtually no activity takes place in Purgatory during the evening. Hugh clarifies this variation somewhat in ll. 118–120, where he notes that the penitents cry out as they are moved by their inner impulses.

24. (p. 115) *"Pygmalion . . . Made his insatiable desire of gold":* In the *Aeneid* I: 340–364, Virgil recounts that Pygmalion, king of Tyre and Dido's brother, secretly murdered Dido's husband, Sichaeus. The murdered man returned to Dido in a dream and recounted what had happened, prompting Dido to make off with all the treasure Pygmalion had acquired by his evil deed.

25. (p. 115) *"avaricious Midas":* This is a reference to the proverbial King of Phrygia who was granted the "golden touch" by Bacchus. But the King realized that since everything he touched turned to gold, he could no longer eat nor drink, and he was forced to beg Bacchus to take the gift back. Dante's source is Ovid's *Metamorphoses* XI: 100–194.

26. (p. 115) *"one needs must laugh":* After losing the golden touch, Midas was asked to referee a contest between Pan's piping and Apollo's playing of the lyre. When only Midas thought Pan's music was more beautiful, Apollo changed Midas' ears into the ears of an ass. Midas' lack of judgment and his avarice have thus given mankind reason to laugh.

27. (p. 115) *"The foolish Achan . . . still appears to sting him here":* In the Bible, Joshua 7: 1–26, Achan's theft of the Israelite treasure causes Joshua to order him to be stoned to death. Now, in Purgatory, Achan lists the items he has stolen, so he still feels Joshua's wrath.

28. (p. 115) *"Sapphira with her husband":* As reported in the Bible, Acts 5: 1–11, Sapphira and her husband, Ananias, sold some of the property that was to be used to support the Church but kept back some of the money for themselves. When Peter rebuked them for their greed, both dropped dead before him.

29. (p. 115) *"We laud the hoof-beats Heliodorus":* In the Apocrypha of the Bible, 2 Maccabees 3: 1–40, Heliodorus is sent by King Seleucus IV of Syria to secure a treasure in the temple of Jerusalem. When he enters that place sacred to God, he is attacked by a man in gold armor and two others who beat him.

30. (p. 115) *"Polymnestor who murdered Polydorus":* Before the end of the Trojan War, King Priam of Troy entrusted Trojan treasure and his

son Polydorus to Polymnestor, king of Thrace. When the Greeks took Troy, Polymnestor took the money and killed Polydorus. Dante also mentions this deed in *Inferno* XXX: 18; his source is Virgil's *Aeneid* II: 19–68 and Ovid's *Metamorphoses* XIII: 429–438.

31. (p. 115) *"O Crassus . . . what is the taste of gold":* One of Rome's richest and most avaricious men, Marcus Licinius Crassus was appointed triumvir with Pompey and Caesar in 60 B.C. While serving as proconsul in Syria, he was killed by the Parthians in 53 B.C., and the Parthian king had liquefied gold poured into the mouth of his severed head to mock his thirst for wealth.

32. (p. 115) *"According to desire of speech . . . No other person lifted up his voice":* We are not told why it was Hugh Capet alone who felt obliged to cry out in this zone of Purgatory. Perhaps the Poet is giving him voice to express hatred of the avarice of his French descendants, whom Dante so despised. We do learn, as Hugh tells the Pilgrim in ll. 122–123, it was simply by chance that he was the only soul to raise his voice when the Pilgrim passed by.

33. (p. 115) *to o'ercome the road:* Once again, the Poet underscores the difficulty of passing through the terrace, because of the large number of souls in their path.

34. (p. 115) *The mountain tremble:* In canto XXI, the reader will learn the reason for this earthquake in Purgatory: Whenever a soul feels that its purgation is complete and is ready to move on to heaven, the mountain shakes and the souls all praise God. The soul now being released, we learn in the next canto, is the Roman poet Statius.

35. (p. 115) *shook not Delos:* Delos is the island to which Latona escaped from Juno's wrath to give birth to Apollo and Diana. The island was unstable and floating until Apollo made it stable. (See Virgil's *Aeneid* III: 73–77.)

36. (p. 116) *"Fear not":* On the rare occasion that a soul is purged and ready to ascend to heaven, the entire community of penitents in Purgatory celebrates this event. Virgil's words here seem to recall those of the angel in the Bible, Luke 2: 10, who bids the shepherds not to be afraid upon arriving to announce the birth of Christ: "Fear not: for, behold, I bring you good tidings of great joy." In Matthew 28: 5, a similar incident occurs at the tomb of the crucified Christ, where an angel

reassures the women who arrive to tend to the body: "Fear not ye: for I know that ye seek Jesus."

37. (p. 116) "Gloria in excelsis Deo": In the Bible, Luke 2: 13–14, angels sing "Glory to God in the highest" before the birth of Christ. The song is also part of the midnight mass at Easter.

38. (p. 116) *Even as the shepherds who first heard that song:* The Poet compares the two travelers to the shepherds who witnessed the birth of Christ.

39. (p. 116) *No ignorance . . . timorous and thoughtful:* Lines 145–151 express the Pilgrim's desire to understand more about the things he has just witnessed, increasing the suspense on the part of the reader to know more as well. Canto XXI will, in fact, be devoted in large measure to providing the Pilgrim, and the reader, with explanations.

CANTO XXI

1. (p. 117) *The natural thirst:* In Aristotle's *Metaphysics* I: i, echoed by Dante's *Il Convivio* I: i: 1, the claim is made that all men naturally desire knowledge.

2. (p. 117) *The woman of Samaria besought:* This is a reference to the Bible, John 4: 3–29, the story of Jesus and the Samaritan woman at the well. The water Jesus offers is the water of everlasting life, or salvation, and the story adds to Aristotle's claim of a "natural thirst" for knowledge the notion that this thirst cannot be satisfied without the revelation of God's purpose through Christ. The revealed truth of Christianity thus completes Aristotle's desire for knowledge.

3. (p. 117) *And I was pitying that righteous vengeance:* The Pilgrim's pity was condemned in Hell as a sign of spiritual weakness, but the sight of the just punishment of the avaricious, "that righteous vengeance," continues to disturb him.

4. (p. 117) *And lo! In the same manner as Luke writeth / That Christ appeared to two upon the way:* In Luke 24: 13–16, two of Christ's disciples are joined by the resurrected Christ on the road to Emmaus but do not recognize him. In like manner, Virgil and the Pilgrim do not recognize the soul of the poet Statius (he remains unnamed until l. 91). This comparison of the risen Christ to a classical poet underscores the fact that purgation is also a form of resurrection and rebirth.

5. (p. 117) *the countersign thereto conforming:* Statius addresses Virgil and the Pilgrim in l. 13 with the words "may God give you peace." This greeting usually would be returned by the phrase "and with your spirit," but instead Virgil makes a sign and does not utter a traditional formulaic reply.

6. (p. 117) *"That me doth banish in eternal exile!":* Here Virgil sadly contrasts his own exile in Limbo without the hope of eternal salvation and the peace that the newly purified soul will soon enjoy.

7. (p. 117) *"If ye are shades . . . If thou note the marks":* Statius has drawn a false conclusion upon seeing Virgil and the Pilgrim, assuming that the Pilgrim is a dead soul. (Remember that elsewhere in *Purgatorio* the Pilgrim's body cast a shadow, revealing the fact that he is a living and breathing human being. But since the sun's rays are in the east and are no longer striking this side of the Mountain of Purgatory, he casts no shadow and in this way is like the souls.) Virgil corrects Statius' opinion of the Pilgrim's status by pointing to the *P*s on the Pilgrim's brow, "which the angel traces" (l. 23) as a special sign of divine favor. This passage has led some scholars to conclude that in Purgatory only the Pilgrim bears such signs and that the ordinary penitent soul does not receive them.

8. (p. 117) *"But because she who spinneth day and night":* In Greek mythology, Lachesis, one of the three Fates, spins the thread of a human life that her sister Clotho winds upon the distaff. The quantity of the wool determines the length of a life, and a third sister, Atropos (mentioned in *Inferno* XXXIII: 126), cuts the thread, thereby ending the life. Virgil is simply saying, in unsimple terms, that the Pilgrim is still alive.

9. (p. 118) *"His soul, which is thy sister and my own":* As all souls are daughters of God, they are each other's sisters. Feminine forms are used here because in the Italian, the word for soul (*anima*) is feminine.

10. (p. 118) *"I was drawn from out the ample throat / Of Hell":* Virgil is saying that Beatrice brought him up from Limbo to act as a guide for the Pilgrim.

11. (p. 118) *"As far on as my school":* In *Inferno* IV: 94, the Poet calls the classical poets that are in Limbo with Virgil the "fair school." Virgil means here that he has been assigned to guide the Pilgrim as best a pagan poet can.

12. (p. 118) *"why such a shudder / Ereswhile the mountain gave . . . as far as its moist feet?":* The earthquake seemed to reach as far down as the foot of the Mountain of Purgatory, which is bathed by the waters of the ocean.

13. (p. 118) *"Naught is there," he began:* In answer to Virgil's expressed question and the Pilgrim's unexpressed but shared one (ll. 38–39), Statius now proceeds (ll. 40–72) to explain the earthquake and the nature of the Mountain of Purgatory. Basically, earthly conditions of weather exist in Antepurgatory up to the gate of Purgatory. Thereafter, nothing typical of earthly conditions occurs, since only the direct influence of heaven controls that realm. Thus, the earthquake celebrating Statius' purification is not really an earthly earthquake.

14. (p. 118) *"Free is it here from every permutation":* Here there are no changes in the weather.

15. (p. 118) *"any higher falls / Than the short, little stairway of three steps":* No earthly weather passes the three stone steps at the gate of Purgatory proper.

16. (p. 118) *"the daughter of Thaumas":* The reference is to Iris, the personification of the rainbow in Greek mythology.

17. (p. 118) *"No arid vapor":* In Dante's time Aristotle's belief that earthquakes were caused by dry vapor trapped inside earth was still accepted in some circles.

18. (p. 118) *"the Vicar of Peter":* This is the gatekeeping angel of *Purgatorio* IX: 103, who becomes Peter's vicar here because he has been entrusted with the Apostle's keys.

19. (p. 119) *"Five hundred years and more":* Statius died in A.D. 96 and has therefore spent almost twelve centuries in Purgatory—five hundred years being purged of avarice and prodigality, and, we later learn in *Purgatorio* XXII: 92–93, another four hundred years on the terrace of sloth. We must assume that the other almost three hundred years were spent either in Antepurgatory or on various other terraces.

20. (p. 119) *"A free volition for a better seat":* Statius' explanation in ll. 59–69 underlines a number of important characteristics of Purgatory that Dante seems to have invented but that make logical sense. The earthquake is a result of a soul's self-conscious realization that it is purged and ready to ascend ("Feels itself pure, so that it soars, or moves / To mount aloft," ll. 59–60) and is accompanied by the cries of all those in Purgatory ("such a cry attends it," l. 60). Although a penitent wants his or her purgation and punishment to end as soon as possible, it is possible to be purified only when the will is no longer divided against itself and becomes whole once again ("Of purity the will alone gives proof," l. 61). When a soul changes its convent (l. 62), or its abode, it moves from Purgatory to Paradise.

21. (p. 119) *"In days when the good Titus"*: Statius (A.D. 45–96) finally identifies himself by name in l. 91, and ll. 81–102 offer a great deal of information about this Latin poet. He was born around A.D. 45 and was therefore living when "the good Titus" (l. 82), the son of Emperor Vespasian who succeeded his father as emperor in A.D. 79–81, destroyed the temple of Jerusalem in A.D. 70. Doing so, according to Dante, he exacted just vengeance for the crucifixion of Christ; Dante repeats this idea in *Paradiso* VI: 91–93. Apparently the Poet accepts this commonplace of medieval Christian thought, attributing the death of Christ to Jews but not so much to his beloved Romans, who obviously played a major role as well. The "name that most endures" of l. 85 is that of "poet," a title that endows eternal fame to those who deserve it. Statius claims he was born in Toulouse, in France ("Me, a Thoulousian," l. 89) but Dante errs here, since Statius was actually from Naples. His two most important works were epic poems mentioned in l. 92. In the twelve books of the *Thebaid*, he recounts the expedition of the Seven against Thebes and the wars between Eteocles and Polyneices, a book that Dante imitates in numerous places in *Inferno*. In the unfinished *Achilleid*, Statius treats the life of the Greek warrior hero Achilles and the Trojan War. Dante was influenced by this work, as well as by Virgil's treatment of the same conflict, since he was unable to read Greek and had no access to Homer's poetry. According to his testimony here, Statius admired Virgil above all other poets, especially his *Aeneid* ("my nurse in song," l. 98).

22. (p. 120) *"More than I must err issuing from my ban"*: Statius claims he would gladly spend another year in Purgatory if he could have lived during Virgil's lifetime.

23. (p. 120) *"Be silent!"*: Virgil warns the Pilgrim not to uncover his identity to Statius.

24. (p. 120) *I only smiled, as one who gives the wink*: The Pilgrim's smile and facial gesture gives Virgil's secret away.

25. (p. 120) *Now am I caught on this side and on that:* Although spoken in the present tense, these words are those of the Poet, not the Pilgrim. This an interesting and important authorial intervention into the fiction of the poem—elsewhere, the Poet only speaks looking backward from the future into the past story of the Pilgrim's journey through the afterlife.

26. (p. 120) *"This one . . . Is that Virgilius":* Given permission by Virgil, the Pilgrim now reveals his guide's identity to Statius.

27. (p. 120) *Already he was stooping to embrace . . . "Do not":* Although shades have embraced in other places (for example, Sordello and Virgil embrace in *Purgatorio* VII: 2 and 15), Virgil refuses to accept the adulation of Statius here. Perhaps the reason becomes clear only after a reading of the next canto, where we learn how important Statius considered Virgil to be as a force behind his eventual salvation, not to mention his poetic development and his moral values. In this context, such earthly considerations as friendly embraces must take second place to more important religious and ethical considerations. Virgil's refusal of Statius' embrace recalls Pope Adrian's refusal to accept the Pilgrim's act of respect in *Purgatorio* XIX: 133–138.

28. (p. 121) *"the sum of love which warms me . . . Treating a shadow as substantial thing":* Statius seems to reconsider his attempt to embrace Virgil here. But he offers the fact that he forgot momentarily his rejection of earthly vanity in his remembrance of Virgil's impact upon his life as a true measure of his love for the Pilgrim's guide.

CANTO XXII

1. (p. 122) *The Angel who to the sixth round had turned us:* Now the three poets—the Pilgrim, Virgil, and Statius—move to the sixth terrace, where gluttony is purged, and another *P* is removed from the Pilgrim's brow. Since each angel represents the virtue opposed to the sin that is being purged and here we are dealing with both avarice and prodigality, this particular angel has been labeled by various editors and translators with such titles as the Angel of Justice (mentioned in l. 4) or the Angel of Moderation. The fact that the Pilgrim mentions the fact that *his* mark is removed and does not note a similar experience on Statius' part would argue for the fact that only the Pilgrim ever receives such marks in Purgatory.

2. (p. 122) "*Beati,*" *in their voices,* / *With* "*sitio*": The Angel recites here only a portion of a beatitude: "Blessed are they which do hunger and thirst after righteousness: for they shall be filled." He also abbreviates the line to "Blessed are they who thirst after righteousness," saving the mention of hunger, appropriately, for the terrace of gluttony in *Purgatorio* XXIV: 151–154. To realize what the Poet has done here, a knowledge of the Latin Vulgate version of the text is required: *Beati qui esuriunt et sitiunt justitiam* is the original line in Latin, but Dante tells us that the angel leaves out the first verb *esuriunt* that refers to hunger and ends instead on the second verb. The biblical source of this beatitude is Matthew 5: 6.

3. (p. 122) *And I, more light:* The way is progressively easier for the Pilgrim as each *P* on his brow and its corresponding sin is removed.

4. (p. 122) "*The love* / *Kindled by virtue aye another kindles*": Virgil's idea that love may kindle love seems to refer us to the famous words of Francesca da Rimini in *Inferno* V: 103: "Love, that exempts no one beloved from loving." Since Virgil has qualified this idea by saying his remark applies only to love "kindled by virtue," his words stand as an implicit criticism of any love stories that are not inspired by virtue.

5. (p. 122) "*Hence from the hour that Juvenal descended*": In ll. 13–24, Virgil reveals that the Roman poet Juvenal (c. A.D. 60–140), upon his arrival in Limbo, informed the Pilgrim's guide of the great affection Statius had for him and his works, and this caused a corresponding affection in Virgil for Statius. Now meeting for the first time, Virgil and Statius treat each other as familiar friends and fellow poets. Of course, the reader should be as surprised to learn of the arrival of Juvenal in Limbo as he would naturally be after a reading of *Inferno* supplies the news that the great classical poets Homer, Virgil, Ovid, and Lucan were there.

6. (p. 122) "*How was it possible . . . For avarice to find place*": Virgil finds it incredible, given Statius' reputation for wisdom, that he could have been guilty of the sin of avarice.

7. (pp. 122–123) *These words excited Statius at first* / *Somewhat to laughter:* Statius smiles at Virgil, who seems to have forgotten the fact that avarice and prodigality are punished together in both Hell and Purgatory. As we soon learn, Statius is repenting for prodigality, not for avarice. The good humor is another indication of the bond of friendship between Statius and Virgil.

8. (p. 123) *"avarice was removed / Too far from me"*: Statius informs Virgil that far from being avaricious, he was prodigal and a waster. For this sin he has been repenting for more than five hundred years, or thousands of months ("lunar periods," l. 36), as he has already noted in *Purgatorio* XXI: 68.

9. (p. 123) *"where thou exclaimest . . . 'the appetite of mortal men'"*: Statius attributes his recognition of his prodigality to an understanding of Virgil's *Aeneid* (III: 56–57), the relevant lines of which he now translates from Latin into Italian. Virgil's text refers to the legend of Polymnestor and Polydorus, already alluded to in *Purgatorio* XX: 114–115. His remarks, though, are aimed against the avarice of Polymnestor, not his prodigality (the sin for which Statius admits his guilt). Apparently, the passage was enough to cause Statius to consider sins in general and to repent of them all.

10. (p. 123) *"the dismal joustings"*: Statius says that if it were not for his moral reaction to Virgil's text, he would now be rolling great stones around in the fourth circle of Hell with the other prodigals or wasters, clashing or "jousting" with the avaricious (see *Inferno* VII: 25–30).

11. (p. 123) *"with shorn hair"*: On the day of the Last Judgment, as we are informed in *Inferno* VII: 57, the prodigal will appear with very little or no hair to symbolize the destruction of their resources.

12. (p. 123) *"Because of ignorance . . . Cuts off repentance"*: Although the prodigal are ignorant of the fact that they sin, this does not alter the necessity for their purgation. This ignorance may, however, lead them not to realize that they need to repent.

13. (p. 123) *"By direct opposition any sin / Together with it here its verdure dries"*: This terrace is the only one on which a sin, prodigality, and its opposite, avarice, are punished. The purgation here is implicitly compared to a leaf loosing its green color, its "verdure."

14. (p. 123) *"the twofold affliction of Jocasta"*: In the *Thebaid*, Statius writes about the civil war in Thebes that emerged from the rivalry between Eteocles and Polynices, the sons of Jocasta by her own son, Oedipus.

15. (p. 123) *The singer of the Songs Bucolic:* Here Virgil is identified not as the epic poet of the *Aeneid* but as the author of the *Eclogues*, referred to here as "the Songs Bucolic," the pastoral poems that play a key role in the conversion of Statius.

16. (p. 123) *"Clio"*: Statius frequently invokes the Muse of History in the *Thebaid*; she is among many muses Dante invokes in *Inferno* II: 7 and *Purgatorio* I: 9.

17. (p. 123) *"It does not seem"*: It is evident from this passage that Virgil, who died in 19 B.C., knows the *Thebaid* of Statius, in spite of the fact that he died decades before its composition. Either Virgil has been doing some idle reading in Limbo or Dante the Poet invents as he pleases.

18. (p. 123) *"That faith without which no good works suffice"*: Virgil implicitly explains his place in Limbo and the fact that any good works he might have accomplished were not sufficient to save him.

19. (pp. 123–124) *"what candles or what sun . . . behind the Fisherman thereafter"*: Virgil wants to know what sources of human enlightenment ("candles") or what divinity ("sun") removed the darkness of paganism from Statius and caused him to follow the Christian religion. Dante symbolizes Christianity here with a reference to the Fisherman, or Saint Peter. In the Bible, Mark 1: 17, Jesus summons Peter and his brother, Andrew, to become "fishers of men."

20. (p. 124) *"Thou first directedst me / Towards Parnassus . . . And first concerning God didst me enlighten"*: Statius claims that Virgil taught him how to write poetry: Parnassus is the mountain sacred to Apollo and the muses and therefore to poetry, and the Castalian spring that flows in the grottoes of the mountain provide poetic inspiration. Virgil was also the first to inform Statius about the true God—a claim meant to be startling and solely Dante's invention.

21. (p. 124) *"as he who walketh in the night, / Who bears his light behind"*: This image of a man walking with a light that guides those who follow him perfectly captures this paradoxical situation in which an unsaved Virgil sheds illumination on a saved Statius.

22. (p. 124) *"When thou didst say . . . 'descends from Heaven'"*: Statius now provides a paraphrase of ll. 5–7 of Virgil's *Fourth Eclogue*. In the Middle Ages, this poetic text was believed to have predicted the birth of Jesus.

23. (p. 124) *"Through thee I Poet was, through thee a Christian"*: Here and elsewhere in the poem, Statius connects poetry with divine inspiration.

24. (p. 124) *"Whence I to visit them the custom took"*: Statius believed that Virgil's poem confirmed the message of the apostles preaching Christianity, and so he began to keep their company.

25. (p. 124) *"Domitian persecuted them":* Born in A.D. 51, Domitian ruled Rome from the year 81 to 96. He was blamed for relentless persecution of Christians. Statius dedicated his *Thebaid* to this emperor.

26. (p. 124) *"And ere I led the Greeks... I was baptized":* Here Statius claims that he was converted to Christianity and received baptism around the time he was composing the seventh book of the *Thebaid*, the section in which the Greeks near the Theban rivers. In *Inferno* IV: 35, we learned that Virgil and the other virtuous pagans were not baptized.

27. (p. 124) *"To circle round more than four centuries":* Because of his fear of openly professing his new Christian faith, Statius was first compelled to remain on the terrace of the slothful (the fourth terrace) for more than four hundred years. Presumably, he has resided on the terrace of the prodigal ever since his departure from the terrace of the slothful.

28. (pp. 124–125) *"in what place is our friend Terentius":* In the next four stanzas Virgil adds a number of Latin and Greek classical poets to the list of those residing with him in Limbo that Dante the Poet could have known only indirectly through remarks about them in Cicero, Horace, and other classical writers. Since most died before the coming of Christ or the announcement of Christ's coming by his disciples, they were denied salvation, as was Virgil. Terentius is the Latin comic poet Terence (c.184–c.159 B.C.). Caecilius' works survive only in fragments; their author probably died in 169 B.C. Plautus (250–185 B.C.) is the famous comic playwright; Varro may be Varius Rufus, a friend of Virgil's; Aulus Persius Flaccus (A.D. 34–62) was a satirist. Euripides (484–406 B.C.) was one of Greece's greatest tragedians. Antiphon was a Greek poet mentioned by Plutarch. Simonides (556–467 B.C.) was a Greek lyric poet; some of his fragments survive. Agatho, or Agathon (448–402 B.C.), was a Greek tragic poet and one of the characters in Plato's *Symposium*. Virgil notes that these five Latins and four Greeks reside "with that Grecian" (l. 101)—that is, the Greek epic poet Homer (see *Inferno* IV: 80–81). Dante the Poet considered Homer to be the greatest poet of all (the muses suckle him more than the rest) even though Dante had never read Homer's works.

29. (p. 125) *"the first circle of the prison blind":* The reference is to Limbo, called here in the original Italian a *cinghio* ("strap"), referring to the fact that the great classical poets are tethered there without hope of the Christian enlightenment of faith. Without the light of enlightenment, it is a blind prison.

30. (p. 125) *"our nurses"*: These are the nine muses who suckle the poets.

31. (p. 125) *"some of thine own people . . . Deidamia with her sisters"*: Virgil now mentions eight additional souls who, according to him, reside in Limbo. They are all characters in the two epics by Statius (the first six from his *Thebaid*, the last two from his *Achilleid*): Antigone and her sister Ismene are daughters of Jocasta and Oedipus. Deiphile and her sister Argìa are daughters of Adrastus, king of Argos, and respectively the wives of Polynices and Tydeus. The woman "who pointed out Langìa" is Hypsipyle, who, according, to Statius' *Thebaid*, pointed the thirsty Greek heroes who attacked Thebes in the direction of a stream by that name during a drought (see *Inferno* XVIII: 92; and *Purgatorio* XXVI: 95). Ismene is another daughter of Jocasta and Oedipus, "mournful as of old" because of the many tragedies she witnessed that destroyed her family. Thetis is the mother of Achilles, while Deidamia is the woman with whom Achilles was left by Thetis in an effort to avoid his tragic death in the Trojan War. The most puzzling fictional character listed here is the daughter of Tiresias, who must be Manto and whom Dante has already placed among the soothsayers in the fourth *bolgia* of the eighth circle of Hell (*Inferno* XX: 52–99). Dante is an exceedingly careful poet, but there is virtually nothing to explain this clash of two different locations of this figure except for the fact that he forgot he had already found a place for Manto in Hell when he wrote these lines. One possible way to explain Dante's "error" is to maintain that he puts Virgil's Manto in Hell and Statius' Manto in Purgatory (since both are literary figures and not real people), but this seems improbable.

32. (p. 125) *From the ascent and from the walls released:* Without much comment about the fact, the two travelers have now neared the sixth terrace, where gluttony is purged.

33. (p. 125) *four handmaidens of the day already . . . the fifth / Was pointing upward still its burning horn:* In *Purgatorio* XII: 81, the sixth hour of the day is described as the "sixth handmaiden." Thus, if the "four handmaidens," or first four hours, have passed and the "fifth handmaiden" is in position, and if the sun normally rises at 6:00 A.M., the present time in Purgatory is between 10:00 and 11:00 A.M.

34. (p. 125) *"I think that tow'rds the edge ... as we are wont to do"*: The correct direction up the Mountain of Purgatory is to head toward the right, and the two travelers are assured by the fact that Statius (who knows the area better than they do) assents to the direction they take.

35. (p. 125) *lessons in the art of song:* The term in the original Italian is much stronger: *intelletto* ("understanding"), which implies that Dante is learning more than how to write poetry. This understanding is much more concerned with the moral and ethical functions of poetry than with the rules of composition. Also, the three epic poets walk in a manner that suggests literary tradition: Dante follows a pagan poet and a pagan poet who was converted to Christianity, while he obviously considers himself the quintessential expression of Christian poetry.

36. (pp. 125–126) *A tree ... that no one might climb it:* This tree that suddenly appears in the path is oddly shaped. The branches bend downward, and the largest branches grow toward the top of the tree. As a result, it is impossible to climb the tree.

37. (p. 126) *"Of this food ye shall have scarcity":* The unidentified voice that speaks from within the foliage seems to be presenting a version of God's first prohibition to Adam and Eve in the Bible, Genesis 2: 15–17. It is interesting that this incident does not accompany an example of a corrective virtue, as has been the case on other terraces of Purgatory. The perfect punishment for gluttony, its "counterpoise," would consist of being surrounded by food without the possibility of enjoying it.

38. (p. 126) *"More thoughtful Mary was ... her mouth which now for you responds":* The voice's second pronouncement begins a series of five examples of temperance, or abstinence, the virtue that corrects the sin being punished in this circle, gluttony. Here the reference is to the Virgin Mary at the wedding of Cana, who thought only of others and not of herself. The Virgin's good deed at this marriage, as told in the Bible, John 2: 1–11, is also cited in *Purgatorio* XIII: 29, and there serves as an example of her generosity. Dante makes a point of the fact that Mary employed her mouth to beg Jesus to perform a miracle rather than to consume food.

39. (p. 126) *the ancient Roman women / With water were content:* This example stresses the Golden Age of temperance in ancient republican

Rome and reminds the reader that Roman matrons did not consume wine or spirits.

40. (p. 126) *Daniel / Disparaged food:* In the Bible, Daniel 1: 3–20, Daniel refuses the meat and drink of Nebuchadnezzar and is rewarded by God with the gift of interpreting dreams.

41. (p. 126) *"The primal age was beautiful as gold; / Acorns it made with hunger savorous":* In the Age of Gold celebrated by the ancients, mankind had yet to be corrupted with expensive tastes (such as fancy food and drink) and was still satisfied with simple acorns and spring water.

42. (p. 126) *the Baptist in the wilderness:* According to Matthew 3: 4, John the Baptist nourished himself on wild honey and locusts in the desert and in so doing earned the praise of God.

CANTO XXIII

1. (p. 127) *Who wastes his life pursuing little birds:* Clearly, Dante feels that hunting birds is not a useful activity, and he uses this idea to give Virgil a chance to chide the Pilgrim for wasting time. Making haste becomes an important theme in *Purgatorio*.

2. (p. 127) *the Sages:* That is, the two poets Virgil and Statius.

3. (p. 127) *"Labia mea, Domine":* The souls are singing an appropriate verse from a song that has already been heard in Antepurgatory (*Purgatorio* V: 24): "O Lord, open thou my lips; and my mouth shall shew forth thy praise" (Psalms 51: 15). The gluttons are learning that human lips should be employed in praising God, not in drinking and gluttonous eating.

4. (p. 127) *"Perhaps the knot unloosing of their debt":* Unloosing a knot is a metaphor for expiating the sin of gluttony.

5. (p. 127) *In the same way that thoughtful pilgrims do:* Here and on other terraces in Purgatory (with the exception of those devoted to envy and avarice), penitent souls are in motion.

6. (p. 128) *Could Erisichthon have been withered up / By famine:* Since the souls of the penitent gluttonous have been reduced to emaciated forms of starving humanity, the Poet appropriately refers to the figure of this man described in Ovid's *Metamorphoses* VIII: 738–878. Erisichthon was cursed by the goddess Ceres and driven to such a hunger that he devoured his own flesh. This passage from Ovid also contains a graphic description of the figure of Famine that probably also influenced Dante's depiction.

7. (p. 128) *"the folk who lost Jerusalem . . . made a prey of her own son":* In Josephus' *De Bello Judaico* (*On the Jewish War*) VI: 3, the historian reports that during the Roman siege of Jerusalem in A.D. 70, a woman named Mary cooked and ate her infant son. The Italian original of l. 30 makes the image even more graphic than Longfellow's translation, for it notes that Mary put her "beak" (not her teeth) into the child. This changes her from a human being into a bird of prey, and Longfellow renders the image skillfully.

8. (p. 128) *Their sockets were like rings without the gems:* The eyes of the emaciated penitents resemble the mountings of rings without the gemstones in them.

9. (p. 128) *Whoever in the face of men reads* omo: In Dante's day, it was believed that God had marked His creation, man, by designing the human face so that a man's eyes formed the two letters *O*, while the nose and the outline of the sockets of the eyes formed the letter *M*, spelling out *omo*—that is, *homo* ("man" in Latin). Here the Poet is saying that the penitent gluttons are so emaciated that only the letter *M* can be discerned on their faces.

10. (p. 128) *"What grace to me is this?":* The yet-to-be identified speaker is referring to the grace, or favor, of seeing Dante the Pilgrim once again.

11. (p. 128) *My recognition of his altered face . . . Forese:* Forese Donati, a friend of Dante's, died on July 28, 1296, only a few years before the fictional date of the Pilgrim's journey to the afterlife. Forese was the brother of Corso Donati, the leader of the Black Guelphs that opposed the faction to which Dante belonged, the White Guelphs. Corso is attacked in *Purgatorio* XXIV: 82–87, while Forse's sister Piccarda Donati is praised in *Purgatorio* XXIV: 13–15; she will also appear in *Paradiso* III: 34–123. Dante exchanged six sonnets with Forese, a facetious poetic argument known as a *tenzone,* and in one of them he accuses his friend of gluttony.

12. (p. 128) *"what thus denudes you?":* The Pilgrim asks Forese for an explanation of his odd appearance, employing a verb in Italian (*sfogliarsi*) that means to "peel off" or "strip" and describes the defoliation of a tree's leaves.

13. (p. 130) *"the eternal council"*: The reference is to God's will and counsel.

14. (p. 130) *"The scent that issues from the apple-tree . . . And not a single time alone"*: The travelers will come upon another tree in *Purgatorio* XXIV: 103–129. The first tree seems to be the Tree of Life, while the second is the Tree of Knowledge of Good and Evil.

15. (p. 130) *"Christ rejoicing to say* Eli, / *When with his veins he liberated us"*: As told in the Bible, Matthew 27: 46, just before dying on the cross, Jesus exclaimed, *Eli, Eli, lama sabacthani* ("My God, my God, why hast thou forsaken me?"). Thus, the penitent gluttons mortify their flesh in imitation of Christ's suffering on the cross.

16. (p. 130) *"I thought to find thee down there underneath, / Where time for time doth restitution make"*: Forese died only a few years before the action of *Purgatorio* takes place, and Dante the Pilgrim is amazed that Forese has not spent more time in the other terraces of Purgatory and wonders why this is so.

17. (p. 130) *"My Nella . . . from the other circles set me free"*: With her prayers, Forese's wife helped to shorten Forese's time in Purgatory. The citation of this faithful wife's piety emphasizes how useful the prayers of the living are to those in Purgatory.

18. (p. 130) *"the Barbagia of Sardinia . . . the Barbagia I have left her in"*: Forese compares the loose morals of the women of Florence to the women of the Barbagia. This mountainous region in Sardinia was said to be inhabited by coarse descendants of the prisoners of the Vandals. They were said to be barbarians, and the women supposedly exposed their breasts.

19. (p. 131) *"the unblushing womankind of Florence / To go about displaying breast and paps"*: Forese delivers a moralistic attack upon the loose morals of the Florentine women. In fact, sumptuary decrees by churchmen in the early fourteenth century did attack the lewd display of the female body made possible by current female fashion.

20. (p. 131) *"They shall be sad ere he has bearded cheeks"*: Forese predicts that Florence's female population will receive the punishment of divine retribution their conduct has deserved in the space of the time it normally takes for a baby to grow into a young man with a beard (fifteen or sixteen years). Since the Poet composes his work long after the date of 1300, he may have meant to refer to any number of military

invasions, defeats, and natural disasters that occurred between 1300 and 1316 and might be interpreted as divine punishment for the city of Florence.

21. (p. 131) *"thou dost veil the sun":* Forese wants to know how it is possible for a living being (one who casts a shadow, or whose body veils the sun's rays) to journey through Purgatory.

22. (p. 131) *"What thou with me hast been ... The present memory will be grievous still":* Some controversy remains over the meaning of the Pilgrim's remarks about his relationship to Forese. It is possible that Dante refers merely to the superficial tone and content of the poetic exchanges between him and Forese (see note 11 to this canto). Other interpretations suggest that the sinful life that Forese and Dante led may cause them both grief. In either case, the rest of the canto provides a summary of the Pilgrim's activities until the end of *Purgatorio*.

23. (p. 131) *the sister of him yonder:* The sister of Apollo, god of the sun, is the goddess of the moon, Diana. The Pilgrim here refers to the full moon shining on the night of Holy Thursday when he entered the dark wood of *Inferno* I, two days earlier.

24. (p. 131) *this one:* The reference is to Virgil.

25. (p. 131) *"That you doth straighten, whom the world made crooked":* The winding or twisting path around the Mountain of Purgatory paradoxically straightens the penitents' souls.

26. (p. 131) *"where Beatrice will be":* Forese is the only penitent to whom the Pilgrim mentions Beatrice's name.

27. (p. 131) *"the other is":* The reference is to Statius.

CANTO XXIV

1. (p. 133) *"he goes up more slowly":* Here the Pilgrim refers to Statius, who is delaying his passage through Purgatory (breaking the rule that the penitents must hastily undergo both their punishment and their expiation) because of his admiration for Virgil. In effect, the Christianized Latin poet is putting his Latin mentor before God. When Dante finally reaches Beatrice in canto XXX, she will scold him severely for doing something of the same with his guide, Virgil.

2. (p. 133) *"Piccarda":* According to early commentators, Piccarda Donati was removed from a convent in Florence by her evil brother Corso in order that she might be married. It was said that she prayed to die in order not to violate her oath of virginity. The reader will meet her again in *Paradiso* III: 49–124 in the heaven of the moon.

3. (p. 133) *"Already in her crown on high Olympus"*: Forese informs the Pilgrim that Piccarda is already among the blessed in heaven, here called Olympus to assimilate into Christianity the mountain sacred to the gods of classical antiquity.

4. (p. 133) *"Buonagiunta of Lucca"*: Buonagiunta Orbicciani of Lucca (c.1220–1297) was a poet of the mid-thirteenth century associated with the imitation of verse composed by Provençal and Sicilian poets. Dante criticizes his language in *De Vulgari Eloquentia* I: xiii: 1.

5. (p. 133) *"and that face . . . Bolsena's eels and the Vernaccia wine"*: Simon de Brie from Tours, France, was elected to the papacy as Martin IV (1281–1285). He was said to have died from overeating eels from Lake Bolsena (a large lake in central Italy north of the city of Viterbo) that had been soaked in milk and stewed in a white wine called Vernaccia.

6. (p. 134) *And all contented seemed at being named*: Unlike the souls being punished in Hell, the penitent in Purgatory are delighted to be mentioned, since their loved ones still alive may help them expiate their sins and shorten their time in Purgatory by the intercession of their prayers.

7. (p. 134) *Ubaldin dalla Pila, and Boniface*: Ubaldino degli Ubaldini dalla Pila, who died in 1291, was a member of the Ghibelline family that also included Cardinal Ottaviano degli Ubaldini (*Inferno* X: 120) and Ugolino d'Azzo (*Purgatorio* XIV: 105); he was the father of Archbishop Ruggieri degli Ubaldini, whose head is being gnawed by Count Ugolino in *Inferno* XXXIII: 15. Bonifazio de' Fieschi was archbishop of Ravenna from 1274 to 1295.

8. (p. 134) *Who with his crook had pastured many people*: Instead of feeding his religious flock of Christians with the good news of the gospels, Boniface instead has used his wealth and influence to feed and entertain the courtiers flocking around him. The bishop's pastoral crook in Ravenna was apparently shaped more like a chess rook than like a shepherd's crook, and in the Italian original Dante specifically calls the pastoral staff a rook (*rocco*).

9. (p. 134) *Messer Marchese . . . for drinking with less dryness*: Marchese (his given name, not a title) degli Argugliosi from the town of Forlì

served as *podestà* of Faenza in 1296 and died shortly thereafter. He had the reputation of being a great drinker, and to this accusation, Marchese apparently replied that people should think of him as merely a man with great and continuous thirst rather than as a heavy drinker.

10. (p. 134) *him of Lucca:* This is the same Bonagiunta of Lucca mentioned in ll. 19–20. Bonagiunta apparently wants to speak to the Pilgrim because he knows him.

11. (p. 134) *He murmured . . . what Gentucca:* Bonagiunta murmurs because his flesh has been plucked away from his jaws, as is made clear in ll. 38–40. His words are difficult for the Pilgrim to understand, and they have presented difficulties for Dante scholars as well. Early Dante commentators took the word *gentucca* to be a pejorative form of the word *gente* ("people"), and thus Bonagiunta's comment would refer to "low people" like the Pilgrim who were members of an opposing political faction. Other, more recent interpretations have argued that the word is a proper name indicating a woman named Gentucca who had befriended the Pilgrim during his exile from Florence.

12. (p. 134) *"A maid is born . . . men may blame it":* Bonagiunta's prediction that a very young and unmarried woman in Lucca will be hospitable to Dante perhaps makes up for the proverbial low opinion that most Florentines had of that city (see *Inferno* XXI: 41–42). This woman would be unmarried because she is described as not yet wearing the "veil," a head cover with a chinstrap worn by married women in Dante's time.

13. (p. 134) *"Ladies, that have intelligence of love?":* Bonagiunta identifies the Pilgrim with the first verse of *La Vita Nuova* XIX. This work marks a turn in Dante's love life from writing poetry in the erotic vein to that of pure and unselfish praise for his lady Beatrice.

14. (p. 134) *"One am I":* Dante here begins a description of his new technique, the "sweet new style" of l. 57. The passages in this canto concerning Dante's poetry have created numerous critical debates, especially about what exactly is meant by the mention of this new style. Most Dante critics generally see the reference as stemming from Dante's self-serving evaluation of his lyric output and desire to emphasize his originality and to shape the literary history of his times.

15. (p. 134) *"the knot":* Bonagiunta asserts that he understands the "knot," or obstacle that prevented the Notary and Guittone from developing the new poetic style Dante claims for his own. The Notary is Giacomo da Lentini, the Sicilian poet of the early thirteenth century who probably invented the sonnet form and who is identified as the major figure in the so-called Sicilian school of poetry. Guittone d'Arezzo (c.1230–1294) was the major figure in the so-called Tuscan school of poetry. Giacomo was primarily responsible for translating the achievements of the troubadour love poetry from Provence into Italian verse. Dante disparages Guittone's language as plebeian and excessive in *De Vulgari Eloquentia* I: xiii; II, vi, even though he often imitated him in his early works.

16. (p. 134) *"the sweet new style that now I hear"*: Note that Bonagiunta identifies the "sweet new style" of poetry with the speech that he actually hears from the Pilgrim's mouth in Purgatory. This must mean that the poetry of *The Divine Comedy* is included in the sweet new style. It is unclear, though, whether or not Bonagiunta is also referring to poetry written by Dante that he had read while alive. Also, he could be referring not just to Dante but to other poets as well: Literary historians have employed the term "sweet new style" (*dolce stil novo* in Italian) to refer to a school that included a number of Florentines in addition to Dante: Guido Guinizzelli, Guido Cavalcanti, Lapo Gianni, Gianni degli Alfani, Dino Frescobaldi, and Cino da Pistoia. What remains clear, in spite of all the controversy, is that Dante identifies himself with a broad intellectual and stylistic change in lyric poetry that moved from secular and erotic focus upon women to the theme of selfless praise of women as agents leading mankind to spiritual salvation (the role Beatrice plays in *The Divine Comedy*). Dante and other like-minded poets moved poetry away from the conventions of courtly, erotic literature toward more elevated goals.

17. (p. 134) *"your pens"*: In the original Italian (*le vostre penne*, or "your pens"), Bonagiunta's use of the plural implies that there are, in fact, a group of like-minded "sweet new style" poets who follow the dictates of love in their verse. At least one critic has also suggested that the passage actually refers to the feathers (*penne*) of wings, a metaphor for poetic flight inspired by love.

18. (p. 135) *Even as the birds... go in file:* The image of cranes seeking a warm place during the winter near the Nile River by flying there in single file may be taken from Lucan's *Pharsalia* V: 711–716.

19. (p. 135) *"sooner in desire arrive":* Even though the Poet has no desire to die immediately, he obviously believes he is destined to be saved and purified in Purgatory. Accordingly, his desire arrives there before his body will.

20. (p. 135) *"is more depleted . . . the body vilely mutilated":* The Pilgrim complains of how his native city of Florence has had the good "depleted"; the original Italian employs the verb *si spolpa* ("stripped away"), a word that reminds us of the punishment of the gluttonous on this terrace. Then we hear a description of the man responsible for Dante's problems in Florence. This is Corso Donati, the brother of Forese and Piccarda and the leader of the Black Guelph faction in Florence (see also note 2 to this canto). Corso received assistance from Pope Boniface VIII to send Charles of Valois to support the Black faction in 1301. After a brief campaign of terror, Charles left the city and Corso was eventually condemned to death as a traitor. He escaped but on October 6, 1308, mercenary troops recaptured and killed him. The beast of l. 83 could well be Pope Boniface, but this may simply be a reference to legends of sinners being dragged off to Hell by various animals. Corso was apparently killed either by being speared in the throat after falling off his horse or by being dragged by his horse's stirrup.

21. (p. 135) *"Not long those wheels shall turn":* Not many rotations of the heavens will take place before Forese's prediction of Corso's demise will take place. In fact, Corso died only eight years after the fictional date of the Pilgrim's visit to the Afterlife in 1300.

22. (p. 136) *those two:* The reference is to Virgil and Statius, neither of whom has spoken in this section of the poem.

23. (p. 136) *Mine eyes became to him such pursuivants / As was my understanding to his words:* Forese departs as if on a battle charger, while the Pilgrim remains behind with Virgil and Statius, referred to l. 99 as the two "mighty marshals of the world." He notes that his eyes could no longer follow Forese, any more than his mind could follow the obscurity of Forese's prophecy.

24. (p. 136) *another apple-tree:* This is the second tree encountered in this terrace. In contrast to the first, which issued words providing examples of the opposite of gluttony, this one provides negative examples of the sin in question. In ll. 116–117, it is made clear that this tree is an offshoot of the original Tree of the Knowledge of Good and Evil, from which Eve tasted the Forbidden Fruit and was subsequently exiled from the Garden of Evil with her consort, Adam. It can therefore be argued that the first tree the travelers encounter on this terrace may be identified with the Tree of Life.

25. (p. 136) *"the accursed ones / Formed of the cloud-rack . . . their double breasts"*: The centaurs—with "double breasts" because they were part human, part horse—were famously gluttonous. They were said to be the offspring of Ixion, king of the Lapithae, and Nephele, a woman born in the clouds ("cloud-rack"). When the centaurs became drunk at the wedding feast of Pirithoüs and Hippodameia, many were killed by Theseus and others (see Ovid's *Metamorphoses* XII: 210–535).

26. (p. 136) *"And of the Jews who showed them soft in drinking"*: In the Bible, Judges VII: 2–8, Gideon selects soldiers for his campaign against the Midianites on the basis of how they react to water when they arrive thirsty at a river. Those who put their faces into the river are rejected as lacking restraint. In like manner, gluttons leap upon their food and drink, while the more moderate act in the manner of Gideon's chosen soldiers, who made a cup of their hands and thereby imbibed less liquid.

27. (p. 136) *closely pressed to one of the two borders:* Virgil, Statius, and the Pilgrim must go around the tree, and to do so they travel very close to the inside edge of the road. In this way they avoid falling off the cliff.

28. (p. 137) *"What go ye thinking thus, ye three alone?"*: This is the voice of the Angel of Temperance, or Abstinence. His appearance is flaming red (as we learn in l. 138); perhaps this color alerts us to the activity on the next terrace, where the lustful are purified.

29. (p. 137) *The air of May . . . So did I feel a breeze strike:* The Pilgrim compares the gentleness with which the Angel strokes his brow to remove the symbol of the sin of gluttony, another letter *P*, to a spring breeze in May.

30. (p. 137) *"Blessed are they whom grace . . . Hungering at all times so far as is just"*: In *Purgatorio* XXII: 4–6, the Poet employed part of the fifth beatitude from the Bible, Matthew 5: 6, but omitted a reference to hungering for righteousness. He uses that reference now, because it makes an appropriate connection to the sin of gluttony. (See note 2 to canto XXII.)

CANTO XXV

1. (p. 139) *To Taurus left . . . to Scorpio:* Once again, Dante tells time by employing the signs of the zodiac. He means to indicate that it is around 2:00 P.M., so the Pilgrim has spent about four hours on the terrace of the gluttonous. Meanwhile, on the opposite side of the globe over Jerusalem, Libra is giving way to Scorpio, which means that it is about 2:00 A.M.

2. (p. 139) *the gap . . . one before the other:* The narrow passageway along which the three poets must now travel requires them to advance in single file. Virgil leads, followed respectively by Statius and the Pilgrim.

3. (p. 139) *"Let fly / The bow of speech":* Virgil anticipates the Pilgrim's unasked question and orders him to speak. The Pilgrim's eagerness to speak suggests the act of an archer drawing the tip of an arrow all the way back so that the tip touches the bow itself, then letting fly.

4. (p. 139) *"How can one meagre grow / There where the need of nutriment applies not?":* The Pilgrim cannot understand how souls, immaterial beings, can grow thin from not ingesting food. He has assumed that this effect occurs only in a mortal, material body.

5. (p. 139) *"Meleager / Was wasted by the wasting of a brand":* In Ovid's *Metamorphoses* VIII: 260–525, the Latin poet recounts Meleager's fate, which was to live only as long as a log burning on the hearth remained unconsumed. In order to prolong her son's life, his mother hid the log. Years later Meleager killed his mother's brothers, so she took the wood and burned it, thereby causing Meleager's death. Virgil offers this story to demonstrate how a result may be far removed from a cause: The wasting away of the gluttonous is not linked to physical deprivation of food, just as Meleager's body was not present when the log was burned.

6. (p. 139) *"sour":* In this case, the word in the original Italian (*agro*) refers to the difficulty of understanding, not to taste.

7. (p. 139) *"Trembles within a mirror your own image":* The reflection of a person's image in a mirror underscores the fact that the body is only a reflection of the soul.

8. (p. 140) *"Lo Statius here":* Virgil courteously asks Statius to provide scientific explanations in response to the Pilgrim's question. His lengthy discourse generally leaves contemporary readers of Dante cold, but it serves to show us the state of scientific knowledge in Dante's time and reveals the prevailing theories about the relationship between the body and the soul. First, he explains the creation and development of the embryo, generally following the theories of Aristotle and those of Avicenna (ll. 37–60). Then, he treats the creation of the soul, employing ideas from Christian doctrine (ll. 61–78). Finally, he discusses how the "formative virtue" creates an aerial body after death (ll. 79–108); much of what Statius says in this last part of the explanation is pure invention on Dante's part.

9. (p. 140) *"If I unfold to him . . . I can naught deny thee"*: Statius declares that he will reveal this specifically Christian theory to the Pilgrim and to Virgil, even though Virgil's pagan beliefs cannot be squared with the information Statius is about to disclose. He will do so out of his love for the Latin epic poet's work and person.

10. (p. 140) *"The perfect blood, which never is drunk up"*: The best part of the blood, designed to become human sperm, does not enter the veins.

11. (p. 140) *"Virtue informative"*: This is the generative power that forms a new organism.

12. (p. 140) *"Again digest . . . 'tis better / Silent to be than say"*: The transformation of blood into sperm apparently takes place before the blood reaches the genitals. Statius modestly refuses to name this part of the body.

13. (p. 140) *"in natural vase . . . with the other mingles"*: The natural vase is the womb, where menstrual blood mixes with the sperm.

14. (p. 140) *"One to be passive meant, the other active"*: The active male blood, now turned to sperm, works on the passive female blood, making it coagulate. As a result, the female blood takes on the informative "virtue" communicated to it by the male blood.

15. (p. 140) *"As of a plant . . . the powers whose seed it is"*: The newly formed soul resembles a vegetable at first. But this vegetative soul develops motion and sensation, turning into a sensitive soul.

16. (p. 140) *"a wiser man than thou once err . . . possible intellect"*: Averroës, the Arab commentator on Aristotle, was mistaken, according to Statius. He believed that the individual soul possessed only vegetative and sensitive aspects but lacked what Christians would call the intellective soul or "possible intellect" required for the soul's immortality.

In spite of such error, Averroës and Avicenna both earn places in Limbo in *Inferno* IV: 143–144, obviously because of their important commentaries on Aristotle's works.

17. (p. 141) *"The primal Motor . . . the juice that from the vine distills":* This is a reference to God, defined in Aristotelian terms as the first motor or mover. The Motor brings life into the fetus by breathing the intellectual soul into it. As a result, the three aspects of the soul—vegetative, sensitive, and intellective—become a single soul. This miracle may be compared to the fact that the sun's heat produces a substance—wine—that is different from the grape juice of which it is made.

18. (p. 141) *"Lachesis has no more thread":* She is one of the three fates who spin out human destiny; when Lachesis runs out of thread, a life ends. (See note 8 to *Purgatorio* XXI.)

19. (p. 141) *"voiceless all":* The voiceless faculties are the vegetative and the sensitive souls.

20. (p. 141) *"far more vigorous than before":* Freed of the earthly body, the memory, intelligence, and will are actually more active than they were when bound to it.

21. (p. 141) *"on one shore or the other":* At the moment of death, a soul falls either on the shore of the River Acheron (if it is damned) or on the shore of the River Tiber (if it is to be saved). The saved souls await transportation to Purgatory.

22. (p. 141) *"So there the neighboring air doth shape itself ":* Dante invents this idea that the informative virtue operates on the air around the soul to produce a visible aerial body, the shades the Pilgrim sees in the Afterlife. Church doctrine, however, generally maintained that after death, the soul remained without any body until Judgment Day, when it would be resurrected as a whole body. Dante invents his notion so the Pilgrim can see real shapes and figures in the Afterlife—necessary, since the poem deals with conversations between a living being and countless shades or souls.

23. (p. 142) *the last of all the circles:* After the lengthy scientific explanations by Statius, it is a relief for reader and Pilgrim to reach the seventh terrace, where lust will be purged. The travelers continue to head toward the right, as usual.

24. (p. 142) *shoots forth flames of fire . . . on the open side:* The wall of flames shoots forth from the inner wall of the terrace all the way to the

outer edge, where a blast of air clears a safe path along the outside edge of the terrace.

25. (p. 142) "Summæ Deus clementiæ": "God of supreme clemency" is the beginning of a hymn once sung at Matins on Saturday. It is appropriate that the lustful sing it, since in the song God is asked to banish lust and to cleanse sinners with his purifying fire.

26. (p. 142) "Virum non cognosco": These Latin words ("I know not a man") come from the Bible, Luke 1: 34. The Virgin Mary utters them at the Annunciation, underscoring her virginity and her status as an emblem of chastity. This is an appropriate text for the realm where the lustful repent.

27. (p. 142) *"Diana ran . . . of Venus felt the poison":* The second example of chastity is taken from classical literature and concerns the goddess Diana, who ran into the woods to protect her chastity. When one of her attendants named Helice (Ovid calls her Calisto) was seduced by Jove and fell in love, Diana dismissed her. Dante's source is Ovid, *Metamorphoses* II: 401–530.

28. (p. 142) *the wives . . . and the husbands who were chaste:* After returning to their song, the penitent lustful shout out the names of wives and husbands who provide examples of chastity within the sacred bounds of marriage. Dante celebrated sexual union within marriage as a form of acceptable lust, while some radical voices in his society called for complete sexual abstinence.

29. (p. 142) *the fire is burning . . . the last wound of all should be closed up:* While the burning fire is traditionally a symbol for lust, here it is a cure. The prayers of the lustful, fortified by their hymns and the examples they recite, provide them with food that closes up their last wound—last because lust is the last sin to be purified in Purgatory.

CANTO XXVI

1. (p. 143) *On the right shoulder:* The sun strikes the Pilgrim low from the right side as he walks around the outer edge of the seventh terrace. Scholars generally calculate that roughly two hours have passed since the travelers left the sixth terrace around 2:00 P.M. So, it is around 4:00 to 5:00 P.M.

2. (p. 143) *"not a factitious body!":* The penitent lustful observe that the Pilgrim's body is not one of the aerial bodies Statius described in the last canto. In other words, his is a real, flesh-and-bone body.

3. (p. 143) *always with regard . . . where they would not be burned:* The penitent come forward to look at the Pilgrim, but they are careful not to step out of the punishing flames, since they are anxious to complete their purification as soon as possible. As usual in the afterlife, souls are puzzled by the presence of a real human being.

4. (p. 143) *"for cold water Ethiop or Indian":* Inhabitants of places with hot climates, such as Ethiopia or India, would naturally be thirsty, just as the penitent lustful in the fire cannot quench their thirst.

5. (p. 143) *Thus one of them addressed me:* This shade's identity will finally be disclosed in l. 92 as Guido Guinizzelli.

6. (p. 144) *kissing one another:* Part of the *contrapasso* ("counterpoise" or "counterweight") of the lustful is that their kisses are now chaste. They are of the kind that Saint Paul recommends in Romans 16: 16: "Salute one another with an holy kiss." The most interesting aspect of this scene is the fact that the remarks of pentitent will soon reveal that the group is composed of both homosexuals and heterosexuals.

7. (p. 144) *"Sodom and Gomorrah!":* The second group of sinners identifies themselves as homosexuals by their reference to the biblical city that has given the name to sodomy. They walk in a clockwise direction while the heterosexual group moves in a counterclockwise direction, underlining the unnatural lust of the homosexuals.

8. (p. 144) *"Into the cow Pasiphae . . . her lust may run":* Pasiphaë, wife of King Minos of Crete, lusted after a mock bull fashioned out of wood, and the result of their union was the Minotaur (see *Inferno* XII: 12–18). It probably strikes the modern reader as strange that the lustful union of a woman and an animal could serve as an image of normal heterosexual lust.

9. (p. 144) *Riphæan mountains . . . those of the sun avoidant:* The Riphæan is a legendary mountain range at the extreme north of the globe. Cranes would obviously not migrate in two different directions at the same time. They recall the cranes of *Inferno* V: 46–47, where the lustful are punished.

10. (p. 144) *their first songs . . . to the cry that most befitteth them:* "Songs" a reference to *Summæ Deus clementiæ* of canto XXV: 121; see note 25 hat canto. The lustful are in two groups and alternate their cries

with this hymn. Their cries, meanwhile, identify their particular type of sin.

11. (p. 144) *"A Lady is above":* This is a reference to Beatrice, although some scholars believe this to be a reference to the Virgin Mary.

12. (p. 144) *"the Heaven may house you . . . and most amply spreads":* Here the Pilgrim refers to a specific part of heaven, the outermost part: the Empyrean.

13. (p. 145) *"Who are you." . . not otherwise with wonder is bewildered:* The shades are amazed by the fact that the Pilgrim has received a special dispensation to visit Purgatory while still alive.

14. (p. 145) *He recommenced who had first questioned us:* Guinizzelli, the shade who first addressed the travelers at the beginning of this canto, remains unidentified.

15. (p. 145) *"The folk that comes not with us . . . by their shame":* The yet-to-be-identified Guinizzelli explains that the sinners heading in the opposite direction are homosexuals, since they practiced the same sin that was associated with Julius Caesar. This statement follows a popular account that claimed the Roman general committed sodomy with King Nicomedes in Bithynia and was hailed by his troops with the title "Queen." Dante may have found this anecdote in either the *Life of Caesar*, by Suetonius, or in a work by Uguccione da Pisa, *Magnae derivationes.*

16. (p. 145) *"hermaphrodite . . . our appetite":* By "hermaphrodite" Dante means heterosexual, and therefore natural. These sinners subjected their reason to their appetite, but they have repented of their lustful behavior.

17. (p. 145) *"Who bestialized herself in bestial wood":* This line, ably put into English by Longfellow, is celebrated as one of Dante's most clever alliterative lines: *che s'imbestiò ne le 'mbestiate schegge.* The literal translation is "bestializing herself with the bestialized splinters." The images of wood and splinters refer to the wooden bull with which Pasiphaë coupled.

18. (p. 145) *"I'm Guido Guinicelli":* Guido Guinizzelli (c.1240–c.1276) is often considered to be a precursor to the so-called *dolce stil nuovo* ("sweet new style") poets. He was most famous for the poem "Al cor gentil rempaira sempre amore" ("Love seeks its dwelling always in the gentle heart"). Guido was from Bologna.

19. (p. 145) *The same that in the sadness of Lycurgus:* According to the *Thebiad* of Statius (V: 499–730), Lycurgus, king of Nemea, bought Hypsipyle, the wife of Jason, and appointed her nurse for his son. In her care the son was killed by a serpent, and Lycurgus was enraged. He ordered her execution, but her two sons by Jason appeared and had her freed. Dante is comparing the Pilgrim's feelings at meeting Guinizzelli, his poetic predecessor, with the complex emotions of Lycurgus.

20. (p. 145) *Of me and my betters:* Given Dante's high opinion of himself, it is difficult to believe that he really considered other medieval poets in Italy to be his superiors. But his declaration here of the poetic paternity he feels for Guinizzelli constitutes an important statement of his intellectual formation.

21. (p. 146) *Nor for the fire did I approach him nearer:* In spite of his enthusiasm at seeing another fellow poet, the Pilgrim is careful not to enter the fire in which Guinizzelli is being purified.

22. (p. 146) *"Lethe":* This is the classical river of oblivion the Pilgrim will soon encounter at the summit of the Mountain of Purgatory.

23. (p. 146) *"Was of the mother tongue a better smith":* Guinizzelli refers to Arnaut Daniel, a Provençal poet who wrote extremely difficult verse. He is credited with the perfection of the sestina form and is identified with an obscure style in troubadour poetry. What Guinizzelli seems to be saying is that Arnaut crafted poetry better than anyone in any mother tongue that was derived from Latin, including Provençal, Old French, and Italian. The reference to "verses of love and proses of romance" (l. 24) has puzzled some scholars, partly because Arnaut wrote only in verse and not in prose. It seems clear that the reference implies Arnaut's poetry surpassed all writings in verse of love and in prose of romance; this would essentially refer to troubadour verse and Old French romances.

24. (p. 146) *"the Lemosin":* This is a reference to Girautz de Borneilh (1175–1220), a troubadour poet from Limoges who wrote in a Provençal style far simpler than that of Arnaut. Both Girautz and Arnaut are mentioned several times in Dante's *De Vulgari Eloquentia*.

25. (p. 146) *"Thus many ancients with Guittone did":* This is Guittone d'Arezzo of *Purgatorio* XXIV: 56 (see note 15 to that canto). Guinizzelli

believes that the many voices who praise a poet may distort his true reputation and worth, as in the case of Guittone.

26. (p. 146) *"the cloister / Wherein is Christ the abbot":* This is the Empyrean heaven, where Christ resides. In ll. 130–131, Guinizzelli asks the Pilgrim to say a Paternoster (Our Father) for him and his fellow penitents but suggests that he not say all of the words of the prayer. Clearly the plea in this prayer that asks not to be led into temptation and to be delivered from evil is no longer necessary for penitent souls in Purgatory. A similar remark is made in *Purgatorio* XI: 23–24 (see note 5 to that canto). There, the souls evoke this prayer and note that they repeat the passage about temptation and deliverance from evil not for themselves, who no longer have any need for this, but for those beloved who remain behind on earth.

27. (p. 147) *"Tan m'abellis vostre cortes deman":* After Guinizzelli's disappearance into the purifying fire, Arnaut Daniel himself steps forward and speaks in his native tongue, Provençal. He is the only non-Italian character in *The Divine Comedy* who Dante permits to speak in his or her native language.

CANTO XXVII

1. (p. 148) *So stood the Sun:* Dante the Poet opens this canto with a description of time in four different places: in Purgatory, in Jerusalem, in Spain (where the River Ebro is located and Libra is at its zenith), and in India (where the Ganges River is located). It is now just before sunset on Tuesday evening in Purgatory; it is 6:00 A.M. in Jerusalem, midnight in Spain, and noon in India. The rest of the events in Purgatory will take place on the following day, Wednesday.

2. (p. 148) *the glad Angel of God appeard to us:* The Angel of Chastity stands on the narrow path outside the fire.

3. (p. 148) *"Beati mundo corde":* This is another beatitude in the Bible, Matthew 5: 8: "Blessed are the pure of heart."

4. (p. 148) *"No one farther goes":* The wall of fire not only purifies the penitent lustful but is a barrier through which all souls must pass in order to advance any farther in Purgatory.

5. (p. 148) *The human bodies I had once seen burned:* Dante the Poet had certainly witnessed execution by burning at the stake in Florence, where it was used for such crimes as homosexuality, heresy, and counterfeiting.

When Dante went into exile, he was himself sentenced to death *in absentia*. Dante the Pilgrim is obviously afraid that the purifying fires so desired by the penitent lustful will work quite differently upon his own mortal body.

6. (p. 148) *"Remember . . . On Geryon have safely guided thee"*: Virgil reassures the Pilgrim, reminding him of the safe guidance he has provided elsewhere in the afterlife. (See *Inferno* XVII for the description of the Pilgrim's fear when he descended down to Malebolge.)

7. (p. 149) *Draw near to it, and put it to the proof:* Virgil encourages the Pilgrim to test the fire with a piece of his clothing. Here, Virgil employs an Italian expression, *fatti far credenza* ("put it to the proof") that was used to refer to having a dog or servant taste the food of an important official to ensure that it was not poisoned.

8. (p. 149) *" 'Twixt Beatrice and thee there is this wall"*: After Virgil's logical explanations and commands fail to move the Pilgrim to pass through the fire, the Pilgrim's guide notes that Beatrice is on the other side of the fire. This is all it takes to move the Pilgrim to action.

9. (p. 149) *As at the name of Thisbe . . . my obduracy being softened:* Ovid's *Metamorphoses* IV: 55–168 recounts the tale of Thisbe and Pyramus, who fell in love and, because their parents were opposed to their love, communicated through a hole in the wall of their adjoining homes. Pyramus came upon a piece of Thisbe's clothing coated with blood. Taking the blood to be that of his beloved, he killed himself, causing the white berries of a mulberry bush to turn red. When Thisbe realized what Pyramus had done, she called out to him with her name. She then killed herself, too, after offering a prayer that mulberries should remain red in their memory. Dante compares Thisbe's calling her name to the dead Pyramus to the effect that hearing the name of Beatrice has upon the Pilgrim.

10. (p. 149) *Then into the fire in front of me he entered, / Beseeching Statius to come after me:* Virgil wants to make sure that the Pilgrim remains true to his resolution to walk through the fire and enters the flames.

11. (p. 149) *into molten glass . . . "Her eyes I seem to see already!":* The Pilgrim says the pain of the flames is so excruciating that molten glass would have been refreshing. Virgil continues speaking of Beatrice to encourage the Pilgrim, telling him that he will see her eyes very soon.

12. (p. 149) "Venite, benedicti Patris mei": The speaker is a second angel on the terrace, perhaps a guardian angel of the Earthly Paradise. The Pilgrim encounters ten angels in Purgatory: the Christianized Mercury who delivers souls to the shore of the mountain (*Purgatorio* II: 43); the guardian angel at the gate of Purgatory (*Purgatorio* IX: 104); seven angels on the seven terraces; and this last angel. The words the angel sings come from the Bible, Matthew 25: 34, and are the words Jesus will speak to the elect on Judgment Day: "Come, ye blessed of my Father." We are probably to assume that the Pilgrim has the final *P* removed from his brow here, either by the purifying force of the fire through which he has passed or by this last angel, although the actual moment that this occurs is never specified.

13. (pp. 150–151) *It was the hour . . . beautiful in dreams:* When Venus (Cytherea) appears an hour before dawn in the eastern sky, the Pilgrim experiences his third important dream. The first was in *Purgatorio* IX: 13–33; the second was in *Purgatorio* XIX: 1–33. Dreams experienced just before awakening, as has been previously mentioned, were considered to be prophetic.

14. (p. 151) *"That I am Leah . . . Her, seeing, and me, doing satisfies":* The tale of Leah and Rachel, the two daughters of Laban, may be found in the Bible, Genesis 29: 10–31. Leah, Jacob's first wife, was fertile and had bad eyesight. Rachel, Jacob's second wife, was barren and had beautiful eyes. Christian theology interpreted Leah as a symbol of the active life and Rachel as a symbol of the contemplative life. The fact that Rachel never ceases to gaze at herself in the mirror (ll. 104–105) should not be read as narcissism but as total immersion in contemplation.

15. (p. 151) *"That apple sweet":* The reference is to earthly happiness.

16. (pp. 151–152) *"no farther I discern. / By intellect and art I here have brought thee":* Virgil now takes leave of his pupil, since he is limited by the fact that he has only intellect and art at his assistance. Because of Virgil's guidance, the Pilgrim has witnessed the "temporal fire" of Purgatory and the "eternal" fire of Hell (l. 127), but he is now spiritually free to continue the journey without his guide.

17. (p. 152) *"Free and upright and sound is thy free-will . . . Thee o'er thyself I therefore crown and mitre!":* Because the Pilgrim has passed through the purifying flames of the final terrace on his journey to Beatrice in Purgatory, his most human faculty, his free will, is now truly free, straight, and

whole again—as it was before Mankind's Fall and the corruption of original sin. It would now be a serious mistake for the Pilgrim not to follow the dictates of his free will. Virgil pronounces a kind of benediction over the Pilgrim that combines the crown and miter of an emperor's coronation. Some scholars have viewed the crown as that of the poet laureate and the miter as that of the Church, thereby attempting to combine Dante's role as a poet with his role as a moral authority. This interpretation is clouded by the fact that both kings and high Church authorities wore miters and crowns. The fact that the Pilgrim is crowned over himself underscores the self-control that he has achieved after his soul has been purged of sin and his free will is liberated.

CANTO XXVIII

1. (p. 153) *the new-born day:* It is now the Wednesday morning after Easter during the Pilgrim's last day of his long journey through the Underworld. In ll. 1–36 the Poet describes an Earthly Paradise. This is a combination of the Garden of Eden from the Bible and any number of pleasances (*loci amoeni*) that pastoral and love poets celebrated in classical and medieval literature and that were associated with gardens, trees, breezes, and singing birds.

2. (p. 153) *Whereat the branches . . . toward that side:* The branches bend from east to west, in the direction the mountain casts its shadow at sunrise.

3. (p. 153) *pine forest on the shore of Chiassi:* Chiassi was the seaport of the city of Ravenna. Since Dante ended his life in Ravenna, he would have known of this particular pine wood from personal experience.

4. (p. 153) *When Eolus unlooses the Sirocco:* Eolus, or Aeolus, was the classical god of the winds; the Sirocco is the southeast wind that blows to Italy from Africa.

5. (p. 154) *a stream cut off:* The reader will eventually learn that this stream is Lethe, in classical mythology a river in Hades where souls of the dead drink to forget their former existence. In Dante's Purgatory the river functions to wash away the memory of sin.

6. (p. 154) *A lady all alone:* We learn later in *Purgatorio* XXXIII: 119 that this figure is named Matilda, although scholars have argued for years over her identity. Many early commentators and a number of recent interpreters of Dante believe she is Matilda of Tuscany

(1046–1115), while others have identified her with a number of nuns or with some of the unnamed women mentioned in Dante's *La Vita Nuova*. It is also important to remember that in the traditional medieval *pastorella* poem, a beautiful maiden was almost always found in the *locus amoenus*, but unlike these sexually available figures, Matilda will prove to be quite a different kind of woman. Commentary on Matilda also associates her with the active life, following Dante's evocation of Leah, the traditional symbol of the active life, in canto XXVII (see note 14 to that canto).

7. (p. 154) *"Ah, beauteous lady":* The Pilgrim addresses Matilda in terms that are traditional in the medieval *pastorella*, but the usual sexual context of such encounters will soon be abandoned.

8. (p. 154) *"Proserpina":* In Ovid's *Metamorphoses* V: 385–408, the Latin poet describes how Proserpina (daughter of Jupiter and Ceres) was carried off by Pluto while gathering flowers in a meadow and became the queen of the Underworld.

9. (p. 154) *with its meaning:* The Pilgrim understands the song Matilda is singing, but the reader of the poem never understands its content.

10. (p. 156) *Venus, when transfixed / By her own son:* According to Ovid's *Metamorphoses* X: 525–532, Venus was kissing her son Cupid when she was accidentally scratched by one of his arrows. As a result, she fell in love with the ill-fated Adonis.

11. (p. 156) *But Hellespont, where Xerxes passed across:* Xerxes, king of Persia from 486 to 465 B.C., invaded Greece by crossing the River Hellespont. But the campaign ended disastrously at the battle of Salamis, where the Greek fleet destroyed the Persian's fleet. This defeat is a proverbial example of arrogance and pride destroyed.

12. (p. 156) *Leander . . . rolling between Sestos and Abydos:* Leander, a young man from Abydos, swam across the Hellespont every night to visit Hero, priestess of Venus at Sestos. When Leander drowned, Hero committed suicide. Ovid tells the story in *Heroides* XVIII–XIX.

13. (p. 156) *because it oped not then:* The Pilgrim declares his hatred for the water separating him from Matilda. Though the distance is only three paces, he does not dare to cross. He wishes the water would part as the Red Sea did for the children of Israel in the biblical story of the exodus of the children of Israel.

14. (p. 156) *"Ye are new-comers"*: Matilda's address in the plural is a reminder that the Pilgrim is still accompanied by Virgil and Statius, although they are clearly secondary figures in this section of the poem.

15. (p. 156) *"in this place / Elect to human nature for its nest"*: Matilda's statement that this pleasance was selected for humanity's abode underlines that it must certainly be the Garden of Eden from which Adam and Eve, and all their descendants, were exiled because of original sin. It's worth noting that in l. 2 of this canto, the pleasance is described as the "heavenly forest."

16. (p. 156) *"the psalm Delectasti"*: Psalms 92: 4–5 of the Bible, the most probable reference here, reads as follows: "For thou, Lord, hast made me glad through thy work: I will triumph in the works of thy hands. O Lord, how great are thy works!" It would seem, given the psalm that Matilda cites, that her song (the content of which is never revealed to the reader but which the Pilgrim seems to understand) is in praise of God, the creator of the universe, and that her love is a chaste love of God.

17. (p. 156) *"The water . . . something which I heard opposed to this"*: In *Purgatorio* XXI: 43–72, Statius explained that there are no changes, such as weather conditions, in Purgatory. The Pilgrim wonders how, if this is the case, there can now be running water from rainfall and the sound of the wind in the forest.

18. (p. 157) *"By his default to weeping and to toil"*: The original sin of Adam and Eve cut short their sojourn in the Garden of Eden. In *Paradiso* XXVI: 139–142 we will learn that Adam and Eve lasted only six hours there.

19. (p. 157) *"That the disturbance . . . And is exempt"*: Purgatory is exempt from weather changes because it is situated above meteorologic disturbances.

20. (p. 157) *"Now since the universal atmosphere / Turns in a circuit with the primal motion"*: In ll. 103–120, Matilda explains how in the Earthly Paradise, the light winds blow constantly and in the same direction (from east to west). This direction is determined by God, the *primum mobile*, referred to as the "primal motion" in l. 104. In contrast, winds governed by earthly weather frequently change direction and force.

21. (p. 157) *"full of every seed . . . never gathered there":* Matilda explains that all types of plants germinate in the Earthly Paradise. Many of these plants are unknown to the inhabitants of earth.

22. (p. 158) *"Here Lethe, as upon the other side / Eunoë, it is called":* Matilda informs the Pilgrim that the water in the Earthly Paradise derives not from rain but from a fountain replenished eternally by God (l. 125). Some of the water from the fountain feeds the River Lethe (the name derives from the Greek word meaning "oblivion"), while part of it feeds the River Eunoë (from the Greek word meaning "knowledge of the good"). The first river removes the memory of sin, while the second river restores the memory of the good. As Matilda says in ll. 131–132, it is necessary to drink the two kinds of water together to enjoy their effects. Matilda's statement in l. 128 that the water of Lethe "takes away all memory of sin" must not be taken literally, since the Pilgrim will meet souls in Paradise who retain that kind of memory. Moreover, it would be counterintuitive for human souls to forget the reason that God's salvation was necessary. Note that in *Inferno* XIV: 136–138, Virgil tells the Pilgrim that he will eventually see Lethe, and here the promise is fulfilled. Also, it is interesting to remember that many Dante scholars consider the "small rivulet" of *Inferno* XXXIV: 130 to be the water from Lethe that flows down from Purgatory to the bottom of Hell, where it freezes around Lucifer.

23. (p. 158) *"Those who in ancient times have feigned in song / The Age of Gold":* Matilda concludes her explanations to the Pilgrim by pointing out that the Earthly Paradise is the place ancient poets celebrated in their descriptions of the Age of Gold and of Parnassus. Dante's original Italian employs the verb *poetaro* ("poetized"), rather than the "feigned" Longfellow uses. When the Pilgrim turns back to see how Virgil and Statius, whom he now calls "my Poets" (l. 146), react to Matilda's remarks, their smiles underscore their acknowledgment that she speaks the truth. The best-known description of the Golden Age in classical literature is that of Ovid's *Metamorphoses* I: 89–112.

CANTO XXIX

1. (p. 159) *"Beati quarum tecta sun peccata":* Matilda sings an abbreviated version of Psalm 32 from the Bible: "Blessed is he [whose transgression is forgiven,] whose sin is covered."

2. (p. 160) *The woman only . . . and for a longer time:* Had Eve not sinned by refusing to wear the "veil" of ignorance that was removed when she ate the apple from the Tree of Knowledge, mankind would still be in the Garden of Eden, enjoying the bliss of living near to God that the souls in Paradise enjoy. Dante was certainly no feminist; he shared the general medieval view that Eve was more at fault than Adam ("the woman only") in earning God's displeasure and expulsion from the Garden of Eden.

3. (p. 160) *O Virgins sacrosanct! . . . Now Helicon:* Here the poet invokes the nine pagan muses, but he Christianizes them by calling them sacrosanct (holy). This is the second of his invocations of the muses in *Purgatorio* (the first was in *Purgatorio* I: 7–12) and one of nine times in *The Divine Comedy* that they are invoked. Helicon was a mountain range of Boeotia sacred to Apollo and the muses, and the fountains of the muses were supposed to be located there. Urania (l. 41) was the Muse of Astronomy, an appropriate choice to assist the Poet in his forthcoming description of heavenly things.

4. (p. 160) *To put in verse things difficult to think:* From l. 43 until the end of the canto, Dante presents a Procession, or a Heavenly Pageant, that will seem to most contemporary readers to be one of the most tedious parts of his entire poem. The Poet will require the inspiration of the muses. The concepts he is about to present allegorically are not difficult to versify (nothing is really difficult for Dante to put into verse), but they are difficult to remember from his physical vision of them in the afterlife and, more importantly, difficult for his readers to understand through his words alone. A synopsis of the procession may prove useful here:

- The seven candlesticks (l. 50): In the Bible, Revelation I: 12, John has a vision of seven candlesticks that are interpreted as seven churches and then as the seven gifts of the Holy Spirit (wisdom, understanding, counsel, might, knowledge, piety, and fear of the Lord).
- The twenty-four elders (l. 83): According to Saint Jerome's count, there were twenty-four books of the Old Testament, and these figures represent God's revelation before the appearance of Christ.

- The four animals (l. 92): The symbols of the Four Gospels—Matthew (an angel or a man); Mark (a lion); Luke (an ox); and John (an eagle).
- A chariot drawn by a Griffin (ll. 107–108): The chariot symbolizes the Church, while the Griffin (both human and divine) represents Christ.
- Three ladies dancing to the right of the chariot (l. 121): The theological virtues of faith, hope, and charity, or love.
- Four ladies dancing to the left of the chariot (l. 130): The cardinal virtues of justice, prudence, temperance, and fortitude.
- Seven men following the chariot: The books of the New Testament, grouped as follows—two men representing Luke and Paul's epistles; then four men (the minor epistles of Peter, John, James, and Jude); then one man alone (the Apocalypse of John).
- A group of one hundred angels.
- Beatrice herself.

5. (p. 160) *"Hosanna!"*: This is the exclamation of joyous praise addressed to Christ as he is about to enter Jerusalem, as told in the Bible, Matthew 21: 9. "Hosanna" is an appropriate form of address here, since the Griffin soon to appear represents Christ in the allegorical procession.

6. (p. 160) *the harness beautiful:* The flames at the top of the seven candlesticks seem to be a single flame, eclipsing even the light of the midnight moon.

7. (p. 160) *With visage no less full of wonderment:* Virgil's pagan education and even his experience in Limbo have not prepared him for the spectacular vision of the Christian Church Triumphant he is witnessing. Along with the Pilgrim, he is spellbound.

8. (p. 162) *Whence the sun's bow is made, and Delia's girdle:* The bow of the sun (Apollo in classical mythology) is the rainbow, and Delia is another name for the goddess Diana, born on the island of Delos. Her girdle is the halo around the moon.

9. (p. 162) *flower-de-luce:* The fleur-de-lis (the lily) is the symbol of purity.

10. (p. 162) *"Blessed thou":* The figures representing the Old Testament sing the praises of the Virgin Mary.

11. (p. 163) *Plumed with six wings:* In the Bible, Ezekiel 1: 6, the animals traditionally said to prefigure the four authors of the Gospels have four wings, while in Revelation 4: 8, they are said to have six wings.

12. (p. 163) *the eyes of Argus:* This is a reference to the hundred eyes of Argus in Ovid's *Metamorphoses* I: 568–723. They are transformed into the eyes in the feathers of the peacock.

13. (p. 163) *Reader!:* This is the fifth address to the reader in *Purgatorio.*

14. (p. 163) *John is with me, and differeth from him:* The Poet is aware of the discrepancy between the descriptions of the animals representing the authors of the gospels in Ezekiel and in Revelation (in which John has a vision). Yet, this important statement underscores his claim that his vision is not imaginary but is the result of a real experience. That is, both Old Testament and New Testament authors must take second place to his firsthand information.

15. (p. 163) *he injured none by cleaving it:* The Griffin's wings appear like a brush stroke over the seven candlesticks, creating a single flame. The Griffin was half lion and half eagle, and the chariot drawn by this singular animal is akin to the two-wheeled chariots that Roman emperors used in their triumphs (the kind of procession to which Dante's entire description alludes). The two wheels are generally understood by scholars to represent the Old and New Testaments, from which the Church derives its dogma.

16. (p. 163) *Not only Rome with no such splendid car . . . That of the Sun:* The triumphant chariot pulled by the Griffin outshines in splendor even that used by Scipio Africanus (185–129 B.C.), the conqueror of Hannibal and victor over the Carthaginians, or that of Augustus Caesar himself (63 B.C.–A.D. 14), the Roman emperor reigning when Christ was born. Even the sun, Apollo's chariot, ridden badly by Phaeton, Apollo's son, cannot hold a candle to the splendor of this vehicle. (For the account of Phaeton's disastrous attempts to ride his father's sun chariot, see Ovid's *Metamorphoses* II: 47–324.) The fact that this procession contains a triumphant chariot underscores the fact that Dante's allegorical vision is that of the Church Triumphant—that is, the Church as it will be in eternity, as opposed to the Church Militant, the actual historical Church of his time.

17. (p. 163) *Three maidens at the right wheel:* The three dancing maidens representing the theological virtues are respectively dressed in red (charity), green (hope), and white (faith), the colors associated with their qualities. They dance on the right of the chariot, underlining the fact that these three virtues are superior to the cardinal, or pagan, virtues on the left side.

18. (p. 164) *Vested in purple:* The reference is to the cardinal virtues of prudence, temperance, justice, and fortitude, which regulate human behavior and form the basis of imperial authority. Since purple is the color of empire, they are dressed in this color.

19. (p. 164) *one of the disciples / Of that supreme Hippocrates:* In the Bible, Colossians 4: 14, Luke is described as a physician. Accordingly, he is a follower of Hippocrates, the famous doctor of the ancient world.

20. (p. 164) *With sword so shining and so sharp:* The sword identifies the traditional iconography of the Apostle Paul and symbolizes the word of God.

21. (p. 164) *four I saw of humble aspect:* These four figures represent the humbler epistles of the New Testament written by Saints James, Peter (two letters), John (three letters), and Jude.

22. (p. 164) *an aged man alone / Walking in sleep:* The reference is to John, author of the biblical Book of Revelation. This is the last book in the New Testament, so the figure representing this writer is the last in the procession. Because the book purports to describe a vision, John is often depicted as sleeping.

23. (p. 164) *Thunder was heard:* With this dramatic halt in the procession just in front of the Pilgrim, the stage is set for a truly unusual sight in the next canto. The fact that the chariot halts directly in front of our protagonist emphasizes that this vision is for his edification alone. This procession does not apparently occur when other penitents journey through this point in Purgatory on their way to Paradise. Once again, Dante the Pilgrim's special dispensation in the afterlife is reaffirmed.

CANTO XXX

1. (p. 165) *the Septentrion of the highest heaven:* The seven stars of the constellation Ursa Major, or the Big Dipper, are here compared to the seven candlesticks leading the procession. The "highest heaven" is the Empyrean where God dwells. The term Septentrion derives from the fact that both Ursa Major and Ursa Minor (the Little Dipper, "the lower" of l. 5) contain seven stars, so they were identified with seven plowing oxen—*septem triones* in Latin.

2. (p. 165) *the veracious people . . . as to their peace:* These are the twenty-four elders symbolizing the Old Testament in the procession. They now turn to face the Griffin and the chariot, acknowledging that the fulfillment of the Old Testament in the New Testament represents the fulfillment of their desires, "their peace."

3. (p. 165) *And one of them . . .* "Veni, sponsa, de Libano": This phrase, "Come with me from Lebanon, my spouse" is from the Bible, Song of Solomon 4: 8. The figure identified as "one of them" may represent the author of the song, Solomon. These words summon Beatrice.

4. (p. 165) *at the final summons / Shall rise up:* A hundred angels arise to sing, just as on Judgment Day the Blessed will take on their physical bodies once more and be resurrected, singing God's praises. The Second Coming, or Advent of Christ, will take place at that time. According to many Dante scholars, there is a conscious analogy between the Second Coming of Christ and Beatrice's appearance here.

5. (p. 165) ad vocem tanti senis: This is Dante's phrase, Latin for "at the voice of such a great elder." Dante thus adds his own Latin phrase to those by Matthew and Virgil that will follow.

6. (p. 165) "Benedictus qui venis": "Blessed art Thou that comest" is a slightly but significantly modified version of Matthew 21: 9 in the Bible. The original in the Latin Vulgate reads *Benedictus qui venit* ("Blessed is he that cometh"). In Matthew, the phrase refers to Christ, while Dante's line refers to Beatrice. Dante retains the masculine *Benedictus* to underline the analogy between Christ and Beatrice.

7. (p. 165) "Manibus o date lilia plenis": These famous words are from Virgil, *Aeneid* VI: 883: "O give lilies with full hands." Anchises speaks the phrase when predicting the early death of the young Marcellus. As Virgil is about to disappear from Dante's poem, the Poet pays him this fitting tribute before his departure. Note that the angels cite both the Latin Vulgate and Virgil's great epic poem as they scatter flowers to welcome Beatrice.

8. (p. 165) *Ere now have I beheld:* Lines 22–33 present a majestic simile of twelve lines devoted to Beatrice's appearance. She is dressed in the symbolic colors of faith, hope, and charity—white, green, and red, respectively.

9. (p. 166) *So long a time had been:* Beatrice died in June 1290, and the date of the Pilgrim's journey is 1300, so a decade has passed since her departure from an earthly existence.

10. (p. 166) *"I know the traces of the ancient flame":* As the Pilgrim turns once again for support from his ancient guide, he employs one of the most famous lines in Virgil's *Aeneid* (IV: 23). The unfortunate Dido speaks this line when she realizes that she has fallen in love with Aeneas and will betray her vow of chastity to her dead husband.

11. (p. 166) *"Dante":* The first word Beatrice speaks is the Pilgrim's name, the only time it is used in the entire poem. If Dante has lost a father ("Virgilius, sweetest of all fathers," l. 50), he now has acquired a very severe mother (see l. 79) who is about to scold him for his childish shortcomings.

12. (p. 168) *I saw the Lady:* That is, Beatrice.

13. (p. 168) *the foliage of Minerva:* This is the olive garland, sacred to Minerva, the goddess of wisdom.

14. (p. 168) *the mother seems superb:* Beatrice seems like a stern and haughty mother because she also represents the Church, and as such she must be both stern and loving.

15. (p. 168) *"In te, Domine, speravi"* . . . *beyond* pedes meos *did not pass:* As the Pilgrim lowers his glance in shame, the angels begin to sing Psalms 31: 1–8 from the Bible, ending with the phrase *pedes meos* (my feet) in the Latin Vulgate: "In thee, O Lord, do I put my trust . . . thou hast set my feet in a large room."

16. (p. 169) *"Ye keep your watch":* Beatrice addresses the angels, who have pled for compassion in the Pilgrim's regard, explaining why her attitude toward Dante is so severe. Even though the angels are all-knowing, Dante himself must learn the nature of his sin, and he must be taught by Beatrice so that he experiences true penitence (see ll. 142–145).

17. (p. 169) *"The work of those great wheels . . . the largest of celestial graces":* That is, the heavenly spheres. The stars were supposed to influence mankind at birth toward good or evil ends, according to their astrological powers. Beatrice also wants to underscore the role played by "the largess of celestial graces" in bestowing gifts upon mankind.

18. (p. 169) *"in his new life"*: Beatrice's use of the term *vita nova* ("new life") and her summary of her relationship to Dante before and after her death refer the reader to Dante's *La Vita Nuova*. Dante composed this important collection of lyric poems and prose commentary to explain his encounters with Beatrice before and after her death.

19. (p. 169) *"my second age"*: Beatrice died in 1290 at the age of twenty-four. She was on the threshold of entering what was then considered to be the age of youth, around the age of twenty-five.

20. (p. 169) *"Himself from me he took and gave to others"*: Here Beatrice accuses Dante of unfaithfulness after her death. Indeed, in *La Vita Nuova* XXXV–XXXVIII, the poet discusses his temporary attraction to other women after Beatrice's death.

21. (p. 170) *"into ways untrue"*: This line recalls the opening of *Inferno* I: 3, where the Pilgrim found himself diverted from the "straight-forward pathway."

22. (p. 170) *"in dreams"*: After her death, Beatrice appeared to Dante in dream visions (*La Vita Nuova* XXXIX, XLII).

23. (p. 170) *"unto him, who so far up has led him"*: This is a reference to Virgil, who has now disappeared but who has led Dante this far to meet Beatrice.

24. (p. 170) *"withouten any scot / Of penitence"*: Beatrice affirms that Dante must experience sincere penitence of the heart and confession before he can obtain the forgetfulness of his sins through immersion in the waters of Lethe. A scot (the Italian original is *scotto*) was a payment of a fee for meals or entertainment at an inn.

CANTO XXXI

1. (p. 171) *"beyond the sacred river"*: Since the Pilgrim still stands on the shore of Lethe, he has not yet purged himself through the act of penance that drinking from the waters of this river symbolizes.

2. (p. 171) *"Thy own confession"*: According to Church doctrine regarding penance, contrition of the heart and then confession by the lips is required before the remission of sin may take place.

3. (p. 171) *Forced such a Yes!*: This single word is the beginning of the Pilgrim's confession as he is forced to admit the truth of Beatrice's

charges. The rest of the confession is contained in ll. 34–36. Dante compares the sudden nature of his confession to the breaking of a "crossbow" (ll. 16–18), and his barely muttered "Yes!" corresponds to the arrow hitting the mark with less force because of the break in the bow.

4. (p. 172) *"turned aside my steps"*: Dante's confession amounts to a simple admission that he derived false pleasure from "present" things after Beatrice's death. This simple confession has occasioned a great deal of commentary, but it no doubt refers to the carnal and intellectual pleasures Dante experienced that were not directed completely toward the love of God that Beatrice had awakened in him.

5. (p. 172) *"by such a Judge 'tis known . . . Against the edge the wheel doth turn itself"*: Reversing the whetstone dulls a blade rather than sharpening it. Thus, if a soul openly confesses the sin that God (the "Judge") knows anyway, the sword of Justice cuts less deeply in its punishment.

6. (p. 172) *"Hearing the Sirens"*: This is a reminder of the dream in *Purgatorio* XIX: 19–33, a vision that warned the Pilgrim against the temptations of the flesh.

7. (p. 172) *"or little girl"*: This female figure (*pargoletta* in the original Italian) may well refer to one of the "other" women to whom Dante was attracted after Beatrice's death (see *Purgatorio* XXX: 126). Indeed, some of Dante's love lyrics do mention a *pargoletta* as the object of his desire.

8. (p. 174) *"lift up thy beard"*: That is, lift up your face. Beatrice's reference to the Pilgrim's beard serves to remind him that he is a mature man whose actions should no longer be regarded as childish.

9. (p. 174) *a native wind . . . from regions of Iarbas*: According to Virgil's *Aeneid* IV, Iarbas, or Hiarbas, was king of the Gaetulians when Dido founded Carthage. The wind from his realm would therefore be from Africa.

10. (p. 174) *Saw Beatrice turned round*: The fact that the angels cease strewing the flowers and Beatrice turns to face the Griffin (the symbol of Christ) implies that Dante's confession has been successful.

11. (p. 174) *To excel, than others here, when she was here*: Caught up in the contemplation of the Griffin (Christ), Beatrice's physical beauty is now far greater than it ever was on earth before her death.

12. (p. 174) *So pricked me then the thorn of penitence . . . O'erpowered I fell*: The original Italian refers to *ortica* ("nettle"), a wild, prickly plant. Dante's true act of penitence is so profound that he is filled with hate

for all those worldly pleasures that drew him away from Beatrice, causing him to faint.

13. (p. 174) *The lady I had found alone:* This is Matilda, who now administers the waters of Lethe and Eunoë to the Pilgrim. Although neither Matilda nor Statius has spoken since the appearance of Beatrice, they have remained present. Virgil has disappeared.

14. (p. 174) *Upon the water lightly as a shuttle:* Matilda is moving over the water as a shuttle used in weaving passes easily back and forth over the fabric being woven.

15. (p. 174) *"Asperges me":* These are the first two words from Psalms 51: 7. Since these are the words a priest repeats when sprinkling a confessed sinner with holy water after confession, thus absolving him or her of his or her sins, Matilda performs the rite of absolution here.

16. (p. 175) *plunged me underneath:* While baptism absolves original sin and need be performed only once (indeed, Catholics accept baptism by other Christian creeds), absolution from subsequent sin is an entirely different matter. So, when the Pilgrim is "plunged" here, he is absolved of sin, not rebaptized. After the completion of his act of penance, he is now ready to dance with the seven handmaidens who accompany Beatrice: first with the four symbolizing the cardinal virtues (l. 104), then with the three symbolizing the theological virtues "who more profoundly look" (l. 111).

17. (p. 175) *"Before the emeralds we stationed thee"... upon the Griffin steadfast stayed:* The Pilgrim's eyes are fixed upon Beatrice's emerald eyes, and her eyes are fixed upon the Griffin, the incarnation of the human and divine nature of Christ. While the Pilgrim sees first one aspect of Christ's dual nature, then the other, Beatrice enjoys the unified vision of Christ's dual nature. The Pilgrim will share this experience when he reaches Paradise. Beatrice thus serves the Poet as a figure of Revelation.

18. (p. 175) *Think, Reader:* This is the sixth of the seven addresses to the reader in *Purgatorio.*

19. (p. 175) *their angelic saraband:* In the original text, Dante calls this angelic dance music a *caribo.* Longfellow renders the word as "saraband," a slow, stately Spanish dance in triple time.

20. (p. 176) *"The second beauty":* The first beauty of Beatrice is her eyes, which reveal the mystery of the dual nature (divine and human) of Christ in the Revelation. The second beauty is her mouth, from

which the inner light of wisdom can be discerned behind a veil. (See Dante's *Il Convivio* III: xv: 2–3 for further details of Dante's thinking on these matters.)

21. (p. 176) *O splendor of the living light eternal!:* Dante the Poet wisely refuses to offer a concrete description of Beatrice's face (her eyes and mouth), stressing instead the impossibility of providing a description of such a unique and marvelous sight. To cap off this statement of inexpressibility, the Poet asserts that any pagan poet who labored at producing poetry or drank from the spring of Parnassus would still be unable to match the beauty of this quintessentially Christian scene.

CANTO XXXII

1. (p. 177) *their decennial thirst:* Ten years have passed since the death of Beatrice.

2. (p. 177) *"Too intently!":* It is clear here that even though the Pilgrim has repented for his past sins and has been cleansed, he still perceives the wondrous beauty of Beatrice in carnal terms. In other words, he is not yet ready to understand the religious nature of this vision—that Beatrice's beauty as a physical woman should be left behind; instead, her beauty will be the cause of his salvation. In short, the Pilgrim perceives spiritual beauty in carnal terms here. It is also possible that the muses warn him not to gaze too intently upon this incarnation of divine Revelation because his vision is not yet prepared for the gaze upon eternal truth.

3. (p. 178) *A squadron turns . . . the chariot had turned its pole:* The precision with which the procession turns around abruptly underscores the Poet's experience with the troops of his native Florence.

4. (p. 178) *The lady fair who drew me through the ford:* This is Matilda.

5. (p. 178) *Followed with Statius:* The reader is surprised by the sudden reappearance of Statius, who has stood by practically unnoticed in the poem since the disappearance of Virgil. He was last explicitly mentioned in *Purgatorio* XXVIII: 146.

6. (p. 178) *By fault of her who in the serpent trusted:* The Garden of Eden would still be inhabited were it not for original sin. Although the Poet's remark seems to place primary blame on Eve, the assembled characters in the procession will murmur Adam's name (l. 37).

7. (p. 178) *when Beatrice descended:* Beatrice's descent from the

chariot marks the beginning of an important shift in theme insofar as the allegorical procession is concerned.

8. (p. 178) *a tree despoiled / Of blooms and other leafage:* This tree can be only the Tree of the Knowledge of Good and Evil that is discussed in the Bible, Genesis 2: 15–17. It is now bereft of its leaves because of the deleterious effects of the Fall. In *Purgatorio* XXXIII: 71–72, Beatrice will remark: "The justice of the interdict of God / Morally in the tree wouldst recognize."

9. (p. 178) *"Blessed art thou, O Griffin, who dost not / Pluck":* Unlike Adam or Eve, the Griffin (a figure of Christ) obeys the eternal interdict not to eat of the tree's fruit, even though it would be sweet.

10. (p. 178) *"Thus is preserved the seed of all the just":* These are the only words the Griffin speaks in the poem. They echo the words of Jesus to John the Baptist in the Bible, Matthew 3: 15: "For thus it becometh us to fulfill all righteousness." It seems clear that this tree represents God's law and His justice, especially since the Griffin repeats the words of Christ.

11. (p. 178) *left bound:* The Griffin removes the pole from the chariot and fastens it to the Tree of the Knowledge of Good and Evil, from which it originally came. Most commentators believe the rejoining of the wood of the Cross to the tree from which it originated underscores mankind's redemption through Christ's sacrifice. Dante's source is probably a very popular bit of folklore popularized by Jacopo da Varagine (c.1230–1298) in his collection of the lives of 182 saints and treatments of the life of Christ and the Virgin Mary entitled *The Golden Legend*. In Jacopo's fanciful treatment of the Legend of the True Cross, Adam's son Seth plants an offshoot of the Tree on Adam's grave. The shoot grows into a huge tree by the time of King Solomon, who cuts the tree down and buries a beam made from it when the Queen of Sheba warns him that it will be used to execute the savior of the world. The beam is eventually employed to crucify Jesus. The legend continues to recount how the Emperor Constantine's mother, Helen, went to the Holy Land and recovered the True Cross, which is why so many relics of the "true cross" were venerated in various Christian churches all over Europe. This legend was particularly popular in Florence and in the rest of Tuscany, and Dante certainly knew of it. The greatest artistic expression of this pious legend is Piero della Francesca's *Legend of the True Cross* fresco cycle in Arezzo.

12. (p. 178) *the celestial Lasca shines:* The reference is to the constellation Pisces.

13. (p. 178) *Less than of rose and more than violet . . . was renewed the tree:* The Tree of the Knowledge of Good and Evil that produces the wood for the Cross is reinvigorated by Christ's sacrifice. The color of the tree, described as being between rose and violet, would be crimson or reddish purple, the noble color of Christ's blood.

14. (p. 180) *how I was lulled asleep . . . picture drowsihood:* With the Pilgrim's sleep, the vision of the Church Triumphant ends, and when the Pilgrim awakens, the procession will have returned to heaven, leaving Beatrice behind. In describing his inability to describe drowsiness ("drowsihood"), Dante refers to the Ovidian tale of Argus in *Metamorphoses* I: 568–723, which he has already used in *Purgatorio* XXIX: 95. Here the Poet compares himself to Argus, who falls asleep when Mercury tells a long-winded story about Syrinx and Pan, allowing Mercury to kill the not-so-vigilant guardian of Io.

15. (p. 180) *"Rise, what dost thou?":* Matilda's voice awakens the Pilgrim from his slumber. Her address to him may recall either the voice of Christ in Matthew 17: 7: "Arise, and be not afraid," or Paul's words in Ephesians 5: 14: "Awake thou that sleepest." The first biblical source is the most likely, since it comes from the description of the Transfiguration that will be mentioned in ll. 75–81.

16. (p. 180) *Peter and John and James conducted were:* This is a clear reference to the description of the Transfiguration in Matthew 17. These three apostles will play an important role in *Paradiso* XXIV–XXVI.

17. (p. 180) *the apparel of their Master changed:* During the Transfiguration, the three apostles ascend a mountain with Jesus and witness the clothing of their Master, his face shining with light, become white. Then they see Him in the company of Moses and Elijah (symbols of the law and of the prophets), who were supposed to have predicted the coming of Christ. The Poet makes an analogy between Christ's Transfiguration and Beatrice's initial appearance—first as a figure of Revelation on the chariot symbolizing the Church Triumphant and later in her earthly guise seated underneath the Tree in l. 87.

18. (p. 180) *that piteous one:* This is another reference to Matilda.

19. (p. 181) *from Aquilon and Auster:* These are references, respectively, to the north and the south wind, both considered to be destructive.

20. (p. 181) *"Short while shalt thou be here a forester":* With these words, Beatrice guarantees the Pilgrim's future salvation. She informs him that after his eventual death, he will spend but little time in Purgatory before joining her in Paradise. In the original Italian, the phrase is *poco tempo silvano*, or a brief time in the forest of the Earthly Paradise, hence the word "forester."

21. (p. 181) *A citizen of that Rome where Christ is Roman:* That is, the Heavenly City of Saint Augustine's *City of God*, which is ruled by Christ as if He were a Roman emperor.

22. (p. 181) *"take heed thou write":* The Divine Comedy, we now learn, originated with Beatrice's command to the Pilgrim to write down what he witnessed during his journey. In the biblical Book of Revelation 1: 11, God similarly commands John: "What thou seest, write in a book."

23. (p. 181) *As I beheld the bird of Jove:* With the appearance of the eagle, the bird sacred to Jupiter (Jove), as well as to the emperors of Rome, Dante presents a succession of seven tableaux (some commentators call them "dumb shows"). These represent the actual history of the Church Militant (as opposed to the Church Triumphant that was represented in the initial procession of the Chariot) from the time of Christ to Dante's own time in 1300. The first calamitous event (ll. 112–117), the one associated with the eagle, is the persecution of the early Church by the Roman emperors.

24. (p. 181) *Of the triumphal vehicle a Fox . . . My Lady put him to as swift a flight:* The Fox, symbolizing the early heresies against which the early Church fathers fought, is driven away by Beatrice.

25. (p. 181) *I saw the Eagle / Descend:* In ll. 124–129, the Poet refers to the Donation of Constantine, the supposed gift of temporal power that Emperor Constantine gave to Pope Sylvester I in the fourth century A.D. Some consider this act to be the beginning of the corruption of the Church. During the Italian Renaissance, Lorenzo Valla proved the actual document to be a forgery.

26. (p. 181) *I saw rise from it a Dragon:* In ll. 130–135, the figure of the Dragon represents the rise of Islam, which Dante considered to be a schism in the Church rather than a different religion. Note that in the

ninth *bolgia* ("ditch" or "pouch") of the eighth circle, in *Inferno* XXVIII, Mohammed is treated as a schismatic.

27. (p. 182) *Reclothed itself:* In ll. 136–141, the Church's increased wealth and temporal power are compared to the additional plumage that covers the Chariot.

28. (p. 182) *A monster such had never yet been seen!:* In ll. 142–147, the Poet describes a seven-headed monster with ten horns (three heads on the pole of the chariot—each with two horns like oxen, and one head on each of its corners, each with a single horn on the forehead). He is indebted to the Bible, Revelation 13: 1, for this image. If we take the seven heads as the seven deadly sins, the Poet seems to be saying that the Church has been completely corrupted by such vices in its quest for temporal power and wealth.

29. (p. 182) *A shameless whore:* In ll. 148–160, Dante presents the seventh and last tableau. This again is an apocalyptic image, similar to that of the Whore of Babylon in the Bible, Revelation 17: 2, "with whom the kings of the earth have committed fornication." Now Dante deals with Church corruption in his own day. The "shameless whore" sits in the Chariot where Beatrice once sat, and the giant she kisses from time to time (l. 142) is probably Philip IV the Fair of France (1268–1314). Philip was responsible for the attack upon the person of Pope Boniface VIII at Anagni in 1303 (see *Purgatorio* XX: 85–93) and also for the so-called Babylonian Captivity of the Church that removed the papacy from Rome in 1305 and established it in Avignon, France, from 1309 until 1378.

30. (p. 182) *her wanton, roving eye / Turned upon me:* While the events of the first six tableaux took place before the fictional time (1300) of Dante's *The Divine Comedy*, the Babylonian Captivity of the Church takes place after that fictional date but, obviously, before the actual composition of the poem. Thus, the seventh tableau is actually a prophetic vision. This scene is complicated by the fact that the giant (the French monarchy) is seen to beat the shameless whore (the corrupt Church) because of the Pilgrim's glance. The fact that Dante injects himself (or his fictional alter ego) into this prophetic scene may suggest that he takes himself to be the representation of Everyman, Every Christian, or simply Every Italian, incensed over the removal of the papacy from its rightful seat in Rome.

CANTO XXXIII

1. (p. 183) "Deus, vererunt gentes": The seven maidens representing the seven virtues open this final canto of *Purgatorio* with a verse from the Bible, Psalms 79: 1: "O God, the heathen are come." As this is a lament for the destruction of Jerusalem, it is an appropriate commentary upon the corruption of the Church outlined in the previous canto.

2. (p. 183) "Modicum, et non videbitis me": Beatrice's answer to the seven maidens is similar to a chorus, and the words she speaks echo Christ's words to his disciples in John 16: 16: "A little while, and ye shall not see me: and again, a little while, and ye shall see me, [because I go to the Father]." Both Christ and Beatrice (His figuration in the poem) announce the eventual triumph of the kingdom of heaven. Thus Beatrice promises Dante that the corruption in the Church previously envisioned will not be the final word.

3. (p. 183) *Me and the lady and the sage who stayed:* These three are the Pilgrim, Matilda, and Statius.

4. (p. 183) *"Why, brother":* Beatrice's familiar address stands in sharp contrast to her scolding manner when she first spoke to the Pilgrim in *Purgatorio* XXX: 55.

5. (p. 184) *"Madonna, / You know":* In spite of Beatrice's familiarity, the Pilgrim continues to address her with a title of respect and, in the original Italian, with the polite *voi* form for "you"—not the informal *tu* form she employs with him.

6. (p. 184) *"Was, and is not":* Beatrice turns back to the previous canto's vision of the shameless whore. Her words echo those of Revelation 17: 8: "The beast that thou sawest was, and is not." She thus reaffirms that this calamitous vision of corruption will not be the final condition of the Church.

7. (p. 184) *"God's vengeance does not fear a sop":* The gist of this difficult passage is that God's vengeance will not be prevented by a mere gesture, but the explanation of the word "sop" (*suppe* in the original Italian) is more complicated. Early commentators suggested that it derived from an ancient practice that was revived in medieval Florence: Vengeance for a crime of violence, such as murder, could be avoided if the murderer ate a ritual meal (for example, a sop of bread and wine) over the tomb of his victim for

some nine days in succession. To prevent this, members of the dead victim's family would apparently guard the grave to guarantee their vengeance.

8. (p. 184) *"Without an heir"*: For Dante, Frederick II was the last Roman emperor. Since Frederick's death in 1250, no heir had appeared to take up his imperial power.

9. (p. 184) *"The stars already near to bring the time"*: Beatrice predicts that the position of the stars is propitious for the coming of a new emperor who will slay both the shameless whore and the giant of l. 45—that is, the corrupt Church and the French monarchy.

10. (p. 184) *"a Five-hundred, Ten, and Five"*: Beatrice's prophecy of a God-sent temporal monarch who will restore the purity of the Church and the Empire has presented commentators with puzzling problems. The Roman numerals for these numbers—DXV—form a word that has sometimes been transformed into the Latin word DUX (leader) by scholars. Some see this figure as the Emperor Henry VII, who invaded Italy in 1310 but died in 1313 before he could accomplish any reform of church and state. However, it seems most likely that both Beatrice and the Poet are being purposely vague here. This prophecy must be compared to that of the Greyhound in *Inferno* I: 101–110, also an extremely puzzling passage for which no satisfying and universally accepted explanation has been produced.

11. (p. 184) *"Like Themis and the Sphinx"*: Both of these mythological figures are associated with obscure riddles or prophecies. In Ovid's *Metamorphoses* I: 262–415, Deucalion and Pyrrah ask Themis how to repopulate earth after the deluge, and he tells them to cast their mother's bones behind their backs (meaning the stones from Mother Earth). They do so, creating a new race of men. The Sphinx was a monster with the head of a woman and the body of a beast who proposed a riddle to those who passed the city of Thebes; those who failed to solve the riddle were killed. Oedipus solved the riddle—what walks on four legs in the morning (a baby), two legs at noon (an erect and mature man), and three legs at night (an old man with a cane)—with the answer "man." Enraged over the ability of Oedipus to solve the riddle, the Sphinx threw herself down from a rock and killed herself. This Sphinx was one of Themis' oracles, and in l. 51, Beatrice mentions the story that Themis avenged her death by dispatching a

monster to attack the fields and herds of the Thebans (see Ovid's *Metamorphoses* VII: 762–765 or Statius' *Thebeid* I: 66–67).

12. (p. 184) *"the Naiades ... Without destruction of the flocks and harvests"*: Appropriately enough in a passage of *The Divine Comedy* that discusses enigmatic utterances, Dante's reference to the Naiades, or water nymphs, is puzzling. Dante maintains that the Naiades helped solve the riddle of the Sphinx, since he used a corrupted text of Ovid's *Metamorphoses* VII: 757 that was the standard edition until the eighteenth century. This version employed the word "Naiades" instead of the more correct "Laiades" (referring to Oedipus, the son of Laius). Beatrice asserts that the prophecy of DVX will be resolved much more easily than that in Ovid and without any destruction of flocks or fields, but Dante scholars have been puzzled by this prophecy for centuries.

13. (p. 184) *"the plant"*: This is the Tree of the Knowledge of Good and Evil in the Earthly Paradise, first pillaged by Adam and then by the corruption of the Church, as represented by the tableaux in *Purgatorio* XXXII: 109–160.

14. (p. 186) *"Five thousand years and more the first-born soul / Craved Him"*: According to the Bible, Genesis 5: 5, Adam lived for 930 years, and in *Paradiso* XXVI: 118, Dante claims Adam waited in Limbo for 4,302 years. The passage makes more sense if the reader bears in mind that Dante accepts the original birth date of Christ as 5200 years after the Creation (a figure proposed by Eusebius) and his death on the cross as 5232 years after the Creation.

15. (p. 186) *"Water of Elsa round about thy mind"*: The reference is to a river in Tuscany flowing through the town of Colle di Val d'Elsa. Because of the river's high mineral content, objects immersed in its waters become petrified.

16. (p. 186) *"And Pyramus to the mulberry"*: Beatrice means to say that Dante's mistaken thoughts ("Thy genius slumbers," l. 64) are staining his mind, just as the blood of Pyramus stained the mulberry (see note 9 to *Purgatorio* XXVII).

17. (p. 186) *"the interdict of God"*: This is a reference to God's command to Adam and Eve not to eat the fruit of the forbidden tree in the Garden of Eden.

18. (p. 186) *"bear it back within thee ... the pilgrim's staff"*: Pilgrims returning from the Holy Land brought back palm leaves as testimony

to their journeys. In like manner, the Pilgrim should bring back his message to the world with his poem. This will be a visible sign of what he has seen, even if he cannot completely explain in words what he has witnessed.

19. (p. 186) *"The more I strive, so much the more I lose it"*: The Pilgrim tells Beatrice that what she says seems clear but that he does not understand its full meaning.

20. (p. 186) *"the school / Which thou hast followed"*: Beatrice accuses Dante of abandoning theology for the study of philosophy—that is, of following reason rather than faith. Dante admits he has done so in *Il Convivio*.

21. (p. 186) *"the heaven that highest hastens on"*: This is a reference to the Primum Mobile, the most distant of the nine heavens, which revolves more rapidly than the others.

22. (p. 187) *"Such an oblivion clearly demonstrates"*: Beatrice notes to the Pilgrim that the very fact he lacks memory underscores the sinful nature of the memories he lost with his immersion in the waters of Lethe. That is, since Lethe erases memory of sin, any loss of memory is proof of sin.

23. (p. 187) *"Be naked"*: That is, simpler and clearer, in keeping with the Pilgrim's limited capacities.

24. (p. 187) *"The sun was holding the meridian circle . . . shifts here and there"*: The time is noon, and the sun seems to move more slowly when it is high overhead than it does when it is nearer the horizon. The sun's meridian point "shifts," since it is always noon somewhere in the world.

25. (p. 187) *The maidens seven:* That is, the seven virtues.

26. (p. 187) *the Tigris and Euphrates:* The Poet is letting us know that even though he has employed poetic invention to place the two rivers of classical mythology, Lethe and Eunoë, in Purgatory, he is well aware of the location of the Tigris and the Euphrates, which are in fact in the Middle East. (According to scripture, Genesis 2: 10 and 14, these two rivers are located in the Garden of Eden.) The Euphrates rises in Turkey and flows across Syria and Iraq into the Persian Gulf after joining with the Tigris. The Tigris rises in Kurdistan and flows through Turkey and Iraq into the Persian Gulf after being joined by the Euphrates.

27. (p. 187) *"O light, O glory of the human race!":* The Pilgrim addresses Beatrice in terms that clearly express her allegorical role in the poem.

28. (p. 187) *"Pray / Matilda":* Dante finally mentions Matilda by name (Longfellow translates the name, while most contemporary translators retain its original spelling in Italian: Matelda). Dante provides no suggestion about which historical figure this woman might represent and, indeed, if he even intended her to represent a real person.

29. (p. 187) *"But Eunoë behold . . . as thou art accustomed":* Just as the waters of Lethe have erased the Pilgrim's memory of sin, now the waters of the second stream must kindle his recollection of the good he has done. The phrase "as thou art accustomed" leads the reader to understand that Matilda performs this ritual for every soul passing through Purgatory toward Paradise.

30. (p. 188) *unto Statius:* The presence of Statius here underscores the fact that all souls must pass through this purifying ritual. Beatrice appeared only for the Pilgrim's edification, but Matilda appears to every purified soul on its way to the Empyrean and eternal beatitude.

31. (p. 188) *If, Reader . . . :* The Poet concludes the second canticle of his poem with his seventh and last address to his reader. In the next two stanzas he claims he is limited for want of space, because of a preordained pattern in his work, "full are all the leaves." Indeed, the three canticles are remarkably similar in length: *Inferno* contains 4,720 lines, *Purgatorio* 4,755 lines, and *Paradiso* 4,758 lines. Dante mentions "canticle" to designate the three divisions of the poem for the first time here. By now, however, the reader surely understands that this master poet could have filled even more pages if he had not preordained a certain symmetrical structure to his entire composition.

32. (p. 188) *unto the stars:* Each of the three canticles ends with the word *stelle* ("stars"), stressing the upward motion of the poem's protagonist toward God.

Six Sonnets on Dante's
The Divine Comedy

BY

HENRY WADSWORTH LONGFELLOW

(1807–1882)

I

Oft have I seen at some cathedral door
    A laborer, pausing in the dust and heat,
    Lay down his burden, and with reverent feet
    Enter, and cross himself, and on the floor
Kneel to repeat his paternoster o'er;
    Far off the noises of the world retreat;
    The loud vociferations of the street
    Become an undistinguishable roar.
So, as I enter here from day to day,
    And leave my burden at this minster gate,
    Kneeling in prayer, and not ashamed to pray,
The tumult of the time disconsolate
    To inarticulate murmurs dies away,
    While the eternal ages watch and wait.

II

How strange the sculptures that adorn these towers!
    This crowd of statues, in whose folded sleeves
    Birds build their nests; while canopied with leaves
    Parvis and portal bloom like trellised bowers,
And the vast minster seems a cross of flowers!
    But fiends and dragons on the gargoyled eaves
    Watch the dead Christ between the living thieves,
    And, underneath, the traitor Judas lowers!
Ah! from what agonies of heart and brain,
    What exultations trampling on despair,

Tenderness, what tears, what hate of wrong,
What passionate outcry of a soul in pain,
    Uprose this poem of the earth and air,
    This mediaeval miracle of song!

III

I enter, and I see thee in the gloom
    Of the long aisles, O poet saturnine!
    And strive to make my steps keep pace with thine.
    The air is filled with some unknown perfume;
The congregation of the dead make room
    For thee to pass; the votive tapers shine;
    Like rooks that haunt Ravenna's groves of pine
    The hovering echoes fly from tomb to tomb.
From the confessionals I hear arise
    Rehearsals of forgotten tragedies,
    And lamentations from the crypts below;
And then a voice celestial that begins
    With the pathetic words, "Although your sins
    As scarlet be," and ends with "as the snow."

IV

With snow-white veil and garments as of flame,
    She stands before thee, who so long ago
    Filled thy young heart with passion and the woe
    From which thy song in all its splendors came;
And while with stern rebuke she speaks thy name,
    The ice about thy heart melts as the snow
    On mountain heights, and in swift overflow
    Comes gushing from thy lips in sobs of shame.
Thou makest full confession; and a gleam,
    As of the dawn on some dark forest cast,
    Seems on thy lifted forehead to increase;
Lethe and Eunoe—the remembered dream

And the forgotten sorrow—bring at last
That perfect pardon which is perfect peace.

V

I lift mine eyes, and all the windows blaze
    With forms of Saints and holy men who died,
    Here martyred and hereafter glorified;
    And the great Rose upon its leaves displays
Christ's Triumph, and the angelic roundelays,
    With splendor upon splendor multiplied;
    And Beatrice again at Dante's side
    No more rebukes, but smiles her words of praise.
And then the organ sounds, and unseen choirs
    Sing the old Latin hymns of peace and love
    And benedictions of the Holy Ghost;
And the melodious bells among the spires
    O'er all the house-tops and through heaven above
    Proclaim the elevation of the Host!

VI

O star of morning and of liberty!
    O bringer of the light, whose splendor shines
    Above the darkness of the Apennines,
    Forerunner of the day that is to be!
The voices of the city and the sea,
    The voices of the mountains and the pines,
    Repeat thy song, till the familiar lines
    Are footpaths for the thought of Italy!
Thy fame is blown abroad from all the heights,
    Through all the nations; and a sound is heard,
    As of a mighty wind, and men devout,
Strangers of Rome, and the new proselytes,
    In their own language hear thy wondrous word,
    And many are amazed and many doubt.

Inspired by Dante and
the *Purgatorio*

Literature

Italy's most esteemed poet has held great sway over generations of writers. The great fourteenth-century English writer Geoffrey Chaucer first encountered Dante's work when he met two other eminent Italian poets, Boccaccio and Petrarch. In "The Wife of Bath's Tale" of *The Canterbury Tales* (c.1390–1400), Chaucer mentions the author of *The Divine Comedy* as "the wyse poete of Florence, That highte Dant," and invokes a passage from *Purgatorio*:

> 'Ful selde up ryseth by his branches smale
> Prowesse of man; for God, of his goodnesse,
> Wol that of him we clayme our gentillesse;'
> For of our eldres may we no-thing clayme
> But temporel thing, that man may hurte and mayme.

Longfellow translates the first three lines above, from the corresponding passage in canto VII, as:

> Not oftentimes upriseth through the branches
> The probity of man; and this He wills
> Who gives it, so that we may ask of Him.

Dante began to be widely read in Britain during the seventeenth century. In his "Lines on Milton" (1688), John Dryden glowingly describes his contemporary John Milton as the summation of Homer's and Dante's graces:

> Three poets, in three distant ages born,
> Greece, Italy and England did adorn.

The first in loftiness of thought surpassed;
The next in majesty; in both the last.
The force of nature could no further go;
To make a third, she joined the former two.

Though Dante's popularity waned during much of the eighteenth century, such important poets as William Blake and Thomas Gray remained steadfast in their admiration of the Italian master. Dante returned to favor in the nineteenth century, when preeminent English poets, including Percy Bysshe Shelley, Dante Gabriel Rossetti, and Thomas Carlyle, claimed Dante as a significant influence and paid tribute to him in their poetry.

In America, Ralph Waldo Emerson celebrated the poet in his short verse "Solution" (1867):

And Dante searched the triple spheres,
Moulding nature at his will,
So shaped, so colored, swift or still,
And, sculptor-like, his large design
Etched on Alp and Apennine.

Another nineteenth-century American, Thomas William Parsons, made a metrical translation of the first ten cantos of the *Inferno* and was moved by a bronze likeness of the poet on the banks of the River Arno in Florence to write "On a Bust of Dante." Florentine streets named Via dell'Inferno, Via del Purgatorio, and Via del Paradiso, form a backdrop for Parsons's musings:

See, from this counterfeit of him
Whom Arno shall remember long,
How stern of lineament, how grim,
The father was of Tuscan song:
There but the burning sense of wrong,
Perpetual care and scorn, abide;
Small friendship for the lordly throng;
Distrust of all the world beside. . . .

The lips as Cumæ's cavern close,
The cheeks with fast and sorrow thin,
The rigid front, almost morose,
But for the patient hope within,
Declare a life whose course hath been
Unsullied still, though still severe,
Which, through the wavering days of sin,
Kept itself icy-chaste and clear. . . .

Peace dwells not here,—this rugged face
Betrays no spirit of repose;
The sullen warrior sole we trace,
The marble man of many woes.
Such was his mien when first arose
The thought of that strange tale divine,
When hell he peopled with his foes,
The scourge of many a guilty line.

War to the last he waged with all
The tyrant canker-worms of earth;
Baron and duke, in hold and hall,
Cursed the dark hour that gave him birth;
He used Rome's harlot for his mirth;
Plucked bare hypocrisy and crime;
But valiant souls of knightly worth
Transmitted to the rolls of Time.

O Time! whose verdicts mock our own,
The only righteous judge art thou;
That poor old exile, sad and lone,
Is Latium's other Virgil now:
Before his name the nations bow;
His words are parcel for mankind,
Deep in whose hearts, as on his brow,
The marks have sunk of Dante's mind.

Not all tributes have been so high-handedly reverential. The nineteenth-century American poet and short-story writer Thomas Bailey Aldrich wrote a delightfully light-hearted verse, "In an Atelier," in which he appropriates Dante's unending love for Beatrice to carry on a sustained flirtation with his muse/model, Fanny. Here are a few stanzas from the poem:

> I pray you, do not turn your head;
> And let your hands lie folded, so.
> It was a dress like this, wine-red,
> That troubled Dante, long ago.
> You don't know Dante? Never mind.
> He loved a lady wondrous fair—
> His model? Something of the kind.
> I wonder if she had your hair!
>
> I wonder if she looked so meek,
> And was not meek at all (my dear,
> I want that side light on your cheek).
> He loved her, it is very clear,
> And painted her, as I paint you,
> But rather better, on the whole
> (Depress your chin; yes, that will do):
> He was a painter of the soul!
>
> (And painted portraits, too, I think,
> In the Inferno—devilish good!
> I'd make some certain critics blink
> Had I his method and his mood.)
> Her name was (Fanny, let your glance
> Rest there, by that majolica tray)—
> Was Beatrice; they met by chance—
> They met by chance, the usual way. . . .
>
> They met, and loved, and never wed
> (All this was long before our time),
> And though they died, they are not dead—

Such endless youth gives mortal rhyme!
Still walks the earth, with haughty mien,
Pale Dante, in his soul's distress;
And still the lovely Florentine
Goes lovely in her wine-red dress.

You do not understand at all?
He was a poet; on his page
He drew her; and, though kingdoms fall,
This lady lives from age to age.
A poet—that means painter too,
For words are colors, rightly laid;
And they outlast our brightest hue,
For varnish cracks and crimsons fade....

Visual Art

Not surprisingly, visual artists have also found inspiration in the extraordinary landscapes of Dante's fertile imagination. Sandro Botticelli, one of the greatest painters of the Italian Renaissance and, like Dante, a Florentine, captured *The Divine Comedy* in a richly colored illustration cycle of which some ninety-two pieces survive. British poet, painter, and illustrator William Blake portrayed Dante's otherworldly landscapes and characters in 102 illustrations. Italian illustrator Amos Nattini completed a lithograph cycle based on *The Divine Comedy* between 1923 and 1941, and Dante's saints and sinners were appealing subjects for the engravings surrealist Salvador Dalí executed in the 1960s to honor the 700th anniversary of the poet's birth. Among the finest works inspired by *The Divine Comedy* are those of French printmaker Gustave Doré, whose prints, completed in the 1860s, grace this volume.

Comments & Questions

In this section, we aim to provide the reader with an array of perspectives on the text, as well as questions that challenge those perspectives. The commentary has been culled from sources as diverse as reviews contemporaneous with the work, letters written by the author, literary criticism of later generations, and appreciations written throughout the work's history. Following the commentary, a series of questions seeks to filter Dante's Purgatorio through a variety of voices and bring about a richer understanding of this enduring work.

Comments

Percy Bysshe Shelley

The poetry of Dante may be considered as the bridge thrown over the stream of time, which unites the modern and ancient world. The distorted notions of invisible things which Dante and his rival Milton have idealized, are merely the mask and the mantle in which these great poets walk through eternity enveloped and disguised.

—from *The Defence of Poetry* (1821)

W. T. Harris

Of all the great world-poems, unquestionably Dante's "Divina Commedia" may be justly claimed to have a spiritual sense, for it possesses a philosophic system and admits of allegorical interpretation. It is *par excellence* the religious poem of the world. And religion, like philosophy, deals directly with a first principle of the universe, while, like poetry, it clothes its universal ideas in the garb of special events and situations, making them types, and hence symbols, of the kind which may become allegories.

—from *Journal of Speculative Philosophy* 21 (1887)

John Addington Symonds

The frigid symbolism which impairs the interest of Beatrice and Virgil does not affect Dante. In him the *Divine Comedy* centres: from him it derives its unity and life.... Were we not held fascinated from the first line of the poem to the end by Dante's stern and vivid personality, as well as spellbound by his marvellous style, few, perhaps, would read his epic. It would be impossible to find any work of art in the whole range of literature which so faithfully depicts a stubborn character in its mental strength and moral dignity.

—from *An Introduction to the Study of Dante* (1899)

E. G. Gardner

Whereas in the *Inferno* sin was considered in its manifold and multiform effects, in the *Purgatorio* it is regarded in its causes, and all referred to disordered love. The formal element, the aversion from the imperishable good, which is the essence of Hell, has been forgiven; the material element, the conversion to the good which perishes, the disordered love, is now to be purged from the soul. In the allegorical or moral sense, since every agent acts from some love, it is clear that a man's first business is to set love in order; and, indeed, the whole moral basis of Dante's Purgatory rests upon a line ascribed to St. Francis of Assisi: *Ordina quest'Amore, O tu che m'ami;* "set love in order, thou that lovest me."

—from *Aids to the Study of Dante* (1903)

William Butler Yeats

> The chief imagination of Christendom,
> Dante Alighieri, so utterly found himself
> That he has made that hollow face of his
> More plain to the mind's eye than any face
> But that of Christ.

—from "Ego Dominus Tuus" (1919)

T. S. Eliot

The *Purgatorio* is, I think, the most difficult of the three parts [of the *Divine Comedy*]. It cannot be enjoyed by itself, like the *Inferno*, nor can it be enjoyed merely as a sequel to the *Inferno*; it requires appreciation of the *Paradiso* as well; which means that its first reading is arduous and apparently unremunerative. Only when we have read straight through to the end of the *Paradiso*, and re-read the *Inferno*, does the *Purgatorio* begin to yield its beauty. Damnation and even blessedness are more exciting than purgation.

—from "Dante" (1929)

Questions

1. Are you satisfied that in Dante's *Purgatorio* the punishments fit the crimes? Are there instances in which the punishment is either too severe or too lenient? Are there instances in which Dante the Pilgrim and Dante the Poet seem to disagree?

2. The *Purgatorio* has a lot to say about eros, love, carnal love, and sex. What would you say is the work's attitude toward sex? Is it an attitude you would attack or defend? Why?

3. Do you agree with Dante's hierarchy of vices? Or would you put some lower down on the scale and some higher up?

4. What is there in *Purgatorio* for a secular, modern person?

5. Is Dante a good psychologist? Does he really understand the inner motivations and intentions of the people in his *Purgatorio*? Though Dante wrote the poem some 700 years ago, do you think some of the same sorts of people are walking the earth today?

6. Do any lines of the poem stand out as being particularly beautiful? To appreciate the beauty of the language and imagery, try reading parts of the poem out loud.

7. Do you like the Pilgrim, Virgil, and the other characters in *Purgatorio*? How about the repentant sinners? Do any seem to be particularly appealing characters?

For Further Reading

Bio-criticism

Anderson, William. *Dante the Maker.* London and Boston: Routledge and Kegan Paul, 1980. The most comprehensive biography of Dante, with extensive information about the poet's life and times.

Auerbach, Erich. *Dante, Poet of the Secular World.* 1929. Translated by Ralph Manheim. Reprint: Chicago: University of Chicago Press, 1961. A classic by the greatest literary historian of the twentieth century; still required reading.

Bergin, Thomas G. *Dante.* New York: Orion Press, 1965. An older overview that is still rewarding.

Hollander, Robert. *Dante: A Life in Works.* New Haven: Yale University Press, 2001. The best book to approach Dante's life through his writings; includes important discussions about the critical problems that have occupied Dante's critics from early to present-day commentators.

Lewis, R. W. B. *Dante: A Penguin Life.* New York: Penguin Putnam, 2001. A brief discussion of Dante by one of America's foremost biographers.

Quinones, Ricardo J. *Dante Alighieri.* Second revised edition. New York: Twayne, 1998. An excellent and very readable examination of Dante's life and works, with useful bibliography and information on translations of Dante's works.

General Criticism of Dante's Divine Comedy

Barolini, Teodolinda, and H. Wayne Storey, eds. *Dante for the New Millennium.* New York: Fordham University Press, 2003. A recent collection of academic essays on all aspects of Dante's literary career.

Bloom, Harold, ed. *Dante's "Divine Comedy": Modern Critical Interpretations.* New York: Chelsea House, 1987. Contains essays by different hands, including some of the most influential interpreters of Dante's poem, including Ernst Robert Curtius, Erich Auerbach, and Charles Singleton.

Caesar, Michael, ed. *Dante: The Critical Heritage—1314(?)–1870.* London: Routledge, 1989. This collection of historically important essays on Dante allows the reader to trace the changing views on the poet and his masterpiece from the first commentaries of the fourteenth century to the nineteenth century. Critics include important figures from Italy, England, France, Germany, and the United States.

Clements, Robert J., ed. *American Critical Essays on "The Divine Comedy."* New York: New York University, 1967. One of the best essay collections on Dante, reprinting classic works by major Dante scholars working in America.

Freccero, John, ed. *Dante: A Collection of Critical Essays.* Englewood Cliffs, NJ: Prentice-Hall, 1965. Contains important essays by such diverse critics as Bruno Nardi, Gianfranco Contini, Luigi Pirandello, and Leo Spitzer.

Gallagher, Joseph. *A Modern Reader's Guide to "The Divine Comedy."* Liguori, MO: Liguori Publications, 1999. The original title was *To Hell and Back with Dante*, 1996. A canto-by-canto discussion of the poem, useful for the student reader.

Giamatti, A. Bartlett, ed. *Dante in America: The First Two Centuries.* Binghamton, NY: Center for Medieval and Early Renaissance Studies, 1983. A fascinating anthology of essays linked to the birth of American interest in Dante created by the writings of Longfellow, Charles Eliot Norton, and James Russell Lowell, plus other more contemporary voices, such as T. S. Eliot, Ezra Pound, and other twentieth-century Dante scholars.

Hawkins, Peter S., and Rachel Jacoff, eds. *The Poets' Dante: Twentieth-Century Responses.* New York: Farrar, Straus and Giroux, 2001. An eloquent tribute to Dante's impact upon working contemporary poets, including essays by Eugenio Montale, Ezra Pound, T. S. Eliot, William Butler Yeats, W. H. Auden, and many others.

Iannucci, Amilcare A., ed. *Dante: Contemporary Perspectives.* Toronto:

University of Toronto Press, 1997. A recent collection of fine scholarly essays on a variety of Dante topics written expressly for this volume.

Jacoff, Rachel, ed. *The Cambridge Companion to Dante.* Cambridge: Cambridge University Press, 1993. Useful introduction by a variety of experts to the major problems of Dante criticism arranged by topic (Dante and the Bible, Dante and the classical poets, Dante and Florence, and so forth). Essays are aimed at the student reader.

Lansing, Richard, ed. *The Dante Encyclopedia.* New York: Garland Publishing, 2000. Indispensable English-language reference to every imaginable topic, character, and problem in Dante's poem, containing nearly 1,000 entries by 144 contributors from twelve countries.

Lee, Joe. *Dante for Beginners.* New York: Writers and Readers Publishing, 2001. The amusing cartoon drawings and sense of humor in this student-oriented guide to the poem do not detract from its excellent canto-by-canto discussions of *The Divine Comedy.*

Mazzotta, Giuseppe, ed. *Critical Essays on Dante.* Boston: G. K. Hall, 1991. A collection of pieces by different authors, particularly useful for its reprinting of a number of the early medieval and Renaissance commentaries on the poem.

Criticism with Special Reference to the Purgatorio

Armour, Peter. *Dante's Griffin and the History of the World: A Study of the Earthly Paradise* (Purgatorio, *cantos xxix–xxxiii*). Oxford: Clarendon Press, 1989. A detailed study of the last part of *Purgatorio.*

————. *The Door of Purgatory: A Study of Multiple Symbolism in Dante's* Purgatory. Oxford: Clarendon Press, 1983. A close reading of Canto IX of *Purgatorio.*

Fergusson, Francis. *Dante's Drama of the Mind: A Modern Reading of the* Purgatorio. Princeton, NJ: Princeton University Press, 1953. Still one of the finest guides to an enjoyment of the poetry and the drama of *Purgatorio.*

Le Goff, Jacques. *The Birth of Purgatory.* Translated by Arthur Goldhammer. Chicago: University of Chicago Press, 1984. The classic study of the invention of the concept of Purgatory, including a consideration of Dante's contribution to this idea. An essential book.

Scott, John A. *Dante's Political Purgatory.* Philadelphia: University of Pennsylvania Press, 1996. A good introduction to the political aspects of this part of Dante's epic poem.

Singleton, Charles S. *Journey to Beatrice.* 1958. Baltimore, MD: Johns Hopkins University Press, 1977. A very influential and learned discussion of Beatrice's role in *The Divine Comedy.*

Williams, Charles. *The Figure of Beatrice: A Study in Dante.* New York: Noonday Press, 1961. An intriguing consideration of the role of Beatrice in Dante's poem by another poet.

English Versions of Dante's So l urces and Dante's Minor Works Mentioned in the Critical Notes to the Purgatorio

Alighieri, Dante. *The Banquet.* Stanford French and Italian Studies, volume 61. Translated by Christopher Ryan. Saratoga, CA: ANMA Libri, 1989. An English version of *Il Convivio.*

————. *Dante's Lyric Poetry.* Edited and translated by Kenelm Foster and Patrick Boyde. Oxford: Clarendon Press, 1967. 2 vols. Dante's Italian lyric poetry with English translations and excellent commentary.

————. *Literary Criticism of Dante Alighieri.* Translated by Robert S. Haller. Lincoln: University of Nebraska Press, 1973. Contains English selections from the various works by Dante (*De vulgari eloquentia, Il Convivio,* the *Letter to Can Grande, La Vita Nuova,* and the *Eclogues*) that discuss poetics, poetry, poets, and allegory.

————. *Monarchia.* Translated and edited by Prue Shaw. Cambridge: Cambridge University Press, 1995.

————. *Vita Nuova.* Translated by Mark Musa. Oxford: Oxford University Press, 2000.

The Bible: Authorized King James Version with Apocrypha. Edited by Robert Carroll and Stephen Prickett. Oxford: Oxford University Press, 1998.

Broken Columns: Two Roman Epic Fragments: The Achilleid *of Publius Papinius Statius and* The Rape of Proserpine *of Claudius Claudianus.* Translated by David R. Slavitt. Philadelphia: University of Pennsylvania Press, 1997.

Lucan. *Civil War.* Translated by Susan H. Braund. Oxford: Oxford University Press, 1999. A complete translation of the *Pharsalia.*

Ovid. *Metamorphoses.* Translated by A. D. Melville. Oxford: Oxford University Press, 1998.

Statius. *Thebaid.* Translated by A. D. Melville. Oxford: Oxford University Press, 1995.

Virgil. *Virgil, with an English Translation by H. Rushton Fairclough.* 2 vols. Revised by G. P. Goold. Cambridge, MA: Harvard University Press, 1999–2000.

Dante Web Sites Useful for a Reading of the Purgatorio

Danteworlds: http://danteworlds.laits.utexas.edu

This is perhaps the most useful site for the student and first reader of *The Divine Comedy.* Created by Professor Guy Raffa of the University of Texas, it includes extensive material on the *Inferno* and *Purgatorio*; a section on *Paradiso* is under construction. An audio component includes readings of important lines of the poem, in Italian; visual material includes works of art indebted to Dante's poem.

Digital Dante: http://dante.ilt.columbia.edu

The juxtaposition of two translations (Longfellow's classic version and the more recent version by Alan Mandelbaum), plus the Italian text, make it possible to compare different English versions with the Italian original. Created at Columbia University, the site also contains other works by Dante and extensive illustrations.

The Princeton Dante Project: http://etcweb.princeton.edu/dante

Created by Professor Robert Hollander at Princeton University, this site is probably best visited by the more advanced reader and requires registration (at no charge). It juxtaposes the recent Hollander translation with the original Italian text and includes much critical and interpretive information.